ALSO BY SHARON WRAY

Deadly Force

Every Deep Desire

One Dark Wish

IN
SEARCH
OF
TRUTH

SHARON WRAY

sourcebooks
casablanca

In memory of

Megan Casey Wray and Courtney Elizabeth Lenaburg

Sisters. Soldiers. Saints.

Published by Sourcebooks Casablanca, an imprint of Sourcebooks
P.O. Box 4410, Naperville, Illinois 60567-4410
(630) 961-3900
sourcebooks.com

Printed and bound in the United States of America.
POD 10 9 8 7 6 5 4 3 2 1

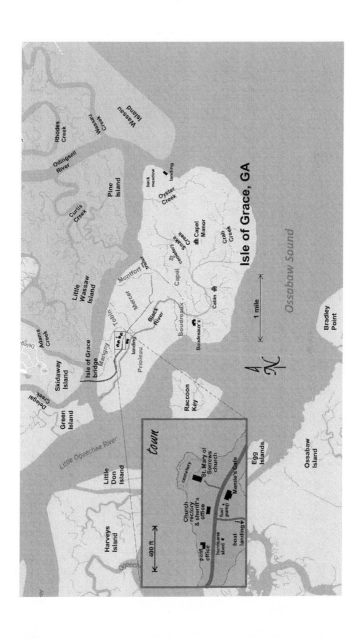

PROLOGUE

"When was the last time you saw a man bow?" Allison Chastain Fenwick led Zack Tremaine onto the courtyard of Le Petit Theatre.

Nestled in the French Quarter of New Orleans, the humid, flower-filled courtyard provided a reprieve from the freezing theater. A breeze tinged with jasmine and white lights wrapped around the trees enhanced the romantic summer night.

"No idea." Zack took two flutes from a server's tray and handed her one.

The champagne tickled her nose. As the courtyard filled with intermission-freed guests, Zack found a clear spot near the raised fountain. "Why?"

"When I was leaving the ladies' room"—she sat on the fountain's edge and her gown pooled on the bricks below—"I bumped into someone. I apologized, but he just wrapped his arm around his waist and bowed. By time I blinked, he'd disappeared."

"Maybe it's a Charleston thing. It's certainly not a New Orleans thing."

She sipped her champagne. "It's *not* a Charleston thing. It's a weird thing. So it has to be from New Orleans, which you'd know about since you're a native Cajun."

Zack threw her a fake-offended look. "Says the woman whose Charlestonian last names are so old she has to use both of them?"

She laughed at their on-going joke about the differences between their hometowns and punched his shoulder. The U.S. Army had turned him into a wall of muscle, so her fist probably hurt far more than his shoulder.

He smiled, took her hand, and kissed her palm.

"Maybe it's a formal thing," she offered to keep the peace. "He *was* wearing a tux." At this last word, she raised her eyebrow. While she'd chosen a long blue satin gown in honor of *Hamlet*'s opening night, Zack rarely wore anything other than jeans and T-shirts. She was happy with his pressed gray trousers, white button-down shirt, and striped tie, despite his almost-shaved black hair.

When he pulled at his collar and scanned the courtyard, she hid her smile behind another sip of champagne. It wouldn't surprise her if he was armed.

Glass broke behind her, and she glanced toward the noise. People were clearing away. As they drifted from the mess, she saw a solitary man in the corner. He stood near a potted palm with his hands in the pockets of his wrinkled, ill-fitting blue suit. The kind of suit someone borrowed or rented, not owned.

The other odd thing? He was staring directly at Zack.

Zack tapped her bare shoulder. "Since we haven't seen each other since graduation, we have some toasts to make. First, to me."

She laughed out loud. "To you?"

"Yes." He held up his glass. "Congratulations to me on completing the Special Forces Assessment and Selection Course. Soon, hopefully, I'll be a Green Beret."

"Oh my gosh!" She stood and gave him a hug. After they'd graduated from Tulane, Zack, who'd been an Army ROTC cadet, had hoped to become a Special Forces officer. So she was very happy for him. When she pulled away, she raised her glass. "May you win every battle and always return to us safe and sound."

"Us?" Zack's brown eyes shuttered and the lines around his mouth seemed deeper than before. "Of course—Stuart."

"Stuart will be happy for you. He's your best friend, besides me." She fluttered her eyelashes until Zack smiled again. "Stuart was sorry he couldn't make the play. He'll meet us for dinner later."

Zack raised his glass again. "Here's to you *crushing* your cultural anthropology PhD program."

They clinked glasses, and Allison ignored Zack's quiet laughter. She knew what Zack and Stuart believed: the only job a cultural anthropology PhD could get was as a barista.

"Despite what you think"—Allison tried to kick him with her high-heeled sandal until he moved—"I'll get a job that doesn't require asking people if they want whipped cream on top."

Now Zack laughed so loudly people glanced their way.

"My turn." Allison lifted her glass and, with her other hand, touched the sapphire-and-diamond engagement brooch attached to her neckline. "To your best friend and my future husband, Stuart. He was just elected Tulane alumni president for our class year. I'm certain he'll become a bank president before he's twenty-five."

Zack nodded, although the shadows in his eyes reappeared. "I have no doubt."

They clinked glasses for the third time, and Allison felt a rare tremble of happiness. She'd always been so alone, but tonight she felt safe. She was engaged to Stuart, and Zack had come home to visit. For the first time in years, she felt like nothing bad could ever happen to her again.

The audience began to file back into the theater, leaving them alone. Neither one of them wanted to return to the play.

"I'm sorry I missed your engagement party." Zack gave his glass to the last server standing. "I was training."

"I understand." She cleared her throat and handed her glass away as well. She'd drunk almost all of it and her head felt fuzzy. "I sent you photos."

"I got them." Zack crossed his arms and his gaze settled on the brooch pinned to her dress. "Allison, are you sure marrying Stuart is the right thing to do?"

"Why would you ask that?"

"I know you. And I love you." The courtyard lights reflected the truth in Zack's eyes.

They stood so close his breath caressed her forehead, and his insanely sexy bay rum cologne sent tingles down her arms.

"Stuart loves me. And I love him. I'm certain of it."

"Certainty is an impossibility." Zack pushed a stray curl behind her ear.

She shivered at the touch of his fingers against her face. "I don't understand."

"You're not in love with him the way a woman is supposed to love a husband."

Her breath snagged, making it hard to breathe without hyperventilating. He'd always discerned all of her insecurities and vulnerabilities. Here, alone in the courtyard, she was defenseless. "Zack—"

"I'm begging you to rethink this marriage. Stuart may be able to give you the security you think you need, but it'll never be enough—not for either of you."

"What are you saying? Stuart will break my heart?"

"No," Zack whispered. "You'll break all of our hearts."

She blinked as he lowered his head. When his lips touched hers, her first thought was that they were so much softer—and gentler—than they appeared. He held her head at the perfect angle so he could deepen the kiss. In all the years they'd known each other, he'd never touched her so intimately, and now that they were locked in this embrace she wondered why.

Horrified at her reaction, Allison pulled back and pressed her fingers against her mouth. That's when she noticed two things: the ill-suited man moving closer and another tuxedoed man following behind. This tuxedoed man with dark skin and green eyes was the bowing man she'd seen earlier in the evening.

Something glinted in the bowing man's hand. A small sword? "*Zack?*"

Zack twisted just as the ill-suited man pulled something out of his jacket.

Zack grabbed her by the waist, and they hit the ground. Her hands took the brunt of her fall, scraping on the bricks. The pain made her dizzy but not enough to ignore the action she saw from beneath Zack's larger body. The bowing man moved behind the ill-suited man and slid his thin sword into the man's neck. The ill-suited man silently slumped to the ground.

Suddenly, with Zack on one knee and holding his handgun, the bowing man pressed his sword point against Zack's heart.

"Hold your peace," the bowing man demanded in a distinct Australian accent. "Do not fear. Tonight's violence has been met and meted."

Zack put his gun on the ground and rose slowly, both hands held up in surrender.

The bowing man retracted his sword, which became a thin, ten-inch-long wand of steel. He slipped it into his jacket pocket. "My name is Laertes. I venture here tonight to bring a message and a warning."

Allison took Zack's hand and he helped her up, making sure she stayed behind him. He didn't speak, so she didn't either—not that she could cobble together any words. All she could do was stare at the dead man and keep the nausea at bay. With no visible blood, he seemed to be asleep.

Laertes took a cell phone from the dead man's pocket and tossed it to Zack.

The dead man's messages were open, and Zack clicked on an image. A short, silent video appeared along with the sent and read receipt.

Allison's body shook. The ill-suited man had texted the video of their kiss to Stuart.

Zack handed the phone back to Laertes.

Laertes glanced to one side, and she noticed another tuxedoed man deeper in the shadows. She grabbed Zack's arm. *There were two of them?*

"My lord has decreed that now is not the time for your understanding." Laertes put the phone into a different pocket than the sword. "'Tis time for a change."

"What are you talking about?" Zack asked.

Laertes hit his own chest with his fist. "My lord believes you are not meant for your life's work. You have other passions he'd encourage you to pursue."

"Was that the message?" She took Zack's hand. "Or the warning?"

"The warning is for you, my lady," Laertes said to her. "Choose your lover wisely."

She took a step back and swallowed the bitter taste in her mouth. The veins in Zack's neck bulged.

Before they could respond, Laertes wrapped an arm around his waist and bowed. "My lord must be cruel only to be kind. Thus bad begins and worse remains behind."

CHAPTER 1

"Who's there?" Allison stopped in the dark Charleston alley, sure she'd heard footsteps other than her own. When no one answered, she rechecked the address on her phone. The building had to be here somewhere. Clutching her phone in one hand, she held up her gown's skirt and walked on the cobblestones.

Now that she was close to the river, she heard waves splashing the wooden wharf and halyards clanging against aluminum masts. Normally, by ten p.m., she'd be tucked into her bed in pj's, grading papers. But tonight's action required full-on body armor: black strapless gown, hair twisted into a braided knot and decorated with crystal daisy hairpins, high heels, and the jasmine perfume she only wore on special occasions.

The hairs on her neck rose, and she paused near an out-of-business bakery. Although the sun had set, the summer humidity pressed down on her like a damp blanket. The air wasn't just hot—its heft and weight carried a warning.

So similar to Laertes's warning seven years earlier.

Voices came from behind her, and she tucked herself into the sunken doorway of a seventeenth-century brick warehouse. A minute later, two men in tuxedoes and black masks covering half their faces walked by at the same time her cell phone buzzed. A light appeared with the message, and she pressed it against her stomach. *Keep moving, gentlemen.*

The first man stopped a foot away. "Did you hear something?"

She almost choked on the stench of moldy bricks.

"Nah," the second man said. "Probably rats."

Rats? She exhaled, making sure to breathe through her mouth so she wouldn't gag. She'd forgotten about the rats, especially being so close to the water.

They moved on until stopping fifty yards away, in front of the last eighteenth-century mansion next to the river. All of its windows, along with the front door, had been boarded up. But it still had its split, semicircular staircase with wrought-iron railings. Instead of going up the stairs, the men went around them and disappeared.

After a few more breaths, she checked her text. It was from Maddie. Except the caller ID name had been changed to MADDIE THE BESTEST FRIEND EVER. Allison smiled. Maddie's almost-eight-year-old daughter had probably changed the ID.

Allison swiped the screen to read Maddie's message.

> *Good luck! Text when it's done.*
> I will. Thanks for the dress.

She left her alcove and stopped near the stairs, where the masked men had disappeared. No one came or went. There was no sound. Yet those men had gone somewhere.

Although she didn't want to call more attention to herself, she used her phone's flashlight. A rat *only a foot away* scurried off. She moved and her light glinted on a polished brass knob attached to a door beneath the protruding staircase. The knob was engraved with *JL* embedded in a lily.

How odd.

She put her phone into her evening bag and opened the door. A dim light appeared, leading her into a narrow hallway. The walls were decorated on both sides with mirrors and candles in sconces.

The hallway veered right, and she climbed a narrow flight of stairs, the sound of electronic music getting louder. Once on the landing lit by candles, she stopped. A man in a tuxedo and a black mask covering his eyes stood in front of another door, arms crossed. Despite his dress clothes, his dark pupils shining through the mask's slits backed up his stance.

She took a coin out of her skirt pocket and handed it to him. "Allison Chastain Fenwick Pinckney."

"Chastain? Interesting." The man tossed the Roman silver denarius into the air and caught it. "*Esse aut non esse.*"

"To be or not to be?" Seriously? "*Id est quaestio.*"

He shoved the two-thousand-dollar coin she couldn't afford into his pants pocket and opened the door. She paused from the heavy reverb caused by too many speakers in too small a room and blinked from the pulsing lasers.

"*Non ruta non dolor,* sweetheart."

Neither rue nor regret? She slipped in, and the closing door hit her back, causing her to stumble in her high heels.

A strong hand grasped her elbow, arresting what might have been a nasty fall. She was grateful for the low light that hid the hot flush flooding her cheeks.

Once she was stable on her feet, the masked man dropped her arm, hit his chest with his fist, and bowed his head. "My lady," he said in a distinct Scottish accent.

She looked around for something—anything—that would help her make sense out of the night. Yet all she saw were grinding bodies on the dance floor. The scent of alcohol and sex masked the cloying smell of incense. Her eyes burned from the smoke drifting in the air.

A sex club?

"Tha...thank you." She stumbled over her words. "I can't believe I'm so clumsy."

The man with dark skin, dark brown eyes behind his mask, and a buzzed head, wore a tux that clung to his wide chest and thick thighs. "I am called Marcellus. 'Twas my privilege to serve you."

Before she could answer, Marcellus disappeared into the crowd.

Allison smoothed down her skirt, hiked her gown's corset, and clutched her handbag. It was time to learn why Stuart had been murdered.

Zack Tremaine halted at the end of Charleston's dankest and darkest alley and answered his cell phone. The ID showed the call coming from Iron Rack's Gym in Savannah. "What?"

"Kells just figured out you left Savannah. Again," Alex Mitchell said in a voice that couldn't have sounded more disinterested. "Your boss is pissed."

"Kells can go to hell." Zack moved toward the building Allison had entered. She'd almost seen him and he'd had to hide behind a dumpster. The chauffeur in a nearby limo had earbuds in and his eyes closed. The rats were doing their own thing.

"Kells is already there. That's why he called a staff meeting. To which I was not invited."

Because, as an unpredictable ex-con, no one wanted to deal with Alex and his moods.

"A staff meeting at this time of night? Why?"

"No idea."

Random staff meetings didn't surprise Zack at all. It'd been almost three months since Zack's Green Beret unit had been suddenly—and dishonorably—discharged and forced to leave Fort Bragg.

Now that he and his men, including their former commanding officer, Colonel Kells Torridan, were managing a run-down gym in Savannah, Zack had adjusted to their new, much quieter life. Unfortunately, Kells hadn't adjusted. He still believed their group of eight men—nine including Alex—who lived above the gym were an active Special Forces unit, with Kells in charge. He even continued to dress the part.

Only now, instead of having missions in the world's worst hot spots, Kells was determined to find out why they'd been dishonorably discharged by a secret congressional committee. Since their new mission to redeem their reputations and reclaim their lives was going nowhere, Kells had decided to channel his anger, paranoia, and frustration into a *let's kick Zack in the ass daily* party.

Not to mention the insults.

Zack rubbed his eyes with his thumb and forefinger. "Alex, is there anything else?"

"Your sister, Emilie, called. Your godmother, Vivienne, told Emilie where you're living now."

Fantastic. Since the night of the dishonorable discharges, he'd been avoiding his family. Not because he didn't love them, but because he wanted to protect them. Unfortunately, Vivienne and Emilie didn't understand that sentiment. "What did you tell Emilie?"

"That you were in a meeting and would call her later."

"Thanks."

"How's the girlfriend stalking going?"

"Allison isn't my girlfriend. I'm just gathering intel."

"*Riiight.* This is only the eighth time in the two months since her husband's murder that you've gone to Charleston to check on her." Alex crunched a chip or a cracker.

"Because her husband was also one of my best friends." Zack peered up at the boarded-up building that Allison had entered. "Can you run down an address for me?" After giving Alex the street name and number, Zack said, "It's an abandoned mansion near the Cooper River."

"I'm checking now."

Zack would've done it himself except all he had was a crappy burner phone. With the state of his permanent record, he wasn't about to take any chances by getting online in a public internet café. "Have you heard of the Satyr Club? Everyone is wearing formal clothes and masks."

"Nope." Typing sounded in the background. "Could be a sex club. Satyrs are those mythical Greek fertility spirits with exaggerated—"

"Never mind." Zack didn't like to think about what Allison was doing in there.

"I found something." Alex paused. "Huh. It *is* a sex club that requires rare coins for entrance payment."

"What kind of coins?"

"Old ones like Roman denarii and gold pieces of eight." Alex whistled low. "These things are expensive. Like thousands of dollars."

"Any idea how I can get into this club without Roman currency or a tux?" Because right then, he wore jeans, a black T-shirt, and combat boots and had eleven dollars in his back pocket.

"Call Vivienne. She might own the place."

"She doesn't own it." Vivienne's exclusive clubs were run out of private homes. "Any other ideas?" Zack wasn't expecting anything. Their unit was in a dismal financial state.

"Uh-oh," Alex whispered. "Kells just came out of the staff meeting."

"No—"

"Zack?" Kells said in a firm voice laced with fury. "Where the *fuck* are you?"

Shit. "In Charleston."

"I distinctly remember *not* giving you leave. *Again.*"

Zack leaned his shoulder against the brick building. "I remember that too." *And, obviously, I didn't care.*

"Yet you went anyway."

Maybe I wouldn't have if you'd apologized. "Yep."

"Against my orders."

"Yes, sir." He'd known when he'd disobeyed orders that Kells would be annoyed. But Zack hadn't given a fuck. He was tired of being Kells's punching bag.

Kells cursed under his breath. "You need to stop trailing Allison. If her husband's death *two months ago* had anything to do with our unit, you would've found it by now."

"Sir, Allison may be in danger." Jeez, how many times did they have to have the same argument?

"You've no evidence she's another target of her husband's murderer. I want you back in Savannah ASAP." Kells softened his tone the smallest bit. "No good will come of spending time with her. Her husband chose to engage with Remiel Marigny and paid the price. Just because we share our enemy—"

"Who's *a vicious arms dealer.*"

"Doesn't mean we need to get involved in Stuart's death."

"But—"

"When you return, we'll discuss your leaving without permission."

Whatever. Zack hung up. Yes, he was all about the insubordination tonight.

"Thou truly art a lily-livered boy." The male voice came from the darkness behind Zack. "A most notable coward."

A loud *whoomph* made Zack duck and turn. The man emerged from the shadows, swinging a two-by-four. Zack slammed his fist into the man's stomach. The man stumbled back and swung again; this time the board clipped Zack's forehead. Pain shot through his head, and he hit the ground hard, elbows first. He rolled to his side and his spit tasted like he was sucking on pennies. His vision splintered.

The man tossed the board away and stepped over Zack's body, saying, "Good night, sweet bastard prince. And flights of angels sing thee to thy rest."

Oh fuck.

Despite Zack's fractured sight, he watched a pair of dress shoes walk away.

The farther the assailant walked, the wider the picture became. Zack blinked as the darkness swallowed him. But in those last few moments of lucidity, he saw a tuxedoed man stop near the iron-railed staircase, wrap an arm around his waist, and bow.

CHAPTER 2

ALLISON PUSHED THROUGH THE DANCE FLOOR AND RUSHED INTO another room where half-dressed people sat at a bar. More bodies wrapped around each other on settees lining the perimeter, and she held her breath until making it into a hallway with a double staircase.

She paused to inhale fresher air. Once she felt less shaky, she hurried up two flights of stairs. On the third floor, she pressed her hand against the carved wooden door that marked the end of the sexy nightclub and the beginning of the *real* club—the *real* club where she might find some *real* answers about Stuart's death.

After more deep breaths, she entered. The parlor was lit by candles, and despite the windows being boarded up on the outside, velvet curtains covered the glass. Men and women in evening clothes sat on sofas drinking green cocktails out of crystal glasses. Two men with masks guarded the entrance into the next room.

"Allison?" A woman with long black hair pulled into a high ponytail and wearing a red one-shouldered silk gown appeared. The woman, older than Allison, walked with such grace her dress moved and shimmered like it'd been melted and poured on her perfect body.

Allison clutched her handbag against her stomach and gritted her teeth. What was Isabel Rutledge doing here?

Diamond earrings sparkled in Isabel's ears and a gold chain around her neck disappeared in her neckline. After kissing Allison on both cheeks, Isabel said in her refined Savannah drawl, "I wasn't expecting you."

Allison didn't want to be rude, but she had more important things to do than talk to Isabel. Especially since Isabel was the kind of person who, because of her beauty and confidence, made every other woman in the room feel less than.

Allison checked out the room again, but no one looked like he was the leader of a 350-year-old antiquarian club. "I'm here to see Hezekiah Usher."

Isabel took Allison's elbow and led her toward the armed guards. "Are you sure you want to do this? Hezekiah has strange...yearnings."

Great. Something else to worry about. "What are *you* doing here?"

Isabel's smile exposed sparkling white, perfectly aligned teeth. "My family is a longtime member of the Usher Society."

Of course it was. As a Rutledge, Isabel was a member of one of the oldest families in the South. Almost as old as the Pinckney and Fenwick families.

Almost as old as the Chastain family.

Isabel motioned to the guards. "Mrs. Allison Chastain Fenwick Pinckney has an appointment."

Allison hated that long name. Yet in this secret world, on the knife's edge of polite society, your names—your people—carried more weight than your reputation and wealth.

The door opened and Allison entered the beautifully appointed room. Despite the mansion's outward decay, this office gleamed with oiled mahogany, polished brass, and low-lit bankers' lamps. Her heels sank into the thick rug as she moved closer to the plumpish bald man sitting behind a desk large enough to land a 747. Again, velvet curtains separated the boarded-up outside from the inside.

The man stood and held out his hand. "Mrs. Pinckney? I'm Hezekiah Usher."

They shook hands over the desk covered with stacks of papers and books and maps. Once he released her hand from his sweaty grasp, she sat in the leather chair across from him.

"Isabel." Hezekiah motioned to the other woman. "Would you leave us?"

Isabel retreated, but Allison, who could read *bitch* as well as the next woman, recognized the anger in Isabel's eyes.

Hezekiah wore a gray suit made of shiny cotton that matched the sweat beading on his head. "Mrs. Pinckney, I want to extend my condolences on the death of your husband."

The desk lamps blinked, then dimmed.

When the lights returned to full power, she said, "Thank you."

"I have to admit I was surprised to receive a call from you on my *private* cell phone."

"Not as surprised as I was when your business card—with your private cell phone number—was found in Stuart's coat pocket. The one he was wearing when he was killed."

Hezekiah leaned his elbows on his desk, tented his fingers, and stared at the map. From her vantage point, it appeared to be a map of the French Quarter in New Orleans. "How…interesting."

"Mr. Usher." Allison sat forward and tried to keep the desperation out of her voice. "Stuart had written the words *Witch's Examination* on the back of that business card. When I contacted my colleague at the University of Virginia, she mentioned you recently acquired an early eighteenth-century—1703, to be exact—witch's examination."

Hezekiah's eyes darkened. "Before I answer any questions, I have to ask: How do you know about the Usher Society?"

"I'm a professor of anthropology at the College of Charleston. *Every* anthropology and history PhD student in this country knows about you—even if they have no idea how to *find* you."

He raised an eyebrow.

Was he daring her? If so, she had nothing to lose by continuing.

"The Usher Society was founded in Boston in 1647 by your ancestor, who you're named after." She exhaled the breath she hadn't realized she'd been holding. "He owned the first bookstore that sold the first books ever published in the thirteen colonies. Since 1647, the Usher Society has been the world's leading archivist of antique manuscripts. The Usher Society studies and catalogs documents for their members' private collections and sells other documents for select clients. Unfortunately, since selling black market antiquities is frowned upon, you must keep your side business quiet. Hence the sex club that fronts your establishment."

Hezekiah's lips looked like two floorboards pressed together. "You're not what you seem, Mrs. Pinckney."

She batted her eyelashes in a lame attempt to ease the tension. "I'm just a cultural anthropologist who'd like to know why your business card was in my dead husband's pocket."

Hezekiah played with the edges of the map. "Stuart was a *member* of the Usher Society. He was on my board of directors."

"Wait." She leaned back in her chair. That's not at all the answer she'd expected. "*What?*"

"Stuart became a member years ago."

"I, uh, had no idea." She cleared her throat delicately. "Doesn't joining the Usher Society cost money?" As in *a lot* of money?

"It does."

"Did Stuart come…" Allison waved her hand to the anteroom where the well-dressed and well-connected drank absinthe and cuddled on velvet sofas. "I mean—"

"He came often. The men and women of the Usher Society were his people."

Her arms felt numb and tingly. Stuart had hung out here and she'd never even known?

"What did Stuart do here?" She shook her head to erase the images of the sex club downstairs. "I mean…*why?*"

"Why was Stuart a member?" Hezekiah picked up a pen and played with the clicker. "Only Stuart can answer that question. I can tell you that he was well liked by the other members of the Usher Society and was *not* a member of the Satyr Club. He disapproved of the things going on below us."

She exhaled her relief. "Did Stuart buy and sell manuscripts?" Because, seriously, she handled the household budget. If he was involved in something like this, she would've known about it.

"Not at first." Hezekiah tossed the pen aside and grabbed a stress ball. His restlessness made her fidget in her seat. "It was only recently that Stuart found a document for which I'd been searching most of my career. When I sold it for him, he requested I use the proceeds to buy another on his behalf." Hezekiah handed her a cardboard tube eight inches long and an inch in diameter. "This is a rare document known as the Pirate's Grille."

She opened the tube's plastic end and slid out a page encased in archival plastic. When she unrolled it, she found a paper with random rectangular cutouts. Someone had also drawn two calligraphy swirls that divided the cutout rectangles into three parts. "Where did you get this?"

"Have you heard of an eighteenth-century pirate known as Thomas Toban?"

She laid the document on the desk and reached for a nearby magnifying glass to study the rectangular cutouts of various sizes. "No."

"Very few have. Unlike most of the buccaneers during the golden age of piracy, Thomas Toban went after other pirates instead of unsuspecting traders."

"Really?" She moved the magnifier and noticed a sketch of a broken daisy in a lower corner. "That's unusual for a pirate to go after other pirates."

Hezekiah, still holding his stress ball, pointed to a painting on the side wall. It showed two eighteenth-century wooden ships in combat, both flying pirate flags. "Thomas had a vendetta against the Prideaux pirate family because they murdered the woman he loved."

She'd recently read about the Prideaux pirates in a peer-reviewed history journal. She got up to study the oil painting, encased in a thick, gilded frame, that was at least three feet wide and two feet tall. "You mean those pirates from Savannah who used to blackmail their victims with poison derived from a rare lily?"

Hezekiah came over to stand next to her. "Yes."

"Didn't the Prideaux pirates also accuse their sister of being a witch and burn her alive in 1699?"

"Yes. But accusing her had been a ruse to commit murder."

Allison had read that as well.

"When their sister attempted to run away with Thomas, they murdered her for her betrayal. This painting represents one of many brutal battles off the coast of Savannah between Thomas's ship, the

Rebecca"—Hezekiah pointed to the black pirate flag decorated with a red heart pierced by a white sword and the words *Noli Oblivisci* below—"and the Prideaux pirates."

Allison stood on her toes to get a better look at both flags. The other pirate flag, also black, had a white skeletal fist gripping a cutlass. Red blood dripped down the blade to form the words *Sans Pitié.* "'Never Forget' versus 'Without Pity.' I bet that was an intense battle."

"Indeed." Hezekiah took her arm and led her back to her chair. "Thomas spent his career destroying the lives of the Prideaux pirates, but they weren't the only men on his revenge list." Hezekiah moved to the other side of the desk again and pointed to the Pirate's Grille. "Thomas believed the Prince, the leader of a secret army of assassins known as the Fianna, was complicit in the death of Thomas's lover. That document belonged to the Prince until 1710."

"What happened in 1710?" *And why had Stuart cared?*

"In 1710, Thomas killed two Fianna warriors in New Orleans and stole that document."

"Do you know what the Pirate's Grille is?"

"I have my suspicions."

She held it up and peered at him through the rectangular cutouts. "This is a Cardan grille used for reading secret messages buried in letters. They were specifically used in the seventeenth and eighteenth centuries."

Hezekiah took it and laid it over a printed page covered with text. Random words could be seen within the cutout windows. "Interesting."

Isabel slipped into the room. She whispered in Hezekiah's ear, and he frowned. "Are you sure?"

"Yes. I've alerted your perimeter guards." Isabel glanced at the desk and sent a fierce frown in Hezekiah's direction. "What's this?"

"The Pirate's Grille, purchased by Stuart and now belonging to Mrs. Pinckney." Hezekiah waved a hand toward Allison. "According to Mrs. Pinckney, that page is a Cardan grille used to decode seventeenth- and eighteenth-century letter ciphers."

"May I?" Isabel held out her hand, and Allison hesitated. Their families had been friends long before either of them were born. Since they'd never gotten along, they only had to put up with each other at random weddings and funerals.

To be blunt, Allison didn't trust Isabel.

Still, not wanting to be rude, Allison handed over the page. "Actually, it's only half of a cipher. You need both the grille and the document that formed the plaintext with the secret message embedded in it."

"This Cardan grille matches up to a specific page of text?" Isabel asked.

"Or pages." While Isabel studied, Allison asked Hezekiah again, "Why did Stuart want this?"

"I don't know." Hezekiah took the page from Isabel and slipped it into the tube. He returned it to Allison yet refused to meet her gaze.

Hezekiah was lying, and none of this made any sense.

Allison held up the tube. "Was this expensive?"

Isabel's cough sounded like a sneer. "It's currently the most expensive document on the black market."

Allison put the tube into her evening bag. "You said Stuart sold another document to help pay for this one. What was it?"

Hezekiah pulled a receipt book out of his desk drawer, flipped to a page, and slid it across the desk so she could read it.

Allison stood, her gaze fixed on the handwritten notation: *The Witch's Examination of Mercy Chastain*. Stuart's familiar signature was scrawled beneath. The rumors she'd heard from her UVA colleague were true. "Stuart somehow found and sold the Witch's Examination of Mercy Chastain, a document stolen from my mother years ago?"

Hezekiah's face reddened by the second.

When he didn't respond, she pointed to the receipt. "That manuscript was stolen from my mother's house sixteen years ago, while I was at my father's funeral. Even if Stuart found it, he had no business selling it. Mercy Chastain is my direct ancestor. It's part of her estate."

That document, or the lack of it, was one of the reasons why she hadn't made tenure yet at the College of Charleston. And Stuart had *known* that.

Hezekiah pulled a white handkerchief out of his pocket and wiped his forehead and upper lip. "Stuart proved provenance."

She was going to ask how, but forged ownership documents for antiquities were a cliché.

She straightened her shoulders and stared at the man who looked like he was melting. "Do either of these items have anything to do with why Stuart was murdered?"

Hezekiah wiped his head again and glanced at Isabel. Now there was a distinct gleam of panic in his eyes. "I know nothing about Stuart's murder. Though he admitted that he sold the Witch's Examination of Mercy Chastain and purchased the Pirate's Grille to protect you."

Allison was about to ask the all-important *how* when Isabel sat on the corner of the desk. The slit in her skirt showed off her perfect skin, but it was the necklace she played with that made Allison inhale a deep breath until her lungs ached. Isabel had pulled the gold chain out of her neckline to show off a sapphire-and-diamond brooch. "Where did you get that?"

Isabel lifted the brooch. The sparkling gems sent prisms around the room. "A friend."

Hezekiah took a drink of water from a crystal glass on his desk. "Isabel."

The way he spoke her name—an admonishment tinged with laughter—made Allison clutch her evening bag. "That brooch is mine. Stuart gave it to me."

"An engagement present." Isabel pursed her lips. "Except you gave it back to him."

"How—"

"Oh, come, now," Isabel practically purred. "Everyone knows."

"Not everyone." Hezekiah took another sip of water. "Don't be cruel."

"What are you talking about?" Allison's voice squeaked, but she didn't care.

"Stuart and I were lovers." Isabel slipped the brooch into her dress's deep neckline, until it rested between her breasts. "This was a lover's gift."

Allison swallowed only to find that her throat had closed up. Stuart and Isabel? *Lovers?* "For how long?"

"Two years. Since the night he told you to throw away that bottle of jasmine perfume Zack sent you from Paris and you refused. The night you returned this brooch."

That night? She gripped the jeweled handle of her evening bag until it cut her hand.

"The night," Isabel continued, "you fought about Zack Tremaine and the kiss you two shared seven years ago, not long before your wedding."

"I don't believe you." The words barely made it out of her throat.

Hezekiah stood and put his hand on Isabel's arm.

Isabel traced the delicate chain that rested on the swell of her breast. "Didn't you ever wonder why Stuart worked late so many nights? Why, after that fight, he never touched you again?"

It was true their physical relationship had been...lacking.

"The tragedy is that Stuart loved both you and Zack. I mean, the three of you were best friends in college." Isabel's voice lowered as if they were speaking secrets between sisters. "Stuart told me you didn't know how to love him, that you're incapable of loving anyone fully. It's no surprise you couldn't recognize that Stuart was in love...just with a different woman."

Allison was heading for the door when Hezekiah said, "One more thing."

She paused, her hand on the door handle, hating the fact that she glanced back. "*What?*"

"The Witch's Examination of Mercy Chastain was incomplete," Hezekiah said. "The appendix was missing. If you can find it, I have a buyer."

Allison left the room and slammed the door behind her. But she couldn't outrun Isabel's self-satisfied laughter. Stuart and Isabel had been lovers, and Allison had had no idea—because what Isabel said was true.

Allison wouldn't recognize love if it hunted her down and killed her.

CHAPTER 3

ALLISON HURRIED DOWN THE STAIRS ON SHAKY LEGS. IN THE SEX club, she slammed into two men. One took her arm to steady her. The same one who'd helped her earlier. Marcellus.

"Madam, may I—"

"No." She pushed past him and headed for the exit. It wasn't until she threw herself against the outside stair railing that she took a breath. The humidity hit her hard, and she coughed to breathe.

Was it true? Had Stuart and Isabel been having an affair?

She sank onto the lowest step. *It couldn't be true.* Closing her eyes, she pressed her cheek against the iron baluster.

Please, God, make it not true.

"Lady Allison, are you alright?"

She heard the Scottish male voice and took out her cell phone to shine its flashlight into the shadows. Marcellus and his friend, also in a tux and a mask, stood nearby. Despite the darkness, she saw the concern in Marcellus's eyes. His buddy stayed hidden in the gloom.

She straightened her shoulders. She had an inherent distrust of men in tuxedoes. "I'm—"

"Allison." Another man came out of the shadows.

Zack? Of all the people she'd expected to meet tonight, he was the absolute last on the list. He hadn't even made the list.

Zack, who stood three feet away from her, had pulled his gun and pointed it at Marcellus's buddy. "Allison, get behind me."

"What are you doing here?" She moved closer to him.

"I'm protecting you."

Marcellus stepped in between his friend and Zack. "What is the cause of this fray between you and my brother Horatio?"

"Ask Horatio," Zack said. "He's the one who hit me."

Marcellus glanced back with one eyebrow raised. "Brother?"

Even though she couldn't see Horatio's face, she heard him say, "'Tis nothing, Marcellus. 'Twas but a disagreement."

Zack snorted. "A disagreement that knocked me out?"

Allison touched Zack's shoulder. "Are you alright?"

With his free hand, Zack took her arm and gently drew her behind him. "Besides the pounding headache, I'm fine."

Marcellus held out his hands, palms up. "We meant no harm."

"Then tell the Prince and his Fianna warriors to stay the fuck away from me, my men, and Mrs. Pinckney."

Allison clutched her purse and her phone. *The Prince?*

Horatio hissed from the shadows, "You understand not—"

Marcellus raised his hand and spoke to Zack. "Your enemy is ours as well."

"If that were true," Zack said in the harshest voice she'd ever heard from him, "Remiel Marigny would be dead."

"He would be if your lord—"

"Enough, Horatio." Marcellus's voice sounded like a bark. "*Dubita veritatem esse mendacem.*"

Horatio responded. "*Sed nunquam non dubitatione.*"

Now they were speaking Latin? "I don't understand. What enemy?" When the men refused to answer, she put her phone into her purse and said sharply, "Does this have anything to do with Stuart's death?"

"Yes, my lady," Marcellus said with an even tone that made him sound like they were at a garden party instead of in a dank alley. "And Stuart's failed task that you must now complete."

She felt Zack's shoulder muscles contract beneath his leather jacket. "What task?"

"Don't listen to them." Zack's voice had a growly undertone. "They're professional liars."

"My lady." Marcellus pressed one fist against his heart. "The Prince regrets that one woe doth tread upon another's heel. Yet time is quickening for you to find the treasure of the dread pirate king."

She squeezed Zack's arm, the leather warming under her hand. This entire situation felt too similar to what'd happened at Le Petit Theatre seven years ago. "I don't understand."

"We're done here." Zack waved his free hand toward the river. "Leave. Now. And take your bullshit with you."

Horatio tapped Marcellus on the shoulder, then he nodded toward the parked car near the dumpster. "Leaving sooner will be best."

With a nod, and no concern for the fact that Zack still had a gun pointed at Horatio's chest, Marcellus and Horatio walked toward the river. The way they moved, so graceful and elegant, almost made them seem like they were floating over the ground. Their walk was powerful and predatory with a side of grace.

A moment later, they disappeared into the shadows.

"Zack?" she whispered. "What was that about?"

"It's—"

"Don't tell me it's nothing." She pointed to his weapon as he shoved it in his back waistband. "Minutes ago, I learned about the Prince and his Fianna warriors—assassins—but I was led to believe they lived in the eighteenth century. They weren't supposed to be wearing tuxes and hanging out in a sex club."

"The Fianna have been around for centuries." Zack's voice carried more authority than she remembered. "They're now in Charleston."

"Like they were in New Orleans seven years ago?"

"Yes."

She deserved more than one-word answers. "You know these Fianna warriors?"

Zack exhaled heavily. Even in the dim light, she noticed his chiseled cheekbones. He'd grown his black hair so long that he kept it tied back at the base of his neck. His shoulders drooped a bit, and he ran a hand over his head. His black leather jacket covered a black T-shirt. Despite the fact that he'd added serious muscle mass, his legendary confidence seemed…less confident. "We're acquainted."

"They said I had to finish Stuart's task. I'm supposed to find a treasure!"

"I know." He led her out of the alley. "That's why we need to get you home."

She had so many questions. So much had happened tonight, and she had so many reasons to be angry, annoyed, confused, and exhausted. In fact, she wasn't even sure she could identify one emotion.

Allison clutched her stomach. She felt nauseated. That's when she ID'd the problem: humiliation. Isabel and Stuart had humiliated her, and Zack was about to witness her complete breakdown.

"Hey." Zack's voice, so gentle and earnest, felt like a cool mist easing her heated body and inflamed mind. The pressure of his hand on her back helped her breathe. "It's okay."

She closed her eyes, and he pulled her into his arms. She smelled his familiar scent of bay rum, and wanted nothing more than to sink into his chest and let him hold her against his hard body. Let him protect her. Let him make everything new again.

When he rubbed her lower back and kissed the top of her head, she almost moaned, almost lifted her lips to his—almost kissed him. Would being with him take away some of her pain? Some of her despair and loneliness? Maybe. But she'd never deliberately hurt him, and using him would just make everything worse.

She opened her eyes and saw a limo near a dumpster, two rats scurrying nearby, and a trashcan on its side. This world she'd stepped into tonight was dark and scary and treacherous. Because of her choices, choices the bowing man—the Fianna—had warned her about years ago, her life was now a mess of secrets and lies and betrayals.

The familiar drowning sensation returned, and when she couldn't breathe, she withdrew from his embrace and faced him head on.

"Zack?" Hating her shaky voice, she hit his chest with her fist. "What's going on?"

෴

Zack's body hardened in the most inappropriate places. He wanted to kiss Allison, lose himself in her scent, but she'd pulled away before he made a fool of himself.

It'd been seven years since he'd seen her last, the night he'd declared his love and kissed her despite the fact that Remiel Marigny's agent and the *fucking* Fianna had been watching.

Since hearing about Stuart's death two months ago, Zack had prepped his heart for this meeting, but nothing could've prepared him for the reality. Seven years ago, she and he, along with Stuart, had been best friends. Now Stuart was dead and Zack was a dishonorably discharged ex–Green Beret.

"I don't know what's going on," he whispered. "I'm here because I'm worried about you."

"Because of the Fianna?"

"Partly." He waved to the building behind them. "You were also in a *sex club*."

"The sex club is a cover for the Usher Society."

Her voice washed over him, and he bit back a growl. In a black strapless gown, with her blond hair twisted into a loose bun, she couldn't have been lovelier.

Every muscle in his body tightened, but he wouldn't let that distract him. He took her elbow and led her in the opposite direction from the warriors. "What is the Usher Society?"

"A secret antiquarian society that buys and sells old manuscripts on the black market." She clutched her purse to her breasts. "What do you think Marcellus meant by finding treasure?"

He squeezed her arm. "I have no idea."

She stopped walking. "Why are you here? The last time I saw your godmother, she told me you were overseas with your Special Forces unit. Something about a rescue."

He only told Vivienne the barest details of his life so she wouldn't worry, but he'd not expected her to share those details with anyone. Especially Allison. "Not long ago, my men and I rescued some of our other men who'd been captured in Afghanistan and held in a POW camp. But I'm no longer in the army. I live in Savannah now and work in a gym."

She watched him for what seemed like minutes. "You, a Green Beret, got out of the army to work at a gym in Savannah. And you happened to show up in a dark Charleston alley the same night I do? The same night I'm confronted by...warriors about my dead husband and treasure? I don't believe it."

He wasn't surprised. She was smart, and his story was mostly bullshit.

"I don't expect you to." He took her hand and started walking again. He'd feel better when they were closer to passing cars and streetlights. "Why were you at the Usher Society?"

"I was hoping to find out more about Stuart's death." When they reached the sidewalk, she dodged a broken curb, and he held her elbow to steady her.

"Allison, let me take you home."

"No, thank you." She waved to a passing cab. "How long will you be in town?"

When the cab stopped, he opened the door for her. "I'm supposed to go back to Savannah tonight."

She nodded, paused as if to say something, then slipped into the cab.

After shutting the door, he double-tapped the top, and the taxi drove away. As he watched Allison leave, he decided that if he ever wrote his memoir, it would be titled *That Didn't Go As Planned*.

Unfortunately, Horatio's hit had knocked Zack out cold, and he knew he was lucky to have woken before Allison appeared. Although he had a vicious headache, he didn't feel like he had a concussion.

His buddy Nate had warned Zack that the Fianna appeared and disappeared at will. Their ghosting act usually happened when things got hot. What Zack hadn't expected was Horatio's insult. *Coward.*

The same word Kells had used earlier that day, before Zack had gone AWOL from the gym.

Now Zack had even more questions than he'd started with. But

Allison's demeanor, not to mention the sadness that swirled around her, told him waiting was the thing to do. The only problem with that plan was that Kells had stripped Zack of time.

Rubbing his head to ease the ache, he headed for his motorcycle, which he'd parked near the river. When he passed the club, a couple emerged. A round man in a suit and a woman in a long red gown and a high ponytail stopped by the stairs. The limo, parked near the dumpster, turned on its headlights and the chauffeur got out to open the door.

Zack tucked himself into an alcove with a "For Rent" sign on the boarded-up door. The woman seemed familiar, but Zack couldn't place her.

She spoke first. "Hezekiah, why did you give the Pirate's Grille to Allison? Why sell the Witch's Examination of Mercy Chastain to the Prince?"

"Isabel," Hezekiah said, "I buy and sell documents for a living. Stuart paid for the Pirate's Grille and I had to deliver it. Same with the Witch's Examination of Mercy Chastain—paid for and delivered."

"I need time to find what I'm looking for," Isabel said. "By selling those documents—"

Hezekiah tapped her arm. "Remind *him* that without the appendix to Mercy Chastain's witch's examination, the Pirate's Grille is useless. Both are needed to find that treasure."

"*He* won't be happy."

"*He'll* never be happy. His unhappiness is not your responsibility. It's time you understood that." After Hezekiah got into the limo, the chauffeur shut the passenger door and walked to the driver's side.

Isabel headed toward the street. When she passed Zack, he held his breath as her red gown swept over his combat boot. Once at the corner, she hailed a cab and disappeared. A second later, the limo's engine clicked twice.

An explosion ripped through the night and Zack hit the ground. Flaming debris rained down and a wave of intense heat swept over him. He rolled until hitting the wall. Once he took in a few breaths, he struggled to his feet. The limo, and the two men inside, had been incinerated.

While he wanted to help, there were no survivors. And there was no way he could be taken in as a witness. Kells would kill him.

Zack ran toward the river. When he reached his motorcycle, his stomach reacted to the stench of smoking oil and he threw up in a storm drain. After the third dry heave, he wiped his mouth. His vision cleared and his training took over. He'd been in worse combat situations than this. But this wasn't a battle. This was a message.

No, this was their new reality. Zack and his men were in a war not of their own choosing, fighting an unseen enemy with an unknown goal. To add to the party, Kells's unit was still on their knees, with no money, no tech, and no support. Hell, their armory, which held five guns and a few knives, was stored in an old filing cabinet with a ten-dollar lock.

Smoke thickened around him and he coughed to relieve the burning in his chest. Sirens sounded closer. Soon the area would be sealed off.

His phone buzzed and he pulled it out to read the text.

> *The play's the thing wherein you'll catch the*
> *conscience of the king. ~ Marcellus*

Zack stared at Marcellus's message and remembered Horatio's earlier nod toward the limo. Had the Fianna set off the explosion? Or Remiel Marigny? When a cop car zoomed down the alley, Zack put away his phone, started his motorcycle, and roared away from the destroyed limousine, which was a hard reminder that when the Fianna told you to leave, sooner was best.

CHAPTER 4

ALEX MITCHELL TOSSED HIS APPLE CORE INTO THE TRASH NEXT to the front desk of Iron Rack's gym. He'd been handling the phone for hours and he was done.

Screw the job. Screw the ridiculous pirate-themed gym. Screw Kells.

Since Kells had gotten Alex out of Leedsville prison two months ago, all Alex had done was sleep, eat, and answer the gym's phones. He wasn't deemed mature enough to attend staff meetings, carry a weapon, or be included in Kells's unit's lame-ass plan to take down that psycho arms dealer who'd set them up and caused their dishonorable discharges: Remiel Marigny.

Alex had spent almost six years in Leedsville, the U.S. Army's secret prison for troublesome soldiers, for a murder he didn't commit. Now, Kells believed Alex had become antisocial and violent—more so than he'd been before his incarceration. While that might have been true, he was tired of being tossed like an unpinned grenade in Kells's war-game version of hot potato.

Nate Walker, the unit's executive officer, came out of Kells's office near the front of the gym. Tonight Nate wore gym shorts with a black Iron Rack's Gym T-shirt. "Kells wants to see you."

Alex kicked back in the chair, boots on the desk, hands clasped behind his neck. "What the fuck for?"

"Does it matter?" Nate picked up the clipboard with the day's chore list.

"You know the quiet isn't good. It means Remiel is preparing his next move."

"I know." Nate dropped the clipboard and answered the ringing phone, making sure to cover the handset as he said, "Kells is waiting."

Alex got up, stretched his arms over his head until his tight muscles eased, and headed to Kells's closed office door. Alex thought about knocking but then pulled a *screw it* and walked in with a sharp "What."

"Sit." Kells, in khaki combat pants and a white T-shirt, sat behind a desk covered in file folders and papers. On the far wall, hidden from the random observer, hung a giant map of Afghanistan. Various colored pins had been stuck in different areas, including the Pamir River Valley—the place where Remiel Marigny began this nightmare.

The map was supposed to live in the gym's storage room—aka command post. But considering the previous owner had been a hoarder and had used the storage room as ground zero for his garbage collection, their CP was currently being treated for mold. Again.

Alex sat in a metal folding chair in front of the desk and crossed his booted ankles. He refused to start the convo he didn't want to have in the first place.

Kells wrote on a pad as he spoke. Legal documents lay nearby. He threw down his pen and sat back, clasping his hands behind his neck and staring at the ceiling. "Zack left the unit tonight without permission."

"Zack is a big boy."

"I think he's...attached to Allison Pinckney."

Alex smirked. "Two points for the observant one."

"Zack's obsession with Allison isn't healthy."

Says the man still in love with the wife who left him years ago.

Instead of stating the obvious, Alex leaned forward, jamming his elbows into his thighs. "Zack isn't obsessed. He's been in love with Allison since college. Now that her husband's dead, what difference does it make if he gets more...attached?"

Alex could've used cruder language, but out of all the men in the unit, he liked Zack the best—except for maybe Nate. Maybe because he, Zack, and Nate had gone to Ranger School together. They'd once been buddies.

"You're rooming with Zack. Has he said anything to you about—"

"No. He never talks about her. At least not to me. Why don't you ask Nate? He's closer to Zack than I am."

"I already have." Kells stood and went toward the window overlooking the dark street. The lower half of the picture window used black Jolly Roger pirate flags for privacy. Someone a long time ago had thought that decorating the run-down gym in a sketchy part of the city with pirate-themed flags would be hip and cool. Now it just seemed kitschy and strange. "I want you to go to Charleston. Tonight. Make sure Zack returns to Savannah."

Uh, no. "The last thing Zack needs is a babysitter."

"The last thing Zack needs is to spend the night in Allison's bed."

With Kells facing the street, Alex moved closer to the desk to see the legal papers. "Zack isn't twelve. He's just…hurt. You shouldn't have said those things to him earlier."

"Maybe not. But Zack isn't free to do whatever the hell he wants." Kells faced Alex again. "We have a mission."

"A mission that's going no-fucking-where fast." Alex leaned his chair back until it balanced on the back legs. His hands shook, so he held on to his seat. Those legal papers from Kells's wife's lawyer just explained why Kells had been so distracted and cranky lately—well, more cranky than usual. "Why can't Zack find some happy on the side?"

"Because I can't have him distracted. I need all of my men—"

"Including me?"

"Including you." Kells sat at his desk again, picked up his pen, and started writing. "I need all of my men focused. We've no idea what Remiel's plan is or when he'll strike next."

Alex stared at the tomato soup can that Kells had been using for years as a pen holder. "Even if I was considering this plan, how am I supposed to get to Charleston?"

Their unit had only two cars—an SUV and a minivan—and two Harleys. Zack had one of the bikes, and the other belonged to Pete White Horse, another man in the unit. There was no way Pete would hand over control of his bike to the antisocial ex-con.

"Take Pete's bike," Kells said.

"Pete will say no. Besides, this plan is horseshit. I'm not going."

Kells focused his intense gray, gold-flecked gaze on Alex. "Excuse me?"

Oh, right. None of the men in their unit contradicted Kells. Ever. "There's no reason for me to go to Charleston to get Zack. If you ordered him back to Savannah, he'll come back to Savannah. An apology from you wouldn't hurt either."

Kells turned away and didn't respond.

Alex moved his gaze to that damn map on the wall. "Unless you want *me* out of town for some reason?"

Kells placed his palms on his desk and used the leverage to stand again. "Alex—"

"It's cool." Alex rose. " I get that I'm not part of your little group here. I'm extraneous."

"You're not extraneous. We need you. There are only nine men, including you, in the unit. Every man counts."

"Is that why I'm not free?"

The only sound in the room was Kells's heavy breathing. "You understood the deal you agreed to."

"Sure. You got me out of prison because Remiel, who I supposedly killed six years ago, is still walking around. Now I work for you. No questions. No arguments. I have to do your bidding for as long as it takes to bring down Remiel again." Alex waved his hand toward the map on the wall.

"Yes," Kells said. "Once we do that—"

"Once I kill Remiel." *Because let's be truthful here.*

"Then you're a free man."

Alex tilted his head. "Yet if you tell people Remiel is alive, then I go free anyway."

"The fact that few people know Remiel is alive is the only advantage we have. I won't give that up."

"Which means that I'm not free."

Kells ran his hand over his head. He'd let his hair grow to half an inch, which only emphasized the fact that he was a ginger. "I'm not just worried about Zack. I'm concerned about you."

"I'm fine." Alex kept his tone flat enough to steady a level's bubble.

"You were in prison for almost six years for a murder you didn't commit."

"A murder I *failed* to commit." He wasn't ashamed of what he'd tried to do, only that he hadn't succeeded. "If I'd killed Remiel when I had the chance, none of us would be in this situation. The Wakhan Corridor Massacre wouldn't have happened. Half of your men wouldn't have been ambushed by local Afghan warlords in retribution. Those same ambushed men wouldn't have spent years in an Afghan POW camp. Some higher-up in the U.S. government wouldn't have accused those same POWs of the massacre after you and your unit rescued them and then sent them to Leedsville prison in the wilds of Minnesota. Finally, the men in your unit who did the rescuing wouldn't have also been accused of war crimes and dishonorably discharged by some secret fucking congressional committee."

"None of that history changes what happened to you in solitary."

"I don't want to talk about this." No good came from rehashing random beatings by the guards or their lame attempt to break his will by starvation. "I don't need me time in Charleston."

Kells sighed. "I want you at the unit's next movie night."

Talk about a change in subject. "Why?"

"It's time you became a more integral part of this unit." Kells picked up his cell phone and typed. "I'm letting Nate know that you're taking over movie night. It'll be your responsibility to pick the movie, order the pizzas, make the popcorn. If you have any issues—"

"I can handle Operation Forced Fun on my own."

Kells put his phone down. "Have you heard from your brother?"

"No. We both know Aidan doesn't give a shit."

"We both know that's not true. Remember the second part of our deal?"

"Yeah, yeah. If Aidan contacts me, I tell you. But Aidan won't. I'm a liability—one of his few failures—that he can't face."

"Still, if Aidan or any of his Fianna warriors contact you, you tell me. Got it?"

"Sure."

Kells's cell phone rang and he answered with a curt "Go."

Without waiting for permission, Alex left the room. Cain and Vane, two other men in Kells's unit, were talking by the front desk while Nate held the gym's phone to his ear. Like Nate, they both wore the gym's uniform of shorts and logo T-shirt. But where Cain's head was shaved, Vane kept his long blond hair tied back at the base of his neck.

"Hey, Alex," Vane said curtly. "Just heard you're in charge of movie night. Think you can handle it?"

"Yep." Alex straightened his shoulders. Since he and Vane had a history that included a fistfight in a Moroccan brothel, they'd spent the last two months playing hide-and-seek. Well, mostly hide. This was, in fact, the first time since Alex arrived that Vane had initiated a conversation. "We had movie night at Leedsville. *Escape from Alcatraz* was always a fave with your imprisoned men."

Vane frowned and Nate gripped Vane's shoulder. Nate hadn't spoken, so he was either listening to elevator music or getting an earful.

"Really?" Cain asked with a seriousness normally reserved for doctors and lawyers. "Did they watch—"

"No, Cain." Alex tried to keep the exasperation out of his voice. "We didn't have movie night. And I've no idea what your men did—or still do—for entertainment. I spent most of my time in solitary."

"Oh." Cain glanced at Nate. "I always wonder what they're doing."

"So do I," Nate whispered.

Alex headed upstairs. He hated talking about the ten of Kells's men who were in Leedsville prison—the same prison Alex had spent six years in—because he had little info. He'd rarely seen them. Those ten men were now serving twenty-year sentences.

"Alex?"

Alex glanced back to see Cain's grin.

"No horror movies. Vane gets freaked when things are too gross or scary."

"Fuck you, brother." Vane stomped toward training room two.

Nate slammed the receiver into the phone's base. "Cain, was that necessary?"

"No." Cain picked up a laundry basket filled with dirty towels and headed for the locker room. When he passed Alex, he winked. "But it was fun."

When Cain disappeared, Nate came toward the stairs. "How was Kells?"

"Pain in my ass." Alex paused, not sure if he should admit what he'd just learned. But Nate, as the unit's executive officer, had a right to know when their dear leader was about to implode. "I just learned Kells's wife Kate served him divorce papers."

Nate's mouth fell open, but since Alex had no interest in gossip, he went upstairs to the room he shared with Zack. Yeah, they all said Alex's middle name was *dick*. But he didn't want to talk about Leedsville prison or Kells's men still there or Kells's marriage. There was nothing Alex could do about those situations, and he had his own problems to worry about—like whether or not *Saw IV* was scary enough for Vane.

He threw himself onto his twin-sized bed that was almost a foot too short and draped one arm over his eyes. His other rested on his stomach. The room barely held two twin beds, two grown men, and their duffels stuffed with clothes.

He'd been out of prison for two months yet still felt the need to hide in the small space. Maybe it was too much time in solitary confinement, but he preferred being alone and able to see the exits. In this case, there was the door leading to the hallway and the window overlooking the back garden that consisted of a sad azalea and a lonely palmetto.

Although he appreciated the fact that he was free, the strings attached made him restless. If his life had been his own, he would have stolen Pete's bike and headed anywhere that wasn't near the South Boston tenement where he grew up—or near Kells and his unit's bullshit.

Alex chewed his lower lip and played his favorite mental game. What would he do if he were free of his past? Where would he go? The beach? The mountains? Would he move out west and live off the grid? Become a farmer?

As Alex imagined waking up in his own cabin on the beach/in the mountains/riding the range, his cell buzzed. The room was dark, but the phone's light shone a bluish-white. The text was in black.

He sat up and swung his legs over the side of the bed. His boots hit the floor with a thud and he reread the message.

Brother, we need to meet. A.

Nonononono. Alex shook the phone like a magic eight ball, as if that would make Aidan's message disappear. Except his brother's words lingered, demanding a response.

What did one say to a brother who'd known, the entire fucking time, that the man you'd been convicted of murdering was still alive?

Brother.

Alex paused in the typing to come up with the right words. Something elegant and unique for this oh-so-special occasion. Fuck. You.

CHAPTER 5

Isabel Rutledge unlocked the Saint Philip's cemetery gate and entered the east churchyard. With the streetlights twenty feet away and only a few spotlights in the trees, the area provided plenty of dark shadows. There were no alarms or cameras. No tourists, like those across the street.

As usual, there was a ghost tour guide with a group of people in front of Pirate House. One of the oldest homes in the city, it also stood next to Saint Philip's west churchyard. The one where they used to bury strangers. At this time of night, since all of the ghost action happened in the west churchyard, no one paid attention to the east.

She slipped the key into her purse and sat on an iron bench behind a gnarled oak tree. She deliberately stayed away from the earth-moving equipment that'd been digging along the back of the cemetery. The last thing she needed was to fall into an open grave.

Even though it was late, the humidity made her dress cling. She closed her eyes and slipped off her high heels. Her feet hurt and her back ached. But that was nothing compared to the migraine brewing behind her eyes. Her plan had yet to succeed. That meant consequences.

The kind of consequences that had killed Hezekiah tonight.

A breeze blew and she raised her face, hoping to catch the cooler air. Sirens sounded in the distance, and she smelled smoke. While in the cab she'd heard the explosion. It'd been closer than she would've liked, but she'd hired a new crew and there were kinks. The irony was if the ambulance sirens hadn't been cutting through the air, it would've been a pleasant evening.

"I'm assuming, from the noise, that Hezekiah is dead?"

She opened her eyes at the male voice and straightened her shoulders. Remiel came closer, pausing near an eight-foot-tall marble column covered in vines. Tonight Remiel wore a tuxedo with his black hair combed back from his forehead.

"Of course Hezekiah is dead." She tried hard to the keep the *duh* out of her voice. "He sold the Witch's Examination of Mercy Chastain to the Prince. He knew the risks."

"I wasn't expecting so much…attention."

"You're the one who suggested Clayborne and his crew."

Even in the shadows, she felt Remiel's frustrated glance. It burned with the coldest regard she'd ever encountered.

Remiel picked a wild daisy from a cluster near his feet and pulled off the petals one by one. "Did you see any Fianna warriors?"

"Two. In the club. I didn't approach them." Because she wasn't stupid. "I know you hate loud noises and high body counts. There was no way to save the driver without tipping off Hezekiah."

"The only reason I've come as far as I have is because I've kept things quiet." He threw down the daisy stem and picked another. "Nothing screams *villain in town* like dead bodies."

She almost brought up the Afghan POW camp where he'd held— and tortured—many of Kells Torridan's men for years, but no good came from contradicting Remiel. Instead, she studied the tourists across the street. They were all looking up at the top floor window of Pirate House. Except for the light next to the front door, the windows and the small alley leading to the back garden were dark. "There's been a development."

Remiel threw away the petal-less flower and sat next to her. "What happened?"

The tourists pointed at the house, and Isabel squinted. Was that a *shadow* in the window?

She shook her head and made her confession. "Stuart sold the Witch's Examination of Mercy Chastain to pay for the Pirate's Grille, and it now belongs to Allison. I couldn't rip it out of her hands."

"I thought you said we don't need the Pirate's Grille." Remiel's exhalation could have been heard by the dead. As long as he didn't stare at his left palm—a tic of his that preceded an episode—she'd be okay. So far, during all the years she'd worked for him, he'd never attacked her. But he was volatile, and a girl had to play the game well to survive.

"We don't. But I would've preferred no one else have it either."

"Allison has the Pirate's Grille, and the Prince has the Witch's Examination of Mercy Chastain. And you don't think that's a problem? Even though you've yet to find the treasure?"

"I'm not worried about Allison or the Prince. Hezekiah told me the Witch's Examination is missing the appendix. It's the appendix, along with the Pirate's Grille, that are the keys to finding the treasure. Since we already know where it's buried—approximately—none of it matters."

Remiel stood again to pace around the small tombstones in front of her. "Does the Prince know the appendix is missing?"

"I'm not sure, but I assume he does." When Remiel frowned, she added, "The Prince has no idea how close we are. By the time he does, we and the treasure will be gone."

"Who are you trying to convince? Me or yourself?" Remiel went back to leaning against the marble column and stared across the street. Now the tour guide had moved his group to the cemetery gates next to Pirate House. They were all pointing, probably convinced they'd seen a ghost. "You've yet to find that treasure."

"That kind of excavation takes time."

"We don't have time. Are you sure Stuart wasn't lying to you? You betrayed and tortured him."

Before you killed him. "He gave me the information before things became difficult."

"We need that treasure, Isabel. If you can't dig it up, I'll find someone who can."

She stood, appreciating the feel of the cooler ground on her bare feet. "Are you replacing me as your second-in-command?"

"I don't want to. But I will."

"I'll find that treasure." She pulled out the heavy brooch that hung on a chain around her neck. "I did make one mistake."

She didn't want to confess this, but if she didn't and he found out, he'd consider it a betrayal. And those didn't end with sunshine and daffodils.

He peered at her. "Excuse me?"

"I held the Pirate's Grille in my hand knowing that if I could destroy it, no one besides us could ever find that treasure. When Hezekiah yanked it away, I was frustrated. I told Allison about my affair with Stuart."

Remiel reached for the brooch, and the sapphire-and-diamond pendant shimmered. The clouds parted and the half moon illuminated his soulless blue eyes. "*Why?*"

She fought against ripping the jewelry out of his hands. He knew why. "I was angry."

"No, you allowed jealousy to ruin your judgement."

"I am not, nor have I ever been, jealous of Allison. Allison is a simple, weak woman who couldn't love a man to save anyone's life."

"'The lady doth protest.'" He dropped the necklace into Isabel's neckline, his tone of voice low.

"What's wrong?"

"Tremaine is in town. He was following Allison."

Remiel turned away again to watch the tourists now taking photos of the cemetery, flashes set on high. Even in the dim light, she saw his shoulder muscles flex beneath the tuxedo jacket. With the hours he spent in the gym, he had the kind of physique that made men jealous and women swoon—until they figured out he was a psychotic fuck. "It's unfortunate I couldn't take Tremaine out of play seven years ago. He was outside the club tonight and you didn't notice."

"How did you know?"

"I had someone follow you."

She bit her lower lip. "Who?"

"Clayborne."

"You're using my own crew against me?"

"Clayborne is desperate for extra money."

"Desperate men don't make great allies." Her dealings with the Fianna, past and present, had taught her that.

"No. They make dirty ones. We're at a critical point. We need to find that treasure before the Prince realizes what we're doing."

"We're close."

"But we haven't succeeded. That means, besides digging for treasure, you must find the appendix or recover the Pirate's Grille. Take one or both out of play. Your position in my organization depends on your imminent success." He reached for her hand and held it to his lips. Instead of kissing it, he squeezed until her knuckles turned white. "Do you understand?"

She nodded.

"Will Tremaine be a problem?"

She cleared her throat and withdrew her hand. It ached, but she'd never show weakness in front of him. He'd lose all the respect she'd worked so hard to earn. "No. Allison is incapable of that kind of trust."

Remiel, always the restless one, paced again, clenching and unclenching his fists. It wasn't a tic, just a sign of his brilliant mind thinking and plotting. His ability to play the mental chess game against Kells and the Prince always amazed her. "Have you seen Alex Mitchell?"

Now that was an unexpected question. In her own best self-interest, she kept her voice even. "No."

"You should renew your friendship."

"Why?"

He lifted an eyebrow. "If the Prince finds the appendix, we'll need leverage."

"Alex isn't useful leverage. The Prince allowed Alex to rot in prison for years. The Prince wouldn't trade anything for Alex."

"The Prince will never allow anyone to hurt his brother."

"Alex is a highly trained soldier who survived years in Leedsville, the army's secret, most secure, most brutal prison. He's not going to allow you to kidnap him." She waved a hand around the churchyard as if that would make Remiel remember what she couldn't forget. "Alex almost killed you the last time you two met."

"Just consider it." Remiel traced the curve of her cheek. His finger was so cold she shivered. "I wish you hadn't told Allison about your affair."

Isabel turned her head slightly, just enough for Remiel to drop his hand. "Allison treated Stuart horribly. She deserves the pain."

"Be careful," he whispered. "Your love for Stuart is showing." When she didn't respond, he added, "And for fuck's sake, stay away from men who bow."

Once he left the churchyard, she sat again. The tourists huddled around the guide and a police car with blue and red blinking lights pulled up next to them.

Her heart skipped around in her chest with that tight, uneasy feeling she despised—the uneasy feeling that told her Remiel was withholding information. The uneasy feeling that Remiel realized how much she had loved Stuart and what she'd been willing to do for him. The uneasy feeling that told her things were not only spinning out of her control, but also that if she didn't succeed—imminently—there would be consequences.

The uneasy feeling that told her she might possibly need an exit strategy.

CHAPTER 6

ALLISON PAID THE DRIVER AND GOT OUT OF THE CAB IN FRONT of Pinckney House. She slammed the door, annoyed at the time it'd taken her to get home. The driver had assumed she was a clueless tourist and driven toward the airport. Once he realized she was a local, he deducted the extra cost and apologized.

When she stepped onto the flagstone sidewalk, she hit a wall of heat and humidity. Her lungs filled with air scented by gardenias and damp bricks. She loved summertime in Charleston.

At least she used to.

As she walked up the pathway to her house, a five-story white building with Doric columns and wraparound porches on the first three floors, trying not to think about the fact that she'd almost kissed Zack or that Stuart had been unfaithful or that the Fianna were back in her life, she noticed a police car had parked under a streetlamp. Detective Hugh Waring hurried over to open the iron gate.

"Mrs. Pinckney." He followed her and latched the gate behind him. Despite the heat, he wore a tan poplin jacket over a white button-down shirt and jeans. Beneath a lapel, a gun rested in a worn leather holster. "I need to talk to you."

She led the way up the steps to her porch. "Is everything alright?"

"I wanted to let you know—" His phone buzzed. He frowned as he read the text. "There's been an incident down by the river."

Now that he mentioned it, she had heard sirens. "I think I smell smoke."

At that moment, the streetlamps and other house lights around them dimmed, then came back on. He shoved his phone into his back pocket.

"I wish I knew what was up with this city's power grid. I lost power for two hours this afternoon and had to hang my laundry to dry in the garden." She was waiting for her neighbors to complain. Line drying wasn't allowed.

"I agree," he said as he returned a text. "It's unsettling."

She sat in one of the porch rocking chairs. "You wanted to tell me something?"

Detective Waring leaned against the railing and crossed his arms. "I got a call earlier." While he spoke, his brown eyes scanned the perimeter, and his foot tapped on the plank floor. His hair stuck up in odd sections, like he'd been running his hands through it. "About Pirate House."

The Pirate House, one of the two oldest in the city, belonged to Allison—a gift from her deceased maternal grandmother. "What about it?"

"The call came from a ghost tour guide. While she was telling stories about the house to tourists, someone saw something in the upstairs window. I went there and...it's the darnedest thing."

"Please don't tell me you saw the ghost of Mercy Chastain." Allison tried not to sound exasperated. "Ghosts are the work of overactive imaginations that lead to mass hysteria and tragedies like the Salem witch trials."

He smiled. "And the witch trial of Mercy Chastain here in Charleston? Wasn't she your ancestor?"

"Yes." Allison clasped her hands in her lap and got back on topic. "What happened when you saw...whatever you saw?"

"I told the tourists to go home and that I'd investigate. I went into the Pirates Courtyard behind the house. There were no signs of forced entry. As I left, I passed the cemetery next door and saw..."

"Good grief." She didn't know whether to laugh or cry.

"A woman in a white gown in the back shadows of the cemetery."

"In the dark? Behind the locked gates? With these crazy dimming streetlights?"

He shrugged and the jacket stretched so tightly across his wide shoulders she wondered if the seams would hold. "Her white gown made her seem like she was floating. Since the gates were locked, I couldn't get in to check it out." His voice lowered to a hush. "It was creepy."

"Detective—"

"I know." He waved his arm like he was swatting gnats. "I don't believe in the paranormal. But this was strange."

She stood and offered a polite smile. "Imagination is a powerful thing, Detective Waring. I have no doubt whatever you saw tonight was disturbing, but it wasn't the ghost of Mercy Chastain. She disappeared centuries ago."

"You're probably right. I'll check out your property and say goodbye before I leave."

"You don't have to do that." Since Stuart's murder, Detective Waring had been doing nightly drive-bys.

"It won't take long." He gave her a half smile. "Besides, I'm not ready to go back to the station."

She smiled back because she understood. He was a new detective, from Boston, who'd admitted the move to Charleston hadn't been an easy one. "Thank you."

When he disappeared around the back, she breathed in the warm, night air and faced her home. White lights outlined the mansion's columns, green shutters flanked the windows, and pink flowers overflowed the boxes attached to the balconies. She loved Pinckney House, as well as the gardens, which encompassed a city block. Except tonight, despite the fact that her home had always offered the comfort and security she craved, the house felt dark and empty.

She closed her eyes and tried to breathe through the tight feeling in her chest. A few hours ago, her home wanted her, welcomed her. Now that she knew the truth about Stuart and Isabel's affair, Pinckney House seemed cool and uninviting.

"Allison?"

She squinted until she saw a man standing in the porch shadows. *Zack?* "What are you doing here?"

He came close enough that she heard the rustling of his black leather motorcycle jacket and felt his breath on her forehead. "Do you hear those sirens?" he asked.

"Yes." Despite the low light, she could see that he hadn't shaved since the morning, and she remembered the way his scratchy face felt against hers the night, years ago, when he'd kissed her. "Why?"

"Hezekiah Usher is dead."

～

Zack held his fists against his thighs to stop himself from reaching for Allison. "After you left, Hezekiah's limousine exploded."

"Hezekiah Usher?" She pressed a hand to her chest. "*Dead?* In a car bomb?"

"Yes." Zack's voice cracked.

"Who would do that? And why?"

"I don't know." He reached for her hand, surprised to find it so cold. "We need to talk about your husband."

Okay. He needed to work on his subtlety.

"About his death."

Yeah. Because that's so much better.

"I mean his murder."

Perfect.

Most of her blond hair, tucked up with crystal daisy hairpins, had come loose. Her shoulders slumped. She'd lost weight since he'd last seen her. Since he'd last kissed her.

He dropped her hand and listened to the summer frogs sing to each other, not sure what to say next.

"Zack—"

"Can we sit?" He pointed to two porch rocking chairs. She sat and he took the chair next to her. "It's possible the man who killed Hezekiah also killed Stuart. Since you're connected to both of them, you may be in danger."

"Stuart's murderer is dead. There wasn't even a trial to set things right." Her voice broke on the final word.

He stared into the garden beyond the porch. Despite the dark night, he saw reflections of white sheets illuminated by the lights strung through the garden's trees. They wafted, ghostlike, on the breeze coming off the harbor. "Stuart's murderer is dead, but he was a minion. There's another man, a more powerful man, who ordered Stuart's death."

She stood. "I haven't heard anything from Detective Waring about a...mastermind."

Zack stood and blinked because, for the briefest second, he thought he'd seen someone in white behind the sheets. When the sheets blew again, the image was gone. "That's because the Charleston PD doesn't know about this man."

"Does this man have a name?"

"It's classified."

She turned away to stand by the railing. With her arms wrapped around herself, she kept her gaze focused on the dark garden. "Did the Fianna—whoever they are—kill Stuart like they killed that man at Le Petit Theatre?"

"No." Zack moved behind her until their bodies almost touched. He raised his hands to place them on her bare shoulders, but dropped them instead. They stood so close, he felt her tremble. "I'm sorry, Allison." He meant it. He'd never wanted her to be unhappy.

She turned, her head tilted. Their mouths hovered inches apart. But her puffy eyes and trembling lips reminded him to keep his own baser instincts in check—not easy since his erection pushed against the zipper of his jeans. Just being near her, smelling the jasmine perfume he'd sent her two years ago, chipped away at his self-control.

Still, he cupped her chin with one hand and ran his thumb over her lower lip until his breathing shorted out.

She moved her head to break contact, but she kept her green gaze fixed firmly on his lips. "You came back after all these years to tell me I might be in danger? That my husband's death was ordered by some mastermind but you can't tell me the details?"

"I know it sounds crazy—"

"Mrs. Pinckney," Detective Waring said as he came around the other side of the house. "Everything looks—who are you?"

Allison touched Zack's arm and sent him a warning glance. "This is a friend. Zack Tremaine." Then she waved toward the other man. "This is Detective Waring."

Fan-fucking-tastic.

Since Zack wasn't ready to play, he shoved his hands in the pockets of his jacket and hid his annoyance. "Hey."

Waring's nostrils flared. "Are you Zack Tremaine who served in the Seventh Special Forces Group at Fort Bragg under the command of Kells Torridan? Part of the same unit that was recently dishonorably discharged?"

Allison inhaled sharply and stared at Zack.

Aaaaand... another fuck.

Before he could think of a more appropriate response, Allison said, "Detective, I hate to interrupt, but can we talk about this tomorrow? I'm tired."

Waring nodded at Allison, sent another glare at Zack, and left with the parting words "Mrs. Pinckney, your property is clear. But if you see anything strange, call my cell phone."

"I will," she said. "Thank you."

Once Waring left, Zack exhaled a sigh of the greatly relieved. "What was that about?"

Allison crossed her arms. "Why don't you tell me, since Detective Waring knows more about you than I do."

Zack reached to touch her hair, except she stepped away, and he dropped his hand. "I believe the man who killed Hezekiah, the same man who ordered Stuart's murder, is responsible for destroying my life as well as the lives of my men. And he may be coming after you."

CHAPTER 7

ALLISON UNLOCKED THE KITCHEN DOOR AND ENTERED PINCKNEY House. The air felt hot and the scent of jasmine and orange blossoms from the plants in the conservatory filled the kitchen.

Zack followed just as her dog appeared with a wagging tail. She tossed her purse on the kitchen table and knelt on the wood floor to bury her head in his neck. No matter what happened, Nicholas Trott was always there to make her feel better.

Except tonight, Nicholas Trott squirmed out of her grasp to jump on Zack.

"Hey, boy." Zack took off his jacket and hung it on a chair. Then he used both hands to scrub the dog's hairy neck. "Who are you?"

"Nicholas Trott. He's part Labrador and part sheepdog. He's a rescue."

Nicholas Trott rolled onto his back for a belly rub and Zack obliged. "I didn't hear him bark while we were outside."

She sighed and went to the fridge while Zack and her dog became BFFs. "He's not a guard dog."

Zack rose and the dog settled onto his bed near the brick fireplace.

She handed Zack a bottle of water and opened one of her own. He stood across the table from her, but it might as well have been an ocean between them. Detective Waring's truth bomb had been more than a surprise. It'd come armed with sharp edges. How else could she explain the hurt deep inside her chest? If Zack had truly been dishonorably discharged—which she couldn't believe—a lot had happened to him that she didn't know about.

Then again, she hadn't been one for sharing her life either. It'd been two years since they'd last had any contact.

They'd once been the closest of friends, and now they knew less about each other than random acquaintances. "Why did Detective Waring know all about you?"

"He knows my boss." Zack opened his bottle and took a long drink. The movement brought attention to his fully-tattooed arms. The dragon was—had always been—extraordinary. She wasn't sure if the tattoo emphasized his wide shoulders or the other way around. "Why was Waring checking out your property?"

Since she had no right to stare at him and wonder if his chest was as heavily muscled as his biceps, she went to the thermostat on the wall and tapped it until the compressor kicked on and cold air blew from the vents. "Detective Waring was looking for ghosts."

Zack laughed, except it sounded like he was choking. "You can't be serious."

"Unfortunately, I am." She adjusted the temp again. When had things gotten so awkward between them? "For the record, I don't believe in ghosts. But Detective Waring does."

Zack picked up the black leash on the table and saw the name *Nicholas Trott* embroidered in white. "Where did your dog's name come from?"

This is how their conversation was going to proceed? Polite questions with no real substance? Since she was tired, she relented. "Nicholas Trott is named after the first attorney general for the colony of Charleston who, in 1702, became the chief justice."

Zack's chuckle quickly moved into a more serious "Uh-huh."

She went to the sink to wash her hands. After everything that had happened tonight, she felt dirty. "Nicholas Trott—the man—is famous for his actions against brutal pirates like Blackbeard and Stede Bonnet. But Nicholas Trott solidified his place in Charleston history when, in 1703, he presided over Mercy Chastain's witchcraft trial." She dried her hands and laid the towel on the counter. "Nicholas Trott's legal arguments saved Mercy's life."

Zack finished his bottle and tossed it into the recycling bin near the sink. "Nicholas Trott saved your ancestor Mercy Chastain, thereby earning the honor of having a mutt named after him."

Allison grabbed his arm and pulled him out of the room, whispering, "Don't call my dog a mutt. He gets embarrassed."

"Really?" Zack tried to glance back until Allison dragged him down the hallway and into the sitting room, turning on lamps along the way.

The sitting room was her favorite space in the house. Her desk where she handled the household accounts, near the picture windows, overlooked the dark gardens. Two yellow chintz couches filled the middle space. She'd placed antique tables around the area, with bookshelves and a colonial-era fireplace dominating the interior wall.

She curled up on the couch and Zack sat on the loveseat across from her. His long legs filled the space between them. She wanted to know why he was here, but she also didn't. His answer might bring up emotions she wasn't capable of dealing with. Everything he'd told her the night of their one and only kiss had been true. She hadn't loved Stuart enough. The affair was proof of that truth.

"Allison?" Zack touched her knee covered by the black silk skirt. "What happened tonight at the Usher Society?"

She closed her eyes and pressed her head back against the couch. "During the investigation into Stuart's death, Detective Waring found Hezekiah Usher's business card in Stuart's pocket. I called Hezekiah, and he told me how to buy a silver coin—which cost way more than I expected—and where to meet him tonight."

"Did you learn anything new?"

Not new. Just life-shattering.

After telling Zack about the two documents and that Stuart was a member of the society, she added, "Hezekiah said that he'd sold the Witch's Examination of Mercy Chastain, but that the Pirate's Grille was now mine. Like a sad consolation prize."

Zack studied his clasped hands in front of him. Every time he squeezed his fingers, the muscles in his forearms rippled, making his dragon tattoo, which started on one wrist, went up his arm, across his back, and down his other arm to the other wrist, move. She couldn't help but wonder if anyone had sat next to him, holding his hand, while the tattoo was completed, like she'd done when he'd started it.

"Zack?" she prompted.

He met her gaze. "What is the Pirate's Grille?"

How could she have forgotten how brown his eyes were? How the dark hair on his arms covered the ink? She looked away, toward the fireplace filled with dried flowers. "It's a Cardan grille." Once she explained what that was and how it was used, she ended with, "This seventeenth-century grille was, apparently, owned by the Prince—"

"The leader of the Fianna?"

She nodded and turned away again before he realized she was staring at the dark stubble on his chin. She could even smell his after-shave, despite the fact he sat a foot away. "In 1710, the Pirate's Grille was stolen by a pirate named Thomas Toban and"—she rested her head against the couch and closed her eyes—"somehow ended up on the current-day black market only to be purchased by Stuart."

"Can you show it to me?"

She opened her eyes to see Zack staring at the floor. "Sure."

She got her handbag from the kitchen, and this time she sat next to him. Her arm brushed his, and she shivered. His hot skin surprised her. She'd forgotten what it felt like to be so close to a man.

She took out the tube and opened the end.

He laid the plastic-enclosed document on the coffee table. "Do you have any idea why Stuart would buy this?"

"No." She rubbed her forehead as if that would make the low-grade pounding go away.

Zack muttered a curse. "Did you ever hear Stuart mention a man named Remiel Marigny?"

"No. But you mentioned him tonight. You said he was your enemy. Why?"

"*Hell.* I wish I could tell you, but I can't." Zack ran his hands over his head. "Didn't the Witch's Examination of Mercy Chastain go missing after your dad died?"

She had so many more questions about things like enemies and Remiel Marigny and the Fianna, but from his tight, closed-off posture, she knew he'd wouldn't answer. Instead, she said, "Yes, it was stolen during my dad's funeral, when I was eleven. And Stuart knew that. If he found it, why wouldn't he tell me? Why would he sell it?"

"Did you ask Hezekiah?"

"I did. He just told me that Stuart sold it to buy the Pirate's Grille to protect me. But I have no idea what that means."

"Protect you financially, maybe? Is the Pirate's Grille worth a lot?"

"Yes. But if Stuart wanted to give me money, why wouldn't he just give me the cash? Why reinvest it in another manuscript?"

"No idea."

"The other strange thing is that I handle the household accounts. If Stuart was a member of the Usher Society, I have no idea how he paid for it."

"Did Stuart have another account? He was a bank president."

"It's possible." It would make sense since he'd had *another life.* "Although…"

"What is it?"

"After Stuart's death, the Pinckney Trust account, which pays for the house, was frozen. My brother-in-law Lawrence wanted an audit done before he'd let me have access to the trust."

"What does that mean?"

"As his wife, Stuart left me his assets that weren't in the Pinckney Trust. But the trust pays for the house itself, with all of its expenses like taxes, insurance, and repairs. Since the trust has been frozen, I've been paying the house bills with my own income and what was in our savings account."

"Has that been hard?"

"His salary as a bank president was far more than I make teaching at the College of Charleston. I've mostly been living off our savings and the life insurance money."

"I hate to say this, but Stuart either used money from the trust or had another account."

Unfortunately, Zack was probably right.

He rolled up the page and returned it to the tube. "Do you have a safe?"

"Yes. In Stuart's study."

Zack took her hand and helped her up. She'd taken off her heels and the thick rug beneath her feet felt soft and warm. So different from the chills that ran up her arms when Zack hesitated to release her fingers.

Trying to hide the awkwardness, she talked as she led the way through the parlor, music room, and foyer, to Stuart's study. "Can I ask about what happened to your unit? Your dishonorable discharge?"

"It's classified."

She wasn't surprised. "Then what about your hair? It's so much longer than when I last saw you."

Last kissed you.

"After I finished my training and joined the Seventh Special Forces group at Fort Bragg, I grew my hair for a mission and haven't been ordered to cut it." He opened the door to the study, and as she passed him, her arm brushed against him. A brief jolt of electricity made the hair on her arms stand up.

And that sound—had he inhaled sharply? Or had she?

She opened the wall safe and placed the tube on top of a vintage metal superhero lunch box that had painted broken daisies on the side.

"Is that yours?" A thread of laughter lined Zack's voice and she exhaled. The tension dissipated as quickly as it had arisen.

"No. It was my brother Danny's treasure box. I kept it after his death."

Zack closed the safe for her. "I'm sorry."

She blinked so she wouldn't cry. "It was a long time ago."

He spun the safe's dial and sighed. "With death, time is immaterial."

She wrapped her arms around her waist and closed her eyes.

"Allison?" Zack's voice sounded closer and he gripped her elbows. She opened her eyes to see his tight lips and dark eyes. His scent surrounded her. "Did someone hurt you tonight?"

Her laugh sounded like a bark. She pulled away and moved toward the French doors that looked out over the other side of her garden. She was glad for the darkness, since she'd had to fire the gardening staff and the plants had gone to seed.

"What happened?"

She didn't want to talk about this, but holding it in was making it hard to breathe. The truth was suffocating her. "Stuart was having an affair."

After a long moment, Zack whispered, "I don't believe it."

"He was sleeping with a woman named Isabel Rutledge. She's from Savannah but now lives in New Orleans. Her people are descended from one of the oldest Charleston families. Almost as old as mine and Stuart's." Allison sniffled and opened her eyes to meet his gaze. "Isabel is older than me by at least fifteen years. Maybe twenty. It's hard to tell because she's so beautiful."

"Was she wearing a red dress?"

She nodded. "How could you know that?"

"I saw her tonight. She left the club with Hezekiah and walked away minutes before the explosion."

"Isabel seemed to be part of Hezekiah's inner circle." Allison picked up a coffee mug with a GOT GHOSTS? logo off the desk and left the study. "Isabel acted annoyed when Hezekiah gave me the document."

Zack pulled out his phone and followed her into the kitchen as he texted. "I overheard Isabel talking about the Pirate's Grille."

Allison loaded the mug into the dishwasher and turned it on. "I'm surprised Stuart didn't leave the Pirate's Grille to Isabel."

Was that her voice that sounded so bitter and tired? She rested her bottom against the counter, gripped the granite edge, and dropped her gaze to the worn pine floorboards. Looking at Zack was too difficult. When she stared into his eyes, all she saw was pity, and that was the last thing she wanted from him.

Zack put away his phone and touched her shoulder. He was so gentle, she hardly felt it. "How did you find out about the affair?"

"Isabel told me. She was wearing my engagement brooch."

"Whoa. How—"

"Where are you staying?" Allison didn't want to talk about this anymore. She just wanted to fall into bed. From the dark circles under his eyes, she wondered when he'd last slept. "With Vivienne?"

Vivienne's mansion wasn't far from Pinckney House.

"No. Someone killed Hezekiah minutes after he gave you the Pirate's Grille." Zack shoved his hands in his pockets. "I'm sleeping here."

She started to protest, then stopped. There was no point in denying that she didn't want to sleep alone in the house. "If the Fianna didn't kill Stuart, do you think it was the same person who killed Hezekiah?"

"I think it's possible...*shit*." Zack gripped his hands behind his neck, and the muscles in his huge biceps rippled. She wondered what he'd look like if he untied his hair. She wondered what he looked like without his T-shirt.

What is wrong with me?

She turned away to wipe down the counter. "Is there a problem?"

"I have to call my boss in Savannah. Let him know I won't be back until tomorrow."

She rinsed the dishrag out beneath a stream of cold water. "Will your boss give you a hard time?"

Zack picked up the dog's leash and wrapped it around one hand. "He always gives me a hard time."

She hung the dishrag over the faucet and wiped her hands on a dry one. "This gym you work at—is it a twenty-four-hour kind of gig?"

Grooves appeared in his forehead, as if he were contemplating something. She wasn't sure what, but considering how he wound and unwound the leash around his hand, she wondered if he was telling her the entire truth. She knew him well enough to believe he'd never lie to her. But omissions were lies' kissing cousins.

"No." He tossed the leash onto the table, and Nicholas Trott perked his ears. "Is this house alarmed?"

Way to change the subject.

Since she *was* tired, and it *was* late, she decided to play along. "No. It used to be, but with the Pinckney Trust being frozen, I canceled it."

Zack ran a hand over his head. Again, the movement showed off the elaborate dragon tattoo that covered his arm in a display of color. "Do you have a gun?"

"Don't you have yours?" She raised what she hoped was a reproaching eyebrow. "The one you pulled on those two men earlier tonight?"

He chuckled and looked around the room as if she had a hidden arsenal in the pantry. "I do but I'd like something…more."

She sighed and the dog wheezed. This didn't surprise her at all.

She led Zack into the laundry room, toward the tall safe that stood against the far wall. She turned the dial a few times—her birthdate—and the door popped open, exposing Stuart's collection of hunting rifles and shotguns. "Take your pick."

Zack found a nine-millimeter pistol and shoved in a fully-loaded magazine. Then he took out the double-barreled shotgun, loaded a few rounds, and charged the weapon. "I'll hold the shotgun, but I want you to keep the pistol next to your bed." He paused before handing it to her. "You still know how to use it, don't you?"

"I may be a widow whose husband cheated on her"—she took the gun and drew back the slide until a bullet clicked into the chamber—"but I'm not helpless."

"I never said you were helpless."

No. He'd said she'd break all of their hearts.

Suddenly the room was too small and she couldn't meet his gaze. "I'm going to bed. I guess this is good night."

And she was glad. No, relieved. After all these years of dreaming about him, wondering what it would feel like to be in his arms again, dealing with him now was the last thing she wanted.

Despite his controlled demeanor, his chest heaved. "I guess so." He reached out to cup her cheek but took her free hand instead. He pulled gently and led her upstairs. Nicolas Trott followed too closely, almost tripping Zack when he hit the second-floor landing. "Which is your bedroom?"

Nicholas Trott stopped in front of the last door on the right and pawed the door open. She'd left her bedside lamp on, and it illuminated pale green walls and a white lace comforter on the king-size four-poster bed with the poles carved with rice stalks. Sheer white drapes hung from the canopy railings. Her favorite jasmine scent wafted out, with no hint of the masculine base notes she'd once taken for granted.

It was a romantic room that reeked of abject loneliness.

A heaviness filled her chest, making it hard to breathe and her sinuses feel tender.

If Zack only knew…

He kissed her palm and wrapped her fingers around it. "I'm sorry."

"You're not responsible for Stuart's death."

"Not that. Despite the violence of that night seven years ago, I've never forgotten our kiss. I replay it in my mind every night before I go to sleep."

She closed her eyes to avoid his intense gaze. An intense gaze that sought a particular truth more than a particular memory. While his kiss had haunted her marriage, she wasn't strong enough to admit that to him. All the truths she'd learned tonight, along with Stuart's death, had left her too raw, too sensitive, too sad. "Is that why you're sorry?"

"No. I'm sorry for this." His lips pressed against hers. His arms wrapped around her, pulling her close until their bodies collided.

She wanted to throw her arms around his neck, move her soft curves against his hard body. She wanted to tilt her head and stand on her tiptoes. She wanted to be held like she mattered, like she wasn't alone, like she was loved.

"*Allison*." The guttural word sounded as if it'd been dragged from his throat.

Her lips softened beneath his…until she tasted salt. From her tears.

Somehow, somewhere, she found the strength to pull away, and Zack let her go. This close to him, she could feel more than see his large body shaking. His wide chest pulsed beneath his T-shirt, and his flared nostrils meant he was trying to drag in gallons of oxygen.

Nicholas Trott worked his way between them and rolled onto his back. The house lights dimmed, went out completely, and kicked back on a second later. The brief power outage knocked her from the sensual kiss-induced fog.

She reached for the doorjamb, needing her house to hold her up.

Her heart raced, and her breasts threatened to push over the top of her strapless gown. She hadn't planned on kissing Zack tonight—or ever again—yet it was the only thing she'd done in the last two months that felt right, that made any sense.

"I need to, uh, go to bed... I mean sleep." Her toes curled against the wood floor. "You can pick any of the eight guest rooms to sleep in."

"Of course. Right." He fixed his gaze on her lips again. "If you need me—"

"I know." She swallowed and it tasted like she'd gargled with salt water. "Good night."

She hurried inside and shut the door. It was only after she'd leaned against the frame, eyes closed, tears coursing, that she realized Nicholas Trott had chosen to stay with Zack. Because the big difference between her and her dog?

Apparently, Nicholas Trott wasn't afraid of Zack, while she was terrified.

CHAPTER 8

Zack had once read that the Knights of the Round Table followed seventeen codes of chivalry, one of which was to honor and respect women. And, as far as he could remember, the list didn't include *be an asshole.*

With Nicholas Trott between Zack's feet, he stumbled downstairs and almost landed on his ass in the foyer that could fit an entire platoon's encampment. He'd not meant to kiss Allison. Hell, he'd not meant to do any of the things he'd done today, including leaving Savannah without permission.

He was usually driven by the rules of combat and the order of his unit, but when it came to Allison, his greater mind caved to his lesser mind. Seven years had passed since he'd last seen her, since he'd last kissed her, and his attraction had matured instead of waned. Proving that his feelings for her were real, had always been real, and would probably never *not* be real.

He was head over heels with no idea what to do about it. She'd responded to his kiss for the briefest moment, yet she'd also pulled away. She hadn't been ready and he'd pushed himself on her. Again, earning him the asshole designation. Maybe he could start a new group called the Order of the Bastard. Since his parents had never married, the double entendre suited him.

One thing that gave him hope was what he saw on her dressing table in her bedroom—the bottle of jasmine perfume he'd sent her from Paris two years ago.

His phone buzzed with a text. He'd expected a return note from Nate, since Zack had texted him earlier about Isabel. Instead, this was from Luke, another one of his buddies at the gym: *Call your sister.*

Right. Zack had forgotten. As he walked to the kitchen, he dialed Emilie. When she didn't answer, he left a message. "Hey, Em. It's Zack. I'm returning your call. I'll try you tomorrow."

The dishwasher rattled on the wash cycle, and he reset the oven's blinking digital clock. He shoved his phone in his back pocket and grabbed the shotgun from the kitchen table. It wasn't until he held the gun again that his breathing evened out. The weapon centered him. The weapon was something he could handle with skill. The weapon was real and true and honest, three things he needed to feel right now because learning about Stuart's affair had been an emotional gunshot to the chest.

An affair was the last thing that he'd ever believe of Stuart. The only reason Zack hadn't stopped the wedding was because he'd known Stuart loved and would honor Allison.

He'd also, at that time, had no understanding of what they'd seen and heard that night at Le Petit Theatre. After the bowing men had disappeared with the man they'd killed, he'd taken Allison home and they'd never discussed it again.

Once he'd joined his Special Forces group and heard rumors about the Fianna, he'd put some of the story together. But he still had a lot of questions about what it all meant.

Carrying the weapon, he and the dog wound their way through three rooms until entering the study. The dog dove for his bed and Zack sent another text to Nate describing almost everything that'd happened, including the fact that Zack wouldn't return to the gym until the morning. Then he searched the room for anything that could link Stuart to Remiel Marigny, the arms dealer who'd been terrorizing their unit.

Nicholas Trott's ears perked and he raised his head.

"It's okay, buddy. She'll never know. I promise."

Nicholas Trott dropped his head and sighed. The dog was… purring.

Ten minutes later, he'd found nothing tying Stuart to Zack's unit or Remiel Marigny. While he closed Stuart's desk drawers, the dog ran toward the window. He stood on his hind legs, paws on the window ledge, and stared into the darkness. His tongue hung out as he panted.

The desk lamp dimmed, flickered, and turned off. Zack stood next to the dog, his handgun drawn, shotgun nearby. He needed a minute for his eyes to adjust to the darkness. This part of the city's power grid had gone down. "What's wrong, buddy?"

The dog barked once.

Zack peered out the window, and Nicholas Trott…growled. Zack knelt and pressed his shoulder against the dog's tense body. The garden surrounded the house on three sides, leaving the shadowed perimeter vulnerable to a nighttime attack. White sheets drifting on a breeze glowed in the half-moon's light, a few getting caught on nearby tree branches.

Was that a shadow behind one of the sheets?

A flash of lightning broke through, then thunder rumbled. He steadied his breathing and pressed his hand against the dog's neck. Nicholas Trott's heart rate increased. His ever-wagging tail was now tucked between his legs.

Another flash of lightning. Then thunder. The woman in a white gown appeared so suddenly, Zack fell onto his ass. Her wide eyes bulged. Her mouth opened in a silent scream. A nanosecond later, she disappeared.

Nicholas Trott tried to paw his way through the window. His nails scraped the glass. Zack grabbed the gun he'd dropped and got up.

What the fuck was that?

He ran to the front door, the dog beside him. Zack took a deep breath and opened the door. Another lightning strike left behind a static charge that raised the hairs on his arms.

Nicholas Trott ran across the porch and turned the corner, disappearing.

Shit. He followed, listening to the night noises around him…except all was quiet. He found the dog on the steps leading to the garden.

He hated admitting that he didn't want to roam the area in the dark. He also didn't want to leave Allison in the house alone. But someone had been outside. He wasn't sure what he'd seen, but he'd never experienced anything like it before. Considering he was a Special Forces officer, with many combat tours behind him, that meant a lot.

He gripped his weapon and went into the garden. Thunder and lightning clapped simultaneously. Nicholas Trott tripped over a wicker laundry basket, and Zack yanked sheets off the line. The least he could do was save Allison's laundry.

When finished, he carried the basket under one arm, kept his weapon ready, and led the dog inside. His timing was perfect, since the rain hit just as he shut the door. "Come on, buddy. I need your help."

He dropped the basket in the foyer and locked the front door. Then he and the dog spent the next hour checking every window and door of the house, which was far larger than he'd ever imagined. It even had a ballroom and an attached greenhouse.

Once assured that the house was secure, he grabbed pillows and blankets from a guest room and made a bed for himself outside Allison's door. Between Nicholas Trott, the shotgun, his handgun, and various knives he kept on himself, he was confident he could prevent whatever the hell had happened tonight from getting close to Allison.

Rain hit the roof and he settled himself on the floor, his weapons within reach. Then the dog decided that Zack's stomach made a better pillow. A few minutes later, while Zack rubbed the dog's head, Nicholas Trott started purring.

Just as Zack began to drift off, he received a text from Nate.

> *Get back to the gym. ASAP.*
> Why?
> *Kells is pissed. And Isabel Rutledge works for Remiel Marigny.*

‿

"*Drown the witch!*"

Allison dropped her book and peeked out the window of her tree house.

A group of kids—her brother Danny's friends—stood on the riverbank, shouting and pointing at the water. She was supposed to be watching them but had retreated to her tree house to read more about Heathcliff.

"He's guilty!" a few shouted.

She squinted against the sun. Danny and his friends knew they weren't allowed to play near the river. She shaded her eyes with her hands until she saw something bobbing in the deeper water. "No!"

She climbed down and ran toward the river on her bare feet, barely noticing the pine straw and rough grass that covered the property of Fenwick Hall. Kids stood along the bank, some even hung off the willow branches that draped over the river.

"Witch, witch, drown the witch!"

More screamed, "He's guilty! Danny's guilty!"

A little girl cried, "I don't want to play Dunk the Witch!"

Please. God. No.

Allison pushed through the crowd and saw a body partially submerged with a rope straggling behind the head. The tide was dragging the body deeper into the river's current.

"Get my uncle Fenwick now!" She jumped into the water. The cold stole her breath and it took her a minute to gain control of her arms and legs. She started swimming toward Danny, wishing she was wearing shorts instead of a dress.

When she reached him, she grabbed his arm. "Danny!"

He didn't respond, only floated farther into the river. She tried to wrap her arms around his body, but something was dragging Danny down. That's when she realized they'd tied a bag of rocks to a rope around his waist. "Danny!"

Water filled her mouth and she coughed because she couldn't swallow the brackish water. She heard screams from the bank, and her uncle Fenwick's voice telling her not to fight the current. She clung to her brother but she was so tired. She kept swallowing water and her brother was sinking. Because she wouldn't let go of him, she was sinking too.

Everything seemed dark and she couldn't move. She couldn't see. She couldn't breathe.

～

Allison opened her eyes and struggled against an unseen force. Her arms and legs refused to move. A huge weight on her chest made breathing impossible. She tried to yell, but nothing came out except for garbled sounds. It was dark and cold and terrifying. She was still in the nightmare but awake at the same time.

While her extremities felt paralyzed, she was aware of both the past and present. She was in the water and in her bed, unable to save herself or Danny. In both situations, she was drowning.

She started hyperventilating and felt lightheaded.

"Allison!" Zack's voice cut through the waking nightmare. "Make fists."

Except she couldn't move.

"Look at me."

Except she couldn't see.

"Find a path back to me."

Except she couldn't find one.

Zack took her face in his hands and brought his mouth close enough for her to feel his breath. His lips pressed against hers and he whispered, "Breathe with me."

She struggled to move until she was exhausted. Her body still wasn't responding.

Zack's breath traced her mouth. "Come on, Allison. *Dammit.* Breathe. With. Me."

Suddenly the force holding her down released her. She expelled the breath she'd been holding, and Zack helped her sit until she fell against his shoulder.

He maneuvered them so he was propped up against the headboard and she lay almost on top of him. His hand ran up and down her spine while she tried to make sense of what had just happened. It took a few minutes until she could breathe regularly and the tingling in her arms and legs went away.

"Sleep paralysis sucks."

"I know." He wrapped his arms around her shoulders and she buried her face against his warm chest, drawing in his scent of bay rum. He still had his clothes on and she rubbed her cheek against the cotton T-shirt. "Were you dreaming about Danny?"

She nodded. When they were in college, she'd told him about her brother's death and how when she dreamt about Danny she suffered from sleep paralysis. "It happens when I'm stressed."

Zack's chest lifted beneath her head. His breathing was strong and steady, unlike hers which was shaky and erratic. "It's been a tough night. And the power has been out for hours."

That must be why the air felt so still and hot. "Did it rain?"

"Thunderstorm. I brought in your laundry."

She raised her head. "Thank you."

He kept one hand on her back while the other pushed strands of hair behind an ear. "You're welcome."

He'd unbound his hair and it was longer than she'd realized. She reached to touch it until she decided she had no right.

"Allison, is this the master bedroom?"

She stiffened. "Why would you ask that?"

"Earlier tonight, I was checking the windows and doors, and I found a bedroom at the end of the hallway. It's larger with an attached bathroom and sitting room."

She closed her eyes. "Since it was his house, Stuart stayed in the master bedroom. Two years ago, I moved in here."

"Why?"

"We had a fight. At the time, he thought it was better if we slept apart...temporarily."

"But it wasn't temporary?"

"No."

"What was the fight about?"

You. She stared at his arm lying across his chest. The eyes of the dragon tattoo shone. It'd always surprised her that the dragon's eyes were sad instead of fierce. In college, he'd let her trace the colorful design, teasing her because while he'd sit for hours in the tattoo shop, she didn't have the courage to get a flu shot. "The fight doesn't matter now."

"Did Stuart's affair begin before or after you had separate rooms?"

"After."

"After that fight, you two never..."

"No. After I moved out, we never again spent the night together as…husband and wife."

There. She'd said it. She'd been a complete failure as a wife and now Zack knew it.

He sighed. "I'm sorry."

She blinked, but it couldn't stop a rogue tear from tracking down her face. "I am too. So very sorry about so many things."

"The affair wasn't your fault."

"I never should have married Stuart. My father's death—"

"Which also wasn't your fault."

"—followed so closely by my brother's death left me unable to love others completely. And tonight's mess is the proof of that."

"You know what I think about that belief. It is, and always has been, horseshit."

Yes, he'd often said that. Yet she hadn't believed it then and didn't believe it now. "My father died because I ran away and he went looking for me in the woods. Then my brother died because I wasn't paying attention."

She didn't deserve love.

"You were eleven when those *accidents* happened. You were a child and were never responsible. Regardless of what your mother has told you over the years." He kissed her head. "One day, I'm going to prove you wrong."

"Good luck with that." She sniffled. "You'd have better luck finding Mercy Chastain's ghost and asking her why she disappeared and how she died."

He chuckled. "Does that matter to you?"

She yawned. "If I can find out what happened to Mercy and write about it, I have a good chance of making tenure."

"That means I'm going to prove you wrong and help you make tenure."

She yawned again. "How?"

"I'm going to find Mercy and ask her." He moved until his head was lying on a pillow and hers was still on his chest. "Because I believe that ghosts are *real*."

CHAPTER 9

THE NEXT MORNING, ISABEL ENTERED WASHINGTON SQUARE AND sipped her coffee.

She buttoned her black sweater over her yellow knit dress, and her sandals crushed oyster shells on the path around the park's perimeter. She preferred meeting her crew early, before tourists appeared and the humidity took everyone hostage.

Clayborne waited beneath a pink crepe myrtle tree. His dirty jeans, black Harley-Davidson jacket lying on a nearby stone bench, and eau de licorice meant he'd come from the barn.

She placed her coffee on the bench and held her clutch handbag against her stomach. "Did you get my message?"

"About not following you anymore?" Clayborne tossed his cigarette onto the grass and ground it out with his boot. "Yep. I did it for the money."

Which was the problem with hired help—she'd been telling Remiel that for years.

Clayborne squinted at her. "Did you know that Tremaine spent the night with Allison?"

Isabel brushed her hand across her forehead. Even though she'd been born and bred in the South, she hated the summer heat. "Tremaine won't be an issue."

"Why do you assume that? Allison is a beautiful—"

"Allison is a sad, pathetic widow."

"One might think you were jealous of your lover's wife."

"That's absurd. Why would I be jealous of her?"

"Because, in the end, Stuart didn't choose you. You fucked him beautifully and betrayed him badly—so badly that he gave up his life to protect Allison."

Isabel tightened her hold on her handbag. She had no intention of confiding her feelings about Stuart to anyone. She knew the truth. She knew Stuart had loved her far more than he'd ever loved Allison. She also knew, in Remiel's world, emotions were not allowed. She may have loved Stuart, but no one could *ever* know that. "Allison is a sad, pathetic widow who is easily manipulated and controlled."

"A sad, pathetic widow who has the Pirate's Grille."

"How do you…? Of course." She moved into the shade beneath a towering oak tree. "Remiel told you."

"He also told me Allison has an armed Green Beret hanging around, desperate to save her or protect her or whatever it is that heroes do."

"Are you scared, Clayborne?"

"Fuck no. I'm just saying if you can't control your emotions, your jealousy may end up biting you in your beautiful, firm ass."

Great. Sexual harassment from the temp. "Right now I need you to set a diversion so you can get into Allison's house and take the Pirate's Grille."

"Why? We don't need it."

"That doesn't mean I want anyone else to have it." She opened her handbag and handed him a slip of paper. "It's probably in Stuart's safe. Here's the combination."

He ran his fingers through his short blond hair. "What about Tremaine?"

"He's on his way back to Savannah." She'd not been thrilled when another member of her crew had told her about Zack staying with Allison, but Isabel wasn't surprised. The protective types did things like that. "With Zack gone, Allison will have no one to turn to. Once we get the Pirate's Grille, we're done with Allison Pinckney."

Clayborne stared at Isabel for a long moment before grabbing his jacket. "You're underestimating Allison and Tremaine. She may be emotionally broken, but she's not weak. And the ex–Green Beret is nothing if not persistent. Jeez, he's been in love with her for years."

Heat crawled up Isabel's spine. She didn't need a reminder that Allison was the original sleeping princess, totally unaware of the two lovers—one dead and one alive—who protected her.

Isabel *despised* helpless, weak sleeping princesses.

She tilted her head and sent another barb. "This is why I'm the boss and you're the help."

Clayborne scoffed. "Speaking of help, our crew at the work site hasn't found what we we're looking for. Are you sure we're searching in the right spot?"

"I'm sure. It has to be there somewhere. Tell them—no, I'll call and remind them. A pirate's treasure worth over sixty million dollars isn't going to be buried in a chest a few feet in the ground. Besides, Stuart confirmed the location."

"You tortured the information out of him."

"That doesn't mean it's not true." Isabel brushed crepe myrtle blossoms off her skirt. "Did you find anything in Hezekiah's office that could incriminate us?"

"No. There've been tons of cops coming and going since the explosion, so I couldn't stay long."

"After you get the Pirate's Grille, send one of your men back there. Although he didn't look it, Hezekiah played his game brilliantly. Make sure he left nothing behind. Now. Have you heard from your lover?"

Clayborne spat on the ground near his crushed cigarette. "That bitch has vanished."

"Is there any chance she's under the protection of the Prince?"

"Fuck if I know. I still can't believe she stole the Witch's Examination of Mercy Chastain from me and gave it to Stuart."

"Bit of advice, Clayborne? Next time you confide in your lover, make sure she's not half your age and desperate for money."

"That's not fair. She seduced *me*."

"Your wife won't see it that way."

"My wife will never know." Clayborne moved into Isabel's personal space until she could smell his sour breath. "*Ever.*"

She waved a hand in front of her face. Men like Clayborne were all the same: insecure and arrogant. "Text me when you've completed your mission."

When Clayborne left, Isabel sat on the bench to finish her coffee and check her phone. After calling the leader of the work site and reassuring him that the treasure had to be there somewhere, she checked in with her crews in New Orleans and Savannah. Thank goodness both places were quiet at the moment.

"'Tis a beautiful morning, Lady Isabel. Is it not?" The male voice, low and melodic, came from a nearby tree.

Isabel looked up and saw two men, a white man wearing a baseball cap and jeans, a black man in a seersucker suit. When she stood, both men hit their chests and bowed at the waist.

Fuck.

She considered her options. She had a gun in her purse, but they'd disarm her before she opened the clasp. While she had decent self-defense moves, she wasn't capable of fighting off two full-fledged Fianna warriors. The only three things in her favor were the time of day, the public space filling with people, and the fact that she was a woman.

Although she'd learned the hard way that the *not hurting women* rule could be lifted.

She shielded her eyes from the sun. "It is a beautiful morning."

The dark-skinned warrior came forward and spoke in a polished British accent. "My name is Marcellus. My brother is Horatio."

Horatio stayed in the shadows, the thug behind Marcellus's gentility.

"What can I do for you?"

"'Tis an unfortunate situation we wish to remedy. The Witch's Examination of Mercy Chastain is without its appendix."

She took a deep breath so she didn't stumble over her words. "What happened to it?"

"Your lover removed it and told not a soul."

Isabel sank onto the bench. *Stuart had removed the appendix?*

Marcellus crouched in front of her. "My lady, do you know where—"

"No." She shook her head for emphasis. "I don't know where it is."

"'Tis unfortunate." Marcellus, still in his crouched position, smiled. "We have a proposition."

Isabel stood again, forcing Marcellus to do so as well. "I don't make deals with warriors because warriors—and the Prince—can't be trusted."

Marcellus held up his phone with an image of a bank account statement. *Her* account. "'Tis a secret from the Fiend. Funded by your lover for your escape."

She swallowed. The irony was the one thing she'd learned from dealing with the Fianna was that her contingencies needed contingencies. This account Stuart had set up for her was her last-ditch contingency in case she could no longer control Remiel's sadistic tendencies. But if Remiel—aka the Fiend—found out, he'd consider it a betrayal. And her punishment would be far worse than what she'd done to Hezekiah.

She sat again and gripped the edge of the stone bench until the aggregate cut her palms. *Please don't let me be sick.* "What do you want?"

Marcellus slipped his phone into his jacket pocket. "Betray the Fiend and accept the Prince's offer of asylum."

She met Marcellus's brown gaze. While his eyes appeared open and honest, he worked for the Prince. "Remiel will kill me."

Marcellus's face softened and he crouched in front of her again. "My lady, let your desperation turn your trust into hope."

Trust? Marcellus must be insane. Then again, he was a Fianna warrior. "I could never trust the Prince, and he will never forgive me."

"What function has mercy except to confront sin?"

Mercy? For me? "The Prince will never offer me mercy. Not after I betrayed his brother. Not after the other things I've done."

Marcellus bowed his head. "Your choices are thin, options deadly."

She closed her eyes and bit her lower lip. Marcellus was right. If she didn't take the Prince's offer of asylum, and the Prince sent that financial file to Remiel, she was a dead woman. The problem was she understood, probably better than Marcellus and Horatio, that the Prince's asylum was almost as terrifying as Remiel's anger.

She opened her eyes. "I request a parlay with the Prince."

Horatio came forward, clutching his own cell phone. "You have no words our Prince needs to hear."

"That's not—"

Marcellus held up his hand. This time Horatio handed her his phone with a photograph on the screen.

"'Tis time"—Marcellus stood—"to consider our offer. You have two days."

She returned the phone and didn't respond because words were pointless.

The men walked away with the kind of smooth gait that took tremendous strength and power to achieve.

She'd no idea how long she sat there, but she eventually texted the leader of her New Orleans crew about what she saw in that photo. Minutes later, she had her answer.

Yes.

In that moment, she knew the truth. If she didn't find that treasure soon, she was dead.

∽

Allison said goodbye to her student and shut her office door. So far this morning, she'd met with three graduate students and approved their research projects, sent off two emails to her boss, and left a message for a colleague at UVA who specialized in seventeenth-century pirates. The same colleague who'd notified her about the witch's examination sale.

She'd also organized her files regarding her Finding Mercy Chastain research project—the one that would hopefully get her tenure—and she'd done an exhaustive internet search into the Fianna and found very little. What she did learn left her uneasy and more convinced than ever that she and Zack had met Fianna warriors in Le Petit Theatre seven years ago.

Fianna warriors—who came into existence in ancient Ireland—tithed their lives to the Prince and had to commit acts of penance. Acts such as only speaking in verse from books of ancient Gaelic poetry or, in later years, Shakespeare. They also learned how to walk in a certain way and had to complete a ruthless training regimen that included running naked and unarmed in the woods in winter while being hunted by other warriors. Then there was the barbaric, bloody rite of passage known as "the gauntlet."

Oh, and apparently they bowed before they killed. Because, yes, the Fianna were also deadly assassins.

And so far she'd met four of these warriors who, also according to her research, weren't supposed to exist. Two in New Orleans seven years ago and two last night. That left her with even more questions, the most important being: What connection did they have with Stuart?

After reheating her coffee in the microwave on her filing cabinet, she returned to her desk to study the Pirate's Grille again. A breeze blew through the open French doors of her College of Charleston office, and Nicholas Trott rolled over on his bed beneath her enormous white board that held photos of her research into Mercy's disappearance in 1704.

She stretched her arms over her head and checked the time. She was meeting her brother-in-law, Lawrence, at Pinckney House at eleven and wanted to get some more work done. But her focus had apparently stayed in bed. Although she tried not to think about the fact she'd spent most of the night in Zack's arms and everything else that'd happened, she couldn't let it go. Not Stuart's affair. Not meeting the Fianna warriors—then and now. Not learning that Stuart had been searching for the dread pirate king's treasure.

Whatever that meant.

As she scrolled through another Fianna search, her phone buzzed. She sipped her coffee, read Pastor Tom's text, and responded. Yes, I'll be at Stuart's memorial service on Friday.

After all, she had been Stuart's wife.

Another text came quickly, except this one was from an unknown ID.

> *What is it ye would see, my lady? If aught of woe or wonder, cease your search.*

"What in the world?" She hurried to the French doors that led into the courtyard garden behind her building, as if the texter would be there, hoping to see her reaction. Of course, the courtyard was empty. The only movement was the water splashing around the fountain where Persephone stood in perpetual running-away motion.

A knock startled her and she spun around to see the door open. When her best friend Maddie's head appeared and her daughter Susan ran in and headed for Nicholas Trott, Allison exhaled. Her heart raced, and she flexed her fingers against her skirt. "Hi."

"I hope we're not bothering you." Maddie came in clutching a bakery bag and shut the door behind her. "Susan wanted to see Nicholas Trott and I knew you had office hours today."

"Hi, Miss Allison!" Susan, in a white sundress and braided brown hair, sat on Nicholas Trott's bed with the dog's head in her lap. "This morning I found a worm on the sidewalk. And I picked strawberries in my mom's garden."

Allison smiled and went over to kiss Susan's head. "I'm thrilled to see you. So is Nicholas Trott. And I can't wait to hear all about the worm."

The dog licked Susan's face and she giggled.

Maddie laid the bag on the desk and went to the coffee machine next to the microwave. Since Allison always had students in her office, she had an entire coffee/tea setup, complete with mugs, sugar, and creamers. Once Maddie poured two, she handed one to Allison.

She took the fresh cup and tried not to think about Zack. He'd made coffee and left before she'd even woken up. She was sad, annoyed, and relieved. And all of it was wrapped up in abject humiliation. Not only had she needed Zack's help to wake from the sleep paralysis, but she'd also admitted that she and Stuart hadn't had a *normal* married relationship for years before his death.

As she put cream and sugar in her cup, she felt like another woman doing the mundane things of life. The separation from herself made her feel lightheaded.

Is this what grief was like? Or was it kissing Zack again?

"Allison?" Maddie touched her arm. "Are you alright?"

"I'm...great."

Maddie took Allison's wrist and led her outside into the courtyard. Once they were seated on an iron bench, Maddie said, "I got your texts this morning. I hate to say this, but you look..."

"Like hell?" Because that's how she felt.

"Exhausted."

Allison focused on Persephone, who ran with her arms over her head and her eyes closed. "I don't know why I feel this way. Tired. Confused. Shaky. I hate women who cry, yet that's all I do now."

"I'm sure it's grief. What else happened last night? Did you get into the Usher Society?"

After telling Maddie about the Pirate's Grille, Hezekiah's death, and Isabel, Maddie said, "Stay here," and left.

A moment later, she returned with the bakery bag and handed Allison the biggest piece of blueberry coffee cake that any woman had ever eaten in one sitting. She bit into it and sighed at the heavenly sweet/tart taste.

Meanwhile, Maddie stared at her with concern in her brown eyes. Today Maddie's long brown hair was pulled back in a clip, so it hung down her back. "Isabel and Stuart were having an affair? For years?"

Allison nodded and took another bite. It was lemony and blueberry-ey and sweet. Yet for the perfectness of the cake, all she cared about was when the pain would go away.

Maddie handed Allison a napkin and laid her own on the skirt of her blue sundress. "I don't understand. How did you not know about it?"

Once Allison had wiped her lips, she said, "Did you know about your husband's affair right away?"

"No." Maddie put her uneaten cake back in the bag. "Although when I look back now, I see the signs. Hindsight and all that."

Allison took Maddie's hand and squeezed. Her friend was in the midst of a vicious divorce that included having to leave her home overlooking the Charleston Battery.

Allison finished her cake and wiped her mouth again. "I want to go back to bed."

"I felt that way for months." Maddie sipped her coffee. "When does your brother-in-law come into town?"

"I'm meeting Lawrence later this morning to talk about *things*."

Maddie snorted delicately. "You had every right to bury Stuart after his death. It's Lawrence's fault for not wanting to leave Paris and return for the funeral. It's also very generous of you to agree to this memorial service Lawrence demanded."

"I didn't have the energy to fight him. But until then, I'm going to see if I can work on my research project."

"Are you any closer to finding out what happened to Mercy Chastain?" Maddie's smile brightened her face and Allison realized that it'd been a long time since she'd seen her friend happy.

"Unfortunately, no." Allison grabbed her cup and savored the coffee. It wasn't quite as bitter as before. "If I can find out what happened to Mercy after she disappeared in 1704, I can get my article published in *The Journal of Eighteenth-Century History*. If I do that, I'm almost guaranteed tenure."

"What about Mercy's witch's examination? If Stuart sold it, can you ask this new buyer to let you read it again?"

"I have no idea who bought it. And Hezekiah is dead. But there is something odd about the Pirate's Grille. In one corner there's a sketch of a broken daisy."

"Why is that odd?"

"It's been years since I've seen Mercy's witch's examination, but I remember there was a sketch of a broken daisy on every page."

"That's odd."

"I know."

Susan appeared with the dog. "May I give Nicholas Trott a snack?"

Allison nodded. "There are treats in the jar behind the sugar. But don't let him see you. I don't want him to know where they are."

Susan's grin showed off her missing teeth. "Thanks!"

Allison shared a look with Maddie. After the long, horrible custody battle that was still brewing, anything that made Susan happy made them happy.

When both the dog and the girl went back into the office, Maddie said, "Are you still having restoration work done on the Pirate House?"

Since Allison didn't live in the eighteenth-century house she'd inherited from her grandmother, she rented it to Maddie and her sister, who owned Ashton Antiques, an appointment-only antiques firm. Maddie used the first floor of the house as an exclusive showcase. "I had to postpone the work due to lack of cash flow. Why?"

"I was there yesterday with a client and thought I heard a noise upstairs."

"It was Mercy Chastain's ghost!" Susan reappeared, this time without the dog. After she took a piece of cake from the bag, she said with her mouth full, "Everyone is seeing Mercy around town. Why wouldn't she be haunting her own home?"

Allison handed Susan a napkin. "Ghosts aren't real."

"Mercy is real. I've *seen* her." After wiping her face with a napkin, Susan added, "I'm doing a diorama about Charleston ghosts and pirates made with marshmallow Peeps for my summer school project."

Maddie raised both hands. "Marshmallow Peeps are not easy to find in the summer, even online."

Allison laughed. "Susan, I hope your research goes better than mine."

"It's so cool that you're related to Mercy," Susan said.

"I just wish I knew what happened to her," Allison said. "Not long after the witchcraft charges were dropped, Mercy disappeared."

"That must be why there are so many ghost stories about her," Maddie said. "I have to agree with Susan. All I've been hearing lately is that Mercy is haunting Charleston again."

Allison offered an exasperated eye roll. "I've been hearing that too."

Susan danced around the courtyard. "I've also been reading about pirate ghosts. Did you know Blackbeard was mean?"

"I've heard"—Maddie winked at Allison—"that he was married fourteen times."

Allison couldn't imagine having fourteen husbands. "Seems like a huge waste of energy."

"That part isn't going in my report," Susan said.

"Susan, have you ever heard of the Dread Pirate King?" Allison asked the girl who was now carefully walking on the edge of the raised pond.

"Yes! He's one of my favorites. He was a famous pirate who taught other famous pirates like Blackbeard and William Kidd. He was super scary. He haunts South Adger's Wharf."

"Does he have a name?"

"Henry Avery."

Allison inhaled sharply. "Are you sure?"

"Yes." Susan jumped off the ledge. "He stole a big treasure, moved to Charleston, and then disappeared, taking all of his loot with him. A lot of people were *very* unhappy."

"Allison?" Maddie asked. "You look pale."

Allison glanced at her friend and whispered, "Little is known about Mercy, but she did have a pirate lover who disappeared the same day she did. And her lover was Henry Avery."

CHAPTER 10

ZACK STILL COULDN'T BELIEVE HE'D SPENT THE NIGHT IN Allison's bed. Although he'd hardly slept due to the night-long hard-on, holding her for hours had been worth it.

Zack parked his bike behind Iron Rack's gym in the not-so-nice section of Savannah. He was half a day late. He was also so deep in *I don't give a fuck about Kells's rules* land that he wasn't about to make excuses. He was still reeling from the night before: Hezekiah's assassination, the ghost, Isabel Rutledge working for Remiel, holding Allison, and her admission about her marriage with Stuart.

The fact that they hadn't slept together in over two years had been the last thing Zack had expected. Why would Stuart send his wife away, to a different room in the house, and turn to Isabel? It didn't make sense.

The other thing that didn't make sense? That woman he'd seen in the window. Once the sun had come up, he'd left Allison asleep in bed and investigated the garden. If there'd been any evidence, the rain had washed it away.

Zack strode into the gym to find Luke, the youngest and most computer-savvy man in their unit, behind the front desk. Today he wore gym shorts and a black Iron Racks logo T-shirt with a skull and cross-bones printed in white, only the crossbones were barbells.

Catering to a primarily male clientele, the gym offered hardcore weightlifting stations and a boxing ring in the center. There were a few cardio machines, but since Pete and Vane started offering Krav Maga and dirty fighting classes, the place attracted more MMA types.

And the gym still smelled like sweaty feet.

When Zack approached the desk, Luke looked up and smiled. He was letting his black hair grow and every day looked less soldier-like. "You're la—"

Zack held up a hand and scowled.

"*Okaaaaay.*" Luke gave Zack a clipboard with a spreadsheet on it. "Nate adjusted the chore chart."

The chore chart was constantly being adjusted since they had more chores than hours and men to do the work. The phone rang and Luke answered with a pleasant "Iron Rack's gym. We now offer self-defense classes for the women in your life."

Because they were so desperate for money, they were offering classes for women. Although why any woman would even want to look in the window of this place confounded him. The new renovations couldn't hide the fact that the centuries-old warehouse-turned-gym still looked—and smelled—like it'd housed Sherman's soldiers during the Civil War.

While Luke talked to a prospective client, Zack scanned the chore list, none of which he had any intention of doing.

"Hey, Zack." Nate came out of Kells's office, also in shorts and T-shirt, a determined smile on his face, which meant one thing: staff meeting.

Fuuuuuck. Zack tossed the clipboard onto the desk.

"Luke," Nate whispered to the younger man with the phone against his ear, "when you're done, meet us in training room two."

Zack followed Nate into one of the two private training rooms they used to teach Krav Maga, jujitsu, and street fighting with knives and chains.

He shut the door behind him.

Kells, in khaki combat pants, stood in front of a semicircle of metal folding chairs with six blank posters on easels behind him. Near the gym mats in the corner, Nate spoke to Pete White Horse and Detective Garza from the Savannah Police Department.

Garza knew about Zack's unit and had been helping them get settled in the gym and in their new lives. Garza's only request in return for his help with certain matters was that their unit fly under the radar. He really, really hated public disturbances. Emphasis on *really*.

Luke hurried in and planted himself next to Ty, who sat in a chair with his legs out, arms crossed, and head down as if he were sleeping. Alex strode in next, which surprised Zack since Alex didn't attend staff meetings or movie night.

It wasn't an idea Zack liked. If Alex was living with them, he was part of the team. And the team always did everything together, including watching monster movies.

Alex threw his ass in a chair near the corner. Cain and Vane were missing, but according to the chore chart, Cain was cleaning and Vane was teaching a Krav Maga class next door.

And this was what was left of the Seventh Special Forces Group that'd once been stationed at Fort Bragg. A unit that had spent most of their time in the hottest combat zones in the world. Eight men—nine if you included Alex who'd been a ranger—left to save the world.

Hoooah. And all that.

Luke, their efficient office manager, got the thing started. "Sir? Is something wrong?"

"Yes." Kells nodded at Detective Garza, who came forward with his trademark frown, complete with brow furrows deeper than a slit trench. "Something's happened."

Ty stretched his arms over his head, then parked his chin against his chest and went back to sleep. The brother became more detached with every passing day.

Garza took off his blazer and tossed it onto the gym mats. His brown holster was a stark contrast to his white button-down shirt. He turned around the first poster, which was a hand-drawn picnic bench, stroller, and tree. A stick man holding a gun stood nearby with a red *X* covering his body. The picture looked like it'd been drawn with crayons by a preschooler. "Before I get to the interesting things that have happened in the past twenty-four hours, Kells and I decided you all needed a refresher in the concept of *No Public Disturbances*."

Everyone in the room looked at Nate, who held up his hands surrender style. "I haven't done anything. I swear."

Zack sat in the closest chair.

Garza spun the next two hand-drawn posters. One was of a building with a hole in the wall near a stack of TNT covered with a red *X*. The other showed Savannah's buildings and skyline outlined in black.

"That's not fair," Luke said. "We didn't set that bomb or take out the city's power for twelve hours."

Garza snorted and moved on to the next poster of a helicopter, or maybe a flying dumpster, hovering over a gun lying on a park bench. Again, everyone looked toward Nate, who just shrugged and said, "Wasn't my fault."

The fourth was of dead cows or horses or some other kind of stick animals lying on their backs with thin legs in the air. Red crayon beneath signified carnage.

"Dude," Pete said. "Are those supposed to be boars? They don't look like boars."

"They look like camels," Alex added. "Except camels have bigger di—"

"They're not camels." Garza spun the fifth poster of a house in flames with dead stick men on the ground. Lots of lines in red crayon, along with the orange flames, added an element of destruction.

"Bro." Nate coughed to hide the laughter in his voice. "You gotta talk to Rafe about that one."

Rafe, technically the tenth member of their unit, rarely came to the gym. Mostly because Rafe and Kells didn't play well together.

Finally, Garza unveiled the sixth poster. It showed a torn-apart car with two dead stick people hanging out the window. For added effect, red crayon stripes shot from their heads.

"Oh shit." Everyone looked at Zack and that's when he realized he'd spoken out loud. Since he'd already incriminated himself, he added, "Is that a car bomb?"

"It is." Garza crossed his arms. "Last night, in Charleston, a car bomb took out a man named Hezekiah Usher and his driver."

"Who is Hezekiah Usher?" Pete asked.

"Hezekiah was the leader of the Usher Society," Zack said.

"I thought you were at a sex club?" Alex said.

"The Satyr Club is a cover for the Usher Society's real business," Zack said. "They buy and sell illegal manuscripts, like ancient papyrus and Gutenberg Bibles." He paused because everyone stared at him. "Stuff like that."

"Hezekiah Usher was the first purveyor of books in Boston in 1647," Kells said, speaking for the first time since the meeting began.

That's right. Kells was from South Boston.

"What does the bombing of that car and the Usher Society have to do with us?" Ty had spoken? A miracle.

Garza nodded at Zack. "A witness also claims to have seen a woman near Hezekiah's car and walking away before the explosion."

"I saw her too," Zack admitted. "It was Isabel Rutledge."

Kells answered in his tough, stern voice that could strip the bravado from the most arrogant teenage boy, "The same Isabel who works for Remiel?"

"Yes." Nate held up his hands. "Just so you all know, she's a quick draw."

"And," Zack said, "Isabel was also having an affair with Stuart Pinckney."

"The same Stuart whom Remiel murdered two months ago?" Luke asked.

Zack nodded.

"According to the witness," Garza said, "Isabel is a high-ranking member of the Usher Society."

"Does this witness have a name?" Nate asked Garza.

"Horatio."

Ohfuckohfuckohfuckohfuckohfuck

Zack stood. "I met Horatio last night. He works for the Prince."

"What did this warrior say?" Kells asked.

"Not much. He was too busy knocking me out cold." And calling Zack a coward. "There was also some Latin thrown around."

Garza took his notebook and a pen out of his jacket pocket. "Do you remember it?"

"Horatio said, '*dubita veritatem esse mendacem*.' His buddy Marcellus responded, '*Sed nunquam non dubitatione*.'"

"There were *two* Fianna warriors there last night?" Pete asked.

Zack nodded. "Rafe told us they work in pairs."

Garza tapped the pen on the notebook. "Horatio said, 'Doubt truth to be a liar.' Marcellus responded, 'But never doubt I love.' It's Shakespeare."

Luke raised his hand. "Wasn't a Shakespearean verse cut in the dirt near where Stuart Pinckney's body was found?"

"Yes." Garza shut his notebook with the pen inside and placed it on the gym mats. Then he pulled out his phone and started scrolling. His jaw cranked as if he were crushing his molars with a hydraulic press. He handed the phone to Kells. "This is a photo of the verse cut in the cemetery near where Stuart was murdered. It's from *Hamlet*."

Nate took the phone out of Kells's hand and passed it on to Pete. From there, the photo traveled to Luke, Ty, and Alex, who handed it to Zack.

"This evidence," Garza said, "never made the news. Detective Waring in Charleston kept this investigation under a media lockdown."

Zack studied the photo of typical Fianna psy-ops bullshit. A warrior, for some unknown reason, had placed small shells and rocks in a perfect square. Inside the square, words had been cut into the dirt and lined with more stones and shells. The letters were in all caps and laid in a precise form that had to have taken time and effort. They spelled the words DUBITA VERITATEM ESSE MENDACEM, SED NUNQUAM NON DUBITATIONE.

"Zack." Pete sat up. "Is Allison okay?"

"She's grieving." Zack handed the phone back to Garza. "Last night, Hezekiah gave her a document Stuart purchased on the black market called the Pirate's Grille. It was owned by the Prince in the eighteenth century and stolen by our favorite pirate Thomas Toban. I also overheard Hezekiah and Isabel talking about two documents: the Pirate's Grille and another called the Witch's Examination of Mercy Chastain. Specifically, the appendix to the witch's examination. The grille and the appendix work together."

"To do what?" Kells asked.

"Not sure, sir. But Isabel did say she was looking for something."

Nate ran his hands over his head. "This is so fucked up."

Agreed, brother. Zack moved his attention to Kells. "Sir, I'd like to go back to Charleston—"

"No. You're not to leave Savannah without permission." Before Zack could respond, Kells left the room, slamming the door behind him.

The silence in the room resonated as if the concrete walls were acoustic tiles.

Had Kells ordered Zack not to leave the city? As if he was twelve?

Zack grabbed Nate's arm and dragged him to the side of the room. "What the fuck?"

"I..." Nate glanced at the other men, who had that glassy-eyed *we've all just been tasered* look. "Take a walk, and later, when things are calmer, I'll talk to Kells."

"That's bullshit." Zack left the training room and passed the front desk. He had a few choice words for his boss.

Nate caught up and grabbed his arm. "Wait."

"For what?" Zack pointed at Kells's closed office door. "For Kells to listen to reason? He's way past that."

"He's stressed. He had difficult calls with the warden at Leedsville prison. There's been a fight, some of our men were injured. And you've been gone—in Charleston—a lot. That leaves the rest of us carrying the chore slack."

"I'm sick of the excuses, Nate. For the past two months, Kells has been an ass." Zack took a deep breath. "I'm tired of being called a fucking coward."

There. He'd said it out loud.

That's when he noticed Pete, Alex, and Garza standing nearby, listening.

"Kells didn't meant that," Nate said. "He's just—"

"Blaming me, Nate." Zack didn't care that the other men were listening. "Kells is still mad about my choices that night five years ago, when everything changed—choices that left you leading two A teams into an ambush and landing in a fucking POW camp."

When Zack's buddies wouldn't meet his gaze, he knew the truth.

They still blamed him as well. "I'm going to Charleston to protect Allison and get us some fucking intel. Are you with me or against me?"

"This is insane." Pete came over and used his middle finger to poke Zack's chest. "You can't run around Charleston on your own. What happens if…something happens? We won't be there to back you up."

"I'm a big, scary ex–Green Beret," Zack said. "I can manage."

"Kells will be pissed," Nate said in a low voice. "There'll be consequences."

"Screw the consequences. Now that Allison has the Pirate's Grille, she's in danger. I can't leave her alone."

Nate glanced at Kells's office door. "How long will it take?"

"No fucking idea."

Alex stood next to Zack. "I'll go with him."

"We don't have enough cars," Nate said.

"Alex can take my Harley," Garza said. "It's parked behind the station."

"Zack." Nate squeezed the bridge of his nose. "I don't have petty cash for a motel—"

"We'll stay with Vivienne," Zack said. "She won't mind."

"I don't like this." Pete's hands landed on his hips. "When the other men find out—"

"We'll cover for Zack and Alex until they return." Nate took out his phone and texted. "Before you go, talk to Rafe. See if he can give you any insight into what's going on Fianna-wise."

Zack nodded. Years ago, Rafe had been a member of their unit until going AWOL to work for the Prince as a Fianna warrior. Now that Rafe had returned to them—kind of—he'd become an excellent source of info.

"Zack," Nate said while he texted, "Rafe is at the church on the Isle of Grace."

"Got it."

"Speaking of petty cash…" Alex held out his palm.

Nate went around the desk, pulled out the cash box, and handed them each forty dollars. "It's all we have."

Better than nothing. "Thank you."

Those two words carried more meaning than Zack could ever express with a million. This plan of theirs was sure to have some serious blowback. But right now, he didn't care. Right now, all he could think about was that Allison was in danger. And that was the only thing that mattered.

CHAPTER 11

Alex drove Garza's motorcycle over the bridge leading to the Isle of Grace, and the paved road turned into gravel.

A few hundred yards down, he followed Zack toward a small white church tucked between enormous oak trees covered in Spanish moss. A white steeple cut through the foliage and black shutters flanked arched windows.

Alex parked next to Zack and removed his borrowed helmet. They fell into step and stomped through wildflowers around the church. Alex was grateful for his boots. He hated bugs and weeds and nature. And heat. Sweat dripped down the back of his neck and drenched his T-shirt. It was hotter on the isle than in his isolation cell at Leedsville prison. Correction: Leedsville Military Correctional Facility. Because fancifying the language always made the horrible more bearable.

They passed orange cones surrounding the church and construction equipment standing nearby. The shutters were open and dripping wet, as if someone had powerwashed them. A generator sat near a stack of red jerricans.

Alex pointed to the church's front door covered by huge planks. "I wonder what this is about."

"No idea."

Alex and Zack found a man in the cemetery, where the grass and wildflowers were higher than the tombs. Rafe Montfort stood on a ladder hanging lights through the trees.

When Rafe saw them, he jumped down.

"What's going on?" Zack asked.

Rafe wiped his forehead with one arm. "Since most of the isle's inhabitants leave in August to escape the storms and the heat, that's when the church maintenance is done. It's on a historical registry, and the isle is required to keep it up. But this year the contractor found termite damage and structural issues. Hence the renovations."

"That can't be cheap," Zack said.

"It's not." Rafe opened a nearby cooler and took out three bottles of water. After handing one to Alex and Zack, Rafe opened his own and drank deeply. "There's a general fund for the church, but we recently had an anonymous donation that's allowing us to do termite remediation and protect the stained-glass windows. We're putting bulletproof glass on the inside and outside."

Zack grimaced. "A bit much."

"Probably." Rafe pointed to the lights in the trees. "Since our sheriff and deputy take off to go fishing every August, I'm also setting up an early warning system."

Alex walked around one of the trees that'd been wrapped in tiny lights. From what little Alex had heard about the former Fianna warrior, Alex knew that Rafe had been born and raised on the island and had recently returned to become the isle's de facto caretaker.

Rafe handed a strand of lights to Zack. "We had an alarm company come out, but there's no Wi-Fi on the isle and electricity is spotty. I'm stringing up white and blue lights we had left over from the isle's Fourth of July party. If the lights are white, the people of the isle know all is well. If someone turns on the blue lights, we grab our rifles."

Rafe moved a ladder to another tree.

"Rafe," Zack said, "did you get my message about what happened last night with Horatio, Marcellus, and the car bomb?"

"Yes." Rafe, wearing a black T-shirt that exposed a series of tattooed names down his right arm, stretched the lights through the branches. "Remiel ordered Stuart Pinckney's death as well as Hezekiah's. Since the Prince is involved in a conflict with Remiel, it's no surprise the Prince has warriors watching things in Charleston."

Alex grabbed a strand and unwound it to make it easier for Rafe to move to another tree. "We were hoping you had more info on the witch's examination's appendix and the Pirate's Grille."

"I don't know." Rafe threw lights over a high branch. "But I'll see what I can find out."

"Can you tell us about Horatio?" Zack asked. "If I contact him, will Horatio kill me?"

"You won't be able to contact Horatio." Rafe grabbed more lights and headed for the next tree. "If Horatio or Marcellus have anything to say, they'll make themselves known."

Alex found a step stool propped against a gravestone. He opened it and moved it to the other side of an oak to help Rafe wrap the lights around the trunk. "Is Horatio a Ghost?"

Zack stretched out a knotted length of lights. "What's a ghost?"

"A Ghost," Rafe said, "is a seasoned Fianna warrior who works autonomously. A Ghost doesn't have to run his plans by the Prince and has more freedom to manage missions. Horatio and Marcellus are both foot soldiers, warriors who gather intel and..."

"Eliminate targets?" Alex offered.

Rafe nodded. "Foot soldiers work in pairs. Where Horatio goes, so goes Marcellus. If one is making himself known, the other is nearby."

Zack remembered that from Le Petit Theatre. "Great."

Rafe paused, holding up a bunch of lights. "Zack, you sure you want to get in between Remiel and the Prince?"

"No. But I don't have a choice. Allison possesses the document Hezekiah Usher may have been murdered for. I need to protect her. *Aaaaand* there's something else—something I didn't tell Kells."

Rafe frowned as he strung. "What?"

"Last night, Marcellus told Allison that Stuart failed in his search for something and that it was Allison's responsibility to find it."

"What the *fuck*?" Alex practically spat out the words. "You never mentioned that part."

"Because I didn't want Kells to have a heart attack or Nate's head to explode."

Rafe came down off the ladder to face Zack directly. "Are you telling me the Fianna gave Allison a task?"

"Yes." Zack swallowed visibly and sweat dripped down his face. "Is that bad?"

"It sure as hell isn't good." Rafe ran a hand over his head, smoothing back his short hair. "What is this task?"

Zack exhaled and looked up at the blue-for-now sky. "To find the treasure of the dread pirate king."

The Prince had given Allison—and therefore Zack—a fucking task? And Zack hadn't said anything before now? "Are you high? No one accepts one of the Prince's tasks unless they're desperate or suicidal or both." Alex hopped off his step stool, ready to slug Zack into unconsciousness. Except Rafe grabbed Alex's arm to keep him from attacking.

"Zack," Rafe said in a low voice that rumbled with threats and darkness, "this is a serious, big-boy problem."

"It gets better." Alex yanked out of Rafe's grasp. "Kells ordered Zack not to go to Charleston, yet we're going anyway."

And because Alex was an idiot, he'd agreed to this plan. He should've known better than to trust one of Kells's men.

"Whoa." Zack held up both hands. "Alex, you volunteered. Where's this pissed-off attitude coming from?"

"It's coming from the fact that I was going to Charleston to get away from Kells, not to complete some task for the Fianna. No one who plays with the Fianna gets out alive."

Zack moved closer to Alex until he could see the black rims around Zack's brown pupils. "If you're scared, go home."

"Enough!" Rafe stepped in between Alex and Zack, one fist pressed against each of their chests. Gently, Rafe pushed them apart. "Zack, are you still determined to help Allison? Without the help of your other men at the gym?"

Zack crossed his arms like a petulant man-child. "Yes."

Rafe glanced at Alex. "Are you still willing to back Zack up in Charleston?"

Fuck. Alex kicked the ground, also like a petulant man-child, but nodded. He didn't want anything to do with the Fianna, but he didn't want to go back to Kells and the gym either.

"Alright." Rafe exhaled and placed his fists on his hips. "Zack, do you have any particulars about this thing Allison has to do? Besides finding some pirate treasure?"

"No. There was a lot going on last night. Marcellus mentioned it, and then they left before the explosion. I'm sure they knew it was about to happen."

"I'm sure they did," Rafe said. "This is what we're going to do. You two go to Charleston and find Allison before the Fianna contact her again. In the meantime, I'll see what I can find out. Once you know the details, call me. But"—he wagged a finger at each of them—"if I think this thing is spiraling out of control, I'm going to Nate. And Nate will go to Kells. And we all know how that will turn out. Got it?"

"Yeah," Zack said. "Got it."

"Good," Rafe said. "Leave now. If the Fianna have already approached Allison once, they'll make contact again soon."

"Thanks." Zack sighed and headed back to his bike.

Just as Alex turned to leave, Rafe gripped his shoulder. "I've wanted to talk to you, but I've no interest in going to the gym and running into Kells."

Alex understood. "I'm not doing anything at the gym because Kells doesn't think I can control my temper."

"I'm not a Kells fan, but he's being cautious. He's worried about you."

"No, he's not. He's using me for his own purposes against my brother, the arms dealer with a God complex who calls himself the Prince."

"How do you feel about that?"

"Not really in the mood to share my feelings with one of my brother's warriors."

"I'm not... Let's just say I have more autonomy now."

"You're a Ghost?"

"Yes. While Nate knows I still have ties to the Fianna, the others don't understand what's required of the men who serve the Prince."

"I'm not sure I know either."

"What I'm saying is that if you need to talk about anything, I can listen and understand and won't tell Kells or the Prince. No psycho-babble bullshit." When Alex stayed silent, Rafe added, "I spent years in prison as well. The difference is I deserved to be there. It can't be easy to have spent so many years in a cell for something you didn't do. Especially when your brother could've freed you just by telling the truth."

Yep. That really sucked. "Thanks, but I'm not one for sharing."

"Your choice. Offer stands." Rafe led the way toward the front of the church. "Just be prepared."

"For what?"

"If your brother wants to see you, he won't take no for an answer."

CHAPTER 12

At eleven a.m., Allison opened the front door of Pinckney House to let in her brother-in-law, Lawrence.

The AC kicked on, sending chills down her arms, and she tightened her black sweater over her black sundress. Her low-heeled sandals clicked on the pine floor as she led the way to the study.

She'd returned home a few minutes earlier. And since she'd worn jeans and a white blouse to her office, she'd used the time to change into *more formal* clothes to meet Lawrence's more formal world.

Lawrence wrinkled his nose. "This house smells like lemongrass oil tinged with mildew. Are you sure you're keeping it up? It is an historic home, after all. It has special needs."

"I'm well aware of Pinckney House's needs." She'd only been living here and managing the house's social calendar for years.

Nicholas Trott bound down the hallway from the kitchen, halted in front of Lawrence, and ran away toward the sitting room.

"You still have that mongrel?"

"Nicholas Trott is not a mongrel." She sat behind the desk and waved to the chair in front of it. "In fact, he's a beloved member of this city. He even has his own parking space at the public library."

Lawrence scowled and sat. Although younger than Stuart, he was taller and leaner. He was also a successful entrepreneur who'd made his money with *Got Ghosts?*, his popular paranormal tour guide business in Charleston, Savannah, and New Orleans.

But today, in khaki pants, a white button-down shirt, and purple bow tie, he appeared more serious than she'd ever seen him before. More like a lawyer than a ghost hunter.

That couldn't be good.

"So, Lawrence, how was your flight from Paris?"

Were the croissants worth missing your brother's funeral?

She didn't say that, of course. No point in poking the tiger who now held the purse strings of the Pinckney Trust.

"Fine." Lawrence cleared his throat. "I have something to tell you that you're not going to be happy about. My accountant and lawyer have finished the audit of the Pinckney Trust, and money is missing."

"Missing?" She sat back in her chair. "I take care of the day-to-day household expenses, but Stuart handled everything regarding the family trust."

Lawrence held up a hand. "I'm not accusing you of anything. But the audit discovered that, over the past two years, almost a million dollars has been siphoned from the estate."

She planted her palms on the desk and stood. "I don't believe it. Stuart wasn't a thief. His books were perfect. He was a bank president."

"Sometimes we don't know people as well as we think we do."

She sat again, her chest feeling suddenly tight. *So very true.* "Lawrence, is that why you put a hold on the account?"

"It's standard procedure to freeze a family trust after the executor of the trust dies. It wasn't personal."

"But it's been difficult—financially as well as emotionally."

"It's only going to remain difficult, financially I mean, until we clear up this mess."

"You still have the crinkled look on your face. What else is wrong?"

"Did you know Stuart added an addendum to his will?"

"No. Stuart's will was straightforward. As his wife, I inherit his assets—those outside the Pinckney Trust, of course." A trust that made her a guest in her own home.

"I was surprised as well." Lawrence took a file out of his briefcase and laid it on the desk between them.

She struggled to keep the rising dread out of her voice. "What's this?"

"My lawyer and I have reviewed this many times." Lawrence put on his glasses and opened the file. "According to Stuart's will, you're the sole beneficiary of Stuart's assets, except for Pinckney House and the proceeds from a secondary life insurance policy."

She shook her head. "I've already received payment from the life insurance company. It's not a huge amount of money but it's helped pay the monthly bills."

It'd also paid for Stuart's funeral.

Lawrence studied her from over his readers. "Stuart bought a second life insurance policy for a million dollars. The beneficiary is Isabel Rutledge."

Allison's voice stopped working. *Stuart had left Isabel a million dollars?*

"I believe," Lawrence continued, "Stuart funded this insurance money with the cash he took out of the Pinckney Trust. Except he took out more than the policy cost. My next question is: What did he do with the rest of the money?"

"I don't know." Her voice rang with a harshness she'd never heard in it before.

Lawrence stood to pace the room. "You've no idea why Stuart would embezzle money and buy a life insurance policy for Isabel Rutledge, an obscure family friend?"

Allison swallowed and stared at her clasped hands on the desk. It would be so easy to pretend that what was true was false. But she'd, apparently, been living a life of lies for two years. And while hiding the truth to protect her bruised ego was a tempting proposition, she now realized that, although lies stole from the truth, they didn't make the truth go away. "Last night, I discovered Stuart and Isabel were having an affair."

Lawrence sat again. He'd paled and was blinking rapidly.

Yep. That's how she'd felt last night.

She went to the bar in the corner of the room, opened a bottle of scotch, and poured some into cut-crystal glasses.

She handed him his drink and placed the bottle on the desk. She sipped hers while Lawrence downed his and poured another. Since her brother-in-law seemed incapable of speech, she asked, "Lawrence, how did you find out about this policy?"

Lawrence finished his second drink. "Stuart sent it to my lawyer a year ago with instructions to show it to me upon Stuart's death. There's one other thing I need to talk to you about."

She wanted to lay her head on the desk and cry. Instead, her phone buzzed with another text from Pastor Tom.

> Can you come by the church so we can talk about Stuart's service on Friday?

She texted back I'll be there soon.

Pastor Tom responded with a thumbs-up emoji and a praying hands emoji. She was going to need a lot more help than that to get out of this mess.

"Allison?" Lawrence barked. "Are you listening?"

She laid her phone on the desk and sent a fake smile to Lawrence. "Yes."

"I've decided to move back to Charleston, and I want to live in Pinckney House."

Her pretend smile turned into a real frown. "Why? You have a huge historic home in Savannah. Your business is based in Savannah."

"This house has been in my family for centuries."

"I don't understand. It's not like I can sell the house. I'm just going to care for it like I've been doing since I married Stuart. Besides, I don't think you understand anything about Pinckney House's full social calendar."

"No, I don't think you understand anything about this situation. Now that Stuart is gone, you don't belong here." He pointed to the folder on the desk. "Now that I know the truth, I don't think you ever belonged here."

"But—"

"I'm the executor of the Pinckney Estate. As such, I'm giving you notice. You have one week."

A second text came in, but this one wasn't from Reverend Tom. It read:

> *Fear not, Lady Allison. What issue this day will come?*
> *Your love and your will shall direct it.*

What did *that* mean?

Lawrence snapped his fingers in front of her face. "Are you listening?"

"Of course." This time she slipped her phone into her dress pocket. "One week to do what?"

"Move out."

⌒

Twenty minutes later, Allison stepped into Saint Philip's Church and inhaled the cold, vanilla-scented air. The church was empty and she wondered if she should go to the parish office.

She shrugged on her sweater and checked her phone. No more strange messages. Good thing too, since all she could think of was the fact that she was a week away from eviction. Needing some peace, she turned off her phone and threw it into her purse.

"Allison?" a male voice said from the doorway leading outside to the east graveyard.

She tried to smile. "Hello, Pastor Tom."

Pastor Tom, in black clericals and white collar, with thinning brown hair, waved his hand that held a metal watering can. "Come with me. We'll talk while I water."

She adjusted her purse on her shoulder and followed him only to immediately shed her sweater and shove it into her bag. She waited while Pastor Tom filled his can from a spigot on a metal pipe sticking out of the ground between two seventeenth-century graves.

Bugs chittered and the hot, humid air shimmered through the overgrown palmettos, orange black-eyed Susans, pink crepe myrtles, and roaming purple salvias. The sunny haze made everything fuzzy. Spanish moss hung like heavy blankets from old and randomly planted live oak trees. Considering how many headstones in the over-three-hundred-year-old cemetery had melded themselves to tree trunks, she'd often wondered which came first: the trees or the dead.

She heard a drilling sound from the darker recesses of the cemetery that extended around the other side of the church. "What's that noise?"

"City is renovating some of the older pipes and sewer lines to alleviate flooding. We've had a lot of rain this summer and, as you know, are always waiting for the next hurricane." Pastor Tom turned off the spigot and led the way down an uneven flagstone path. As he walked, the foliage he disturbed hit her bare legs.

"Pastor Tom, I'll never understand how you can keep track of everyone buried back here." She brushed away a palm branch, praying no spiders fell out of the tree, because that sometimes happened. "Most of the names and dates are worn off."

"That's what historians are for, my dear."

She stopped when he paused to water a daylily. Waving an arm around the cemetery which was an overgrown garden filled with dearly departed, she asked, "How do you decide what to water?"

"The plants tell me."

That wasn't at all helpful. She blew a strand out of her eyes and sat on an iron bench next to a stone obelisk draped in ivy. "Is there something you wanted to talk to me about?"

After watering a few more plants in between gravestones, then ferns in urns on top of columns, he sat next to her. It always amazed her how, despite wearing black all the time, he never seemed to look hot. "I'm concerned you don't want to speak at Stuart's service tomorrow. Is there a reason?"

She turned toward the iron fence that separated the church from the road and the other cemetery across the street. "I..." She clasped her hands in her lap. "I don't know what to say."

"Then speak from your heart."

Except her heart was so closed down from pain and betrayal—past and current—she wasn't sure words could escape. "If I spoke from my heart, those attending would trample each other running for the door."

He smiled and sat back to survey his deceased flock, most of whom had passed on centuries ago. "Allison, I understand there's hurt—"

"You couldn't possibly."

He glanced at her, his gaze softening as if knowing she was on the verge of tears. "Stuart and I talked about it. I know."

"Know what?" She stood and kept her voice deliberately vague. It was possible that Stuart had other secrets besides Isabel, insurance policies, and rare manuscripts.

Pastor Tom watched her, and she warmed beneath his regard. Still, she was going to make him say it. She needed him to say it.

"I know Stuart desecrated his marriage vows." Pastor Tom now stared at his shiny black shoes. "I begged Stuart to confess his affair to you and make amends, and he'd finally agreed."

She sat again because her legs were no more stable than if they'd been soggy Pixy Stix. "When?"

"A few days before his death, we spoke about…the situation. He told me he was going to end the affair and tell you all about it. As well as other things going on."

"He didn't."

Pastor Tom raised an eyebrow. "How did you—?"

"Stuart's lover told me."

"I'm sorry." He stood and she followed him toward the front of the church, where he stopped to water a clump of wild daisies. "I understand why you don't want to speak, but Stuart was your husband. I know how much you loved him and he loved you."

"Not enough, apparently." All this talk made her feel worse. "The truth is, Pastor Tom, I have nothing to say."

"The irony is," he said as he watered a wild flowering fern, "you have many words. You just can't say them to Stuart."

She followed Pastor Tom toward another spigot sticking up out of the ground next to a limestone tomb covered in spotted mold. He filled his watering can again while her mind raced.

Pastor Tom was right. She had a million questions, but Stuart wasn't here to answer them.

She was a walking contradiction. She felt so detached yet so filled with pain. And the thought of speaking in front of others made her throat close up and her palms itch. A few more wildflower waterings led them to her brother's grave. A skull with wings had been carved above the name *Daniel Fenwick*. Below that were his birth and death dates. Then there was the quote she'd never fully appreciated until today. *When sorrows come, they come not single spies but in battalions.*

She avoided a nearby stretch of dirt without a headstone that signified a newly buried body. Stuart lay deep beneath, and soon his headstone would be placed next to her brother's.

She turned away. "Pastor Tom, did Stuart ever mention finding the Witch's Examination of Mercy Chastain? Or buying the Pirate's Grille?"

"Yes." Pastor Tom watered the wild violets in front of Danny's grave. "Stuart said that the Witch's Examination of Mercy Chastain and the Pirate's Grille, if used together, was one of two ways to find the dread pirate king's treasure."

"What was the second way?"

"Discover what happened to Mercy in 1704. Stuart believed that if he could find Mercy, she would lead him to the treasure."

Great. "This dread pirate king—would it be Henry Avery?"

"Yes." Pastor Tom pulled wild purple clematis vines off a marble column. "You don't seem surprised by all of this."

"I am and I'm not." She licked her dry lips. "Did you know Henry Avery was, supposedly, Mercy Chastain's lover? And that they disappeared *together* in 1704?"

"I did." Pastor Tom pointed to Pirate House across the street. "Henry Avery met Mercy in the Pirate House when it was an alehouse—"

"Brothel—"

"And then built the nearby Pink House for her after she bore him a child. Yet, while I've seen Mercy's ghost, I've never seen Henry's."

Allison coughed politely. "Did Stuart say anything else about why he was looking for this treasure?"

"Stuart was supposed to find and give the treasure to someone named the Prince before another man found it."

"Does this other man have a name?"

"Remiel Marigny."

She sank onto a raised flat tomb, not caring that it was covered in green lichen.

Hadn't Zack mentioned Remiel Marigny last night? Twice?

Pastor Tom gently touched her shoulder. "Stuart told me if he could find Mercy and the treasure, he could keep you safe."

She might have believed that yesterday, but today? Not at all. She stood and followed Pastor Tom to the front gate.

"There is one other odd thing that happened not long before he died. Stuart asked to borrow a small hammer and chisel. The kind one uses on a headstone."

"Why?"

"He didn't say."

"This all seems far-fetched," she said. "Stuart was a bank president, after all."

"We are not always who we appear to be to others." When they reached the gate that led to the street, he frowned. "Is that your mother in Pirate House?"

A woman in a long orange-and-red-striped skirt and black camisole had her hand on the knob of the front door of the white stucco building. "What is Rue doing here?"

Pastor Tom gave her a half smile. "Please give her—"

He stopped speaking, probably because of the disgusted look Allison sent him. "Rue doesn't care about well wishes or other people. You know that better than anyone."

He cleared his throat. "Will she attend the memorial service?"

"No. And please don't lecture me about inviting her."

"I won't." He gave her a chagrin-tinged smile. "Everyone in town knows Rue Chastain Fenwick could start an argument with an empty room."

"Truer words and all that." Allison hiked her purse on her shoulder. "I'll take care of it."

"Good luck," Pastor Tom said as he walked away.

Taking a deep breath, she opened the iron gate and hurried across the street toward the house with red shutters and a huge anchor on the outside wall. It was called the Pirate House because it'd served as an alehouse and brothel for eighteenth-century rogues and villains. People still thought it was the oldest building in the city not because of its hurricane-proof engineering but because it had once belonged to Mercy. It'd once been protected by a witch.

At this point, Allison would take her protection any way she could get it.

CHAPTER 13

ZACK FOUND ALEX STRETCHED OUT IN A LOUNGE CHAIR ON THE patio behind his godmother Vivienne's mansion, drinking lemonade, eyes closed. The walled patio overlooked a garden filled with flowering trees twice the size of the house. Two symmetrical spray fountains flanked the swimming pool.

On the road, Zack had called Vivienne to ask her if he and Alex could spend the night in her house. She hadn't answered, so Zack had left a message. He'd no doubt Vivienne wouldn't mind. She was always berating him for not calling or coming home enough. He just hoped she stayed in New Orleans and didn't come rushing back to Charleston for a quick family reunion.

Until this thing with Remiel Marigny was over, he needed to keep his soldier life away from his family life. It was the only way to keep those he loved, including Vivienne and his sister, Emilie, safe.

He checked his cell, and so far there'd been no stressed texts from Nate. That meant that Kells didn't know yet about Zack and Alex leaving. Now that they were settled, Zack was off to find Allison. But first he needed to make sure he and Alex were on the same team.

"Alex, are you sunbathing in jeans and a T-shirt?"

"Yep." Alex smiled, his eyes closed. "As soon as you leave, brother, I'll be swimming in that pool. Naked."

Not something Zack needed to see.

He tossed a burner phone onto Alex's stomach.

Alex sat up, almost knocking over his glass. "What's this for?"

"That is our Charleston mission phone. I also have one and they're both programmed with our new numbers. No one, besides the two of us, knows about these cells. They're for this operation only. Got it?"

"Yep." Alex pocketed the phone and went back to sunbathing.

"Hey." Zack hit Alex's shoulder. "This isn't a vacation."

"Miss Isabel Rutledge." The housekeeper disappeared as soon as the words were spoken.

A moment later, Isabel appeared in a sleeveless yellow dress that clung to every gorgeous curve. Her long dark hair had been swept into a side ponytail to show off diamond drop earrings. She glided across the patio, laid her purse on the wrought-iron table, and poured herself a lemonade from the crystal pitcher.

Zack sent Alex a raised *what's going on* eyebrow. Alex returned a shrug.

Isabel sipped her lemonade and ran her tongue over her lower lip. "Mmmmm. That's refreshing."

Alex moved to sit on the wide, white concrete railing separating the patio from the garden. He leaned against one of the pillars covered with wisteria and jasmine.

Zack stood on the other side of the table, so he wouldn't have to smell Isabel's sandalwood perfume. "You're Isabel." He ignored Alex's frown. It wasn't a great opening, but Zack wanted to get this thing started in order to end it.

"I am." Isabel looked at Alex. "Still playing games, Alex? I thought prison would've matured you."

Alex closed his eyes. "Not playing games. Just not caring about what you want."

"I don't believe you. I think you do care and you're desperate to know what I want."

"Wait," Zack said to Alex. "Do you and Isabel *know* each other?"

She chuckled. "You didn't tell Zack about our past friendship."

"Friendship?" Alex scoffed, eyes still closed. "I fucked you to get close to Remiel. You knew it. I knew it. It was mutually agreed upon self-destruction."

Holy. Shit. Zack rubbed the back of his neck. "You two were lovers."

"Yes," Isabel said as she sipped her lemonade.

Alex grunted. "There was no love involved. Now, what can I say that will make you go away?"

She moved until she touched Alex's chin with a manicured fingernail. "Why would you want me to leave?"

Alex opened his eyes and pushed her hand aside. "Because you're a coldhearted bitch?"

"Says the cold-blooded murderer?"

"Killing Remiel would've been a public service."

"Not according to the U.S. Army." She caressed his bicep and he jerked away.

Alex's fists clenched, and Zack pushed his way between them. The last thing he needed was Alex in fight mode. "What do you want, Isabel?"

She smiled at Alex. "I need you to set up a meeting for me with the Prince."

Zack laughed first, but Alex laughed loudest.

Finally, Alex was able to drag in enough breath to ask, "Why?"

"It's personal." She found her purse on the table and took out her cell phone. "I have something to give you in return, Zack."

"You have to be insane." Alex snapped his fingers. "Oh, that's right. You *are* insane."

Zack forced Alex back to the lounge chair. "Why do you think Alex can get you a meeting?"

She scoffed. "Alex is the only person to whom the Prince would grant such a request. I need to see him soon. It's important."

"Jeez, Isabel," Alex sneered, "why would I do anything for you? Because we once fucked in a closet?"

She handed Zack the phone. "Convince Alex to help me. If you do, I'll tell you everything I know about her."

"Her?" Zack stared at the phone. At first, he couldn't comprehend what he was seeing so he tried to enlarge the photo, then move it around the screen. His throat went dry and he blinked. "Where did you get this?"

"It doesn't matter." She took her phone back. "What does matter is that the Fianna have her, and I know where she is. You help me get a meeting, I'll help you save her."

Alex grabbed the phone from Isabel and stood next to Zack, shoulders touching. "Isabel lies, Zack. You can't—"

"You have to talk to your brother."

"Hell no—"

"Alex." Zack kept his voice low and level when what he really wanted to do was destroy everything around him. "You have to."

"Why?"

"Because"—Zack pointed to the photo of the blindfolded woman holding today's newspaper—"the Prince has my sister, Emilie."

Now it was Alex's turn to push Zack aside. "Isabel, why did the Fianna take Emilie?"

"Where's my sister!" Zack moved until Alex shoved him into a chair.

"If you fuck up now," Alex whispered in Zack's ear, "you'll never see your sister again. Keep your mouth shut while I deal with this."

Before Zack could agree or disagree, Alex faced Isabel. "The Fianna wouldn't kidnap a woman for no reason."

Isabel's smile exposed straight white teeth that could've been fangs. "No more information until you promise me a meeting with your brother."

"I can't just call him."

"Alex?" Zack's exasperated voice told Alex he was running out of time.

"You always were so childish, Alex. I'm surprised prison didn't toughen you up." Isabel ran her hands over his biceps and beneath his T-shirt sleeves. Her hands felt cold against his hot skin, and his muscles bunched involuntarily. Yet he didn't move. He didn't want to give her the satisfaction of thinking she unnerved him—or turned him on—in any way. "Although it did *build* you up."

Five years of push-ups and pull-ups in a solitary cell did that to a man. When she licked her lips again, he grabbed her wrists and pushed her away. "Tell me why they took Emilie or I'm not helping you."

She sighed and paced the patio. All of her graceful movements, from her swinging arms to swaying hips, were intended to seduce and entice. The problem was he knew her. He'd *had* her. She'd been a great fuck but was an even better liar. He'd taken a calculated risk in screwing her to get close to Remiel, and because she'd betrayed him, he'd ended up arrested for murder.

"I don't know why they took Zack's sister."

Alex tossed the phone onto the table. "Does Remiel know you want to meet the Prince?"

Isabel clasped and unclasped her handbag. "No."

Interesting. Dissension in the enemy's ranks.

"Okay." Was Alex agreeing to this? "I'll try. I can't promise he'll say yes."

"After you speak to Marcellus"—Isabel glanced at the darker recesses of the garden—"call me. I'll leave my number with the house-keeper." Isabel kissed his cheek and left the patio.

Marcellus?

"Fuck." Zack stood and pointed beyond the pool.

Alex squinted and it didn't take long to see a shadow in the back of the garden. The warrior wore a starched and pressed seersucker suit. He stood on spread legs, his head bowed over his phone. Even as he texted, he was a silent dare of a man.

Alex's new phone buzzed, and he read the text.

> So full of artless jealousy is guilt, it spills itself in fearing to be spilt.

Zack read it and said, "What the hell does that mean?"

"No clue."

Alex and Zack hopped over the wall, passed the fountains, and walked toward the shadow man. Alex would love to know how the warrior got Alex's burner phone number when it'd just been activated. Then again, the Fianna probably owned the telecom company that made the damn things.

Alex and Zack stopped two yards away, making sure to stay within the shade of an oak tree. It was too hot to be doing this in direct sunlight.

"Zack? Let me do the talking."

Zack grunted and crossed his arms.

Alex moved closer. "Marcellus."

Marcellus hit his chest with his fist and bowed his head. "Welcome home, Master Alex."

Alex held up his phone. "Translation?" He wasn't too proud to ask for one. He wasn't a Fianna warrior. He hadn't memorized every play Shakespeare had ever written and didn't speak only from words within those texts.

"Your guilt leads to suspicion and paranoia that reveals itself precisely because it fears to be revealed."

"I don't feel guilty. I didn't kill Remiel, yet I suffered as if I had."

"Your failure to murder the Fiend fuels your guilt. Your failure to end this civil war between the Prince and the Fiend, when you had the chance, fuels your hopelessness. Your failure to save—"

"This nightmare isn't my fault."

"That doesn't mean you don't feel some responsibility for the tragedy that set this play in motion."

"Screw you." Alex waved a hand to get rid of the gnats around his head. "I'm not going to argue about what I do and don't feel guilty about. And I sure as hell am not going to discuss the past with you."

"Then why do you serve Colonel Torridan?"

"I don't serve anyone. Kells got me out, which is more than my brother has ever done for me."

"My lord was protecting you."

"Whatever."

Zack barreled between them, stopping inches from Marcellus's face. "Where the fuck is my sister?"

Alex took Zack's arm and pulled him back. Unfortunately, Zack was as strong and tall as Alex. "Let me handle this."

Zack hissed, "You're *not* handling this."

Alex pointed to the iron bench beneath the tree. "Sit. Now."

Zack sent a fierce scowl at Marcellus and sat.

Finally. "Marcellus, Isabel said you have Emilie Tremaine. Is this true?"

Marcellus centered his gaze on Zack. "'Tis true. 'Tis my reason for visiting."

Alex moved in between Marcellus and Zack. "Yesterday, my brother asked for a meeting."

Zack stood again. "What?"

Alex pushed him back to the bench. "I declined, but today I'm saying yes on one condition. I'm requesting a parlay between him and Isabel. It's a simple thing."

"Yet it's not." Marcellus texted while he talked. "You'll meet your brother tomorrow night. Ten p.m. The Best Friend Lounge. Mills House Hotel."

Alex felt a pain in his jaw and let up on the teeth grinding. "Isabel?"

"You can discuss it with the Prince."

Zack pushed his way back into the convo, fists fully formed. "How do I get my sister back?"

Marcellus slipped his phone into the inside pocket of his jacket. "Lady Allison must complete her dead husband's task."

"Why?" Alex asked.

"Stuart Pinckney was indebted to the Prince. To pay off that debt, he was supposed to find Henry Avery's treasure. Now that Stuart is dead, Lady Allison must retrieve the treasure and return it to the Prince four days hence. In return for the treasure, the debt will be paid and Lady Emilie will be released unharmed."

"You want Allison to pay back Stuart's debt? Which is why *you* don't search for the treasure? Even though the Fianna have way more resources than Allison?"

"Aye."

"This is bullshit," Zack said.

Yes, it was. Dealing with the Fianna was always a back-and-forth of veiled threats and unfulfilled promises.

"Henry Avery's treasure?" Alex asked. "In four days? And that's all the intel you're going to give us?"

"The Pirate's Grille and the appendix from the Witch's Examination of Mercy Chastain may help."

"*Fuck!*" Zack slammed his fist into a tree.

Marcellus scowled at Zack, turned, and left.

Alex wanted to hit something too. Instead, he ran after Marcellus. Something wasn't right. An impossible task and no info? What the hell was that about? "Do you have a problem with Zack?"

Marcellus sent a look of contempt at Zack, who was wrapping his hand with a bandana. "Many years ago, another Prince offered Tremaine a choice. He refused. As the former Prince predicted, Tremaine has proven himself to be a coward from a family of cowards."

Alex stepped back. He'd not been expecting *that*.

Marcellus left and Alex returned to Zack, who was muttering curses and nursing his fingers. Alex dragged Zack to the patio and poured more lemonade, hoping to cool down both their tempers.

While Zack paced the patio, flexing his bruised fingers and cussing loud enough to scare the birds, another text came in to Alex's phone. *See you tomorrow night, little brother. Don't be late.*

Alex almost threw his phone into the lemonade pitcher. Life had been so much easier in prison.

CHAPTER 14

By the time Allison made it across the street, her mother had gone inside. Allison had only two questions for Rue. What was she doing here and how the hell did she get a key?

As Allison turned the knob, the back of her neck tingled. Next to the house was an iron gate that led to the narrow alley and the Pirates Courtyard behind the building. Adjacent to the gate was a pilaster holding up the elaborate iron railing that protected the cemetery. The sun partially blinded her, but she saw a man standing beneath the shade of a pink crepe myrtle tree. He wore a black T-shirt and an Atlanta Braves baseball cap.

He seemed familiar.

The moment he realized she spotted him, he hit his chest with his fist and bowed his head. Because that wasn't at all creepy or strange.

She entered the house, shut the door behind her, and breathed in the cold, lemon-scented air. Since she leased out the building to Ashton Antiques, the first-floor rooms were filled with an array of furniture that required the house to stay in a ridiculously cold state. A stairway in the center hall led to the second floor that was closed off due to termite damage. "Rue?"

When she heard grunting and banging, she went to the end of the hall and entered the kitchen with windows overlooking the Pirates Courtyard. Her mother was lifting cardboard boxes and dropping them onto the kitchen table. Each of the four boxes had Stuart's name printed on the side. They were personal items from Stuart's office.

"What are you doing here, Rue? You're going to wake the dead."

Rue spun around and held a hand to her heart. "Oh, Allison. I didn't hear you."

"Probably because you're making so much noise." She pointed to the cemetery she could see through the patio walls made of brick and iron railings. "Seriously. They're just over there."

"Don't disparage the deceased." Rue lowered her voice. "You don't know which spirits are listening."

"Save the ghost tour nonsense for Lawrence." Allison dropped her purse onto the table. "You didn't answer my question. I'd also like to know how you got a key."

"The bank told me they'd sent Stuart's boxes here and the door was unlocked." Rue started opening boxes and laying items on the table. "You should take better care of this place."

Unlocked?

She grabbed a sweater out of Rue's hands. It still smelled like cigar smoke mixed with pine. She folded it and placed it next to a stack of books and office supplies Rue had already unloaded. "These aren't your things to go through. And in case you've forgotten, you're not supposed to be here. I have a court order."

Rue's green eyes flashed, and she tossed a book onto the table. Yet, instead of hitting back verbally, she offered that sickly sweet smile Allison dreaded. "I thought we were way past *that* by now."

Allison retrieved the book, closed up one box, and moved it near the colonial-era fireplace that dominated the small room. "We're not."

Like a defiant teenager, Rue opened another box and pulled out a stack of ledgers. "Is that why you didn't invite me to Stuart's service?"

Allison took a stapler out of Rue's hand. She wanted to throw it against the wall but instead placed it near the other supplies. Her hard-won self-restraint may have saved the eighteenth-century wall but didn't soften her tone. "How'd you find out about that?"

Rue laughed. "It's a small town, Petal."

Allison refilled one of the boxes and moved it near the fireplace. She despised that nickname and Rue knew it.

"You do know that Stuart was having an affair, don't you?" Rue opened the third box. "I told you that would happen."

Allison ignored the taunt and took that box away as well. "It's time for you to leave."

"Fine." Rue threw a pencil holder onto the table. "It's not here anyway."

"What's not here?"

"Something Stuart saved for me." Rue left the room and headed for the front door.

Allison followed, and just as Rue reached for the knob, Allison placed her body in front of it.

"Please move," Rue said. "My acolytes are waiting."

"Why are you really here?"

"It doesn't matter." When Allison still didn't move, Rue spewed her favorite taunt. "You're a stupid, naive fool, Petal."

Even though Allison knew better than to engage, she couldn't help herself from responding. "Go back to your cult, Rue."

"Raven's Retreat isn't a cult. It's a lifestyle choice."

"The deluded people who give you money to listen to your pseudo-pagan-divination-doomsday nonsense who must live and work on your property with your husband/my uncle have a choice?"

"Of course they do." Rue clenched her hands against her skirt, wrinkling the fabric. "My acolytes can leave at any time."

The very word *acolyte* made Allison sick to her stomach.

Rue and her husband—Allison's uncle—Fenwick were con men. Ever since Allison's brother's death, Rue and Fenwick had been making their living from siphoning money off their cult members, forcing those same cult members to run their absinthe distillery and work in the Pink House. The Pink House, the other oldest structure in the city also originally owned by Mercy Chastain, was Rue's art gallery. It specialized in female creations inspired by the goddess.

It would be one thing if Rue practiced those pagan or wiccan beliefs, but she was too pragmatic. The only thing Rue believed in was money and her own ability to generate it.

Allison moved away from the door. "Go back to Fenwick Hall. Your minions await."

Rue sent Allison a sly, serpent-like smile. "I told you not to marry Stuart. That you had no business marrying anyone ever. That your heart, so hard and ugly, would never be able to love. Especially not a man."

Allison opened the front door. "Leave. Or I'll have you arrested for trespassing."

It wouldn't be the first time.

Rue put her hand on the jamb. "Your father and brother are dead because of your selfishness and inability to love others. Because you're a closed-hearted, frigid bitch. You're a brittle, dead petal."

Unfortunately, Rue's voice carried. A group of tourists, listening to their docent and taking photos in front of the Pirates Courtyard gate, turned to stare at them.

When one tourist pointed a camera in Allison's direction, she lowered her voice. "Rue, it's time to go."

"I saw it all in my visions, Petal. I saw Stuart betray you. I saw you loveless and alone."

Allison swallowed a bitter taste and noticed the man with the baseball cap beyond the tourists, now leaning against the gate. Allison forced a smile for the sake of whatever cameras were on her now and gently forced Rue onto the front stoop. "Thanks for coming by."

With that, Allison shut the door and locked it. Then she leaned against it and closed her eyes. She focused on taking long, deep breaths and reminded herself that this was why she stayed away from Rue. This was why, when she was fourteen, she ran away to New Orleans to live with her grandmother. A decision that led to her attending Tulane and meeting Stuart.

And Zack.

Opening her eyes, she went into the kitchen to get her handbag and found a piece of paper on the floor. A receipt for a local garden center dated a few days before Stuart's death.

Had it fallen out of a box?

Not only had he bought rosemary, lilies of the valley, and thistle, he'd paid in cash.

How odd.

She shoved it into her purse and turned on her phone. She had a few messages from Maddie and called her back. When she heard Maddie's friendly voice, she exhaled loudly. What a relief to talk to someone sane.

"Allison?" Maddie asked. "Susan made something for Nicholas Trott. May we stop by later today after ballet class?"

"Of course." Allison shoved all of the office supplies back into the box, rearranging things so they'd fit. She didn't have the mental energy to sort through it all now. Besides, she might turn up actual evidence of his affair. "Maddie, when you were last at Pirate House, do you remember locking up?"

"Yes. Why?"

"Rue was here and she said the door was open." Allison grabbed her purse and unlocked the back door to enter the courtyard, where a fountain in the shape of a Green Man face spewed water into a raised brick basin. The spray cooled her hot face as two koi swam around the pond. Purple violets had worked their way through the cracks in the brick-and-mortar background.

"That's strange," Maddie said. "Was dealing with Rue difficult?"

Allison dropped her bag onto the wrought-iron table near the fountain. "It's always difficult."

"I'm so sorry. Is there anything I can do?"

"No. But thank you. I'll see you soon." After hanging up, she slipped her phone into her pocket and sank into the iron chair next to the table.

Non ruta non dolor. The phrase the guard had spoken the night before tumbled through her mind. But today *neither rue nor regret* took on another meaning. For all the problems lying in her lap, all the questions burning in her brain, two things she knew for certain: Rue could not be a part of her life, and Allison couldn't spend the rest of her life regretting that decision.

"Allison?" She stood and saw Zack striding toward her. Today he wore jeans and a dark blue T-shirt. Even his tattoos seemed more intense in the daylight. She was getting used to the long black hair tied at his neck. It made him look more like a biker than a soldier.

Maybe that was the point.

Zack grabbed her shoulders, pulled her against his chest, and kissed her.

His lips tilted over hers and he took charge of the motion. It was hard and fierce, and heat rushed through her body. The moment her body softened against his, he let go.

"I'm sorry." He sat on the edge of the raised pond and dropped his head into his hands.

She went over on shaky legs and laid a hand on his hair. It was so much softer than it looked. His body shook. His right hand was bruised, the knuckles covered in dried blood.

A man didn't kiss a woman like that if everything in his life was great. "What's wrong?"

He didn't answer. Instead, he raised his head, and she swallowed hard. She'd never seen so much pain in another person's eyes.

She sat on the brick edge next to him, the fountain water misting her back, and took his hands in hers. "I thought you went back to Savannah?"

He cleared his throat and stared at the violets pushing up between the bricks. "I told you I'd be back."

Except she hadn't believed it. "Why did you return to Charleston?"

"To protect you." He stood and shoved his hands in his pockets. "But now I'm asking for your help. Remember last night when Marcellus said you needed to retrieve that pirate treasure that Stuart failed to find?"

"Yes."

"If I want to save my sister, we need to find it within the next four days."

"Why?" Allison stood and touched his arm. "What happened to Emilie?"

"She's been kidnapped."

⧜

Had he just kissed Allison?

What was wrong with him? Zack flexed his aching hand and paced the courtyard. A restlessness had taken hold of him, and he felt manic and feverish. After talking to Alex, Zack had called Allison but she hadn't answered. So he'd gone to Pinckney House and seen Lawrence. Lawrence, who'd remembered Zack and for some reason had been measuring the hallway, sent Zack to Pastor Tom who'd pointed to Pirate House.

Zack's sister was missing and the only way to save her was to find some old pirate's treasure? He despised the Fianna almost as much as he despised Remiel.

"Zack." When he passed by, Allison grabbed his hand, forcing him to stop moving. "What's going on?"

Zack stared at their clasped hands. So many thoughts tumbled in his brain he didn't know how to sort them. "The Prince and his Fianna warriors kidnapped my sister. The only way to save her is to find Henry Avery's treasure. To do that, we need the Pirate's Grille—"

"And the appendix to the Witch's Examination of Mercy Chastain." Allison released his hand to clasp hers in her lap.

"Which we don't have because Stuart sold it to the Prince."

"According to Hezekiah, Stuart sold the Witch's Examination of Mercy Chastain without the appendix. Which means it's still missing." Allison rubbed her forehead with her fist. "There might be another way."

Zack knelt in front of her. "What?"

"Mercy Chastain and Henry Avery were lovers who disappeared on the same day."

Zack grimaced. "Really?"

"Yep." She waved her hand around the courtyard. "They met when Mercy worked as a barmaid here at Pirate House. They started their affair, and after she had his baby, he built her another house called Pink House. A year later, she was accused of witchcraft."

"Any idea why?"

"None. According to her witch's examination, it was an anonymous accusation. Eventually Nicholas Trott, the chief justice, got her exonerated. Although Trott believed in witchcraft, he'd seen the paranoia and fear caused by the Salem witch trials only a decade earlier and refused to let that happen in Charleston." Allison stood because now it was her turn to pace. "After Mercy's release from prison, she came back to Pirate House to work, but a few months later, she and Henry disappeared. It was only after their disappearance that people realized Henry the barkeeper was actually Henry Avery the infamous pirate who'd been hiding in plain sight from the authorities."

"And this pirate Henry Avery had a treasure?"

"Yes." Allison came back to take his hand. "Before hiding out in Charleston, he took the largest prize ever taken by a pirate. But then he went missing and so did his treasure."

"Then he came to Charleston to do what…hang out?"

"Yes, actually." Allison quickly told Zack about her conversation with Pastor Tom. "Since Stuart didn't have the Pirate's Grille, he believed that if he found out what happened to Mercy, she would lead him to the treasure."

"Why would he think that?"

"I have no idea. And here's the problem."

Zack sank down onto the edge of the raised pond again. "There's always a problem."

"I've been looking for Mercy my entire life."

He glanced up at her. "What are you talking about?"

"Ever since I read Mercy's witch's examination when I was little and learned that she disappeared, I've been obsessed with finding her. This obsession led to my PhD in cultural anthropology, and finding her is the best chance I have of making tenure. Except there's no written record of her death or burial. I've spent years searching for her. Talking to historians. Poring over old records. She simply disappeared."

"There's nothing simple about this." He sighed. "Where do we start?"

"Let's go back and study the Pirate's Grille again. There's got to be another clue." She rubbed her forehead with her fist and frowned. "Zack, last night you mentioned a man named Remiel Marigny. I know it's classified, but if I'm going to help you, you need to trust me."

Zack leaned his forearms on his thighs and let his head hang low. "You can't tell anyone."

She knelt before him and raised his chin with her finger until their gazes met. "I would never betray you."

After a long moment, he said, "Remiel Marigny didn't just order the deaths of Hezekiah and Stuart. Remiel accused my unit of a horrible event called the Wakhan Corridor Massacre—a massacre he orchestrated and that led to half my unit being ambushed in the Pamir River Valley. The other half of the unit rescued them. The POWs were then sent to a secret army prison while my men and I were secretly and dishonorably discharged."

"Why?"

"Because the army believed that our entire group was responsible for the massacre." He took her face in his hands. "I swear we weren't."

As if she'd ever believed he could have been responsible. She sat next to him. "There's something you should know. Stuart left Isabel a million-dollar life insurance policy."

Zack's eyes widened. "Excuse me?"

When she finished telling him about her meeting with Lawrence, he said, "This isn't a joke?"

"Nope. None of this makes sense. I mean who is this Remiel Marigny?"

"A vicious arms dealer who's in a war with the Prince. I don't know why. All I'm sure of is that my men and I are caught in the middle."

"How did Stuart get involved with all of this?"

"No idea. Although if I had to guess, I think Isabel is the key. She works for Remiel."

Allison paled. "That means she's partly responsible for Stuart's death."

Before Zack could respond, Allison's cell phone rang and she answered, "Hello, Detective." A moment later she said, "We're on our way."

"What's wrong?"

She threw her purse over her shoulder, took his wrist, and ran out of the courtyard, pulling him with her. "Pinckney House is on fire."

CHAPTER 15

ZACK PARKED HIS BIKE BEHIND ALLISON'S CAR, FOUR HUNDRED yards from her house. The street was blocked off by fire trucks, police vehicles, and lots of bystanders. He took her hand and led her down the crowded sidewalk.

When they arrived, Detective Waring helped them cross the barricades. From there, Zack saw smoke coming from the back garden. Yet the house appeared unharmed.

"Detective," Allison said in a breathless voice, "what's going on? How's Nicholas Trott?"

On cue, Nicholas Trott ran off the porch to greet them.

Detective Waring took Allison's arm and led her toward the back of the house. "There was a fire in a garden building."

"The gardener's shed?"

"Yes. The firefighters put it out, but the building has been gutted."

Zack followed them. "And the main house?"

"The fire was contained to the dependency and part of the west garden." Waring stepped over a ladder. "The fire inspector is checking the main house now. There's smoke damage."

When they turned the corner, Allison gasped. Black soot coated the house's wooden clapboards.

"I'm sure the soot can be washed off," Waring said.

Nicholas Trott ran into the house, and they headed toward the wood-and-brick building in the far corner of the property. A shell of its former self, the roof was charred timbers, and the windows and doors were gone. Only the brick supports remained. A few firefighters were still spraying the area with hoses.

"Those eighteenth-century bricks are sturdy," Waring said. "I bet it can be renovated with insurance money."

Allison sighed. "Lawrence isn't going to be happy."

A few minutes later, they entered Allison's kitchen.

Waring took out a notebook and pen. "Mrs. Pinckney, do you have any idea why someone would burn down your shed?"

"No," she said. "It's historically significant, but there wasn't anything in there of value."

"You should call your insurance company. Once the investigation is done, they'll give you contacts for cleanup crews and builders." Waring snapped his notebook closed. "After the inspector finishes his work, it'll take at least a week to get the report finished and filed."

When Waring left the kitchen, she called the insurance company and Zack heard a knock at the back door.

He found Alex standing there, hands in his jean pockets. "I got your text."

Since Allison was preoccupied with insurance people, Zack went outside with Alex. Nicholas Trott followed for belly rubs from the new guy. Most of the fire trucks had left, but one remained with the firefighters still soaking the gardens.

When Alex stopped rubbing, Nicholas Trott returned to the house. "What happened?"

"Allison's shed burned down."

"Burned? Or had been burnt?"

"Not sure yet." They walked the path together while Zack told Alex about Isabel's insurance windfall.

When Zack finished, Alex said, "Isabel is a conniving, manipulating bitch."

"I feel bad for Allison. She's acting like she's okay, but that news had to have hit hard."

"Allison is strong. And she has you." Alex gripped Zack's shoulder. "Have you called Nate to tell him about Emilie?"

"I'll call when I have more intel." Zack leaned against a palm tree and crossed his arms. This garden was larger than he'd realized. "Do you want me to go with you to meet your brother?"

"No." Alex took out a hand-rolled cigarette and lighter. "What are you going to do now?"

Zack was about to give Alex the smoking lecture but figured there was no point. From what Zack had witnessed since Alex had arrived in the unit, the brother hardly ever smoked. The only time he lit up was after an argument with Kells. "Right now I need a plan."

Zack stopped talking because Allison appeared, looking paler if that was at all possible.

"Allison, this my buddy Alex. He's in town to help."

She shook Alex's hand and smiled. "I'm grateful, Alex. We're going to need it."

Zack heard the tension in her voice. "What happened?"

"Remember the Pirate's Grille I put into the safe last night?"

Zack nodded.

"It's gone."

Four hours later, Allison said goodbye to the fire inspector and escorted Detective Waring back to his patrol car he'd parked down the street.

"Mrs. Pinckney, do you have any idea who would've stolen that document from the safe? It wasn't broken into, so the thief must've had the combination. There's no sign of forced entry into the house. Was the alarm set?"

"I had to suspend service to cut expenses." She then told Detective Waring about Lawrence being at the house and how she'd left him alone so she could meet Pastor Tom. "I know he didn't have the new safe combination, and I've no idea when he left. It's possible Lawrence forgot to lock the front door."

"Do you have a number where I can reach him?"

"Of course." After giving him Lawrence's contact number, she said, "For the record, I don't believe Lawrence set the fire. He loves this house."

"Still, I'd like to talk to him. We also dusted for prints and took photographs." Detective Waring stared at the last firetruck pulling out. "It's possible the fire was a cover for the burglary."

"I was thinking the same thing."

He touched her elbow. "Mrs. Pinckney, if you remember anything else, let me know."

"Thank you, Detective." Once he left, she went through the garden and stopped a few feet away from the burned-out shed, which was now surrounded by yellow police tape. She heard rustling sounds and saw a man's dark-haired head.

"Zack?"

His head poked through a broken window. "I'm checking everything out."

"We're not supposed to go in there. There's police tape around the perimeter. And a yellow sign that says DANGER. DO NOT ENTER. You walked past it."

"Huh." He leaned out to see the sign posted on the doorframe. "Must've missed that."

She laughed when she should've scolded. "Did you find anything salvageable?"

"Come take a look." He disappeared again.

Taking a deep breath, she ducked under the tape and went inside. She wasn't one for breaking rules. But it was her husband's family's property.

On cue, thunder rumbled and dark clouds rolled in.

Zack stood in the center of the burned-out room. "See? Nothing to worry about. I left Nicholas Trott with your girlfriend Maddie and her daughter, Susan. They're waiting for you in the house."

"I forgot they were coming over."

He touched what was left of the wood mantel over the colonial-era fireplace. "I introduced myself, but I think she already knew all about me."

Allison walked around, avoiding blackened debris. Since the building, which had once been a colonial-era kitchen, was partly made of brick, the walls were still upright. Inside, the remaining crossbeam over her head dripped with dirty water. The only thing left were the metal parts of gardening tools hanging on walls and lying on the floor. What hadn't burned was now wet and mangled. "Maddie is my best friend. She knows *all* about you."

He waggled an eyebrow. "*Everything?*" Allison laughed in that knowing, female way that made Zack frown.

"Maybe." Although she teased him, the truth was that there wasn't anything to tell. Yes, he'd spent the night with her but it wasn't like they'd done anything other than kiss.

Twice.

He moved and a brick mantel support fell out, missing his foot by an inch.

She took his arm. "We should get out of here."

He shoved his hand into the hole left by the brick and pulled out a bag. "What's this?"

"I don't know." She opened the bag and found a white handkerchief with an *SP* monogrammed on the edge. "This is one of Stuart's handkerchiefs."

She unrolled the white cotton and discovered a heavy iron key.

She held it up and saw the unusual markings on the key's handle. A *JL* in the middle of a lily. "I've seen this before. This is the same marking as on the door handle going into the Satyr Club/Usher Society building."

Before Zack could answer, Maddie appeared in the doorway. Her body shook and her eyes were wide. "Susan is missing."

CHAPTER 16

ALEX SHOVED HIS CELL PHONE INTO HIS BACK POCKET. According to his most recent texts with Marcellus, the Prince was not responsible for the fire. And, in typical warrior form, wouldn't admit whether or not he knew who was responsible.

After the firefighters left, Alex discovered a hidden path lined with rose bushes and boxwoods. The huge garden had multiple hidden ponds and seating areas. Despite its formal design, the area had gone wild. Rose branches snagged his pants and he couldn't help but stomp on daisies and violets that refused to stay within their boundaries. The live oak trees carried Spanish moss like it was a burden they couldn't shed, and the smell of jasmine soaked the air.

It was a mess, but he didn't mind. He related to the inability to follow rules.

When he turned a corner, he found a raised fountain held up by the tabby wall. A Pan statue sprayed water out of two flutes into the basin filled with white and purple water lilies. Hidden from the world, he took his sharpening stone and knife out of the pocket of his motorcycle jacket. After dipping the stone in water, he sat on the edge of the pond and sharpened his blade. He was still annoyed over the fact that Kells didn't think he was mature enough to carry a gun.

A few minutes later he heard barking and a soft female voice calling out, "Nicholas Trott! Come here, boy!"

He put the stone away and stood, still holding the blade. When Nicholas Trott appeared, the shaggy mutt jumped on Alex with his tongue out.

"Nicholas Trott!" the feminine voice shouted. "Get down!"

The dog ran back to a tiny girl. She wore a purple leotard and net skirt that sparkled in the sunlight. Her brown hair had been pulled tight into a bun and someone had attached glittery purple wings to her back. She dropped to her knees and buried her face in the dog's neck. When the dog pulled out of her embrace and loped away to chase a squirrel, she stood. She barely came up to his waist yet stared with brown eyes that showed a soul as old as his.

Shit. He and kids didn't mix well.

She watched him with a wariness that made him feel as if he'd crawled out of hell. Which he had done. Twice.

"Why are you holding a knife?" Her voice had an innocent, singsong quality that reminded him of someone he didn't want to remember. Someone he'd loved, lost to death, and still missed.

"For protection." Which was better than admitting he was waiting to kill that evil fuckface Remiel Marigny. Alex shoved the knife into his boot. "Why are you wearing wings?"

"For my ballet class." She twirled, the wings fluttering as she moved. "We're practicing for our fall recital, *A Midsummer Night's Dream*."

"Huh." He wished he had a cigarette but he'd smoked his last one.

She held out her hand. "I'm Susan Ashton. I'm almost eight. My cat is named Mrs. Pickles and I'm looking for a leprechaun."

Not only did he know nothing about kids, he knew even less about precocious little girls. Since he couldn't leave her hanging, he shook, taking her much smaller hand in his. "Alex Mitchell."

"I'm not allowed to call adults by their first names." When he dropped her hand, both of her palms landed on her hips. "I'll call you Mr. Mitchell."

"That's cool." Not sure what to do next, he said, "You know you're not supposed to talk to strangers, don't you?"

"Of course. My mother says now that we're alone in my grandmère's house, we need to be extra vigilant."

"Why are you living alone?"

"My dad is staying with his girlfriend. Except my parents aren't divorced yet."

"Oh." Wow. What did one say to that? "Are you sure you're only seven?"

"I'm almost eight." Her lower lip quivered. "I listen a lot. That's how I knew my parents were getting divorced before they told me."

He raised an eyebrow. He wasn't sure how he felt about having something in common with a young girl, but it sure as hell didn't feel manly. "I listen a lot too."

"Really?" The yearning in that question made her seem closer to seven instead of eight.

"Yep." He crossed his arms. "I listened to my older brothers argue." Mostly about him.

She dropped her head, all bravado gone. "I don't like it when adults argue."

He knelt in front of her and waited until she met his gaze. "Most of the time when adults argue, they're doing it because they're scared."

Her eyes widened. "Scared of what?"

He shrugged. "Adult stuff. Stuff that has nothing to do with you."

She leaned in to whisper, "I still don't like it."

He whispered back, "I don't either."

Finally, she smiled again. "Mr. Mitchell, may I see your knife?"

"Sure." He stood and took his bowie out of his boot. "Don't cut yourself. I'm in enough trouble."

"I promise." She took it and started waving it around. "It'll be our secret."

"Susan!" Another female voice sounded out through the garden.

Susan answered, "I'm here, Mom!"

Alex heard footsteps, and then a woman in a strapless blue sundress and white sweater appeared. Her long brown hair had been pulled back, but damp curls framed her face. Her low sandals crunched on the oyster-shell walkway as she hurried over.

"Susan… What is that?"

Susan waved the bowie around again. "It's Mr. Mitchell's knife!"

Susan's mother stopped, and her chocolate-brown gaze met his. "Why does she have your knife?"

All of the breaths he'd ever taken and would ever take rushed out of his chest. Where Susan was cute, the mother was stunning. Of course, he had a fondness for great breasts, lean legs, and flashing eyes. "Susan asked to see it."

"When a seven-year-old wants to see something, you let her have it?"

"Mom!" Susan's eyes widened. "I'm almost eight!"

He shoved his hands in his pockets. "Sure."

Susan slashed the air once more before handing him the knife. "I'm not a baby."

Alex slid the knife into his boot as Zack arrived with Allison.

Zack grabbed Alex's arm. "What's wrong?"

Alex yanked away. "Nothing."

"Maddie?" Allison touched her friend's shoulder. "Is everything okay?"

"I guess. Come on, Susan." Maddie took her daughter's hand, and they walked toward the house. But not before Susan waved goodbye.

Allison's quizzical glance moved between Zack and Alex. "I'll go back to the house with Maddie."

When the women disappeared, Zack glared at Alex. "What did you say to Susan?"

"She asked to see my knife. No big deal."

Zack's sigh reminded Alex of Kells: one part frustration, one part annoyance, one part disgust. "I need you in the game, Alex."

"I'm in the fucking game. Hell, I'm meeting my brother to win the fucking game."

Zack shook out his swollen, bruised hand. "This whole day has been an epic failure."

Alex thought about Maddie's silky hair, almond-shaped eyes, soft skin, and firm… "The day's only half over, brother. There's still time to turn it around. You gotta have faith."

"You're lecturing me on faith? Do you know how fucked up that is?"

For the first time since Alex could remember, he smiled—a genuine grin that almost turned into a chuckle. "I do. And you know why I'm smiling?" Alex slapped Zack on the back. "Because fucked up is what we do best."

"Glad you think that way, bro. Because I have a job for you."

Alex cocked his head. "What?"

"I'll call Rafe to see if he can find out anything about where the Fianna are holding Emilie. I want you to find Isabel—"

"*No.*"

"—and steal back the Pirate's Grille."

Fuck.

Allison poured lemonade as Maddie hung up the house phone. Susan sat at the table with a book. Sighing, Allison found a hair band in her dress pocket and pulled her hair up. The day's heat had won, and it was time for the high ponytail. "Thank you for taking that call, Maddie. I can't deal with Lawrence anymore."

"He told me some of the Pinckney relatives have arrived for Stuart's memorial on Friday."

"Ugh. It's only Wednesday."

"I know." Maddie shrugged. "Because of the fire, Lawrence is settling everyone, including himself, at the Meeting Street Inn. He said if Detective Waring contacts you with more information that he wants to know ASAP."

"Of course he does." Allison placed a glass of lemonade and a plate of brownies on the table for Susan. Thunder rolled again and the first big splats of rain hit her kitchen window. It was almost six p.m., but with the dark skies, it felt more like midnight.

Zack entered the kitchen, shoving his phone in his back pocket, and she met his gaze. Then he winked. Thank God Susan had only been exploring the garden and not missing. To be fair, Maddie had been under enormous stress lately and was more protective than normal.

"Did Mr. Mitchell leave?" Susan turned the page of her book.

Zack patted her head. "Yes. I told him next time he wants to show you his knife to ask your mom first."

"Okay." Susan smiled around her lemonade glass. "Thanks, Mr. Tremaine."

Maddie frowned, and Allison sat to squeeze her hand.

Zack took water bottles from the refrigerator and handed them out. With all the going in and out of the house, as well as the approaching storm, the humidity had overpowered the AC.

"Thank you," Maddie said, opening her bottle. "It's so awful that someone set your shed on fire. Can you talk to Lawrence about restarting the alarm?"

"Oh, I'm sure it'll be restarted in a week." Allison played with the bottle cap, hating the fact that she had to break this news. "Once he moves back into Pinckney House."

Maddie placed her bottle on the table. "What are you talking about?"

Zack spun another chair around and straddled it. "That's what I'd like to know."

Susan ate her brownie and stared at the adults.

"This is the situation." First, Allison told Maddie about Stuart leaving Isabel the life insurance money. Before Maddie's eyes fell out of her head, Allison added the news about Lawrence moving in and her moving out. "In a week, I'll be living at Pirate House full-time. Since the upstairs isn't safe, I'll put a cot in the kitchen. At least there's a half bath with running water."

"Can Lawrence do that?" Zack asked.

"Yes."

Susan paused, mid-brownie bite. "Miss Allison? You have to move?"

Allison nodded at the little girl.

"What a nightmare." Maddie leaned back in her chair. "Do you want me to take out the antiques?"

"No. Honestly, I need the rent and I don't require much room. I don't want to live there permanently."

"Because it's haunted?" Susan said with a chocolatey smile.

Zack laughed, and Allison threw a napkin at Susan, who giggled.

"For the record," Zack said to Susan, "I think Pinckney House is haunted."

Maddie's eyes widened as she sipped her water. "Have you seen a ghost here?"

"I'm not sure…"

"I cannot believe," Allison said to Zack, "that the big bad Green Beret believes in the paranormal."

"I grew up in the number one most-haunted city in America, I live in the second most-haunted city in America, and today I'm in the sixth most-haunted city in America. So, yeah, I do."

"It's okay, Mr. Tremaine," Susan said in a whispery, little-kid voice. "I've seen ghosts here too."

Allison took a bite of her brownie and almost sighed. It'd been hours since the blueberry coffee cake and she was starving. "That's the thinking that got Mercy Chastain accused of witchcraft and led to the panicked frenzy of Salem, where over two hundred were accused of witchcraft, about one hundred fifty people were arrested, four died in prison awaiting trial, nineteen were hanged, and one was pressed."

Zack smiled. "That's why Salem is the fifth most-haunted city in America."

She tapped him on the head. "Ghosts aren't real."

"I hope not." Maddie stood and touched Allison's shoulder. "We need to get home."

Allison stood to give Maddie a hug and kiss Susan on the head. "I'm okay. I promise."

Once they were alone, Zack tossed out his water bottle. "I'm so sorry you have to leave your home."

She ate another brownie, not caring about the calories. "At least I don't have to move any furniture. None of it belongs to me."

He took her arm and forced her to look at him. "You don't have to pretend to be strong or that this entire thing isn't freaking you out. A few months ago, I lost everything as well. After we were dishonorably discharged, the army kept our bank accounts and many of our belongings."

She touched his chin. "Zack, I am so sorry. I had no idea."

He took her hands and pressed them against his chest. Beneath her palms, she felt the hard muscles moving from the force of his breathing.

"Zack, I have no idea how, but I promise you we'll find the treasure and save your sister. If anyone in this nightmare deserves a happy ending, it's you."

"What about you?"

"It's too late for me. My marriage to Stuart taught me that."

"I disagree—"

Her cell phone buzzed and she stepped away from Zack's warmth to find it in her purse.

"Is anything wrong?"

She handed him her phone with the text: *For women's fear and love holds quantity, in neither aught, or in extremity.*

"It's the third of these I've gotten today."

Zack frowned and scrolled through her phone to find the other odd texts. "This first one is telling you to stop searching for something. What were you doing when you received it?"

"Searching the internet for information about the Prince and the Fianna. Although apart from Irish folk tales written almost a thousand years ago, there wasn't a lot of information."

"They scrub the information. I've heard that the Prince updates his own online encyclopedic entries." He glanced at her. "These texts are from the Fianna. Probably Marcellus."

"The warrior we met last night?"

"Yep." He pointed to the second text about the day's issues. "This one is basically saying that whatever task you have to do today, your love will help you find the way."

"Huh." She moved in close to read as well. Why did Zack always have to smell so good?

"Look at the time stamp." Zack expanded the screen. "It's about the same time Alex and I were learning about my sister and how I needed your help to save her."

"It's also the same time that Lawrence was telling me I need to move out." She glanced at Zack. His lips were so tight they'd whitened around the edges. "It's not a coincidence, is it?"

"No." He handed her the phone and started pacing the kitchen. "The third text is more cryptic."

"Not really." She finished her water. "It means that a woman's worry and her love work together. A woman either doesn't worry at all because she doesn't love, or she worries too much because she loves too much." Neither description really fit her. "The question is, now what do we do?"

Zack took a brownie and ate it in one bite. "First," he said with a mouthful, "we get something to eat."

Her stomach gurgled on cue, and she nodded. As she shoved her phone in her pocket, she felt something else and pulled out the key. "I have an idea. After we eat, of course."

He took the key from her and turned it over. "You want to return to the Usher Society?"

"I want to scour Hezekiah's office and find everything I can about what Stuart was doing."

"It may be under surveillance." Zack's phone buzzed. He checked it, frowned, and shoved it into his pocket. "It'll be dangerous."

"Not as dangerous as our next meal is going to be. I haven't gone food shopping in weeks." She opened the fridge and stared into the empty recess. Finally, she pulled out a jar of grape jelly and a can of tuna.

Zack took the food and gently pushed her aside. "I'm not just eye candy."

She laughed. "You're handsome, you're a highly trained soldier, and you can cook? I've never heard of such a thing."

He found a flowered apron in a drawer. "I also kiss really, really well."

She blushed and turned away to get the plates. Yes, he really, really did.

And she couldn't help but wonder if he'd ever kiss her again.

CHAPTER 17

Isabel paced the garden courtyard behind the Gibbes Art Museum. The fountain's mist cooled her, helping to soothe her racing mind. Gravel crunched beneath her sandals. Flashes of lightning and random raindrops forewarned an impending storm.

Seeing Alex again had been harder than she'd expected. She'd never loved him. She'd never even liked him. Yet she was torn. Stuart had been a kind and generous lover, and her feelings for him had been real. But Alex? No woman could forget the kind of passion a man like Alex brought to bed.

A whistle came from behind her, and she turned as Clayborne appeared at the cemetery gate near the corner of the courtyard. It seemed like every building in this city backed up to a cemetery.

She met him at the gate. "Any trouble?"

"No." He handed her the tube and shoved his hands into his jeans pockets. "I gotta tell ya—Allison and her soldier are looking mighty tight."

Isabel honestly didn't understand what Zack saw in that milquetoast Allison. "I'll deal with it. Now for your next assignment. I need you to find the appendix to the Witch's Examination of Mercy Chastain. Check every library, special collection, and magazine rack in this city. Also, double-check Hezekiah's office."

"Why? Now that you have the Pirate's Grille, it shouldn't matter."

She hated explaining herself to the hired help. And she was sure if Remiel had done the asking, Clayborne wouldn't have questioned him. "Remiel will feel better if we take it out of play."

"Right. My boys are on it." Clayborne pulled out his phone and texted. "What about you?"

"I'm going to destroy this." She raised the tube. "Then I'm going to pick a time and place to tell Allison what really happened in Afghanistan. I'm going to make sure she knows the truth about her hero Zack. Make sure she knows he's a liar and a coward."

Thirty minutes later, Isabel let herself into her suite on the top floor of the Belmond Hotel. She'd had to hide the Pirate's Grille and had barely made it to the hotel before the storm hit. While she'd told Clayborne she wanted to destroy it, she'd had another idea. Once she found the treasure, she'd secretly sell the Pirate's Grille and the witch's examination appendix. As long as no one knew the treasure had been found, those two manuscripts would still be worth a ton of money. Money that could supplement her getaway account.

She dropped her handbag onto the couch...and froze. Alex Mitchell sat in the opposite chair looking masculine and bored.

"How did you find me? And how did you get in here?"

"I came to the most expensive hotel in the city and paid off the housekeeping staff."

"With what? You're broke."

"Money isn't the only currency." His smile was deceptive. It drew you in until you realized his dark amethyst eyes were almost as cold as Remiel's. "You're looking chipper, Isabel. Could it be you found the Pirate's Grille?"

She poured herself a seltzer water and took out a ginger ale from the fridge. Yes, she remembered his favorite. "Drink?"

"Sure." He came over while she filled the glass with ice. "Tell me, did you set the fire? Or did you have hired help?"

She popped open the soda and waited for the initial fizz to settle before pouring the ginger ale over the ice. "I don't know what you're talking about."

"Okay. I'll play your way." Alex took the drink and went to the window. Normally, at this time of day, one could see Fort Sumter in the harbor. But with the driving rain, one could barely see across the street.

A huge clap of thunder hit outside the window and the electricity dimmed, only to come back on a second later.

Isabel kicked off her shoes, curled up on the couch, and drank her water. It was cold, and she was hot. Actually, she was exhausted. For the last few months, Remiel had had her moving at such a rapid pace, she wasn't sure if she could keep up anymore. "Alex, why are you here?"

Alex came back to his chair and sat across from her. He placed his glass on the table between them and closed his eyes. "To find out more about Emilie. Except you don't know anything else."

"Alex?" Isabel kept her voice whisper level. "Do you ever just want to…run away?"

He opened his eyes, his focus entirely on her. While he watched her movements, she took out her hair band and let her long black curls fall over her shoulders. His eyes narrowed and his hands gripped the chair. "Why do you ask?"

"Because I do. I dream of running away to an island somewhere—an island with no tourists, no noise or tall buildings, just the sea breeze and lots of sunshine."

"You sunburn." Alex took a sip of his soda but kept his gaze on her. "I've seen it."

Yes, he had. In Jamaica. "I remember that trip. The heat. The blue sea. The red bikini."

Alex stood to pace the room. "There's no running away for either of us. We've done too many things."

When he walked by her, she grabbed his arm, forcing him to stop and look at her. "Alex, we've both been used—me by a Fianna warrior first and then by Remiel, you by your brother and Kells. We've been lied to, mistreated, and blamed for things that weren't our fault. We've even suffered abuse, albeit in different ways."

Alex pulled out of her grip. "It doesn't matter, Isabel. We've caused suffering."

She stood. "Because we were forced to."

"No one forced you to work for Remiel."

"Remiel saved my life. After I was attacked when I was only seventeen, he took me in when no one else in my family would look at me. And your brother—"

"Did not save my life." Alex waved her off as if she were an irritant, like a buzzing fly. "My brother used me and discarded me. Just like Remiel is using you. And trust me when I say this, Isabel. Remiel will discard you. Eventually. He has to. You know everything about him."

"That knowledge protects me."

"No, it makes you too dangerous to keep alive."

"Remiel would never—"

"I'd beg to differ except I don't beg anymore. Ever. And if you think either of us is due a happily ever after, you're even more deranged than Fuckface."

She hated when Alex called Remiel that awful name. She went back to the couch and sat, her feet tucked beneath her body. "What do you want?"

"The Prince told Allison and Zack they need to find Henry Avery's treasure if they want to save Emilie's life."

She had figured that would be the plan. "So?"

"There are two ways to find that treasure: find out what happened to Mercy Chastain over three hundred years ago, or combine—and somehow use—the Pirate's Grille and witch's examination's appendix."

"No one knows what happened to Mercy because she disappeared."

"Correct. That leaves the appendix and the Pirate's Grille." Alex sat next to her so he could meet her gaze head-on. "And we both know you have the latter."

She shrugged.

"I want to offer a trade."

She lowered her eyelids halfway and gave him a once-over. "You'd be willing—"

"Hell no." He grabbed his soda and finished it. Ice cubes and all. "Earlier today you mentioned a meeting with my brother."

"I'm not trading—"

"If you want to see the Prince, I want the Pirate's Grille. That's the deal."

She rubbed the couch's crushed-velvet armrest back and forth, forcing the nap to change colors from light to dark. "Remiel will kill me."

"Not if you accept asylum."

"I don't trust the Fianna. Not after what they did to me."

"No one should trust them." Alex stood. "That doesn't mean they can't help you."

She stood, her bare feet cushioned by the soft carpet. Without her heels, Alex towered over her.

"I need to think about it. I'm going to an event tomorrow." She grabbed a piece of paper from the desk and wrote down the information. "Meet me in the bar. You'll have my answer."

Alex took the paper and turned to leave. He paused, one hand on the doorknob. "I know you're scared, Isabel. But if I had the choice between facing Remiel's wrath or the Fianna's offer, I'd take the latter. The latter is more likely to offer you mercy."

He left and she sank onto the couch, knowing in her heart that Alex was right. The Fianna might be brutal, but Remiel was merciless.

Allison stood in front of the door of the Satyr Club/Usher Society and turned the key.

Lightning flashed and Zack held the umbrella over them. "We should hurry."

She nodded. Most of the alley had been blocked off with yellow police tape, and an empty police car sat at the other end. Zack had scouted the area and found no security cameras, curious tourists, or other cops. Still, someone belonged to that patrol car.

"I hope this place isn't alarmed." She swung the door open and they entered.

They waited for a moment and both exhaled at the same time when they realized no alarms had been tripped. Then she sucked in her breath at the AC. She was so acclimated to the city's heat and humidity it was hard to go back and forth between Charleston's suffocating outsides and frigid insides.

She'd no idea what they'd find, but since they had the key, it was the only plan she had.

Zack propped the umbrella by the entrance and took two flashlights out of her tote bag that had her dog's face on it. Zack had filled the bag with a variety things they might need, like her pistol, extra ammo, and duct tape. She wasn't sure why they needed the tape, but she wasn't about to argue with a Special Forces officer.

"Allison"—Zack took out his weapon—"why do you have your dog's face printed on your bag?"

"I made the bags for last year's Fourth of July parade."

"Interesting." Zack turned on his light, but since she'd been here before, she led the way. The door where she'd paid her silver coin was unlocked, and inside all she found was an empty room. The bar, DJ table, couches—all gone. And there was no light switch. All the windows were boarded up; the only light came from their flashlights.

"Last night this place was full of people and furniture." She walked across the dance floor, her sandals clip-clopping along the way. "It smelled like sweat and incense."

"Now it smells like lemon furniture polish."

Chills scurried up her arms. The sooner they did this, the sooner they could leave.

A minute later, she entered the Usher Society's anteroom where she'd met Isabel. This room looked exactly the same, except without the people. Like the first floor, it was completely dark and they had to swing their beams around to see the situation.

Couches and velvet curtains? Check.

A bar in the corner? Check.

The double doors leading into Hezekiah's office? Check.

Zack tried the office doors, but they were locked. She handed him the key, and, thank goodness, the office doors swung open.

She stepped into the room only to find documents strewn about everywhere. The floor, the desk, and the nearby credenza had been torn apart. Even the painting of Thomas Toban's pirate ship was askew, as if someone had searched behind it.

Zack walked the room's perimeter. "We're not the only ones with this idea."

"Apparently not." She picked papers off the floor and threw them onto the desk. All of the credenza and desk drawers had been pulled out, emptied, and tossed into a corner. "This is a mess. I'm not sure where to start."

"First, see if there are any electronics—computers, flash drives, hard drives." He handed her the tote bag. "Second, we take every piece of paper we can find."

"Why?"

"Because we don't have time to sort through it here and we have no idea what's of value."

"Okay." She laid her flashlight on the desk and started stacking papers and maps. "Everything?"

"Yes." He knelt next to the credenza and felt beneath it. He even peered into the open holes where the drawers had been. While she tried to organize the papers on the floor, he searched baseboards, beneath the chairs and desk, and every item that could hold anything.

Fifteen minutes later, she'd stuffed the tote bag, and he replaced the pirate painting on the wall.

"That's it." She shrugged the bag onto her shoulder. "Whoever got here first took the good stuff."

Zack stood in the center and, using both flashlights, scanned the room. "With the appalling lack of security, I don't think Hezekiah would've stored stuff in his drawers. There's no wall safe. There's no place to hide anything important."

"Last night, I didn't see a computer."

Zack glanced at her. "If you were the oldest black-market book proprietor in the U.S., where would you hide those things you didn't want others to find?"

"In books?" She took one of the lights and studied the room again. "Except there are no bookshelves. That's strange."

"Very strange." Zack led the way back into the anteroom and did another perimeter search. He even tapped the wood-paneled walls. When one tap sounded hollower than the rest, Allison used her fingers to feel around the edges of the paneling.

"I don't feel anything."

He hit the wall with his fist. "I don't—"

The wall suddenly swung open and Zack shone the beam into the closet.

"It's a…library. I think." Allison went in, dropped the bag, and stood in the center of a room that had floor-to-ceiling bookcases. Except there were only a few books on the shelves. She coughed as the musty smell hit her sinuses hard. There was no window to open to get some desperately needed fresh air.

"It's not climate-controlled." Zack came in, taking up the rest of the floor space. His light rested on a few volumes. "Considering the heat and dust, this has to be temporary storage."

Allison swung her light and noticed a book on the shelf lying on its side. "What is this doing here?"

Zack came over and took it from her. "*Stories Out of Stone* by Allison Chastain Fenwick Pinckney, PhD. Did you write this?"

"Yes. My dissertation was published last year. I wrote about Southern headstones as forms of colonial-era personal narratives." Zack stared at her with a quizzical look until she added, "It's about how the symbolism in tombs and headstones, especially during the sixteenth and seventeenth centuries, told the stories of the deceased and their families."

He handed her the flashlight while he flipped through the pages. "It says it's a bestseller."

Allison scoffed. "In a narrowly defined field."

"What's this?" He took an envelope out of the book and read the return address. "It's from the anthropology department at the University of Virginia."

"I've been looking for that." She shoved it into the tote bag. "It's from a colleague of mine. I gave a presentation for their graduate students. It's a thank-you note."

Zack frowned and took the letter out of the bag. "Why would it be in your book that was stashed in an Usher Society closet?"

"It's possible…" She tucked a stray curl behind her ear. "Stuart may have hidden it here because a few months ago they offered me a job.

Stuart and I got into a huge fight about it. It's not like I wanted to leave Charleston, but it's a wonderful opportunity."

Zack stared at her for a long moment. He opened his mouth as if he were about to say something, then went back to her book. He studied photographs she'd taken of tombs around Charleston. "This is an unusual topic."

"You don't have to look interested. I started the research because I was looking for clues about Mercy's disappearance. And it just morphed into this *thing* about funerary symbolism and the stories it told."

He glanced at her. "A *thing* that got you a job offer from UVA?"

"Yes." She pulled a few books off the shelf and read the spines.

"Allison? Were you considering leaving Stuart?"

She placed the books onto another shelf. There wasn't anything here related to their search. "No..." She swallowed a few times. "I don't know."

Instead of asking her more questions, he shut her book and shoved it into the tote bag. "Allison, why have you been so intent on finding Mercy?"

She went back to reading the book spines. "Besides wanting to know for my own sense of personal history, I believe there's a story there worth telling. Mercy was—is—the *only* unnamed accused witch in the history of the United States. The unnamed accused witch who disappeared and is now a ghost hunted by tourists. And tenure at the college is extremely hard to get. If I can find Mercy and tell her story—in a peer-reviewed journal—it would go a long way toward helping me achieve that goal."

One by one, Zack pulled out each book from the shelves, shook the pages, and placed it back. "In all of these years, have you found any clues?"

"One. A broken daisy. It stands for the loss of youth, innocence, and hope. There were broken daisies on the pages of Mercy's witch's examination. I know from a jailor's letter that she carved broken daisies, along with other graffiti, into the wall of her cell while she was awaiting her trial. And there are broken daisies carved in one of the original wooden bed frames in Pirate House."

"How old was Mercy when she disappeared?"

"Twenty-four." Allison took an untitled book off the shelf only to find it was a leather journal. The front was embossed with a sword piercing a heart. "Henry was forty-five."

Zack moved quickly through the books, shaking and reshelving. "Are there any broken daisies on any of the tombs in Charleston?"

"No." She turned the journal pages filled with intensely neat scribbles and notes. "I've been through every public cemetery in the Low Country, and I didn't find any from Mercy's time. Although there are private colonial-era cemeteries I didn't see because it's hard to get permission to search them."

Zack glanced at her. "Could Henry and Mercy have run away together?"

"It's possible, but I don't believe she'd leave her son behind. Although he was raised by relatives, I still have a tough time believing a mother would abandon her child."

Except for mothers like Rue, of course.

Zack went back to the bookshelves. "What do you know about this treasure?"

"It's still the largest score ever taken by a pirate." She scanned the pages and her heart rate kicked up. The handwriting was familiar. "In 1700, when Henry moved to Charleston under an assumed name, his treasure consisted of six hundred pounds of gold and silver and precious gems. In today's market, over sixty million dollars."

"*Whoa.*"

Allison bit her lower lip. She understood the tremor beneath his voice. His sister's life was now worth sixty million dollars—which they had to find in four days. "Look at this."

Zack stood behind her and held the light over her shoulder. "What is it?"

"A planner." She turned to the first page, where the owner had written his name. "It belonged to Stuart."

"Why would Hezekiah hide Stuart's planner in a hidden vault?"

"That's a good question." She turned the pages until stopping on a calendar layout. Above the calendar, Stuart had written a quotation.

"'When sorrows come, they come not single spies, but in battalions,'" Zack read aloud. "Where is that from?"

"*Hamlet*. It was my brother Danny's favorite and is on his tomb." She turned another page and gasped.

Zack took the book out of her hands and flipped through pages. From January until the end of May, at least three days per week had an *I* marked in the upper corner. "We don't know the *I* stands for Isabel."

"Of course the *I* stands for Isabel. They were sleeping together multiple times every week for two years."

Zack pulled out something that'd been stuck in the back of the book—a photo of Isabel in between two men wearing tuxedoes. Stuart was on her right; another man he didn't recognize stood on her left.

"I don't remember this night." Which meant she hadn't been there. "And I don't know the other man."

Zack shoved the photo into the planner. "They might have been meeting every week, but you don't know what they were doing."

She put a finger against Zack's lips. "You don't need to protect me. I've been living a lie for so long, I need to know the truth regardless of how much it hurts."

"I hate to see you sad."

She closed her eyes. "I need to be sad. I need to feel something."

"We both felt something earlier, in Pirates Courtyard."

She opened her eyes and met his gaze. She had felt something. More than something. She just wasn't ready to talk about it yet. "Seven years ago, you were right about me breaking all of our hearts." She took the planner out of his hands and held it against her chest, like a shield. "This book proves it."

"That's bullshit."

She stared at Zack for a long time, watching the light reflecting off his brown eyes. "Zachariah Tremaine. Do you know one of the things I've always loved about you?"

"No idea." He smiled wide. "But you could tell me."

"Your fearlessness. You always say exactly what's in your mind." She touched his lips. "Even when you're completely wrong."

Zack kissed her fingers and moved them to press against his heart. He hated seeing Allison sad. But that wasn't the only thing, at this moment, that he hated. His righteous rage was focused on Stuart.

Because of Stuart's stupidity in getting involved with Remiel Marigny, Zack's sister was in danger and Allison was struggling with all these new truths. No one could learn the things she'd learned about her husband and be okay. That emotional storm was coming, and he hoped it'd hit quickly so the air between them would clear.

While she read the planner, Zack went back to the shelves. So far none of the books seemed to be anything other than old novels one would find at a garage sale.

"Zack? Look at this."

She'd pulled a piece of tracing paper out of the planner. Someone had used a charcoal pencil to do a rubbing of three long ovals that touched in the center. The design resembled half of a flower. Faint, random lines appeared on the side of the half-flower.

"I know these petal-like designs. They're carved in the wood around the fireplace on the second floor of Pirate House, in the same room as the bed with the carved broken daisies. Why would Stuart sketch them?"

"No idea." Zack turned the paper over and found the words *Finding Mercy Chastain*. Below that title, Stuart had listed three places: Pirate House, Pink House, Fenwick Hall. The Pirate House was crossed out. "If these sketches came from Pirate House, maybe Stuart didn't have a chance to check the other two locations."

She sniffled from the dust overload. "Do you think these markings will help us find Mercy?"

"I don't know. But it's the only new clue we have."

"Which means we need to check the other two places out." She shoved the planner in the tote bag. "Awesome."

He held her elbow until she faced him. "That wasn't a happy awesome. That sounded more...resigned."

"That's because both places are owned by my mother."

He kissed her forehead. "It'll be—"

The lights suddenly turned on, blinding Zack. At the same time, a male voice said, "This is unexpected."

A man in dark jeans and black hoodie aimed a gun at Zack's chest. The man stood six feet away, and Zack had no space to make any quick moves. They were trapped.

"Allison." Zack raised his hands and used his steadiest voice. "Move behind me."

Allison did as he said, and he felt her take his weapon out of his back waistband.

The man laughed and leered. "Don't bother, sweetheart. This won't take long. Then you and I will have some alone time to get...acquainted."

"Never going to happen," Allison said in a surprisingly calm voice. "Who are you, and what do you want?"

The man pushed back his hood to expose his bald head and blue eyes. "Aren't you the bossy one. Not that I mind. I mean, I like it when women take control."

Allison snorted.

The man used his gun to wave them toward the anteroom. "Toss me that bag and come out of the closet."

Zack kicked the bag toward the man and moved slowly, making sure that Allison and the gun stayed behind him. The other weapon, unfortunately, was in the tote bag he'd kicked across the floor.

Once they were out, and with the lights now on in the room, Zack had a better view of the situation. One man with a gun pointed at Zack. Tote bag near the man's feet. Allison behind him, one hand on his shoulder and the other holding his weapon. Zack's arms still raised.

The man, shorter than Zack and of slighter build, moved with a sureness that proved he worked out regularly. The man also bounced from foot to foot, like a kid having to go to the bathroom. And his pupils were dilated. Was he both strong and high?

Fan-fucking-tastic.

"Now it's my turn to ask the questions." The man nodded toward Allison. "What are you looking for in that closet?"

Allison shifted so her hand holding the gun pressed into his back and her body came alongside his. "A place to have sex."

The man coughed on his own spit and Zack moved fast. He grabbed the man's wrist and disarmed him, but not before a bullet fired into the floor. Zack slammed his fist into the guy's stomach and followed that up with a few right and left hooks to the jaw. He ended with a kick in the groin.

Now the man lay on the floor. Zack, meanwhile, felt heat rush through this body. His heart pounded against his ribs and his hands ached.

"Allison." Zack shook out his hands and flexed his fingers before they swelled. "Grab the tote bag and toss me the tape. While I secure him, keep my weapon on him."

She did, and within two minutes, he had the man trussed up with silver duct tape. When he was finished, he wiped the sweat off his forehead and took the gun out of her shaking hands. He had no idea what to the do with the man, but right now, he was more worried about Allison. "Grab our things. We have to leave."

"Pray tell, what has happened here?"

They both turned to see Horatio in the doorway leading to the hall. In jeans and baseball cap, he entered with that strangely graceful gait that ID'd him as a Fianna warrior.

Allison pointed to the man on the floor. "He held us at gunpoint."

Horatio raised one eyebrow and looked at Zack. "You lowered your guard?"

Since that was the truth, all Zack could do was say, "Yes."

He wasn't going to qualify it with the fact that they were in a closet, it was dark, or that he'd thought they were alone. The truth was he'd let the man sneak up on them, leaving Zack in a position where he'd given up his weapon to Allison. He'd no doubt she could've shot the man, but that did nothing for his pride.

After a long moment, Horatio nodded. "'Tis time you left. The officers will seek the source of the gunshot."

"And this asshole?" Zack kicked the man on the floor.

"He works for the Fiend. Marcellus and I will care for him." Horatio pulled out his cell phone. "The hours are passing. Lady Emilie awaits."

CHAPTER 18

ZACK AND ALLISON LEFT THE USHER SOCIETY AND WERE WALKING briskly through the pouring rain when a string of police cars—complete with sirens and lights—descended on the alley.

Zack kept the umbrella over their heads. "Don't look back."

Allison glanced back anyway, watching as another police car rounded the corner. Once they reached the Cooper River, Zack pulled Allison against his chest, making sure the umbrella protected them. As the cruiser passed, he kissed her. It was supposed to be a soft, gentle kiss, meant to soothe. Instead, it became a fierce, needful demand. He tilted his head, and she threw her arms around his neck to deepen the kiss. A random whistle broke them apart, and they rested their foreheads together. His breath roared in his head, and Allison's breasts heaved with exertion.

After he counted to ten, he kissed her forehead and they started walking again. Neither of them spoke, but they held hands as they headed for the car.

Once they were both buckled in, Zack checked his texts. No message from Alex or call from Rafe. But there was a text from Nate.

> *What the hell is going on in Charleston? Call me*
> *ASAP.*

Zack shut down his phone and tossed it into the back seat. He knew he had to deal with Nate soon, just not now.

"That warrior." She closed her eyes and leaned against the headrest. "I saw him earlier today at Pirate House."

"That's Horatio." He turned on the ignition and then the wipers. "We met him last night. Now what do we do?"

She checked the dashboard's clock. "The Pink House is closed and it's too late to go to Fenwick Hall. So we can't check out what Stuart might have been looking for at either place. The only thing we can do is go home and sort through the papers we took from Hezekiah's office."

Zack pulled into traffic and slammed on the brakes before he hit a horse-drawn carriage that had stopped for no apparent reason in the middle of the road.

Allison touched his hand. "It'll be okay. We'll find the treasure and save Emilie."

He nodded, although he had doubts. They had few clues and time was slipping away.

Two hours later, after he'd stopped by Vivienne's to get his duffel bag and returned to Pinckney House to make them a snack of tea and egg sandwiches, he pressed his fists on the kitchen table. It was covered with the papers from Hezekiah's office they'd finished sorting through. "There's nothing here."

Allison checked the dog's food and water bowls and began loading the plates into the dishwasher. "I think we should go to bed and start with Pink House tomorrow morning."

He dumped the papers into a cardboard box waiting to be recycled. "That was a giant waste of time."

Allison touched his arm. "We found Stuart's tracing paper with those rubbings. They have to mean something."

"What if they don't?"

Before she could answer, one of Zack's phones rang. It was his Charleston mission phone and he answered with a brusque, "What?"

"I'm here at Vivienne's," Alex said. "The housekeeper made dinner, in case you're interested."

"I'm not." Zack left the kitchen and headed out into the garden. The rain had paused and everything around him was too wet and overly green. He really needed to pull himself together. "I'm sorry," he said to Alex. "How'd it go with Isabel?"

"She knows nothing more about Emilie. I'm working a deal with her to get the Pirate's Grille. What about you? Find anything at the Usher Society?"

After filling Alex in, Zack admitted in a defeated voice, "I have this awful feeling we're going to fail."

"We still have time. The best thing we can do now is get some sleep." Alex paused to eat something crunchy. "Have you talked to Nate? He's been texting me and I've been ignoring him."

"I'll call him." Zack watched Allison through the kitchen window. She was cleaning the kitchen. "You're right. The best thing we can do is sleep and start again in the morning."

"I'm all set here. There's even a game system in my room. I assume you're spending the night with Allison?"

"Yes." Although he'd be on the floor with the dog again, and this time probably all night. "If anything happens, call me."

"Will do."

After Alex hung up, Zack went inside to find Allison folding a dish towel.

"Everything okay?" she asked.

He nodded. "Just filling Alex in on what we didn't find."

Allison took his hand, led him and the dog through the hallway and into the foyer, then up the stairs. She paused near a door next to hers. "While you made dinner, I put your duffel bag in this guest room. It has an adjoining door to my room and a private bath."

She refused to meet his gaze and bit her lower lip.

"Right." He opened the door and went into a room decorated in dark blue with white trim and heavy mahogany furniture. The aesthetic reminded him of a china pattern he'd never be able to name.

Nicholas Trott bounced in and found his bed near the fireplace.

"I hope you don't mind." Allison pressed her hands against her stomach. Her black linen dress had dried and wrinkled, and her blond hair had fallen around her shoulders in soft curls. She was even more beautiful in her disarray. "I knew Nicholas Trott would want to sleep here. He likes you."

"Thanks." He sighed heavily because there was nothing else to say.

She reached out to touch his arm, then dropped her hand and said, "Good night."

Once she left and he was alone, he threw himself onto the bed. At least it was comfortable and clean. Everything even smelled citrusy, like the bedding had been freshly laundered.

Despite spending time with Allison, today had been a total disaster.

To make sure the day ended on a crappy note, his phone rang. He knew before looking that it was Nate. "Hey."

"Listen," Nate said in a harsh voice, "I have no idea what's going on there, but right now, I'm your best friend. I convinced Kells that you and Alex are spending the night with Rafe on the isle. You two were helping him string lights or whatever around that church and are crashing out there. Kells bought it. For now."

"Thanks, brother. I owe you."

"Do you have anything to tell me?"

Zack covered his eyes with one arm. He wasn't ready to talk about the mess with Emilie and the Fianna. The news would surely make its way to Kells, and that was the last thing Zack wanted. "Not yet."

"Well, I have news I probably should've told you before you left. Something for you to keep in mind. Kate filed for divorce."

Fuckety-fuck-fuck-fuck. "We knew this would happen eventually."

"It explains Kells's mood."

"It doesn't excuse it though."

"No. I guess not." Nate sighed. "Just remember—I am the *fucking* loop."

"Got it." Zack closed his eyes and listened to the dog purr nearby. "I mean it. I couldn't do this without you."

"I know you need to prove something to yourself, but you're not alone. Regardless of what happens, we're all in this mess together."

CHAPTER 19

THE NEXT MORNING, ZACK PACED ALLISON'S STUDY. "I CAN'T believe Pink House doesn't open until ten a.m."

Allison shut her laptop and took off her glasses. She'd been trying to enter grades, but Zack's restlessness was too distracting. "Rue runs the shop according to the whims of her astrological sign."

Zack grunted and ran his hands over his head. He wore his beat-up jeans, a green T-shirt, and combat boots. "Why aren't we on our way out to Fenwick Hall? That was the other location on that page of rubbings that wasn't crossed off."

"Because we need permission to go to my childhood home. And I'm hoping that if we find what we're looking for at Pink House, we won't have to go out there."

She picked up her coffee mug and headed for the kitchen. She'd woken up early and found Zack downstairs, ready to go. He'd made coffee and homemade biscuits and was cleaning his pistol on her kitchen table. After telling him they couldn't go to Pink House until it opened, he'd settled into a nerve-wracking funk of loading and reloading weapons.

Yet for all of his worry about Emilie, Allison couldn't help but wonder if something else was bothering him. Maybe it was the fact that she'd insisted on separate rooms? While a part of her had desperately wanted him to sleep in her bed again, she just wasn't ready.

No, to be truthful, she wasn't that brave.

"Allison?" Zack appeared as she poured herself another cup of coffee. "We've never talked about what happened at Le Petit Theatre—not the kiss, the other...the warning."

She placed her mug on the counter and faced him. His eyes seemed darker, with circles beneath as if he hadn't slept well. His hands were fisted, and he wore a scowl she'd never seen before. "After you returned to the army, I spent the next few weeks thinking about what that warrior had said while at the same time trying to convince Stuart that our kiss meant nothing."

"Has it ever occurred to you that—"

"That I made the wrong choice?" She took a damp dish towel and folded and refolded it. "At first, it didn't. Stuart and I got married and were happy. Sure, Stuart was insecure where you were concerned, but we never saw you. Eventually, I forgot about the bowing man's warning. Then you sent that bottle of perfume from Paris. And all of those memories came crashing back, for both me and Stuart."

Zack crossed his arms over his chest and stared out the window into the garden. He stood in the sunlight, which only emphasized the black hair covering his muscled, tattooed arms. He looked…fierce. More so than she'd ever seen him.

"Stuart began to withdraw, and I let him. Then the little fights started, leading to bigger fights. Bigger fights caused long silences. No matter what I said to him, how I reassured him, he withdrew further. Eventually, I stopped trying. It wasn't until I left his bedroom that I realized the truth of the bowing man's words. Since then, I've just wondered how he knew."

"I am so, so sorry," Zack said in a strained voice. "I never should have said those things to you that night. All I did was add to your doubts."

She came up behind him and, before she talked herself out of it, wrapped her arms around his waist and laid her cheek against his back. His bay rum scent tickled her nose, and she could hear his steady heart-beat. Since she wore a sundress, she felt his denim-clad legs against her bare skin. "The thing is, Zack, you were right."

He covered her hands with his, and she felt him sigh. "I'm sorry I'm a grump today."

She chuckled. Yes, he was being a grump. But for the moment, he was her grump.

And despite all the danger and worry, she wouldn't have it any other way.

౷

At exactly ten a.m., Zack parked in front of Pink House and stepped onto the cobblestone street to open Allison's door. He'd never admit out loud that he appreciated how her navy sundress rose up her thighs as she exited the car. But he did. Very much. "This house really is pink."

As in bubblegum pink, with a dormer window lined with black shutters. Like most of the historic houses in town, this one was only one room wide.

"Hey, Mrs. Pinckney! Give Nicholas Trott a hug for us!" They saw two young women in colorful dresses wave from the other side of the street.

Allison waved back. "Two of my students."

He took her arm and led her to the front door framed by side iron railings. Before they went in, he tilted his head. "Will Rue be here?"

"No. She's too busy conning people out of their livelihoods." Allison glanced at him as she turned the knob. "The staff doesn't know I'm Rue's daughter. I'd like to keep it that way."

"Got it. Any idea what you're going to say? We don't know what we're looking for."

"I'm still working on that." As she opened the door, she smiled as if she had a secret. "Ten bucks the employees are named after herbs or plants."

"No way. I don't have enough money to gamble with you." He escorted her inside, where the AC cooled his hot skin. Pink House was a three stack: three floors, one room on top of the other. The bottom floor was a thirteen-foot square with a fireplace and a tight spiral staircase leading to the second floor. Every inch of wall space was covered with framed prints and watercolors. A counter stood on the left side.

A young female shopkeeper offered them a wide smile. She had braided hair, an apron with the words *Be the Goddess* painted on the front, and was wrapping framed prints in brown paper. She wore her glasses on a chain around her neck, granny-style despite the fact that she looked no older than eighteen. "Welcome to the Pink House gallery. I'm Primrose. Is there anything I can help you find?"

He heard the laughter beneath Allison's voice as she said, "I came from Pirate House—"

"Oh!" Primrose stopped wrapping, picked up a flashlight, and moved around the counter. "You must be from the Usher Society. I've been waiting for you."

"Yes," Zack said, ignoring Allison's surprised gasp. "We are."

Primrose led them toward the colonial-era fireplace. "Pink House only has a few marks, and they're over the door. These marks date to 1703."

Primrose shone the light onto the crossbeam until Zack held out his hand. "May I?"

"Of course." She handed him the flashlight. "I'm packing up a big order, so I'll be at the counter if you need me."

"We will," Allison said. "Thank you."

Primrose turned, then stopped. "Where are your tools?"

Zack glanced at Allison, whose wide eyes told him she was as clueless as he was. "Excuse me?"

"Aren't you here to take rubbings? That's what the previous man did."

Allison put a hand on Zack's arm and said, "You mean we're not the first?"

"No. A man who said he was from the Usher Society came by to study the marks and said he'd send his colleague. A woman." Primrose crossed her arms over her chest. "He didn't mention another man though."

Zack offered his gentlest smile. "I'm here because I'm tall and can reach the carvings."

"Oh." She smiled slightly. "Okay."

Before she could ask more questions, Allison showed her the photo of Stuart and Isabel they'd found in the planner. "Is this the man you met?"

After putting on her glasses and studying the photo, Primrose pointed at Stuart. "He came in a few months ago." She paused with a new wariness in her gaze. "He also had tools."

"We did too but the airline lost our bags," Allison said with a breathy voice that reminded Zack of other things he really shouldn't be thinking about now. "You wouldn't have a piece of paper and a charcoal pencil we can borrow, would you? That way we can get started."

"Let me see what I can find." Primrose hurried up the stairs.

Zack shone the light over the door to expose faint carvings in the dark wood. He could tell they were there, but not what they looked like.

Primrose returned with a pad of tracing paper and a charcoal pencil. "Will these do? We have a studio upstairs with some art supplies, but this is all I could find."

"It's perfect." Allison took them. "Did my colleague tell you what he was looking for?"

"He said he wanted a tracing of the marks to help him with some research about the witch who used to live here."

"You mean Mercy Chastain?"

Primrose nodded. "Did you know she was almost burned at the stake?"

"Actually," Allison said, "if Mercy had been found guilty, she would've been hanged. In the colonies, witchcraft was a felony—a crime against the state—and its punishment was hanging. In Europe, witchcraft was a heresy—a crime against the church—so its punishment was burning."

"Interesting." Primrose smiled tightly. "I need to go back to work. Let me know if you need anything else."

When she left, Zack handed Allison the light and took a sheet of paper and the pencil. Then he whispered, "Know-it-all."

"It's a terrible problem," she said with a laugh because she clearly wasn't sorry. "Use the edge of the pencil. You'll get a better impression between the different depths of the carvings."

"Have you done this before?"

"Yes. For my thesis I did hundreds of rubbings in tons of cemeteries."

"Sounds lonely."

"It kept me busy."

He heard the soft hitch in her voice but didn't want to bring up her marriage again.

A few minutes later, Zack handed Allison the page. The rubbings were another group of long petal-like ovals connected in the center with small rectangles off to the side. Almost identical to the other page of rubbings.

Primrose appeared next to him. "The man who came before said the marks had held up for centuries because they'd been carved in rowan wood."

"I've never heard of rowan wood," Zack said.

Allison squinted at the rubbings. "In North America, rowan wood is called mountain ash. It grows in colder climates."

"It's also an oak epiphyte," Primrose said, "and carries magical qualities."

Allison glanced at Primrose. "Rowan wood was used in colonial buildings in Jamestown, Plymouth, and Boston. Sometimes the rowan seeds would land within the branches of an oak tree and grow. That offshoot is called an epiphyte. Because rowan and oaks were considered sacred trees, this epiphyte wood would be considered blessed and used to ward off..." She stared at the page of ovals again. "Oh. My. Gosh."

Her last three words sounded so hushed, he asked, "What's wrong?"

"I know what these are. These long ovals are apotropaic marks." She took another piece of unused paper and went to the counter.

Zack and Primrose followed.

Allison drew a circle and then made concentric ovals inside a circle, like kids made with Spirographs. "This one is called a daisy wheel because it looks like daisy petals within a circle. They were marks made on beams to ward off witches and curses. By carving apotropaic marks in *magical* rowan wood, you could block witches from causing mischief."

"That's so cool," Primrose said.

Allison drew more circles with different designs in them. "They're common in New England but not down South."

"Why?" Zack asked.

"Rowan wood is rare this far south. And since so many of the buildings in Charleston, Savannah, and New Orleans were built after 1700— after the Salem witch trials—people didn't worry about curses. They were more worried about pirates and taxes."

"Primrose," Zack said, "do you have something we can put our sketch in?"

"I'll be back." Primrose wiped her hands on her apron and went up the spiral stairs again.

Once Primrose disappeared, Allison said, "I think Stuart was collecting these apotropaic marks hoping they'd lead him to Mercy. Only I have no idea how they'd lead anyone anywhere."

Zack took Allison into his arms and felt her heart racing as fast as his. His cell phone buzzed, and keeping Allison tucked against him, he checked the message from Nate.

> *Your godmother Vivienne called Kells. She wants to talk to you because she can't reach your sister. Call her so she'll stop calling Kells.*
> Okay. Has Kells noticed I'm not there?
> *Not yet. He still thinks you're with Rafe. Coming back sooner is better than later.*

Zack had no response to that.

Primrose appeared with a manila envelope, and they separated.

He put the rubbing and extra pieces of tracing paper into it. "You've been a great help."

"Yes," Allison said. "Thanks."

Primrose led them to the door. "You're welcome."

Zack noticed a calendar on the wall and paused. The August photo was of a dog in a garden with wildflowers between his teeth. A black cat stood nearby, sneering as cats do. "Is that Nicholas Trott? On a calendar?"

"Yes," Primrose said proudly, as if she were the owner of the pin-up dog. "That's Nicholas Trott and the cat is Mrs. Pickles. This calendar is famous in Charleston. It sells out every year before it's even printed!"

Before he could respond, Allison drew him outside. Once near the car, she put her hands on his shoulders and said solemnly, "I can explain."

He kissed her hard. Before she could pull away, he broke the kiss and opened the car door. "I can't wait to hear it, but first I need to call Vivienne."

He shut her door, got into the driver's seat, and dialed.

Vivienne picked up on the first ring. "Zachariah, have you heard from your sister?"

Since he wasn't ready to tell her what had happened, he stuck to the absolute truth. "No."

"Emilie is so strong-willed."

And you're not? Instead of stating the obvious, he offered a vague, "Try not to worry. I left you a message yesterday. A buddy of mine and I are staying in your Charleston house. Just for a few nights."

"That's why I came to town. I got your message and want to see you. It's been too long."

Fuck. "Great. Can't wait."

"And Zachariah, I expect you and Allison to meet me and the Pinckney family for luncheon today. They're in town for Stuart's service on Friday. The lunch is at Husk on Queen Street and starts in an hour."

"Nénaine." He slipped into his Cajun accent to appease the only mother he'd ever known even if she could be annoying and controlling. "I'm not—"

"Nonsense. I know you're with Allison."

"How—"

"Now that Allison is a widow, where else would you be?"

"What's wrong?" Allison whispered.

Zack muted the phone and told her, "Vivienne wants us to go to lunch with the Pinckney family."

Allison shook her head, and Zack unmuted the phone and said, "I don't think—"

"No excuses, dear. You're both expected and I hope you'll dress appropriately."

"Nénaine, why are you going?"

"Our families have been friends for generations. I'm in town for Stuart's service and Lawrence invited me to lunch."

"We'll be there. But I'm wearing what I'm in."

"Alright." Vivienne's response sounded like a sigh of defeat instead of the victory she'd just claimed. "Tell Allison not to fret. And remind her that better dressed means better armed."

"I will."

When he hung up, Allison hit him on the arm. "I'm not going to lunch with my in-laws."

"You have to." He started the car and drove back toward Pinckney House.

"Why? We have things to do."

"Because if we're going to figure this out, we need to be smart. Stuart may have mentioned his plans to find Mercy to his family. This lunch might be our only chance to ask them." He turned right and tried to keep the laughter out of his voice. "But first I want to hear about how Nicholas Trott became a pin-up calendar dog."

CHAPTER 20

An hour later, Allison tied Nicholas Trott to a tree outside Husk restaurant near a water bowl printed with his name.

Zack patted the dog's head. "The restaurant won't mind? Or do they love having a pin-up celebrity as a guest?"

She hit him in the chest. She'd explained the whole *Nicholas Trott and Mrs. Pickles have their own calendar* situation, but he'd laughed so hard she wasn't sure he'd even heard her. "The owner loves Nicholas Trott. Last year, when the owner was having trouble with mimes—"

"Mimes?" He covered his eyes with one hand. "You're kidding."

She took his arm and led him inside. "I was walking by with Nicholas Trott, and one of the mimes, a former student of mine, was trying to order dinner. I stopped to see if I could help, and he let Nicholas Trott order dinner for them all. They spent a fortune. Ever since, Nicholas Trott has been known as the top menu picker in Charleston. He's even been written up in the restaurant magazines."

"I don't think I can stop laughing," Zack said as they walked onto the second-floor porch.

She tugged his arm and whispered, "Please try. I don't want anyone to notice me."

Luckily, no one was paying attention, and she let out a grateful sigh. The reprieve from stares and whispers gave her a chance to peruse the crowd.

Zack wrapped an arm around her waist. "If I didn't mention it earlier, you look lovely."

"Thanks." He had mentioned that a few times since they'd left her house, but she didn't mind hearing it again.

After leaving Pink House, they'd gone home so she could change. While Zack walked the dog, she put the apotropaic marks into the gun safe. Then she'd changed into a navy silk dress with an off-the-shoulder neckline, sheer cap sleeves, and a flowy skirt in varying shades of darker blue and black chiffon. She hadn't been sure what to wear, but Vivienne's advice about dressing well was true.

Vivienne Beaumont was a woman of the world who'd navigated multiple husbands, built many businesses, and lived with an outlook that took no prisoners and suffered no fools. She also owned upscale, invitation-only salons for discriminating clients. Salon being a discreet code word for brothel.

Zack hadn't changed his clothes, but she didn't mind. Jeans worn out in all the right places topped with a dark green T-shirt suited him perfectly.

They stepped aside as a waiter appeared with a tray of cheese biscuits. Oak trees on either side of the building shaded the wide porch overlooking the enclosed patio and fountain below. Tiny lights encircled the balustrades while overhead fans provided a breeze. The bar had been placed at one end while Lawrence held court at the other.

Zack rubbed her lower back. "We should greet our host."

Allison groaned.

They made their way toward Lawrence, who sat at a table with a beer. One by one, the people Lawrence had been talking to disappeared.

"Hello, Lawrence." Allison didn't hold out her hand. "And before you ask, I don't have any more news about the fire. Although I did give the insurance agent your number."

Lawrence scowled but then stood and straightened his jacket before shaking Zack's hand. "We met yesterday. But I didn't realize you're Vivienne Beaumont's godson. That also makes you the grandson of the governor of Louisiana, doesn't it?"

"Former governor," Zack said. "We're going to greet my godmother now. We'll see you later."

Before Lawrence could speak again, Zack took Allison's hand and pulled her toward the other end of the porch. More people filled the area, most of whom Allison knew. She hoped they could make their social rounds and leave before the meal was served.

When Zack said, "Nénaine," Vivienne turned with a wide smile. Although Allison hadn't seen Zack in seven years, she saw Vivienne whenever she was in town. As usual, she was the loveliest woman in the room.

In a gold dress and with her silver hair piled elegantly on top of her head, she shone like the sun and the moon. "Zachariah. Are jeans, T-shirts, and boots the only clothes you own? Couldn't you have worn your dress blue uniform? Or are you saving that for the service?"

His arm muscles tightened beneath her fingers and his nostrils flared. Instead of correcting his godmother, he kissed her on the cheek. "I told you I had nothing to change into."

She shook her head, kissed Allison's cheek, and then tapped Zack's arm. "Tell me, Zachariah. What's this business of you leaving the army to live above a gym in Savannah? Why would you do such a thing? Is it as gross and filthy as it sounds?"

"The gym is temporary, Nénaine. Until I figure out what I want to be when I grow up."

"That's ridiculous."

Maddie and Susan crossed the threshold and came onto the porch. Susan, wearing a backpack decorated with a puppy's face and her hair in a long braid, ran over to the bartender to ask for a Shirley Temple. Maddie gave Allison a hug. Then Maddie greeted Vivienne. Maddie—through her parents who were from old Charleston families—knew almost everyone in town.

"What are you and Susan doing here?" Allison asked.

"Vivienne commanded us," Maddie said with a smile as a waiter handed her a club soda.

"Nonsense." Vivienne offered a graceful wave. "It was a simple request. I knew Allison would want you here."

"Thank you, Vivienne," Allison said, trying to ignore Zack's exasperated sigh.

"My, my." Vivienne looked over the balcony. Susan had taken her drink downstairs to the courtyard below the porch. Now she sat at a table near the fountain, sipping her soda and reading a book. She'd moved Nicholas Trott's leash so he could lie at her feet. "Susan is quite the young lady now."

"She's almost eight," Maddie said as she sipped her club soda.

Vivienne allowed a small frown to crease her forehead. "Susan isn't still working on that ghost report, is she? That seems very dull for a young girl."

"According to Susan," Maddie said, "ghosts and pirates were interesting people."

"What about treasures, Vivienne?" Allison asked. "Have you ever heard of Henry Avery's treasure?"

"Of course I've heard of it," Vivienne said. "How else do you think Henry was allowed to live in Charleston under a false identity while Nicholas Trott—the attorney general, not the dog—hanged pirates up and down the East Coast?"

"Huh." Zack frowned. "You think Henry paid off the local officials with his treasure?"

Even Vivienne's shrug was elegant. "That's what I'd do."

Allison noticed a boy around Susan's age throwing rocks at Nicholas Trott. Then she nudged Maddie.

Allison handed her drink to Zack and took Maddie's arm. "We'll be right back."

Zack watched Allison and Maddie leave until Vivienne tapped him on the arm. He could smell the bergamot notes of her favorite perfume: Chanel No. 5. Even the slightest whiff sent him straight back to his childhood. Although he and Emilie had been loved, they'd been alone.

"Zachariah, how is Allison doing?"

"Her husband is dead, Nénaine. She's grieving. You, more than most, should know how that feels."

"I've no doubt she'll recover. She's a towering woman."

"What does that mean?"

Vivienne pressed one hand against her chest. "Grief doesn't ask, or wait, or cajole, or bargain. It hits hard and fast. Grief has a way of knocking you down, then demanding you rise taller than you were before. I've no doubt Allison will come out stronger for it. So much so that when the next round of grief appears—and it always does if one lives a full, rich life—she'll handle it with even more grace and dignity."

Zack stared into his glass. That was lovely.

"Zachariah, can I assume you'll be properly dressed for Friday's service?"

He was about to ask why she always fussed about his clothes when he decided not to argue with her. "I'll try."

Vivienne stared at him for a long moment before peering over the railing to watch Allison and Maddie sit with Susan. "Does Allison know about Stuart's affair with Isabel?"

"Yes." Zack studied his godmother's profile. "How do you know?"

"Last year Stuart and Isabel attended one of my salons here in Charleston."

"You didn't say anything to Allison?"

Vivienne raised a delicate eyebrow. "If I break confidences, my business is over."

Because Vivienne's business wasn't actually about sex. It'd always been about the buying and selling of information.

Zack pulled out the photo and handed it to her. "Do you know the other man?"

Her lips thinned. "Isabel brought him as her guest."

"I don't understand." Zack tried to keep the accusation out of his voice. "You select those who come to your salons, the women *and* the men. Yet you didn't know him?"

She waved a hand as if swishing away the question. "He came with Isabel."

He slipped the photo into his back pocket. "Nénaine, do you know Remiel Marigny?"

Vivienne wiped her lips with a white cocktail napkin. Her red lipstick left a stain on the paper. "I've never met the man."

"But you've heard of him."

Vivienne offered a single nod.

Seriously. Dealing with Vivienne was like talking to a teenager. "What do you know?"

"Very little," Vivienne said. "His family is from New Orleans. Although he has people in Savannah."

"Did you know Isabel works for Remiel?"

"No."

And for the first time in his life, Zack didn't believe her. What—or who—was she protecting? Or frightened of?

"If you'll excuse me, I want to pay my respects to Lawrence." Vivienne left on a perfume-scented breeze.

Zack stared into the courtyard where Susan sat with Maddie and Allison. Nicholas Trott hopped on Susan's lap, and a man stood off to the side watching the women.

"Dammit." Zack hurried down the stairs to meet Alex.

Alex paused near the oak tree protecting the entrance to Husk's courtyard and focused on the table near the fountain.

Susan sat between Maddie and Allison, and Nicholas Trott jumped off the little girl's lap to sleep beneath the table. Alex had only come because this was where he was supposed to meet Isabel. Although the thought of dealing with Isabel again made him feel dirty, seeing Maddie filled his chest with a lightness he hadn't felt in years.

Maddie wore a green halter dress and her hair down, curling over her bare shoulders. She'd pinned a sparkly brooch to the bottom of her V neckline, which brought attention to her full breasts.

He glanced at his black T-shirt, jeans, and black combat boots. He owned nothing. Had nothing. Was nothing. He'd once slept with women like Isabel and had tried to kill another man. He had no right to go over to Maddie, talk to her, or even look at her. And...he had his meeting with his brother to worry about.

Good thing he didn't care about any of that.

He halted in front of the table, and all three women looked up at him. Susan was the only one who offered him a smile. "Hi, Mr. Mitchell!"

Allison stood and offered him her chair. "You can sit here if you want. I need to find Zack." Then she nodded toward Maddie. "Will you be staying for lunch?"

"No," Maddie said. "I'll offer my condolences and go home."

Allison kissed Susan on the head and left.

Alex moved closer but didn't sit. Since Maddie used a hand to cover her face from the glare, he moved until he stood between her and the sun.

It was so pathetic that the best he could offer her was shade.

"What are you doing here, Mr. Mitchell?"

"Passing by."

"I'm so glad." Susan slurped her drink through a straw. "Would you like a soda?"

Maddie took Susan's glass and placed it on the table. "I'm sure Mr. Mitchell has better things to do than talk to us."

"Actually," Alex said, "I'd love a soda."

"I'll go ask!" Susan jumped up and ran toward the restaurant. As she passed the fountain, she turned back to him. "What kind?"

"Ginger ale, please."

Maddie stood. "What are you really doing here?"

"Like I said—"

"I know you weren't just passing by." She nodded toward Zack, who was coming toward them, his stride a study in earnestness and intention. "And I know you weren't one of Stuart's college buddies. Stuart never mentioned you."

"That doesn't mean anything."

She leaned in close enough for him to smell her light floral perfume. "Who are you?"

No one. He took a step back just as Zack arrived.

"Everything okay?" Zack's gaze bounced between the two of them.

"Sure." Alex ran a hand over his shorn head. "Got a minute?"

Zack looked up at the balcony, where Susan was talking to the bartender. "Yes."

Maddie grabbed Susan's book. "Excuse me. I need to talk to Lawrence before we leave."

When she entered the restaurant, Zack hit him on the arm. "What's wrong?"

"Come on." Alex left the courtyard and slipped into the alley next to the restaurant. "Have you heard from Rafe? Any information about Emilie?"

"Rafe is still checking into it. But he has no new info."

Alex leaned his shoulder against the wall and stared at the cobblestones below his feet. "There's something else. Nate called me a few minutes ago."

"Why would he do that?"

"Nate, probably through Rafe, learned about the Fianna having Emilie."

"Fuck." Zack ran one hand over his head. "Was Nate pissed?"

"Oh yeah. Nate told me to tell you that if you don't call him within the hour, he's going to tell Kells."

CHAPTER 21

Allison was determined to say her goodbyes. The restaurant upstairs was full. With the talking, laughing, and music, the event reeked of a wedding instead of a funeral.

Although Zack's idea of coming to get more information had been a good one, there was no one here she wanted to talk to. No one here, that she knew of, who'd been close to Stuart.

She elbowed her way onto the porch until she found Lawrence talking to...Isabel. They had their heads together, laughing. Allison didn't flinch when someone stepped on her toes. Her throat closed up, and her sinuses felt hot and tender. A man jostled her, and she stumbled against the railing. Both Lawrence and Isabel looked over.

Isabel touched the brooch pinned to her dress and smirked.

Allison made it into the dining room but had to wait for waiters carrying trays to pass. The air in the room had reached an unbearable temp because the humidity coming in through the open balcony doors had burned up the AC. Between the heat, the crowds of people she didn't know, and the scent of sandalwood, she felt light-headed.

She needed fresh air and...Zack.

Someone jerked her arm, and she turned to find Isabel holding her elbow.

"We need to talk," Isabel said. "I know Stuart took the appendix out of the witch's examination. That means he hid it and I think you know where."

Allison pulled herself free. "I know who you work for. And that means despite the fact you were sleeping with Stuart, you knew Remiel was going to torture and kill him."

Isabel backed up a step. To her credit, her face paled. "I didn't—"

"Remiel wanted Stuart dead, and *you* allowed it."

"Lower your voice." Isabel took Allison's arm again and yanked her behind a fern. "There's something you need to know about your lover. Zack isn't the man you believe him to be."

Again, Allison freed herself. But now she was stuck between the plant, Isabel, and the wall. "I don't—"

"If you know about Remiel, then you also know about the Seventh Special Forces group's mission in Afghanistan. The one where two A teams were ambushed."

Allison nodded to make this conversation end more quickly.

"The A teams were sent to a POW camp—"

"Run by Remiel."

"And two commanders were singled out."

"So?"

"So, one wasn't leading his own team. He was leading *Zack's* team. Zack chose not to lead his men that night. Zack chose to deal with a personal issue. A *female* issue. When he returned, his best friends—his team—had been captured. They remained in that POW camp for two years. Zack is nothing but a coward."

Allison gritted her teeth. "That's absurd. Zack is the bravest man I know."

Isabel smiled and played with her brooch. "Why don't you ask him? Maybe that's why, seven years ago, the Prince asked Zack to change careers."

"I'm done listening to your lies." Allison forced her way through a group of men and found the stairs amid the low whispers of "That's the widow," "It's so tragic," "Did you know Stuart was having an affair with Isabel?"

Allison made it halfway down the stairs when she bumped into Zack coming up.

"Hey." He took her arms and steadied her. "What's wrong?"

"Leave. Now."

Zack's face hardened and Allison noticed Isabel on the top step, watching them. "Come on."

He took her hand and led her into the courtyard. They retrieved Nicholas Trott from under the table where Susan had been sitting.

Zack's phone buzzed, and he dug it out of his pocket. "It's my buddy Nate."

She took Nicholas Trott's leash and nodded toward the restaurant next door. "I'll wait in the Poogan's Porch garden. It's quieter."

He touched her cheek gently. "I'll be there soon."

She tried to ignore the heat that shot through her every time he touched her and left Husk's patio. Poogan's Porch Restaurant had a front garden instead of a courtyard, and after talking to the hostess who'd been in her Intro to Folklore class last spring, she sat on a porch bench. Shaded by trees surrounding the building, she relaxed, appreciating the cooler air. A fan above her head kept the bugs away. The hostess brought out a water bowl for Nicholas Trott and a glass for her.

Nicholas Trott leapt up to the seat and assumed his favorite position: facing the street, sitting on hind legs, fronts legs straight. He panted and watched the world go by.

Allison drank her water and closed her eyes. Even if Isabel spoke the truth, it didn't matter. If Zack hadn't led his team that night, he must've had a reason. And the guilt he probably carried over that decision had to weigh on his heart.

She prayed it wasn't true, but if it was, she hoped she could offer some solace.

Except he hadn't told her and she didn't know how to bring it up.

Her phone rang and she answered.

"Mrs. Pinckney? I'm the insurance agent in charge of your case regarding the fire at your property. I've received a preliminary report from the fire inspector and would like to meet with you. Are you home this afternoon?"

"Shouldn't you be talking to my brother-in-law, Lawrence Pinckney, about this?"

"I did. He's busy and suggested I call you."

She brushed a loose curl off her shoulder and said, "I'll be home within the hour."

She hung up and stood when she saw Zack coming. Nicholas Trott took the lead until his tail went straight and still. She looked in the direction of the dog's line of sight to see a man in a baseball cap across the street, near the entrance to the Mills House Hotel. *Horatio.*

"Allison!" Zack's voice boomed, and Nicholas Trott sprinted toward him, pulling her along.

Zack's long stride caught up with the dog first. He took the leash and gave Nicholas Trott the love he demanded. Then Zack stood and she walked into his arms. One arm held her around the waist while the other held her head. "Ready?"

"Yes." She glanced across the street again, but Horatio had disappeared. Her phone buzzed with a text.

Time is passing, Lady Allison. Remember the urgent acting of your dread command.

"I think it's from Horatio." She showed it to Zack and his body stiffened.

He scanned the area around them, gripped the leash, and put one hand on her back. "Let's go home."

∽

Isabel found Alex sitting in Husk's downstairs bar. He was sipping ginger ale. After her disastrous encounter with Allison, Isabel was just glad he'd shown up. For the second time, she'd overplayed her hand with Allison. Just like the first time in Hezekiah's office, Isabel's hatred of the simpering widow had made her strike from emotions, not logic. "I've made a decision."

Alex lifted his drink and used a bar napkin to wipe the granite counter. "Good for you."

Isabel laid her purse on the bar, ordered a martini, and turned sideways to face his profile. They were only inches apart, but Alex's gaze was fixed on the liquor bottles shelved on the wall.

The bartender placed her drink in front of her, and she said, "I've decided to take you up on your offer. But you don't get the Pirate's Grille until after I meet with the Prince."

He took another sip and wiped down the granite again. "No deal."

Really? He was the most stubborn, frustrating male she'd ever had. Unfortunately, he was also the best in bed that she'd ever had. Even though it'd been years since they'd been together, she still remembered everything. "You can't expect me to hand it over before the meeting. I don't trust you."

"Then we're at an impasse." Alex graced her with a sideways scowl. "Because I don't trust you."

More people arrived at the bar, and Isabel moved until her breasts brushed against his chest. He sucked in a breath. They were blocked by patrons ordering drinks before Lawrence shut off the open bar.

She whispered, "I remember, Alex. And I wouldn't mind if—"

"Mr. Mitchell!" A little girl suddenly appeared. She carried a book under one arm and a soda in the other hand. "Here's your soda."

Despite the fact the child was completely out of place, she carried herself with a poise Isabel respected.

Alex took the glass and frowned. "What are you still doing here?"

"My mom saw one of her clients and couldn't get away. I was looking for you outside, but it got too buggy."

Just as she said that, another woman's voice said, "Susan?"

Isabel found the source of the voice near the stairs leading to the second floor. The stunning brunette stood on the second step, scanning the room. Maddie Ashton? Isabel hadn't seen Maddie in over a year and was surprised at how...lovely she'd become.

"Bye, Mr. Mitchell." Susan found her mother near the front of the restaurant.

"That was..." Isabel stopped talking when she realized that everything about Alex—from his gaze to the turn of his body—was fixated on Maddie.

Once Susan and Maddie left, Alex released a deep breath.

A hot flush rose up Isabel's neck. She'd never been disregarded for another woman—and certainly not by the likes of Alex Mitchell. Alex might be the brother of one of the most dangerous men in the world, and he himself considered as violent and tough as men come, but he was still a poor kid from South Boston. He was as far beneath her as a man could be, yet now he was dismissing her?

"Alex." She ran her hand up and down his arm until she rested her palm against his warm bicep underneath the sleeve of his T-shirt. The muscles bunched beneath her fingers. "How about a compromise? You come back to my hotel—"

Alex removed her hand. "How many lovers have you had, Isabel?"

She licked her lips. "Does it matter? If it makes you feel better, you were the best."

"Don't you get tired of giving pieces of yourself away? Tired of being hollow inside?"

She traced his lips. So many people moved against the bar now, their bodies touched again. Her breasts against his chest, her hips against his hard thighs. She stood on her toes—because Alex was impossibly tall—until she could feel his breath. Until her lips almost rested against his. "I would never tire of you."

"Bartender, have you seen a backpack with a puppy face?"

Alex's head turned, and Isabel smiled at Maddie, who stood on the other side of Alex. Maddie was taking a backpack from the bartender—until she stopped and noticed Alex. His breaths sounded like roars, and Isabel moved in closer to Alex's side, making sure Maddie saw Isabel's breast against his arm.

Alex didn't move, and his gaze on Maddie didn't waver.

Maddie swallowed and disappeared into the crowd.

Isabel used a finger to trace the outline of muscles through the black T-shirt until Alex grabbed her wrist.

"Tonight, Isabel. Meet me at the Mills House Hotel bar. Bring the Pirate's Grille or—"

"Or what?"

"I'll tell Remiel all about how five years ago you helped me try to kill him."

CHAPTER 22

EIGHT HOURS LATER, ZACK LEANED BACK IN THE IRON CHAIR IN Allison's garden and sighed. She seemed distracted, probably because she was tired and overwhelmed.

They had returned to the house, and Allison had spent the *entire* afternoon dealing with the insurance agent.

Allison had told him of her run-in with Isabel and the fact that she thought Stuart had hidden the witch's examination appendix. Frustrated because time was passing and they were no closer to finding Emilie, Zack had decided to search the entire house, which had to be larger than the Pentagon.

He'd torn apart every drawer, closet, and wardrobe. He'd even searched through the Christmas ornaments in the attic and the flower pots in the conservatory. Not to mention the gun cabinet that he unloaded, cleaned, and reorganized.

After seven hours of digging through the house and finding nothing, he decided to scrounge through her freezer and make dinner.

While he searched, he'd also been processing the call he'd gotten earlier from Nate. Nate had indeed learned about Emilie's kidnapping from Rafe *and* that the Prince wanted Allison to find the treasure in exchange for Emilie's safe return. Then Nate lectured him about how secrets were bad and that since Nate had been covering for Zack for two days, he deserved to be kept informed.

While Nate was correct, Zack wasn't sorry. He needed to prove to himself that he wasn't a complete fuckup. He needed this second chance.

Then Zack called Rafe *again* to make sure that the Fianna wouldn't hurt Emilie while Zack searched for the treasure. Rafe reminded Zack about the rules of leverage. The conversation helped Zack's worried mind, but it didn't alleviate it.

Zack tossed his napkin on the table. "That shrimp étouffée was delicious."

Allison laughed and stacked the dishes. "You made it."

"Is that why you didn't eat it?"

"I'm not that hungry."

Zack touched her arm. "Leave the dishes. I'll do them later."

She sat with her hands in her lap and stared at the salt shaker. She still wore her dress but had traded her heels for flats.

"What's wrong?"

She shrugged. "When I think about Stuart, I miss what our life could've been together. I'm also angry. He decided we should have separate rooms. He decided to have an affair and get involved with Remiel."

Zack took her hand and rubbed the finger where she'd once worn her wedding band. "You've every right to be angry. But Stuart's behavior is on *him*. You're not responsible for his choices."

"I took off my wedding band." She pulled her hand out of Zack's grasp. "After Stuart's funeral, I took it off and shoved it in my jewelry box."

Zack kept silent. He wasn't sure what to say. She'd retreated so far into herself he didn't know how to reach her. He didn't want to lose the tenuous connection they had at the moment.

"The ring felt heavy." She rose to pace the garden. "I was at the funeral and couldn't stop twirling it. I must've spun it a thousand times. By the time I left the cemetery, the gold was hot."

Zack leaned forward and clasped his hands.

"When I got home, I took a cold shower just to make myself feel something. But it left me more numb than I'd ever been in my life. That's when I took off my ring and put on my pajamas."

"That's not a crime."

"It was noon, Zack. I'd buried Stuart without his family—who wanted to wait—and I was supposed to have a potluck here at the house.

Except I couldn't." Her voice cracked. "I told everyone to take their food to the church hall and that I'd meet them there. Except I came home, put on my pajamas, and didn't leave the house for four days. If Maddie hadn't come by each day, I wouldn't have bothered eating."

"I'm glad you have such a wonderful friend."

"I was horrible to the people who wanted to celebrate Stuart's life. I was horrible to Maddie. I even yelled at her to stop bringing me food."

Zack finally stood. "Why are you so hard on yourself? You were grieving, are still grieving, and everything you've done is what people who are grieving do."

She shook her head until her blond hair fell out of its clip. "I took my ring off because I couldn't handle the weight of it. When I put it into my jewelry box, I wasn't sad. I was *relieved*."

He took her shoulders. "It's okay—"

"It's *not* okay. The day I buried my husband, I took off my ring, and for the first time in years, I felt free."

"Allison."

She hit his chest with her fists. "For the first time since you kissed me, I was free. No more pretending to be the loving wife desperate for her husband's attention yet unable to give him the intimacy he wanted. Sure, we slept together before our big fight, but it wasn't enough for Stuart. I couldn't give him everything he needed."

"That wasn't your job. His issues belonged to him."

She picked up the dishes and he followed her to the kitchen with the rest of the food. She didn't say anything while he loaded the dishwasher, while she put leftovers in the fridge, while he fed Nicholas Trott, who'd been waiting patiently for dinner, while she cleaned the counters.

When they were finished, he grabbed the open bottle of wine and the Bluetooth speaker with a flash drive attached, and went back outside to the garden. He forced himself not to look back to see if she was following. The sun had gone down, and small white lights sparkled in the garden's trees.

It took him two wrong turns before he found the small table where they'd eaten dinner. It was tucked in the side garden near the Pan fountain attached to a brick wall. He'd deliberately left the wineglasses on the table and now poured them each another glass. Then he turned on the speaker which started a song that had been preloaded onto the flash drive.

Thank goodness it was a slow song so they could dance.

By the time he finished, he noticed Allison in the darker shadows. "Zack? What are you doing?"

"This." He took her hand and drew her close until his other arm wrapped around her waist. When she relaxed against him he said, "Allison, everyone's life is driven by decisions based on incomplete facts and powerful emotions that aren't always based on truth."

She rested her head against this shoulder. "I don't understand."

"Faith and reason, not emotions, are sources of truth. Truths discovered by faith and reason never contradict each other. Truths discovered by faith and reason are immutable."

She looked up at him. "What are my truths, Zack?"

"You were never able to fully give yourself to Stuart because he wasn't the right man for you. You wanted him to be the right man. You wanted him to be the perfect husband who could shield you from Rue's abuse, your father's death, and your brother's drowning. Jeez, Allison, you were eleven when that all went down. It's no surprise when Stuart offered you a life protected by these garden walls, you jumped at it."

"What kind of person does that make me?"

"A wounded one. Like all of us. You know how to love as deeply as everyone else. You're just afraid that if you admit it, you'll get hurt again." When she didn't answer, he continued, "Another truth? Stuart was emotionally abusing you."

She tried to pull away.

Zack tightened his hold. "Withholding sex is a form of emotional abuse."

"The night of our big fight, we argued about the bottle of jasmine perfume you sent me from Paris. Then I found out that you'd called the house and Stuart hadn't told me."

"I did call, and Stuart told me you didn't want to talk to me." Zack paused, trying to decide what to say next. "He was angry about the perfume. Finally, I hung up. I was on my way to a mission in Afghanistan and had other things to worry about."

Like rescuing his men from Remiel's POW camp.

She slowed her steps until their dance turned into a sway. "That was the night Stuart told me I was broken, that I'd never be able to love another man completely."

If Stuart had still been alive, Zack would've killed him.

Since he couldn't seek retribution on her behalf, he kissed her head and then rested his cheek against her hair. "Stuart always had passive-aggressive tendencies."

She met his gaze. "How do you know so much about the subject?"

"My parents. My mother, despite having two children with my father, refused to marry him and never gave a reason. Vivienne thinks my mother's constant rejection was her way of controlling my father. My father, in return, had a horrible temper. He'd withhold affection and disappear for months. Then he'd show up with presents and promises that we'd be a happy family. It was a perfect storm of codependence, enabling, and mental illness that lead to their deaths at my grandfather's estate, Bayou Saint George."

"I thought you grew up in the Garden District?"

"I did. We only went to the country for summer holidays. Mostly, it stood empty. Now, Bayou Saint George belongs to Vivienne."

"You inked your family's devastation on your arm—your dragon slayed by Saint George."

"I needed that tattoo to remind me of my truths. That I want—no, I *believe* in happy families and love ever after. I deserve those things as much as you do."

Allison leaned her head against his shoulder again. "I'm so selfish. I'm wrapped up in my emotions while you're desperate to find your sister."

"I am desperate, but a buddy of mine, Rafe, reminded me that if the Fianna hurt Emilie, we won't do what they want." He stopped dancing and rested his hands on her waist. Slowly, she raised her head and he lowered his lips. The kiss threatened to drop him to his knees. He drew her in until her breasts pressed against his chest. His lips tilted over hers, and she sighed. A hot force rushed through him, hardening every inch of his body.

When she stood on her toes, he swung her around to press her against the nearest tree. Her hair hung in curls around her shoulders, and her skirt bunched up between them, allowing his thigh to fit between her bare legs. When she tightened her arms around his neck, he made sure his hips met hers. She moaned; he growled. He needed her to understand what she did to him, what she meant to him. He so desperately wanted to wipe away their pain, to bury himself inside her until this nightmare melted away. Although he wasn't a man to run and hide, he was finally realizing the toll the last few years had taken.

He was tired of being tossed around by forces not under his control. He was sick of lies and secrets that left him in reaction mode. He was done letting fate limit his choices.

"*Zack.*" Her breathless word wasn't a statement or a demand. It was a plea that made his heart swell until he was sure it would break his ribs.

Using his body to keep her against the tree, he held her face in his palms and planted tiny kisses on her cheeks, her forehead, her nose, before resting his lips against hers again.

She ran her fingers through his hair until reaching the tie behind his neck. A brief tug and his hair fell down, closing them in a world of their own. "I love your long hair."

He moved his hands to her rib cage, his thumbs perilously close to her breasts that swelled at the attention. "I'd cut it if you wanted me to."

"No." She took his hands and moved them until they held her breasts through the thin silk. "I like it. It makes you look wild. Like my wild man."

He ran his thumbs over her nipples, and they hardened instantly. She closed her eyes and leaned her head against the tree. With both their hands on her breasts, he drove his hips against hers. It was important that she understood what she did to him, understood how he needed her, understood that they were hitting the moment where ending this would take every last ounce of willpower.

She threw her arms around his neck and kissed him with a force he didn't expect. He held her waist so her legs could encircle his hips. Using his body to hold hers up, he planted his hands on the tree. Their bodies connected at every soft curve and hard angle. Her breasts flattened against his chest; his erection between her thighs strained against his jeans. Their bodies were as close as two could be with clothes on.

A situation he hoped would be addressed soon.

As if understanding his need, Allison broke the kiss to whisper, "Please don't stop."

He met her gaze. "Are you sure?"

She bit his earlobe. "*Yes.*"

Fuuuuuck. His body jackhammered against her. He didn't want to do this outside against a tree, but he'd no strength to move elsewhere. It took a moment to unzip his pants, slip aside the tiny scrap of lace separating them, and move his cock to her entrance. He held her waist again and lifted her up. He felt her intake of breath and pulled her down until he'd buried himself so deeply inside her he wasn't sure where she began and he ended.

She gasped and tightened her hold on his neck, her lips taking his hostage.

Using his strength, yet trying not to hurt her, he lifted her up and down again. She moved her hips until he repeated the driving action, over and over, the entire time listening to her labored breaths.

Her core tightened around his cock and he increased the speed. What kind of man was he to treat her so wretchedly? Forcing himself deeply inside her, her back against the rough bark, his hands squeezing her waist?

Despite the tightening in his balls, he paused the motion and slowed the kiss. She clenched her thighs, but since he had the greater strength, he was in control. Without a word, he swung her around and lowered her to a patch of damp grass nestled between the pond and a row of white daisies, the entire time keeping himself inside her.

Once beneath him, her body protected by the soft earth, he adjusted himself between her legs and placed his hands on either side of her head.

Her blond hair shone from the tiny lights around them; her green eyes glimmered. He began the driving motion again—slowly, then not so much. It took barely a moment to reach the intensity that obliterated everything around him.

"Zack," she whispered. "Please."

Oh. Shit. He closed his eyes and allowed his body to tighten and clench and slam until he had only one conscious thought: *Allison.*

Was this what sex was supposed to be like?

Allison closed her eyes and gripped Zack's strong shoulders while he drove into her with a power and force she'd never before experienced—a passion she'd never even imagined. She arched her hips and met him thrust for thrust, desperately seeking to fill the emptiness. For the first time in forever, she felt warm and wanted and desired.

Without opening her eyes, she traced the muscles from his shoulders to his biceps beneath his T-shirt, feeling how cold her hands were against his hard, hot skin. She gripped his arms and relaxed into the damp ground. It'd been so long since she'd made love, she wasn't expecting to climax. And she was okay with that. It was the closeness she craved, the pressure of his thighs pushing her own apart, his weight on top of her body, his ragged breath on her forehead.

A light rain began, and she heard *plit-plats* on the pond. She appreciated the cooler air because an unfamiliar heat had started in her toes and was working its way up her bare legs that were rubbing against his jeans. Her heart filled with a happiness so intense it left her as fragile as glass.

Suddenly, his thrusts sped up and then stilled, like the moment between when a drop forms on an icicle and the time it falls.

She opened her eyes to see his own were closed, his face raised to the sky, his nostrils flared. His muscles bunched beneath her fingers. *Had he stopped breathing?*

He pulled back for a moment, then released himself inside her with a powerful thrust and a growl that sounded like an animal. *Her wild man.*

He collapsed on her and his weight drove the breath from her lungs. She wrapped her arms around him and held him close. Burying her head into his neck, she took three deep breaths. His powerful, masculine scent filled her lungs and her eyes burned with unshed tears.

How could anyone call this man a coward?

Zack kissed her face. "Did I hurt you?"

She shook her head because she didn't want him to see her tears. "I'm so happy."

He frowned and moved off to lie next to her. He pulled her into his arms until her head rested on his shoulder and her clenched fist lay on his chest. Her legs were intertwined with his, her skirt bunched up around her hips. The rain had turned to mist, but she had no intention of moving.

When she shivered, he took her fist and brought it to his lips. "I didn't give you enough time."

She raised up to meet his gaze. His eyes shone in the reflection of the white lights strung through the trees. "I'm fine."

He snorted and started to roll her over again, but she pushed him until she lay on top of him. "Honestly, Zack—"

"I didn't do my job because I'm a selfish bastard."

She placed one hand over his mouth. "Shh. You gave me such a priceless gift, more than any climax could." She removed her hand and kissed him thoroughly. When she was done she rested her head on his chest and counted his heartbeats. "You made me feel desired. You made me feel beautiful. Two things I haven't felt in years."

The way his hands rubbed her back, up and down her spine, told her he was mulling.

She snuggled closer into his embrace. Although the mist was abating, she shivered.

Zack's hands stilled and he whispered, "Do you hear that?"

"It's Nicholas Trott. He always makes that noise when he looks for me."

Zack laughed. "I've never heard a dog purr before."

"Please don't talk about it in front of him. He's sensitive."

A second later, Nicholas Trott lay on top of her, turning Zack into a heavily muscled mattress. While she didn't love the wet-dog smell, she loved the warmth that came from the man below and the dog above.

"Ugh," Zack said. "How heavy is Nicholas Trott?"

She whispered, "I don't talk about his weight either. It makes him sad."

Zack tightened his hold on both her and the dog. Just as she drifted to sleep on top of Zack, not caring about her dirty hair or the dog smell, the rain started again.

When it began to pour, she scrambled off and discovered Zack had already adjusted his zipper. On the ground, fully clothed in his jeans and T-shirt, he still had his boots on. The only thing undone was his hair.

They'd made love, but the only skin she'd touched on his body was on his face and his arms. She'd never seen him naked. Yet she'd begged him to do this outside in the dark, with their clothes on.

He took her hand and she dragged him up. Why did she always forget how tall he was, how small she felt next to him?

He picked her up in his arms.

"By the way," he said as he carried her to the house, "your house is haunted."

She tightened her hold on his neck. "Ghosts aren't real."

"Tonight, while we were all falling asleep, I saw a flash of white through the bushes. I think it was Mercy Chastain."

CHAPTER 23

AT TEN P.M., ALEX ENTERED THE LOBBY OF THE MILLS HOUSE Hotel and took off his leather jacket. The crystal chandeliers, silk upholstered furniture, and thick floor rugs told him this wasn't a jeans-and-boots kind of place. It wasn't his kind of place.

A uniformed man hurried over, exuding earnestness and polished perfection. "May I help you, sir?"

"I'm meeting someone in the Best Friend Lounge."

The bellboy pointed to the right of the split staircase. "Around the corner." He stared at Alex's motorcycle jacket. "Sir, would you like me—"

"No, thanks." Alex found his way to the corridor and straightened his shoulders. He'd yet to see Isabel or the Pirate's Grille. While he was committed to this meeting with his brother, he wasn't going to hold up his end of the bargain if she didn't show.

He entered the tiniest lounge he'd ever seen. The bar took up most of the length of the far wall and small tables were placed in the open spaces. A jazz trio played in the front corner. Low lighting, partitions, and couches gave the space an intimate feel.

He found Marcellus at the bar drinking a club soda. "I'm here."

"And Isabel?"

"She will come." Marcellus waved toward the back corner behind a partition. "My lord awaits."

Great. Alex headed over, wishing he were back in solitary at Leedsville. He stopped when he got to the table. He wasn't going to sit until his brother stood.

Aidan put down his drink and rose. He wore pressed black wool slacks and a blue dress shirt with a matching silk tie. His dark hair was longer than Alex's and styled with a cut that had to cost a ton of money.

Aidan's brown eyes glinted. He sat and waited for Alex to do the same. A waiter appeared with a cold ginger ale, placed it on the table, and left.

"I preordered it for you," Aidan said.

Alex sipped it, savoring the sweetness. One of the things he and his two older brothers had in common was that they rarely drank alcohol. Shitty childhood memories and all that. "Why'd you take Emilie Tremaine?"

"Why do you want me to meet with Isabel Rutledge?"

"Isabel stole the Pirate's Grille from Allison. In exchange for a meeting with you, she will give the Pirate's Grille to me. That way Allison and Zack can get on with the impossible mission you've tasked them with." While he waited for a reply, he sipped his soda.

"Isabel can't be trusted."

"I'm not stupid."

"Alex." Aidan was now staring at his club soda with lime. "I want you to leave Charleston with me."

"Why?"

"I want to take you to Italy. I have a place there, a safe haven I've set up for my warriors."

"Fianna rehab?"

Aidan glanced at Alex, but he wasn't laughing. "I can give you refuge, all the money you'd ever need. You can work or lie around reading and sketching."

"Again, why?"

"You're in danger here."

"The time for saving me has passed, Brother. Next you're going to tell me your decision to make sure I was convicted of a murder I didn't commit was for my own safety."

Aidan's glance bounced around the room. "It was."

"You know what I think?" Alex leaned forward to whisper, "Your fake concern, your fake promises coming from fake guilt are bullshit."

Aidan grabbed Alex's wrist and pulled him in even closer. "If you stay with Kells and his men, things will get hot."

"Things are always hot." Alex yanked his arm out of his brother's grasp. "All this, the manipulations, the bribery, the threats, all the Fianna nonsense is for one reason: power. You want to stay in power because you like power."

"You don't have a clue what you're talking about."

"Why is that? Because I'm the stupid younger brother? The one who can always be counted on to fuck up? The one who's self-destructive, antisocial, and violent? Who the hell do you think made me that way? And while you're thinking, remember this: out of all of us, I'm the only one who had the balls to go after Remiel even though I knew the consequences."

Aidan's eyes narrowed. "Remiel knows you're free and will come after you."

That deserved a giant *duh*. "Tell me, Brother. When did the Fianna start targeting women? I don't mean evil cows like Isabel, but women like Emilie. I thought those were the ones you were supposed to protect? Or have things changed since I've been gone?"

"You don't understand the consequences, Alex."

"No? Then why don't you tell me? Because I don't see the honor in terrorizing a woman who's caused you no harm."

"She's leverage I need to get what I want."

"You mean Henry Avery's treasure? You don't need money."

"I don't want to spend it. I want to destroy it. If Remiel finds that treasure first, I'll have to trade Emilie for the treasure."

Alex sat back and took a breath. He'd not seen that move coming. "Remiel is a soulless bastard. He'll torture and kill her. You don't even know if he'd trade the treasure for her."

"Remiel will trade if it means one of Kells's men, like Zack, will suffer. But"—Aidan waved to the waiter who brought another club soda—"I'd prefer to take the treasure out of play."

Alex sipped his soda. What Aidan said was true—Remiel could so easily kill Alex or Kells or any of Kells's men, but that would take the fun out of things. Remiel was a sadist. He'd rather cause continuous suffering than actually murder the men he hated. The same men he held responsible for his own tragic life. "Stuart was indebted to you, but why put that on Allison? Why don't you have your men find the treasure?"

"Stuart was the last person to have the witch's examination's appendix. He hid it because he was trying to protect her. In the process, he put her in even more danger."

"And Zack? Marcellus called him a coward."

"Zack is a coward." Aidan took a drink. "If you don't believe me, ask his team that are still in prison."

Alex looked away. He'd heard rumors in prison about Zack's team being in the field without him. But Alex had served with Zack and knew the truth. Zack would never abandon his men. He must've had a damn good reason for not leading his team that night. "I'm not going to Italy with you."

Aidan took Alex's arm. "Please, Little Brother. Rein in your self-destructive tendencies and listen to reason."

Alex finished his soda and watched the ice melt. "I like my self-destructive tendencies."

Aidan sighed and stood. "Horatio is waiting."

Alex noticed another warrior in the shadows and stood. "Where are we going?"

"Zack will want proof his sister is safe." Aidan gripped Alex's shoulder. "Horatio will take you to Emilie."

Alex pulled away from his brother. "And Isabel? If you agree to meet with her, she'll give me what I want."

"I've already issued an invitation." Aidan raised an eyebrow. "That means I doubt you'll get what you want from her."

Undermined by his brother again. Why was Alex not surprised? "Thanks."

Had Aidan caught the sarcasm?

Aidan shoved his hands in his pants pockets. "Isabel has good reason not to trust the Fianna."

"What happened to her when she was seventeen had nothing to do with you."

"It's not about me. Since the man who attacked her when she was a teenager went unprosecuted and eventually became a warrior—"

"A warrior *you* beat in the gauntlet."

"She distrusts everything about the brotherhood. I don't blame her for that."

Since Alex didn't blame her either, he followed Horatio and left his brother—hopefully for good.

∽

An hour later, Isabel stood in the courtyard of the Mills House Hotel, yet couldn't make herself enter. If she did—no, *once* she did—Remiel would see it as a betrayal and her life would be forfeit. If she entered that hotel, she'd be at the mercy of the Fianna. Something she'd promised herself would never happen again.

Her phone rang and she moved closer to the center fountain, away from milling guests. "Yes?"

"We have a problem," Clayborne said. "The Fianna took one of my men from Hezekiah Usher's office."

She sat on the edge of the fountain, appreciating the cool mist on her back. The sunset had done nothing to alleviate the day's humidity. "*What?*"

"Yep. And from what I can tell, he's still alive. That means one thing."

"If the Fianna haven't killed him, he's talking." She raised her face to the night sky. "He knows nothing."

"He knows the location of the work site."

The place where they were digging for the treasure. She flexed her free hand and closed her eyes. "You need to find him and take care of this."

"You're fucking crazy. My crew and I are *not* going up against Fianna warriors. They'll slaughter us."

As usual, the men in her life were cowards. "Any idea where they're holding him?"

"No."

She straightened her shoulders, opened her eyes, and glanced around to make sure no warriors were present. She needed to find that treasure ASAP. "Any leads on the witch's examination's appendix?"

"Yes. I'm checking a solid lead now. Meet me in thirty minutes. Our usual place."

Isabel shut her phone and stared at the hotel entrance again. If she went in, she'd be at the mercy of the Fianna for the rest of her life. If she left, she still had a chance to find the treasure and reassure Remiel of her loyalty. If she did that—if she could buy herself a bit more time—she could escape both the Prince and Remiel and be free of them all. Forever.

And she could keep and sell the Pirate's Grille that she'd promised Alex.

Shoving her phone in her purse, she left the courtyard, and the Fianna, behind.

Thirty minutes later, Isabel used her family's key to enter Saint Philip's east churchyard. The key was one of the benefits of having generations of family members buried there. With her cell phone light, she made her way to her family's raised mausoleum topped with an angel statue. A few minutes later, she heard Clayborne's whistle and saw him approach with a penlight.

"Well?" she asked when he stopped a foot away.

Clayborne crossed his arms over his chest. Even in the dim light, she noticed his bruised knuckles. "Nothing."

The blood rushed to her heart and she felt light-headed. What had she done? She'd walked away from a parlay with the Prince because *Clayborne* had made promises? She stumbled back and sat on a raised tomb. "Please tell me you know how to the find the appendix."

He rocked back on his heels. "Nope."

She closed her eyes and reminded herself that she still had the Pirate's Grille. She still had the work site. She still had more than Allison did. And she really didn't need the appendix. It was just another layer of protection. Especially since, so far, they hadn't found the treasure.

She opened her eyes, stood, and smoothed her skirt. "We need to find your lover. If she gave the witch's examination to Stuart, she may know where he hid the appendix."

"She's disappeared."

"She didn't disappear. She was *disappeared*. On purpose. By the Fianna." Isabel took out her phone again and dug into her encrypted photo file. When she found an image of the warrior, she held it up for him to see. "Find Horatio and follow him. Maybe he'll lead you to your lover."

CHAPTER 24

ALLISON HEARD NOISES AND ROLLED OVER IN BED ONLY TO realize that Zack wasn't there, and the dark garden outside the windows told her the power was out.

She sat up and pushed the hair out of her face. After they'd come inside, he'd walked and fed Nicholas Trott so she could shower. It was as if he'd understood her need to be alone. By the time he came upstairs, she was in pajama pants and a cami and tucked into bed.

At first it'd been awkward, but Zack's smile and teasing way had eased her anxiety. After brushing his teeth, he'd come out of the bathroom in gym shorts and a T-shirt. She wondered if he'd chosen not to sleep naked—which he'd once told her he did—because he knew all of *this* was a bit overwhelming for her.

Then he went to her fireplace and started a fire. Despite the fact it was August, the rain and AC had chilled the air. The fire also offered a muted light, not too harsh but enough to watch him while he worked. He built the fire, moved Nicholas Trott's blanket into the room, and crawled into bed next to her. All of which he did with quiet assurance and graceful strength. When he reached for her, she clung to him with her head on his chest and his arms around her. He didn't pressure her for any more than she had to give, and she was grateful.

The fire crackled, sending shadows around the room. Between the sound of his heartbeat, his heat that scorched and protected, and Nicholas Trott's purring, her mind slowed. The moment she felt Zack's breathing even out, she'd allowed her eyes to drift closed.

Except now she was awake, and Zack was gone.

She peered over the side of the bed to see Nicholas Trott missing as well. A noise came from down the hallway, and she got up, throwing on her Tulane sweatshirt. She found Zack at the other end of the hall, standing in the middle of the master bedroom, staring at his phone. His gun lay on the four-poster bed, next to Nicholas Trott, who was in his lounging-yet-observing position. An LED lantern lit up a corner of the room.

She paused in the doorway. "Looking for ghosts?"

Zack glanced at her. "I'm looking for the appendix. *Again.* Alex texted earlier. He learned that Stuart was the last person to have it. He had to have hidden it somewhere."

"After his death, I went through this room looking for answers. Every drawer. Every closet. I didn't find anything unusual. No rare documents, and no sign of his affair."

"His clothes are gone."

She stopped in front of the closet that once held expensive suits, silk ties, and rows of leather shoes. "Last week I packed everything and gave the boxes to the church."

Zack shoved his phone into the pocket of his gym shorts and picked up his gun. "What about personal effects? Loose change? Random receipts? Knives? Keys? Lighters? A wallet?"

"I didn't find anything like that." She ran her hand over one of the bed's carved poles that held up the canopy. "Every drawer had a purpose. Socks in sock drawer. T-shirts in another. Even his closet was color-coded. Stuart didn't believe in junk drawers or coin jars."

"That's not right," Zack said softly, more to himself than to her. "Don't you think it's weird Stuart didn't keep any personal stuff in his room?"

She sat on the edge of the bed to rub Nicholas Trott's neck and then got up. She hadn't been on that bed in two years and didn't want to remember the time when it'd been hers. "I guess."

Zack went to the window overlooking the dark garden. "I currently live with eight men above a pirate-themed gym once owned by an old man who was a hoarder. I've also lived in barracks, BOQs, Quonset huts, and tents. And I can tell you that men always have tons of things in their pockets, in duffel bags, on tables. Everything from condoms to gum wrappers to lottery tickets. It's odd that you found nothing like that."

She stood next to him. "The night after Stuart asked me to leave our bedroom, I returned the engagement brooch he'd given me." She shivered and Zack put an arm around her shoulder. "When I cleared this room, I didn't find it either. Now I know he'd given it to Isabel."

She rested against his chest and watched the lights in the garden flicker on, and then go out again. *What was up with the power?*

Zack rested his chin on top of her head. "Allison?"

She closed her eyes. "*Hmm.*"

"Did you ever come back into this room while Stuart was alive?"

She shook her head. No point in stating the sad truth out loud. "When I had a housekeeper, she kept it clean."

"Did you choose what Stuart was buried in?"

She stiffened. It was an odd question, but she had nothing to hide. "Maddie picked out his suit. After I saw his body at the morgue, I couldn't come in here."

"It's okay, sweetheart." He rubbed her back. "No one knows, do they?"

The whispered words struck her heart with the force of a broadsword. She tried to swallow, but her throat was too dry. She blinked a few times and her face felt hot. The still air had made it hard to breathe.

No. No one knows.

Except she couldn't get the words out.

"I know how hard it is to carry a secret. To act normal in public, like you're happy and everything is great, only to know that it's all a lie."

She clenched her fists until her nails cut into her palms.

Was he thinking about what happened to his men in Afghanistan?

She felt him swallow and studied his face. Dark stubble lined his jaw, his lips had thinned, and his gaze was fixed out instead of in, as if he were looking for someone.

"When my parents killed themselves at Bayou Saint George, my grandfather was governor of Louisiana. He was obsessed with things like family name and had never been able to accept the fact that my mother refused to marry my father. Or my mother's mental illness. Grandfather floated the story that they'd gotten married and, after going to Bayou Saint George for their honeymoon, had been murdered by escaped convicts."

"You never told me that."

"My grandfather and Vivienne turned Emilie and me into coconspirators. We were kids, terrified and alone, so we went along with the bullshit story. Years later I went to college and met Stuart. While Stuart's family can be difficult—"

She snorted.

"—they were emotionally connected. They had traditions and memories. They'd built a foundation that, while not friendly, seemed honest and true."

She agreed reluctantly. She didn't like Stuart's family, mostly because they'd never accepted her and hated Rue, but they stuck by each other.

"That's when I decided I wanted a real family—a real family who lived by the truth instead of falsehoods."

Again, she agreed.

"Then I met you, a beautiful woman who had a family history filled with as much violence as mine. Watching you was like looking in a mirror. I saw the pain and loneliness caused by silence and fear. For the first time, I realized how the weight of secrets and lies could crush a person—or at the very least, cause a person to make choices out of fear."

Her shoulders shook. She sank to the floor and struggled to breathe.

Zack sat down next to her. "You're hyperventilating."

Her breaths came out faster and shorter.

"Allison." Zack held her face between his hands. "Look at me."

She closed her eyes and tried to lie down. If she could get to the cooler floor, she'd be okay.

"It's okay." Zack's voice softened. "You don't have to keep this secret anymore. I know."

Besides Zack and Maddie, no one else knew.

Except for Isabel.

"Stuart is dead." Zack's voice was so soft, it wouldn't even be defined as a whisper. "You don't have to pretend any longer. Stuart had no right to throw you out of this room, no right to shut you out like you were worthless, like your feelings didn't matter. And he sure as hell had no right to make you feel like this was all your fault or make you believe you were incapable of loving others."

She hiccupped a few times before saying, "I couldn't be what he needed."

Was that her voice? So shaky and low? Trembling like a daisy stripped of its petals?

"No. Stuart couldn't be what *you* needed. He failed you. When he realized that, he was so wracked with guilt he had no idea how to handle it. He shut you out, not because he hated you but because he couldn't bear to hurt you anymore. Not being able to love you the way you needed to be loved was his greatest shame. Not being able to protect you was his greatest failure."

"How could you possibly know this?"

"Stuart was one of my best friends as well. Before I left for the army, we used to talk."

"About what?"

"Things that men talk about." Zack pulled her onto his lap and held her against his chest.

She turned until she faced him. Nicholas Trott now lay half on her lap, while she was tucked into Zack's. She was surrounded by the two heartbeats of those she loved the most.

Her chest tightened, and she closed her eyes again. *Did she love Zack?* She honestly didn't know.

"Allison." Zack trailed tiny kisses along her face and down her neck. "You're not alone. You no longer have to carry the burden of being the abandoned wife in private and the loving wife in public. You no longer have to be anything other than who you were meant to be."

"*Zack.*" She barely recognized her own voice. "I don't want to be alone anymore."

"You're not, sweetheart. The sad truth is you never were alone. The irony is that somehow, seven years ago, even the Fianna knew that."

She was too busy gasping for air to argue. She'd confessed her greatest secret to the man her husband had always been insecure around and felt lighter than she'd ever felt in her life. What kind of woman did that make her?

Zack stood, pulled her up as well, and they followed Nicholas Trott to her room. When they got there, the power clicked on again. The AC fans whirred and the outdoor garden lights bathed the room. That's when she saw, in the shadows near her bed, a man holding a gun.

∽

Zack drew his weapon and kept Allison behind him. Of course Nicholas Trott had already welcomed the warrior and was now in his dog bed. This visit was the absolute last thing Zack needed tonight. "What do you want, Horatio?"

The warrior hit his chest with his hand and bowed his head. His other hand held his weapon. "My lord sends reassurance and seeks to remind."

And Zack came that much closer to the *lose his shit* line. "How's my sister?"

Horatio pointed to a photo on the bed. Zack picked it up and his mouth fell open. It was a photo of Emilie standing next to Alex. She wasn't gagged or bound in any way but her eyes were as angry as he'd ever seen them.

"Your sister," Horatio said, "remains a guest of the Fianna until you find that treasure. Pray tell, my lord, have you?"

Seriously? "No, Horatio. Because we have shit for intel. What about that man you took yesterday? He worked for Remiel. Did you get anything out of him?"

"Nothing about the treasure." Horatio motioned to Zack's gun. As soon as Zack shoved it back in his waistband, Horatio put his away as well. "Lady Isabel failed to appear as well."

"Wait." Allison drew her hair back from her face. "I thought Isabel was trading the Pirate's Grille for her meeting with the Prince."

"She declined."

"She still has the Pirate's Grille?" Zack kicked a pillow across the floor and started pacing. "Fuck."

Allison took his arm to stop him. "Horatio, is there anything else you can tell us about this treasure?"

Horatio nodded once. "Until recently, 'twas the legend that the Pirate's Grille and the witch's examination's appendix, when used together, deciphered a code that would lead to the treasure of the dread pirate Henry Avery."

"We know the story." Allison released Zack's arm and pointed toward the master bedroom. "If Stuart had the appendix, I would've found it by now."

"'Tis quite the quandary."

Which left them exactly where they started: completely and utterly screwed.

Horatio walked closer to Zack and said in a low voice, "This search is far larger than you or me. If you wish to learn the truth, ask your lord."

Ask Kells? What kind of bullshit was that? "Thanks for the tip, but I'm not sure how Kells has anything to do with this."

Besides, if Zack went to Kells now, there'd be all kinds of hell unleashed.

"'Tis your decision."

Zack flexed his free hand instead of reaching for his gun, which was what he really wanted to do. "What happens if we don't find the treasure by Sunday?"

Horatio moved past them with that eerie way of walking. "The Prince will turn Lady Tremaine over to the Fiend."

CHAPTER 25

ALLISON SAT ON THE FLOOR AND HELD NICHOLAS TROTT.

Zack had followed Horatio downstairs to make sure the warrior left. She could still hear Zack stomping around the house, probably trying to work off his temper before he came back upstairs. Because her digital clock had been blinking and she had no idea what time it was, she'd unplugged it.

Watching time tick down served no purpose.

She pressed her head into Nicholas Trott's neck until he whined. She released him with a "sorry, boy" and went over to the fireplace. While the lights in the garden had come back on, it wasn't enough to dispel the shadows. Yet she wasn't ready to turn on the room lights. They seemed too harsh and real for a situation that defined harsh and real.

Instead, she stoked the fire. Minutes later, the fire was crackling and she was tucked in bed, thinking about everything that had happened. She lay on her side and buried her head in her pillow. She felt so raw, like she was a hot wire sparking around the room, ready to electrocute anything that came too close.

Zack came in and shut the door. A loud click echoed when he turned the seventeenth-century lock. Her heart thumped as he pulled off his T-shirt. Backlit by the fire, she had a full profile view. His loose hair reached his shoulders. His dark stubble made him look fierce. The way he poked the logs—jabs instead of pushes—made his muscles ripple and his tattooed dragon appear alive. He was the epitome of male perfection. Her wild man.

Stuart had always kept himself in excellent shape, but he'd also had a desk job. Zack's physique didn't come just from a gym. It'd come from a lifetime of hard physical labor. When a log rolled, he knelt to catch it with the iron poker. As he moved the log back, she saw his leg muscles contract and relax. That's when it hit her: all he wore was a pair of gym shorts.

She inhaled sharply and he came over. She had to fight to keep her hands to herself. Even though they'd made love once and were sleeping in the same bed, she had no right to expect anything from him. One thing she was grateful for though was that he knew her darkest secret—he understood how hard it had been for her to live a double life of happiness and sadness.

He pulled the covers over her shoulder. "Are you okay?"

She nodded.

"Do you mind…" He looked toward the other side of the bed.

She shook her head.

He came around the other side, but she didn't have the courage to roll toward him. She stayed on her side, facing the fireplace, all her insecurities hounding her.

Zack rolled until his arm wrapped around her waist and he pulled her close to his body. The man had to have an internal temperature that would melt the ice caps. His breath tickled her hair and she snuggled against his bare chest.

"Are you tired?" she asked.

"I'm overtired. I can't shut off my mind."

"I feel the same way."

His arm tightened, and she couldn't help but rub his wrist and forearm. The hair on his arms felt so…masculine. Then there was his smell. That intoxicating scent of bay rum. She closed her eyes and relaxed, amazed at how well his larger angles fit against her smaller curves.

As she listened to his breathing and the logs crackling and the dog purring and the AC humming, she felt his hand move. The slightest pressure against her stomach. She held her breath and, just as she released it, felt his hand again.

His breathing in her ear sped up. Slowly, his hand edged down until his fingers found the waistband of her pj's. He paused for a moment. When she didn't move, he slipped his hand inside...until he stopped. He must have realized she wasn't wearing any panties.

"*Allison.*" He whispered her name. "If you want me to stop, you need to say something. Now."

"Don't stop, Zack. *Please.*"

He pressed his lips against her shoulder at the same time his hand reached her most sensitive center.

She bucked at the unexpected pleasure. Heat spiraled low, contracting her lower stomach, and she arched her back.

His other arm reached beneath her body and his hand found her breast. Her nipples tightened, and he moaned against her shoulder. "Can you feel what you do to me?"

Yes. His erection pressed into her back and his fingers between her legs caressed and teased, building a tension she wasn't sure she'd survive. His body clenched around hers, and although they were both on their sides, he forced her legs apart. When one finger reached inside her, she shoved her face into the pillow to hide her moans.

The building pressure was almost too much to bear.

He increased the speed and forcefulness of his movements, always tender yet demanding a response—a response she couldn't help but offer. When the tension became too much, she reached down and covered his hand with her smaller one. He paused for half a second until she taught him the rhythm, a perfect blend of hard and fast that brought her to a climax far more quickly than she expected.

Before she was even finished with her last wave of the most intense pleasure, he used the arm around her waist to draw her up higher against his body. A moment later, he entered her from behind.

She gasped at the intrusion. Not because it was unwanted, but because he filled her to a point where she wondered if he'd even fit. She squeezed her legs together, and he began a driving motion that pushed the breath out of her body. He held her almost completely immobile, one arm around her breasts, the other around her waist, and had complete control of both of their movements. He kept hers small and tight while he drilled, as if making sure she knew he was offering her everything he had to give.

His thumb teased a nipple and she raised her free arm to hold his head. With her head against his shoulder, and his face buried in her neck, he increased the speed until they were both gasping. Without warning, he reached down to press his fingers against her core. He held her body between his palm and his erection and whispered, "Come for me, Allison. I need you to."

She released his head because she'd no strength left in her arm. But she could lower her hand until her fingers covered his, forcing him to press into her harder. "Faster."

Zack took her request seriously and gave her three more strokes that sent her shattering like a thousand shards of light cracking open the night sky. Her body stiffened and her toes curled. She arched her back and cried out, "*Zack.*"

Zack tightened his arms around Allison, one hand holding her breast and the other buried deep in her sex. He had no control over his body; his hips drilled and his balls constricted until the pain/pleasure was too much. He exploded inside her, stroke after stroke, draining himself and filling her. He arched his neck, keeping her within his arms, and let out a raw, guttural growl.

Daaaaamn.

Thank goodness breathing was part of the autonomic nervous system because otherwise he would've stopped that as well.

Holding her close, he rolled onto his back. That left her sprawled on top of him.

"Zack." She squirmed until he used his strength to keep her still, his hands still in place. "What more do you want from me?"

"I've been dreaming of this night my entire adult life. I've fantasized about making love to you in every position possible, in every situation possible."

Her sharp intake of breath eased the constriction in his chest.

She hadn't been ready earlier when they'd made love in the garden. Her body had been ready—her body had wept for his—but she hadn't been emotionally prepared. Yet despite knowing that, he'd been unable to stop. Then when she'd broken down in the master bedroom, he'd understood the depth of her loneliness, the weight of that secret, and how sad she must've been despite her outward appearance of happy wife.

When he'd come back into her bedroom, he'd been determined to give her time and space. But as soon as he'd held her in his arms, smelled her jasmine scent, and felt the softness of her skin, all resolve melted away. He was, no kidding, the biggest ass in the world.

"Zack?" She squirmed. "What are you—"

"Shh. It's going to be okay. I promise." Before she could argue with him, he began to move his fingers between her legs again.

He had nothing to offer her other than this. He had no home, no real job, no security. And so far, he'd done a shitty job of protecting her and figuring out what the hell was going on. *But this?* He slipped two fingers inside her while his thumb found her most sensitive part. *This* was what he had, so *this* was what he was going to do.

And never again would they make love without her finishing with him. He was an ass, but he wasn't a selfish bastard.

"I can't," she whispered. "Really. I'm tired."

He gently bit her earlobe. "I believe in you."

She laughed and when she shivered, he caressed one breast while he made love to her with his fingers. The more she squirmed, the harder he held her. Her ass moving over his hips was just a penance he'd have to suffer if he was going to offer her this gift.

He loved her little moans and kissed her shoulder. She tasted sweet, like sugar cookies and cinnamon. "It's okay, sweetheart."

A few moments later, she stiffened and her hand tightened on his, pressing him in deeper. He felt the vibrations roll through her body, felt her core tighten around his fingers, felt each breath as they got shorter and shorter until she stopped breathing altogether.

When he knew she was finished, he just held her. He didn't want to remove his hands. Didn't want to let her go. Didn't want this moment to end. But like all moments, a few passed and she shivered again.

He rolled her off yet arranged her so she was curled up around him, her head on his shoulder and her hand on his lower stomach. Sure, he had a raging hard-on. But he'd been in far worse physically painful situations.

She smiled, nuzzled against his shoulder, and met his gaze. Her eyes were shadowed in the dying light of the fire, her blond hair was spread across his chest like a silk blanket. He was sure he'd never get tired of seeing her soft, pale body against his darker, harder one. "Zack Tremaine, you are the most amazing man I've ever known."

"You're only saying that because I gave you three climaxes."

"True." She kissed his chest. "You also brought in my laundry, cooked me dinner, and make me laugh."

"As long as I don't have to do it all at the same time, I'm good with that."

She closed her eyes, and he brushed stray curls off her cheek. Her skin was so soft, like satin, yet his hands were hard and scratchy. He didn't want to hurt her.

"I love it when you touch my hair," she said in a muffled, almost-asleep voice.

"Good. Because I intend to do a lot more touching."

She rubbed her face against his chest and her breath tickled. As he settled himself, making sure she was comfortable and his arms weren't going to go numb, he felt a *thump* on the bed. Nicholas Trott now lay at their feet.

"I know your mother doesn't allow this," Zack said to the dog. "You're going to get me in trouble."

Nicholas Trott sighed and rested his head on his front paws. Before Zack could kick him off, Nicholas Trott started purring.

Without looking, Allison asked, "Is the dog on the bed?"

Zack glared at the dog, who was now so settled that there was no way to get him off without moving. That meant letting go of Allison. "No."

"Good. He's not allowed on the bed except in certain circumstances."

"What are those?"

"When he's lonely, when he's hungry, and when he sees the lady in white."

Zack glanced at her, but she was so buried in blankets, her face pressed so tightly against his chest, he saw only a wild mass of blond hair. "Who is the lady in white?"

"You know," she said in a lilting, drifting voice that almost sounded like she was smiling. "The woman you saw outside Stuart's study and in the garden. The ghost of Mercy Chastain."

CHAPTER 26

THE NEXT MORNING, ZACK POURED HIMSELF ANOTHER CUP OF coffee and made room at Allison's kitchen table so Alex could sit. He and Alex had already shared texts about everything that had happened last night and agreed to meet this morning to come up with a new plan.

Zack and Allison had woken early and gone to her office to get all of her research on Mercy Chastain. Then after they'd returned home, he'd made breakfast. Now he had a bread pudding in the oven and a whiskey sauce on the stove. While he stirred the alcohol into the melted butter, Nicholas Trott napped on his bed and Allison was responding to emails on her laptop. Apparently, her UVA professor friend had emailed with some information on Henry Avery.

Zack was still processing the news that Allison had considered taking a job at UVA. Yesterday, while going through Hezekiah's papers again, he'd found the UVA letter again and read it without telling her. She'd not just been offered a job. She'd been offered a full tenured professorship. A professorship that didn't require her to find a centuries-old witch or publish in obscure history journals. A professorship that would've set her free from her life with Stuart.

Instead of asking her about it, he'd folded up the letter and placed it on top of Hezekiah's papers and maps. Maybe, when all of this was over, they could discuss it. Until then, he had to focus on finding that treasure.

As if realizing his thoughts were all about her, she smiled at him and he winked.

Today she wore a long chiffon skirt, made with layers of different shades of blue, and a navy T-shirt. Except it wasn't like any T-shirt he'd ever seen. This one had a scoop neck, tiny sleeves, and fit like it'd been painted on. Between the tight top, flowy skirt, and her hair pulled back from her face with a clip, she reminded him of why men went to war, welded steel, and rocketed to the moon.

"Alex," Allison said as she sipped her coffee and typed, "did you know Zack could cook?"

"Nope. To be fair, there's no kitchen at the gym. Just a hot plate and a slow cooker." Alex poured himself a cup of coffee and sat next to her. "Did you find anything in that stack of paper you took from Hezekiah's office?"

Zack used the spatula to point to three stacks of paper he'd retrieved and organized on a nearby credenza. "No."

"Too bad." Alex drank his coffee and looked at the tracings Zack had removed from the envelope. "What are these?"

Allison closed her laptop and, after telling him about the apotropaic marks they found in Pink House and in Stuart's planner, she said, "These apotropaic marks mean something. I'm just not sure what."

"And you think they'll lead you to Mercy Chastain? Maybe tell you how she disappeared and what happened to the treasure?"

"Yes. The only place we haven't checked yet is Fenwick Hall."

"Fenwick Hall is where Allison grew up." Zack put a bowl of strawberries he'd picked in her conservatory on the table. "That's our next stop."

Alex took a pencil and a clean piece of tracing paper and placed it over the Pink House rubbings. Once he retraced those, he did the same with the rubbings they'd found on the page in Stuart's planner. When he was done, he drew an outline around all of the ovals. The two rubbings fit together making one full circle. He even added the odd lines around the perimeter of the circle. "These ovals are part of a hexafoil. Overlapping ovals that form a flower within the confines of a circle are called a daisy wheel."

"That's right." Allison studied the new tracing. "How'd you know that?"

"I'm from Boston but my mother was from Ipswich. These things are all over that area, mostly in barns." Alex opened the planner. "Is breakfast ready yet?"

"It's coming," Zack said.

"It smells delicious." Allison smiled at Zack again, and he saw the secret happiness hiding in her gaze. It had been an incredible night, but since they'd woken, they'd barely spoken about what they'd done. They showered separately and dressed quickly. It was as if they'd both been hit with the shyness bug.

Considering the work ahead of them, Zack was relieved by her distance. Everything they'd done together carried emotional weight. And to be honest, he wasn't sure he could carry that weight along with his worry about Emilie. And that just made him feel guilty.

Could he be even more of an ass?

At least he could make Allison a decent breakfast. After he took the bread pudding out of the oven, he ladled whiskey sauce over the top and served three plates. Then he sat next to Allison, across from Alex. It was time to get to work. "Alex, what happened last night?"

Alex swallowed a bite of pudding and followed it with a gulp of coffee. "This is good."

"No," Allison said with a mouthful, "it's incredible."

"Thanks." Zack kicked Alex under the table. "Focus."

Alex wiped his lips with a napkin. "Aidan asked me to leave town with him."

Zack hadn't expected that. "And?"

Alex waved his fork around. "I said hell no. Then Horatio took me to see Emilie. He drove me around for at least an hour."

Zack pushed his plate away. He didn't feel like eating. "That doesn't mean she's an hour away."

"True. I was blindfolded. They could've driven in circles. Once they took off my blindfold, I saw Emilie sitting on a bed. She wasn't bound in any way. She recognized me from Ranger School graduation and gave me a hug."

Zack gripped his mug until Allison touched his wrist. "Was there a stench?"

"No," Alex said as he went for another cup of coffee.

Allison glanced at Zack. "What does that mean?"

"In a hostage situation, there can be adrenaline, fear, urine, sweat, vomit—it all has a terrible smell."

"Fear has a smell?" Allison asked.

"Yes," both men said at the same time.

"Last night, there was no smell." Alex added a shit ton of sugar to his coffee and leaned his ass against the counter. "I mean, no *human* scent. I did recognize three other things though: rosemary, lavender, and something else I couldn't identify."

Allison released Zack's wrist to take a bite of pudding. He was glad she was eating.

"You think that Emilie isn't in desperate straits?" Allison asked Alex.

"She's been kidnapped, but she's not being tortured or made to eat her own vomit or forced to sit in her own shit."

When Allison's eyes widened, Zack glared at Alex. While they'd both seen a number of terrible hostage situations and had heard Nate's story of torture at the POW camp in Afghanistan, Allison didn't need to know the gory details.

"Was Emilie scared?" Allison asked.

"Yes, but she's tough. I told her that her big brother was going to save her."

Good. "Did she talk?"

"She rambled about how sorry she was for something. Then she cried. But when Horatio walked away to make a call, she told me in an extremely calm voice that she heard two other warriors talking. Apparently, they'd interrogated someone and learned about the city of bell towers." Alex drank his coffee, his brow furrowed. "I think she was fake crying."

"That sounds like my sister."

Allison touched Zack's arm. "I wonder what the city of bell towers means?"

Her touch sent shivers down his leg, and his foot tapped the floor beneath the table. "It's probably Charleston, Savannah, or New Orleans. All three are known for having more churches than people."

Alex found her folder that held her Mercy Chastain research. "Do you think this city of bell towers is where Stuart hid the appendix?"

"I don't know," Allison said.

Alex took out some photos and laid them on the table. They were images of a wooden beam with broken daisies carved into them. "What are these?"

"Photos I took as part of my search for Mercy Chastain. After her arrest, Mercy was held in an early version of Saint Philip's Church on Meeting Street. While she awaited her trial, she carved these daisies. The church was nearly destroyed by a hurricane in 1710 and rebuilt in its current location on Church Street. Because building materials were scarce at the time, they reused what they could. These beams, with Mercy's carvings, are now in the choir loft."

Alex sorted through the other photos. "Why a broken daisy?"

"I don't know," Allison said. "I noticed broken daisies sketched on the Pirate's Grille. And I know they're on the pages of the witch's examination."

While Zack ate, he studied each photo as Alex finished with them. Despite the camera's flash, the photos were still dark. "Allison, do you have a magnifier?"

"I do." She stood and laid her napkin on her chair. "I'll be right back."

When she left the room, Alex lowered his voice. "I can't believe Isabel blew off the Prince."

Zack laid all the photos on the table in a long row. "What do you think that means?"

"No idea," Alex said. "It can't be good."

Allison returned, handed Zack the magnifier, and he laid the glass over one of the photos. "Do you see what's near the broken daisy?"

Alex and Allison leaned over to look. He adjusted the glass to get the best view, then pointed to the carvings in the edge of the image. "Those look like apotropaic marks."

Allison glanced at him with wide eyes. "They do. I was always so fixated on her broken daisy, and there's so much other graffiti, I never noticed."

Alex grabbed another plate of pudding and ate standing up. "Is it possible that Mercy made the Pirate's Grille to help Henry hide his treasure?"

"I guess...but that would mean she'd have known about Henry Avery's treasure."

"That's a good point," Zack said. "Did Hezekiah mention where the Pirate's Grille came from?"

She shook her head. "All I know is that the pirate Thomas Toban stole it from the Fianna in 1710."

Zack stood and stretched his arms over his head. "Thomas Toban must've known about the treasure if he went looking for the Pirate's Grille."

"It's possible. Thomas knew Henry." Allison opened her laptop again. "Yesterday I emailed my colleague at UVA. She sent me back some notes."

"The one who offered you the job?" Zack got up to pour more coffee.

"Yes." Allison typed instead of looking at him. "My colleague specializes in lesser known seventeenth and early eighteenth century pirates. This morning she sent me information on Thomas Toban. In 1700, Thomas bought Henry's ship the *Fancy* and renamed it the *Rebecca*."

"That was *after* Henry stole his treasure?" Alex asked.

"Yes." Allison scrolled. "Henry stole the treasure around 1695 and disappeared with the loot. In 1700, Thomas met Henry in Nassau and bought his ship. In 1701, under an assumed name, Henry moved to Charleston and built Pirate House as an alehouse and a brothel. In 1702, he started his affair with his barmaid Mercy, they had a son, and he built Pink House for them.

"In 1703, Mercy was accused of witchcraft and eventually exonerated. In 1704, Mercy and Henry disappeared forever. Yet despite never marrying Mercy, Henry left Pink House, Pirate House, and a lot of money to their son. Henry also directed that if anything should happen to him and Mercy, the boy would be cared for by relatives."

"That," Alex said as he licked the whiskey sauce spoon, "sounds like premeditation."

Zack grabbed the spoon out of Alex's hands and dropped it into the sink. "It also means Mercy probably knew Henry's true identity."

"But would she have known about the treasure?" Alex asked.

"Everyone knew about the treasure," Allison said. "It was such a huge deal when it happened that Daniel Defoe and Robert Louis Stevenson wrote novels about buried treasure based on Henry Avery's exploits."

"What if Mercy was in on the gig?" Zack covered the bread pudding with tinfoil and slipped it into the fridge. "What if she and Henry made their getaway with the idea of taking the treasure and living the rest of their lives together in peace?"

"Why?" Allison asked. "They had a life here with a child, and no one knew who Henry was until after they disappeared."

"Leverage." Zack snorted because he was annoyed he hadn't thought of it earlier. "What if Mercy's accusation wasn't about witchcraft at all? What if it was blackmail?"

Allison stood, her arms wrapped around her waist. "You mean someone was using Mercy to blackmail Henry to give up the treasure?"

"It's possible."

"I have to admit," Alex said, "it makes sense. It's what the Prince is doing with Emilie."

Allison frowned. "Other than going out to Fenwick Hall to find more daisy wheels and hope they lead us to Mercy, we don't have many more clues. I can't find the witch's examination's appendix and we don't have the Pirate's Grille."

"I'll go to Saint Philip's," Alex said. "See if I can find the apotropaic marks Mercy carved."

Zack pulled the photo from his back pocket and threw it on the table. "This is our only other clue. This unknown man. He might be some random dude Isabel hooked up with."

Alex took the photo and frowned. "I know this guy. Not his name, but I've seen him before. He works for Remiel. At least, he used to."

"Are you sure?" Zack asked.

"He was there the night I tried to kill Remiel."

"Wait." Allison glared at both of them. "Alex, you did *what*?"

"It's a long story." Alex smiled at her. "I'm sure Zack can fill you in."

Allison blinked a few times and then started putting her photos back into her Mercy Chastain file. "The problem is I grew up in that house and I don't remember seeing any markings like that anywhere. My mom was obsessed with Mercy Chastain. If we'd had apotropaic marks in the house, she would've known. Then there's the issue that I don't have permission to go out there."

Alex opened his mouth until Zack shook his head. That was a *later* kind of conversation.

Alex picked up the tracing he'd done of the daisy wheel. "These things are often in the barns. Are there older buildings on the property?"

"There is a barn, and it's older than the house by two hundred years. There are some old carvings on the second floor, but they're not apotropaic marks and they're later eighteenth century. But the original barn was built in 1710…the same year the original Saint Philip's church was destroyed." Allison went back to her laptop and typed some more. "It says here that Pink House and Pirate House were also damaged during that hurricane."

"Is it possible Mercy carved the apotropaic marks while being held in the church?" Zack said. "Then, after the hurricane, the church's wood was divided up and used to rebuild Pirate House, Pink House, the new Saint Philip's Church, and the barn at Fenwick Hall?"

Alex flipped through the planner again. "Why would they do that?"

Allison shut her laptop and brought dishes to the sink. "Because there were no hardware stores. In colonial days, everything was reused."

"If we're right," Zack said, "Mercy carved the apotropaic marks while in captivity in 1703. Then, after the hurricane in 1710, the wood she'd carved was distributed throughout the city with no one realizing."

Alex picked up the planner again. "Did you see this?"

Zack read one of the calendar entries. Almost all of the days had an *I* in them, except for one with the notation *CAB/ILL 9 a.m.* "Allison, what does CAB/ILL stand for?"

She rinsed the plates and Alex went over to load the dishwasher. "It stands for Charleston Architectural Board. It's a group that watches over all of the renovations and new construction in the city. Stuart was one of its directors and went to monthly board meetings."

Zack scanned the other pages, but there were no other notations for CAB. "I don't think this was a board meeting."

Allison wiped the counter with a dishrag. "The CAB has a library and bookstore on Meeting Street. The ILL probably stands for Interlibrary Loan. Maybe Stuart borrowed a book?"

Alex cleared the table of crumbs and offered, "After I go to Saint Philip's, I'll check out the CAB. Is there anything else you need me to do? I gotta make up for not getting back the Pirate's Grille."

"Nate keeps texting. Help him come up with a story to keep Kells off our asses."

"Okay." Alex grabbed his motorcycle helmet off the counter. "I'll let you know when I find something."

Allison's phone rang and she excused herself to talk to her UVA colleague.

Zack walked Alex out to his bike that he'd parked near the burned-out building. "Horatio told me something last night."

"I'm not sure you can trust anything a warrior says, even if you can understand it."

Probably true. "Horatio suggested Kells was somehow involved in this mess."

Alex put on his helmet and mounted his bike. "Any idea what that means?"

"I was hoping you could find out if Kells and the Prince have a history. Maybe Kells has intel we could use."

Alex stared at the ignition until Zack hit his shoulder.

Alex nodded, turned the key, and gunned the engine.

As Alex drove away, Zack was sure of one thing: Alex knew more about Kells than he was sharing. And Zack hoped that wasn't going to be a problem.

CHAPTER 27

ALLISON FLIPPED THROUGH STUART'S PLANNER WHILE ZACK drove them in her car to Fenwick Hall. Nicholas Trott sat in the middle of the back seat and stared out the front window.

Zack glanced in the rearview mirror. "Does Nicholas Trott need a seat belt?"

"He won't wear one." She pointed to the light ahead. "Turn left here. The causeway to Hoopstick Island will be on your right."

Zack turned and slowed down on the gravel road. "I wish you'd put that planner down. You're torturing yourself."

"I know." She tossed it into the back seat. "I still can't believe Alex tried to kill Remiel and even went to prison for it."

"Remember, no one else can know."

"I promise I won't say a word."

Zack had told her the story and it was almost unbelievable. In fact, if it'd been a regular day on a regular week without Fianna warriors, impossible tasks, and a kidnapped woman, she wouldn't have believed it.

Zack parked the car outside a set of locked gates decorated with wrought-iron ravens. A sign off to the side read RAVEN'S RETREAT AT FENWICK HALL. PRIVATE PROPERTY. NO TRESPASSING.

She sighed. Part of the restraining order deal she'd made years ago to keep Rue away included the stipulation that Allison needed permission to return to Fenwick Hall. She'd emailed Rue yesterday and had left a message, but hadn't heard anything. Not surprising, considering their latest fight.

Now Allison wasn't quite sure how this unexpected visit was going to turn out.

Since Nicholas Trott was trying to open his door, Zack got out and freed him. Nicholas Trott ran toward the gate, and Zack opened her door. "Prepare yourself. It's humid."

She got out, slung her Nicholas Trott tote bag filled with tracing paper and pencils over her shoulder, and sucked in her breath. Although it was still midmorning, the temp had hit the high nineties and the humidity level had to be as high. Sweat formed between her breasts, and she took off her sweater and tossed it into the car. "Let's get this over with."

At the fence, she typed in numbers on a security keypad, and the gates swung open. Nicholas Trott raced down the lane in front of them. "We can't drive onto the property—Rue won't allow it. But we can walk to the house. We need to go there first since the barn will be locked."

Zack took Allison's hand and squeezed. "It'll be okay. I promise."

"I hope so." She started walking with Zack next to her. Except he glanced back a few times. "What's wrong?"

"There are cameras in the trees."

"There are also armed guards in the woods. My uncle Fenwick and his men are always patrolling." She tugged on Zack's hand to keep him moving. She didn't want to be here. And she hated the fact that she had to ask permission to visit her childhood home, the home her father had renovated for his family. The home her uncle usurped after her father's unexpected death. "Are you armed?"

He looked down at her with a serious gaze she'd never seen before. "I'm always armed."

She nodded and went back to studying the lane ahead of them. She wasn't surprised; she just wasn't sure where he kept his weapon. He'd left his jacket in the car, and today he wore jeans and a black T-shirt. Maybe he'd tucked it into one of his combat boots?

She brushed away gnats that hovered beneath the canopy of oak trees lining the drive. "Zack, if I see my uncle Fenwick, you'll have to intervene before I beat him with a pitchfork."

Zack chuckled. "Although I'd love to see that, I promise. I'd hate to have to visit you in prison."

She glanced at him, wondering if he would visit her in prison. Or if, once this was all over, he'd just disappear. That thought had been running through her mind since she'd woken up this morning. Last night, in his arms, had been amazing. But this morning it felt like things were all business with a side of shyness.

Of course, she'd left the bed first to shower alone and had been distant all morning.

She wasn't being bitchy; she just didn't know what to do with all the emotions burning through her blood like rocket fuel.

Zack waved away his own gnats. "What did your UVA colleague say on the phone earlier?"

"That job opening I turned down last year is open again. The professor who they hired instead has another opportunity. And school starts in a few weeks."

He glanced at her, but she kept her gaze on the long, tree-lined stretch ahead. "Did your colleague offer it to you?"

"Yes." Allison swallowed and wiped her forehead with her forearm. "I told her I was on deadline until Sunday and asked if we could talk about it after that. She agreed."

Zack nodded and they followed the road's turn. "Where's Nicholas Trott?"

Relieved at the change of subject, she pointed toward the water peeking through the trees. "Sitting on the riverbank, watching the birds. I'm not worried about him though. Since an incident with a copperhead last year, he knows better than to go into the water."

The lane made a sharp left and opened up to show the white house that guarded the river. They both stopped, and he said, "This place is amazing."

"Don't let the beauty fool you." She nodded toward the white clapboard house. Three stories high, with balconies on all four sides held up by Doric columns, the mansion had all the elements of Southern architecture including brick fireplaces in every room. "The house was built in 1900. My father, who was an architect, renovated it. The only original thing on the property is the barn."

He pointed to a gray barn tucked behind a grove of pine trees. An oak next to the barn still held the tree house her father had built. "Is that where we should start our search?"

"Yes." She pulled on his hand. "But our first stop is the herb garden."

A few minutes later, Allison was desperate for air-conditioning. Instead, she stood beneath a pergola covered in wisteria in the center of the circular herb garden. Young women in long skirts with kerchiefs in their hair pulled weeds and cut stems off the herb bushes. One of them, upon seeing Allison, had run off to find Rue.

"Who are these women?" Zack whispered. "They seem young."

"Rue's acolytes. They are young. In exchange for her pagan wiccan goddess wisdom and room and board in the mansion, they work in her gardens which, in turn, provide the main ingredients for her Raven's Retreat absinthe business."

"Does she pay them?"

Allison snorted. "No."

"Oh." Zack leaned against a pillar holding up the pergola. "Does she have male acolytes?"

"Yes. They live in another building on the other side of the property. They work in the distillery and as security."

"Is this really a cult?"

"I think so."

"Allison." The female voice came from behind, and both Allison and Zack turned to see Rue. Today she wore jeans and a black T-shirt. Her red hair had been braided and hung down her back. "Why do you want to see the barn?"

"It's personal."

Rue crossed her arms. "If you can't tell me, you can't see it. You haven't lived here since you ran away when you were fourteen."

"I want to see it, Mrs. Fenwick," Zack said in a low-yet-firm voice. "I asked Allison to bring me."

Rue moved close enough for Allison to smell her rose-scented perfume. "Who are you?"

"I'm Zack Tremaine. Allison's friend from college."

Rue's green eyes widened. "You were Stuart's friend as well."

"Yes, ma'am."

"Why do you want to see the barn?"

"Like Allison"—Zack smiled at her—"I was a history major. I'm interested in architecture."

Rue glanced at Allison. "I'll agree on one condition. Your uncle Fenwick and I want to come to Stuart's service. He was our son-in-law, after all."

Zack touched Allison's trembling shoulder. The last thing she wanted was Rue at the service, but time was running out to play games. "Okay. It's at—"

"I know when and where." Rue stared at Zack's hand on Allison's shoulder. "Zack, are you fucking my daughter?"

Allison clenched her fists, and Zack tightened his grip.

"With all due respect, Mrs. Fenwick, my relationship with Allison is none of your business."

"She's my daughter."

"I'm a grown woman." Allison threw that in because she hated the fact that they were talking about her as if she weren't there.

Rue brushed away a bug. "Even if my daughter were capable of loving another, I wouldn't want her loving you."

Zack's nostrils flared. "Excuse me?"

"You're an ex–Green Beret whose unit was charged with the Wakhan Corridor Massacre. Half your men are in prison, the other half dishonorably discharged. I also know that you refused to lead your team on a mission, and they ended up spending two years in a POW camp."

"How could you possibly know that?" Zack's voice had gone dangerously low.

"Stuart told me all about you, your unit, and your commander, Colonel Kells Torridan." Rue lifted her chin. "I know what Colonel Torridan did, what he's capable of, and I don't want you anywhere near my daughter. Because you, sir, are a coward."

"*Mother.*" Allison grabbed Rue's arm and dragged her toward a row of lavender bushes. "What is wrong with you?"

"Zack's dangerous, Petal. The man he works for is dangerous. You have no idea what you're involving yourself in. Zack will get you killed. He let another man lead his team."

"I'd think you'd be relieved to get rid of me."

Rue's eyes glinted in the sunlight. "Even though you caused your father's death and allowed Danny to die, you're still my daughter."

Allison released Rue's arm and went back to Zack. His hands were still fisted, his gaze fixed firmly on her. "Let's go."

"Wait." Rue's voice rang out.

Allison waited while Rue talked to an acolyte who'd been cutting lavender. "Why?"

"I'll give Nicholas Trott a treat while you look at the barn," Rue said. "And I'll see you at Stuart's service."

Allison was about to tell her mother to go to hell when Zack took her hand.

"Thank you," Zack said.

Before Allison could argue, Zack started walking and pulled her hand until she followed.

"We need to do this." Zack kissed Allison's palm and held it against his chest. "For Emilie."

Allison took one last look at her mother and said, "For Emilie."

Zack held on to Allison's hand while they headed for the barn. He wanted to address some of the things Rue had said, as well as Allison's job offer, but now wasn't the time.

They left the garden along a crushed shell pathway that led down along the riverbank. Meanwhile, Nicholas Trott bounded toward the house where he knew, apparently, there'd be treats.

Allison grimaced. "He needs a bath before the fourth Saturday of the month."

"Does that matter?"

"The fourth Saturday of every month, from nine a.m. to eleven a.m., my college students and Susan help Nicholas Trott give autographs in my garden."

"I don't understand," Zack said. "How—"

"Paw prints," Allison said. "He dips his paw in a bowl of mud and presses it onto whatever people want. Except their bodies. I drew the line at that."

They left the path and followed a worn trail that led to a gray barn on a ridge a hundred yards away from the river.

"Are you serious?" Zack coughed, probably to hide his laugh.

"Yes. In fact, one of my graduate students has a tattoo of Nicholas Trott on her butt."

Zack stumbled until Allison grabbed his arm. When they reached the barn, she held the padlock. She had no idea what the new combination was but didn't want to go back to ask Rue. After three failed tries, Allison spun the number for her brother's birthday. It worked and the lock opened.

Zack helped her slide open the barn doors, and Allison turned on the light. The center room was filled with boxes.

"Wow. What is that smell?"

"Dried herbs for the absinthe. Rue's acolytes grow all of the herbs on the property and dry them in the rafters."

Zack looked up to see dozens of dried plants hanging on hooks. "That licorice smell?"

"Green anise. One of the main ingredients in absinthe." She wandered around with her hands on her hips. "What is that fan sound?"

Zack pointed to the loft, which had been closed off. The door over the top of the stairs had a yellow-and-red sign that said DANGER. TERMITE REMEDIATION.

"Jeez," Allison muttered. "I hate termites."

Zack frowned. "Why do they need fans?"

"No idea."

He maneuvered through the towers of crated bottles of Raven's Retreat Absinthe. The room had such a heavy scent of herbs it was hard to discern one from the other. "Is it difficult seeing all these people living in your childhood home?"

"Sometimes. But I left at fourteen to live with my grandmother in New Orleans."

He reached for her, but instead she walked around the barn, looking up at the ceiling. "There are some interesting carvings of skulls upstairs, but they're not old enough. The original woodwork would be on the first floor."

There was so much he wanted to say, to try and reach her, but she'd closed herself off. Then again, so had he. As much as they needed to talk, as worried as he was about her job offer, they also needed to work the mission. "I'll check the support beams while you look at the door lintels and window frames."

"Good plan." She left him to check out the front door while he examined the perimeter.

Minutes later, she said, "I found one."

He met her by the back entrance. She stood on her toes and ran her fingers over the lintel above the door. "Feel this."

Being taller, it was easier for him to see the wood. "Do you have the flashlight?"

She pulled it out of her tote bag and handed it to him. "What do you see?"

He felt the indentations more than saw them. "Can you hold the light, so I can do a rubbing?"

"Yes." She traded him the light for a piece of tracing paper and a pencil.

A few minutes later, he'd traced a daisy wheel with other markings around the edges.

Allison held it up to the light.

"What are you doing here?" a male voice said from behind them.

Zack turned and saw a man in the doorway holding a gun against his thigh.

Allison shoved the paper into her tote bag. "Put away the gun, Fenwick."

This was her uncle/stepfather, Fenwick?

The man had blond hair cut in a military style. He wore a

sleeveless white T-shirt, black combat pants, and boots. But the thing that concerned Zack the most was that Fenwick had fixed his gaze—and aim—on Allison.

Zack moved until Allison stood behind him. "We're leaving now."

Fenwick used his gun to wave them outside. "Let's go."

CHAPTER 28

Isabel entered Vivienne's sitting room on the second floor of the mansion and waited for the maid to announce her. So far there'd been no word from Clayborne. Supposedly he was still tracking down the appendix.

Vivienne stood in front of a full-length window and studied a French desk from the Napoleonic period. "I'm not sure, Maddie."

Maddie moved the desk so it faced the garden instead of the room's interior. "If you don't like it, I can find something else for this space."

Vivienne walked around the furniture. Today she wore her silver hair in a braided coronet, as well as a blue linen sheath and matching Louboutins. Diamond earrings enhanced her patrician jawline.

Isabel had to admit the older woman was aging beautifully.

"Miss Rutledge has arrived," the maid said. "Would you like me to serve tea?"

Vivienne waved a hand. "We'll take tea in the drawing room."

"As you wish, ma'am." The maid left.

Maddie adjusted the desk away from direct sunlight. The room, with many windows overlooking the water gardens the mansion was known for, was one of Isabel's favorite. Filled with sunlight, eighteenth-century antiques, and a fireplace one could walk into, the room was elegant and cozy.

The kind of home Isabel hoped to have one day. She forced a smile. "I didn't know you were redecorating."

"Just freshening up the house." Vivienne nodded to Maddie. "I love the desk. But now I need a chair to go with it."

"I have one on order." Maddie picked up her phone and texted. "My sister found it in Paris. It'll be here next week. Although"—she paused in her texting and winked at Vivienne—"you may have to fight Pastor Tom for it."

Vivienne winked back. "I have no doubt I'd win."

Isabel wrinkled her nose. "What would a pastor need with fine furnishings?"

Maddie sent Isabel a frustrated glance. "Just because he's a man of God doesn't mean he can't appreciate fine things. He is, after all, a member of the Charleston Architectural Board with me and Stuart."

Maddie's voice hitched on Stuart's name, and she turned away until Vivienne touched Maddie's arm.

"I know you were friends," Vivienne said to Maddie. "I'm so sorry."

Sick of Maddie's exaggerated grief, Isabel moved to trace her finger over the wood inlays. "Vivienne? Why all the fuss for a house you rarely visit?"

Vivienne glared at Isabel until she lifted her finger. "My next salon will be in Charleston in a few weeks. I'm also hosting the governor's birthday party."

"Hmm." Isabel sat in one of the yellow chintz arm chairs. "I RSVP'd for that event. Are you going, Maddie?"

Maddie glanced at Isabel, and there was no denying the chill in the air didn't just come from the AC. Maddie's glare could freeze oil. "I haven't decided."

"You should come, Maddie." Vivienne opened and closed the desk drawers one at a time. "It'll be good for you."

"I have Susan." Maddie checked her watch. "She should've returned by now."

"She's outside with a butterfly net." Vivienne moved to the window. "My garden needs a child's laughter."

Maddie stood next to Vivienne. "I hope Susan is laughing."

Vivienne put a hand on Maddie's shoulder. "Susan will come out stronger for all of this. No girl needs a weak man for a father. The stronger and more secure the father is in his masculinity, the more confident and powerful the girl becomes in her femininity."

Isabel crossed one leg over the other. "You are the expert in male-female relations."

"Yes." Vivienne gave Isabel a backward glance. "I am."

Seeing how close Maddie and Vivienne appeared sent a rush of heat through Isabel. Why was she always on the outside? "It might be better if you don't go, Maddie. Your husband is bringing his girlfriend."

Maddie kept her gaze on the garden below. "He can bring whoever he wants. Our divorce should be final by then."

"Look at you, all emancipated."

"Isabel." Vivienne turned, her sharp voice cutting through the room's chilled air. "I assume you came for a reason?"

"Yes." Isabel stood, took a deep breath, and put on her brightest smile. She couldn't let petty emotions get in the way of her plans again.

"Excuse me, Vivienne," Maddie said. "I'll meet you downstairs for tea. I want to check on Susan."

Once Maddie left, Vivienne said, "I don't appreciate rudeness."

Isabel clasped her hands in front of her. "Forgive me. I speak my mind and forget that not all women—or men—can handle that."

Vivienne came up so close Isabel could smell her bergamot-tinged perfume. "As one strong woman speaking to another, I'm reminding you that humility and grace are the true source of attractiveness between the sexes. Regardless of how hard one likes to fuck."

Isabel nodded. She'd allowed her temper to take over and that wasn't going to get anything accomplished. "I came to tell you something about your godson."

"Zachariah?" Vivienne led the way downstairs to the drawing room, where the maid had laid out the table with a silver tea service, original blue willow teacups and saucers, sandwiches, and scones. "I wasn't aware you knew each other."

"We don't. Not directly."

Vivienne poured tea for both of them and sat in a Louis XVI chair covered in brown silk decorated with white embroidered flowers. She crossed her legs and pointed to a chair across from her instead of next to her. Upstairs, Vivienne had been annoyed. Downstairs she was guarded. "What do you need to say?"

When Isabel was seated, she stirred the spoon in her teacup. "I'm worried about Zack. He's becoming attached to Allison Pinckney."

"I don't understand." Vivienne sipped her tea. "What business is that of yours?"

"I feel guilty—"

"You should. You carried on an affair with a married man."

Criticism from a woman who made her living off other peoples' affairs? "Since Stuart's death, I understand how much pain I've caused Allison. I believe she's become less stable."

"Hmmm." Vivienne watched Isabel with those eyes that judged everything.

"To your comment earlier about humility and grace." Isabel placed her cup and saucer on a nearby table. "I'm trying to mitigate the damage I've done. I know I've hurt Allison—"

"Do you?" Vivienne tilted her head, and the sunlight hit her diamond earrings, sending prisms around the room.

"Yes." Isabel stood and moved toward the window overlooking the water garden. A tall bronze statue of Hermes appeared to be running away. Off to the side, Maddie sat on a bench with Susan, who was holding purple violets. "The other day Allison and her mother argued at Pirate House. Allison yelled at Rue in public."

"Rue needs a good yelling at."

"Vivienne." Isabel came back to her seat. "I don't think it's a good idea for Zack to get involved with Allison. She's unhappy—"

"With good reason."

"She's depressed." Isabel touched Vivienne's arm. "We're friends, and I don't want to see Zack, or any of the people you care for, get hurt."

Vivienne removed Isabel's hand. "If that were true, you wouldn't be working for Remiel Marigny."

Isabel straightened her shoulders. "What are you talking about?"

Vivienne poured herself another cup of tea. "I'm not stupid, Isabel.

You believe I don't see what's going on, who you work for, the men you fuck"—she took a sip—"Hezekiah's death."

Isabel swallowed hard.

Vivienne placed her cup on the silver tray and stood. "I've known for years that you work for Remiel. I also know how dangerous he is and that his power is only growing."

"I'm not sure—"

Vivienne held up a hand. "Remiel, for some reason, has gone after my godson's Special Forces unit. Now, I admit I don't know much since it's classified, but I do know that whatever Remiel has in play won't stop until he either wins or is defeated."

"Miss Vivienne!" Susan ran into the room holding a butterfly net and wilted flowers and threw herself into Vivienne's arms. "I saw a leprechaun!"

Vivienne kissed Susan on the cheek. "Leprechauns love my koi pond."

Maddie followed, pausing when she saw Isabel. "You're still here?"

Isabel picked up her handbag and stood. "I'm leaving. I'm seeing an old friend." As she passed Maddie, she whispered, "Actually, I'm seeing an old lover."

Maddie gave her a tight smile. "How nice for you."

Isabel glanced at Vivienne, who was now pouring tea for Susan. "He's recently been released from prison so"—Isabel offered a secret smile—"I'm seeing to his *needs*."

Maddie wrinkled her nose. "I don't care."

"Oh." Isabel licked her lips. "I shouldn't tell Alex you said hi?"

Maddie's eyes darkened, and Isabel heard a sharp intake of breath.

Smiling, Isabel went over to Vivienne and bent down to whisper in the older woman's ear, "The Fianna have Emilie. They're using her as leverage in a game against Remiel."

Isabel smiled when Vivienne's face paled and the hand holding her teacup shook.

Susan took Vivienne's arm and said, "Is everything okay, Miss Vivienne?"

Before Isabel could hear the answer, she left the room. As she headed out the front door into the garden and past the spray fountain, she dialed Clayborne.

He answered on the first ring. "I can't find the appendix. Horatio is a ghost. My man is still with the Fianna. And our diggers have dug up nothing but bones."

Dammit. "You may have been right about Allison and her soldier. They're closer than I thought. That makes them a larger threat."

"What do you want to do about it?"

"While you keep looking for Horatio, check out Pastor Tom at Saint Philip's Church. Apparently, the pastor and Stuart were friends. Maybe he'll know something we don't. In the meantime, I'm going to make a call. I think it's time that secret congressional committee knows what Kells's men are doing in Charleston."

Alex folded the tracing paper and shoved it in his back pocket. He'd gotten the apotropaic tracing from Saint Philip's and was walking toward the Charleston Architectural Board building.

The church had been surprisingly deserted. He'd had no trouble getting into the choir loft and taking the rubbings. He wiped his forehead, not sure whether he hated the heat or humidity more. He also had another chore to deal with and decided that calling sooner rather than later was a better plan.

He paused in the shade of a pink crepe myrtle tree and called Nate.

Nate answered on the first ring. "Tell me you're on your way back here."

"Nope. Does Kells know what's going on?"

"Not yet." Nate sighed like a preschooler. "Now he thinks the two of you spent all night cleaning the locker room. Luckily, Kells is distracted by issues with our men in Leedsville prison. I feel awful for saying this, but I'm grateful for prison fights."

Alex unloaded everything that had happened including meeting Aidan, seeing Emilie, and everything he knew about the apotropaic marks. The only thing he left out was the part about Horatio blaming Kells for this clusterfuck. No reason to dig through that worm can.

Nate sighed. "We need to get this sorted ASAP. Any idea where the appendix might be? Or how to find Mercy Chastain?"

"I'm working on a clue." Alex went up the steps of the white building with two levels of porches held up by columns. The gold sign next to the door said *Charleston Architectural Board*. He prayed they had AC. "Just promise me that whatever you do, you won't tell Kells."

CHAPTER 29

Zack kept his hand on Allison's back as they walked into Vivienne's drawing room. After being escorted from Fenwick Hall, Zack had received a call from Vivienne. She wanted to see them immediately, no questions allowed.

Nicholas Trott ran toward the tea table covered with cookies until Susan's voice said, "Nicholas Trott!"

The dog jumped onto Susan, who sat on a sofa near the window. Nicholas Trott rested on her lap with his front legs around her shoulders, as if hugging her. The book she'd been reading fell onto the floor, next to the leash's handle.

"Hi, boy." Susan buried her face in the dog's neck. "Oooooh. You smell like river mud."

Allison dropped her tote bag on one of the chairs surrounding the tea table. "He needs a bath."

Vivienne swept in on high heels, and Maddie followed with a leather portfolio. Vivienne kissed Zack on the cheek and then Allison.

"Susan." Maddie smoothed back her brown hair which had been pulled into a tight bun. "It's time to leave."

Susan, with her head still tucked into Nicholas Trott's scruff, gave a muffled "No."

Allison took Maddie's hand. "Is everything alright?"

Maddie lowered her voice. "Susan is supposed to go to her father's this afternoon, but she doesn't want to go."

"Daddy's girlfriend is a cow," Susan said without lifting her head.

Maddie frowned. "That's not nice."

"That's what Miss Vivienne calls her." Susan sniffled into the dog's fur.

Zack, Allison, and Maddie stared at Vivienne, who threw up her hands. "It may not be nice, but it's true."

Maddie sat next to Susan and rubbed the dog's head. "It may be true, but it doesn't help."

"Nonsense." Vivienne went to the table and poured a cup of tea. "Lying to a child only causes more problems. I learned that the hard way."

Zack knew that comment was directed at him. He'd gone through a period of life—called middle school—when he'd resented Vivienne for what she'd told him about his parents' death. No kid wanted to know that their mentally ill parents had killed themselves, but they also didn't want to believe they'd been murdered.

"I'm still not going." Susan had her arms wrapped so tightly around Nicholas Trott now he began to squirm. "You can't make me."

Zack knelt in front of Susan and drew her hair away from her damp face. "Hey, kiddo. I have an idea. Why don't you and your mom take Nicholas Trott home for a bath and a nap. He's had a busy day and needs to rest before the service. Then, you can bring him to the church. I'm sure your mom can make your dad understand."

Maddie snorted elegantly, but Susan raised her head to ask, "Can we, Mom?"

Maddie rubbed her forehead, then nodded.

Susan took a deep breath and looked at Vivienne. "May I give Nicholas Trott a treat?"

Vivienne picked up a bell from the tea service and rang. "Of course."

Susan got off the couch and released the dog. "Will Mr. Mitchell be at the service?"

"Why?" Zack stood and handed Susan the leash. "Would you like Mr. Mitchell to be there?"

She nodded. "I think he's lonely."

"Then I'll text him and make sure he comes."

Maddie picked up the book from the floor. "Please tell Mr. Mitchell no knives."

Zack tried not to smile. "I'll let him know."

"Mr. Mitchell?" Vivienne handed Allison a cup of tea. "Is that your friend who's staying in one of my guest rooms? Next to your room that doesn't look like it's been slept in at all?"

"Yes, Nénaine." Zack wasn't about to discuss his sleeping arrangements. "Alex has been helping us with things."

"You mean your missing sister?" Vivienne glanced at Maddie. "Yes, I know all about your sister being kidnapped and I told Maddie about it."

He drew in a breath. "*Why?*"

"Because I know Emilie," Maddie said. "I run an antiques shop with my sister who lives in Paris. When we were opening an auction house in New Orleans, I needed a lawyer. Vivienne mentioned your sister, and we became friends."

"You do understand that no one can know about this, right? My sister's life—"

"Zachariah." Vivienne tapped him on the arm. "Maddie is not stupid. And neither am I. Once I heard your sister was missing, *less than an hour ago*, I had a friend go through Emilie's cell phone record, and Maddie was the last person Emilie called. Therefore, I took it upon myself to investigate."

Zack pulled out his phone and texted Alex. Then he reminded Alex about the service and what time to be there. "Maddie? What did you and Emilie talk about?"

"Emilie called me about a project we're working on together. I've had a number of requests recently for decorative iron objects and was worried one was stolen. Emilie knew of a firm in Boston who could help. That's the last I heard from her."

"What's special about iron objects?" Allison asked.

"I'm searching for ironwork wrought in the early seventeen hundreds. Since Stuart and I were both directors on the Charleston Architectural Board, he'd been helping me identify the iron pieces."

Zack glanced at Allison. Maybe that's why the *CAB/ILL* notation had been in Stuart's planner.

Allison took a cookie from the tray and asked Maddie, "Any chance Stuart mentioned Henry Avery's treasure?"

"Unfortunately, no. Too bad you don't have a treasure map."

Zack glared at Vivienne. "I think we need to discuss the idea of operational security."

Vivienne waved, brushing away his concerns.

"Mom?" Susan said with a mouthful of cookie. "Henry Avery didn't like treasure maps. In the pirate ghost stories I've been reading for my summer project, I learned that Henry Avery changed how pirates hid their treasure. He made his men measure things in leagues, he liked ciphers, and he used Poland coordinates to get around."

"Polar coordinates." Zack took a few cookies himself and popped them in his mouth. He was on the edge of starving. "What else did your book say about Henry Avery?"

"Not much." Nicholas Trott pressed up against Susan again, and she rubbed his neck. "Henry Avery was really superstitious. His ship had special witch marks carved into it because he was so afraid of ghosts and curses."

"When one has a treasure worth millions," Vivienne said, "one would be paranoid."

"Susan," Allison said, "do you have any idea where Henry hid his treasure?"

"Henry was too afraid to bury it, so his friend Thomas Toban, another pirate, helped him hide it with a fifolet."

"Ridiculous," Vivienne said.

"What's a fifolet?" Maddie asked.

"It's a pirate ghost legend," Allison said. "When pirates buried their treasure, they'd kill a crewman and bury his body on top of the chest. This ensured the murdered man's spirit would bind to the treasure and become a ferocious guard. If the location was disturbed, these ghosts would manifest as blue lights. When treasure hunters saw a blue light—a *fifolet*—they'd follow it to a remote area, where the spirit would kill them."

"If Susan is right," Vivienne said, "if Henry Avery was smart enough to steal the world's largest treasure and bold enough to hide himself in plain sight in Charleston, he wouldn't have done something as ordinary as bury his treasure."

A maid appeared with a silver tray and a rawhide bone. "Master Trott's snack."

"Thank you!" Susan gave the bone to Nicholas Trott. "Can we go now, Mom? Mrs. Pickles is waiting and Nicholas Trott needs his bath and his nap."

After saying their goodbyes, Maddie and Susan left with the dog.

Vivienne poured herself another cup of tea. "Zachariah, I assume you have a plan to save your sister?"

Zack squeezed Allison's hand before sitting. He wasn't a tea drinker, but he did love scones. "First, we need to find the appendix, figure out how to decipher it without the Pirate's Grille, and get the treasure. Or we figure out what happened to Mercy Chastain and discover the treasure. Either way, we trade the treasure for Emilie."

That didn't sound so bad. It wasn't until one tried to define the details that one realized the entire situation was a clusterfuck.

Vivienne sipped her tea and raised a single eyebrow.

"We've found apotropaic marks, but I'm not sure what they mean." Allison told Vivienne how Stuart had been looking for the apotropaic marks and what they'd been doing for the past few days—except for the private things.

Zack didn't stop Allison from giving away all of their intel because there was no point. The big a-ha moment of the day? Vivienne didn't blink when Allison told her about the Prince and the Fianna. Clearly, Vivienne ran in circles far beyond Zack's imagining. Then again, Vivienne had always kept her business separate from her life. If she knew Remiel Marigny, then she'd know about the Prince.

What irritated him was that he'd never realized it before.

Vivienne peered at them over her teacup. "Do you have any clues to the location of the appendix or Mercy or the treasure?"

"One. Emilie mentioned a bell tower in a city of bell towers." Zack sat back and closed his eyes. "I have no idea what to do next."

Allison took his hand and he opened his eyes to meet her gaze. She was so quickly becoming his touchstone he knew he couldn't live without her. He even wondered if he could leave his men and start his life over—again—in Virginia.

Vivienne went to a desk near a picture window. "I know where you can start. An invite-only restaurant called the Belltower. It's on the second floor of a nondescript building in the French Quarter of New Orleans."

She wrote something on a piece of paper and handed it to Zack. "A man's life depends on your discretion, Zachariah. Talk to him, but don't allow yourself to be followed."

Zack stared at the address and name she'd written. He didn't know the man, but he knew this street. It wasn't far from Vivienne's mansion. Not the one he grew up in. The one where she held her salons.

"Zachariah, I didn't used to care who won this war between the Prince and Remiel. But now I know Remiel was responsible for what happened to your men—"

"Wait!" Zack stood, his clenched fists pressed against his thighs. "How could you know what happened to my men?"

"Almost three months ago, Stuart told me his problems. I knew about him and Isabel." Vivienne nodded toward Allison. "Yes, dear, I did try to talk him out of the affair. But he believed himself to be besotted."

Allison put down her teacup. "You don't think he was besotted?"

Vivienne scoffed elegantly. "He was lonely. While a woman's greatest need is to be desired, a man's is to be loved."

Zack squeezed Allison's shoulder. "What does Stuart's affair have to do with my men?"

"I'm not sure. All I know is Stuart was afraid. He'd discovered Isabel worked for Remiel and had begun to realize the danger he'd put Allison in and came to me for help. I'd heard rumors that the Prince and Remiel had had dealings, so I asked a friend to contact the Prince."

Now it was Zack's turn to raise an eyebrow. "You asked a friend to call the Prince?"

She clasped her hands in front of her. "Yes."

"Because reaching out to a man who leads a secret army of assassins isn't suicide."

"Not for me. The Prince—three different Princes—have attended my salons in the past."

Zack sat down because his legs wouldn't hold him anymore. "Why didn't you tell me this last night?"

"Last night I didn't know that Emilie had been taken."

He hated it when she was right. "What happened?"

"The Prince met with Stuart in private, here in this house. Stuart made a deal with the Fianna. After Stuart left, the Prince stayed for a nightcap."

"You drank with the Prince?" *Please God, let that be all that happened.*

"Yes, and that's when he told me about you. The boy I raised on my own who has kept me out of his life for years."

"That's not fair. I'm a Special Forces soldier. It's not like I can talk about what I do—did—at the dinner table."

"Perhaps not." Vivienne picked up her teacup again. It was as if she drank it just to keep her hands busy. "The Prince told me about the Wakhan Corridor Massacre, the ambush in the Pamir River Valley. The two A-teams sent to POW camps in the bowels of Afghanistan. How you and your men spent two years trying to rescue them. Then the convictions of these two A-teams, their imprisonment, and the dishonorable discharges for the rest of the unit."

"And?"

Vivienne lifted her chin. "The Prince also told me you refused to lead your men into the Pamir River Valley. That you weren't fit to be a Special Forces Officer. He believes you're a coward."

"What do you believe, Nénaine?"

"What I believe doesn't matter. It's what you believe about yourself that's important."

Zack stood to pace the room. It was either that or hit something. "Why would the Prince tell you any of this?"

Vivienne raised an elegant eyebrow. "You know what I do, Zachariah."

"You're a madam. A high-end one, sure. But—"

"I do *not* manage prostitutes," she said with enough disgust in her voice that he took a step back. "The men and women who attend my salons come voluntarily and only by my invitation. Those who seek my favor will never be invited.

"The men and women I choose are always equal in wealth and power and social status. My guests are from every country, and of all races and religions and political beliefs. The women pick their lovers, not the other way around. There is no coercion or payment between parties, and I never invite anyone under the age of twenty-six."

"Huh." He crossed his arms. He'd not known about the age restriction.

"My guests, both male and female, pay the same entrance fee and are guaranteed access to others with power, money, and influence."

"Why?" Zack asked.

"Because those with power, money, and influence appreciate others with the same traits. How do you think your grandfather became governor of Louisiana? How do you think I was able to hide your parents' codependent mental illness for so long? The fact that your mother killed your father and hanged herself? How do you think I was able to raise two orphaned children in a protected household and send them to the best private schools without any hint of scandal?"

"I don't—" He ran a hand over his head. "I never thought about it."

Now Vivienne stood to meet his gaze. "For all your experience with death and destruction, you're naive about the world. I offer a safe place for the powerful, wealthy, and influential to meet, deal, and fuck. That includes the Prince."

"And his warriors?"

"No. I don't issue invitations to foot soldiers. But at the Prince's behest, I have offered invitations to Remiel...which he's turned down."

Zack narrowed his gaze. "You told me you'd never met Remiel."

"I haven't. That doesn't mean I don't know who he is and what he's capable of. Information is my currency." She came over to touch his chin. "Hezekiah Usher was my friend. He was also my business partner. He had a small stake in my salons, and I had one in the Usher Society. I don't appreciate it when men like Remiel kill my friends."

Zack held up the address. "This man in New Orleans? Is he a friend?"

"An acquaintance. That man used to work for Remiel until he came to Hezekiah for asylum. Hezekiah and I helped him escape Remiel's wrath, although Remiel doesn't know my part in that yet. I'd like to keep it that way."

Zack leaned a shoulder against the window and watched two birds play in a long fountain with four sprays. "Remiel killed Hezekiah because he helped this man escape?"

"That's one of the reasons." Vivienne touched his shoulder. "Go to New Orleans, Zachariah. Find the appendix, dig up that treasure, and save your sister."

"It's a twelve-hour drive each way. I have less than two days left."

"Then it's lucky for you I just inherited a plane."

He met her brown gaze that reminded him of his sister. "You're joking."

"Compliments of the Usher Society." Vivienne found her cell phone on the desk and dialed. "I'll have the plane ready for you at a private airfield on John's Island. You can leave after Stuart's service."

She held the phone to her ear and looked at her watch. "We don't have much time. You two should get ready."

Zack took Allison's hand and pulled her up. She hadn't said anything during Vivienne's confession. "Are you alright?"

She smiled but it didn't reach her green eyes.

"Zachariah?" Vivienne put a hand over the phone. "May I speak with you alone for a moment?"

"I'll wait for you outside." Allison touched Zack's shoulder and nodded to Vivienne. "Thank you for the tea."

Once Allison left the room and Vivienne hung up, she said, "I'll bring the details of the flight with me to the service."

"Thank you."

"There's one more thing." She went into the foyer and paused at the front door. From the side windows, Zack watched Allison wait near the fountain outside the front door. "Allison is a strong woman, but she's also fragile. Fragile women fear being broken and run before they shatter. I know you love her. You've loved her since you were in college."

It wasn't as if it was a big secret. "And?"

"I don't want you to get your heart broken."

"I'm a grown man."

"Who's in love with a woman who can't let go of the guilt surrounding her dead husband. She doesn't feel like she served him well in life. Now that she knows he'd chosen another, she may try to prove to herself and others that she loved him, that she was worthy of being his wife."

Zack crossed his arms over his chest. "What are you talking about?"

Vivienne touched his wrist, near the eyes of the dragon tattoo she'd been against. "This is my job, dear. I read men. I read women. I know the difference between lust and love. While Allison is attracted to you—of that there's no doubt—I don't know if she loves you."

"Again, Nénaine, I'm a grown man. I've spent my adult life in hostile countries getting shot at. I think I can manage a broken heart."

"How many women have you dated seriously?"

"I brought a girlfriend home for Thanksgiving once."

"She left the next morning." When he stepped back, she asked, "How many women have you fucked?"

He exhaled loudly. He didn't want to discuss this with her, yet she was the closest thing he'd ever had to a parent. He knew she was worried about him. "A lot, actually."

He just didn't like to think about all the women he'd given himself to in a desperate attempt to forget Allison.

"Don't hand your heart to a woman who doesn't know what to do with it."

He kissed her on the cheek and, for the hell of it, pulled her into a hug. "You don't have to worry about me. I'm well trained and hard to kill."

"But I do." She wrapped her arms around his waist. "Some wounds are worse than death."

He let go of her, surprised to see her eyes full of tears. In his entire life, he'd only ever seen her cry twice—the first time at his mother's funeral, the second time when she and Emilie pinned his Special Forces tab onto his uniform. Vulnerability was not a trait Vivienne fostered. "I'll see you at the service?"

She nodded and opened the door. "You should know..."

Uh-oh. "Know what?"

"I asked Berlin's Tailoring to send clothes to Allison's house." Vivienne motioned to his jeans and boots. "When I see you next, I expect you'll be properly dressed."

ᔕ

Alex stood in front of the computer terminal in the Charleston Architectural Board building. Apparently, one had to be a member to log in and search the catalog.

The building, as well as being blessed with the world's strongest AC, had three floors. The first was a bookstore, the second held reading rooms, the third contained the library. Other than the teenager handling the cash register on the first floor, there was no one around to help.

"Nicholas Trott!" Susan's voice rang out in the hallway. "Wait!"

A moment later, Nicholas Trott ran in and jumped on Alex's legs. Alex rubbed his scruff. "Whoa, boy."

Susan appeared, out of breath. "Nicholas Trott! Where—oh. Hi, Mr. Mitchell!"

"Hi, Susan. What are you doing here?"

She grabbed the dog's leash. "My mom is a member of the board and had to pick up some papers."

"Susan?" Maddie appeared in the doorframe in a pink A-line dress and flat sandals, her hair pulled back into a braided bun. "Mr. Mitchell. I didn't expect to see you here."

"I'm just helping Zack and Allison with...things."

"Henry Avery's treasure?" Susan asked.

Alex tilted his head at the little girl. "How could you know that?"

"Remember, Mr. Mitchell"—she lowered her voice to a whisper—"I listen."

"Oh." He smiled at her. "Right."

"Actually, Mr. Mitchell..." Maddie paused just beyond the ray of sun that cut across the mahogany table and settled on the polished wood floor. "Vivienne told me about Emilie and how Zack and Allison have to find the treasure."

So much for operational security. "How does Vivienne know?"

"I'm not sure, but Zack and Allison confirmed it." Maddie motioned toward the computer while Susan and the dog crawled beneath the table. "I hope you don't mind my saying, but you look lost."

"I am." He ran his hands over his head. After telling Maddie about the CAB/ILL notation in Stuart's planner, he said, "Allison thinks Stuart requested a book on interlibrary loan."

"It's possible." She laid her purse on the table and came over next to him. "May I?"

He stepped back. "Please."

"A few months ago"—Maddie clicked on the login button—"I found Stuart here doing research. Since he couldn't remember his password, I let him use mine."

After Maddie logged in, she clicked on the Recent Transactions button. "He didn't tell me what he was looking for, but at the time I had no reason to ask."

Alex glanced at her profile. Her long eyelashes made tiny shadows on her cheeks. Her lips were red, but not too red. When she breathed, her breasts rose just enough to show the outline of a lace bra.

And she smelled like fresh air and lilacs.

He wiped his forehead and leaned forward to put his arms on the raised table. He didn't want her to see his very physical reaction.

She squinted at the screen. "Stuart requested a book titled *Notorious Pirates and their Secrets, 1650–1781*. According to the log, Stuart checked it out and it hasn't been returned."

"Shit." He looked at Maddie. "Sorry."

Susan and the dog crawled out from under the table. "Mom, Nicholas Trott needs his bath and his nap."

Maddie glanced at her watch and nodded. "You're right."

"I appreciate your help, Maddie." Alex swallowed at the realization that that was the first time he'd said her name aloud.

As if realizing that as well, her face reddened. "You're welcome. I hope you find it."

"*Mom*," Susan said from the doorway, clutching the dog's leash.

Maddie paused on her way out. "Are you going to Stuart's service later today?"

"Yes." He didn't want to, but Zack had asked him, so he'd agreed.

She took Susan's hand and said, "I'll see you there."

When she left, Alex sank into a chair and covered his eyes with one arm. While he was annoyed at the dead-end, he had another more important concern. His intense attraction to a still-married woman with an almost-eight-year-old daughter.

And if his brother—or Isabel—found out? That wouldn't be good for any of them.

CHAPTER 30

ALLISON STOOD BENEATH THE SHOWER AND LET THE WARM WATER run over her hair.

Vivienne knows the Prince and owns the private plane that belonged to Hezekiah Usher? And Stuart went to her for help?

Allison closed her eyes and leaned back against the cold tile wall. They were running out of time. To find the treasure. To save Emilie. To love Zack.

She'd learned so much about Zack in the past few days—things he'd hinted at but never shared—and she wasn't sure which shocked her most: the truth about his parents' death or what had happened to him and his men. POW camps and daring rescues seemed like something out of a horrible movie, yet it was all true. And it had all happened to Zack.

Zack had shared some of his childhood during college, but Vivienne's descriptions added Technicolor to the memories.

Allison heard the glass door move and opened her eyes. Zack stood in front of her completely naked. His long hair hung around his shoulders. This was the first time she'd seen the muscles cut across his chest, the thickness of his arms, the dark hair sprinkled on his legs, the black line that started below his belly button and led down to his...hand holding his full erection.

He reached past her to increase the temp and flow of the water. The movement brought him close enough for her nipples to rub against his pecs. Heat, not from the water or the day, flooded her body. Her lower stomach cramped and her breaths came out in short, choppy bursts.

She was supposed to be getting ready for her dead husband's service, yet here she was, desperate for another man's touch. For another man's taste and smell. For another man's hardness deep inside her.

Zack reached for her breasts. His warm, wet hands raised them gently, one at a time, to his lips. He kissed and sucked and licked until she was sure his hands on her breasts were the only things holding her up.

"*Zack?*" Had he even heard her plea? Between his rough breaths and the sound of water hitting their skin, she wasn't sure.

"Allison." His voice was just as fractured as hers. "This isn't the best timing, but I need you. Fuck, how I *need* you."

She needed him too, in a way that demanded faith over reason, love over logic. In a way that defied expectations and beliefs and even words. His gaze drew her close, demanding things she wasn't sure she could give. Last night, in the dark, she'd allowed him to remind her of everything she'd been missing in her life. But now? He clearly wanted more than consent. He wanted more than her body. When he pulled her against his hard chest, when he held her head at just the right angle, when his lips demanded a response, she knew he wanted her heart.

His lips traced her cheek, down her neck, and he murmured, "I can't lose you again."

She tangled her hands in his hair and drew his head up so she could kiss him. For the first time, she took the initiative. She set the pace, demanded the speed, and drew herself into his body so the water had to wash over them instead of between them.

His thigh parted her legs, and with his hands on her bottom, she wrapped her legs around his waist. His erection pressed against her sex and she moaned. While she wanted him inside her, she refused to end the kiss. Over and over again, holding his head still, she kissed him the way she'd always dreamed of kissing him—like he was hers, and she was his. As if they belonged to each other. As if they loved each other.

Finally, he broke the kiss by pulling back his head to stare at her with those amazing brown eyes. "I have to know that you need me as much as I need you."

She pressed her forehead against his and whispered, "Yes."

"Say it." He closed his eyes. "Please, say it."

"I need you too."

She moved her hips higher, but he held her in place and swallowed hard. "Once I start, I won't be able to stop."

"Once you start, I won't want you to finish."

"*Fuuuck.*" He drew back his hips, then drove deep inside her, pushing her back against the tile wall. He began a rhythm that pushed and pulled until she could feel all of him in all of her.

She clenched her legs around his hips. He raised his head, allowing the water to fall over his face, and growled. She tried to adjust the speed, but since he held her entire weight, she was at his mercy.

"Zack? Please. *Harder.*"

His response came in a powerful pistoning motion. He'd moved his hands to hold her higher, and now his fingers dug into her waist while she clung to his shoulders. With her face buried in his neck, the water spraying over them, and his masculine smell of bay rum and sex, the tightening began in her toes, and by the time she felt the heat in her womb, she was riding wave after wave of pleasure. Her entire body stilled as the intensity took her breath away.

Her climax happened so suddenly she wasn't sure Zack was even aware. He was in the midst of his own final moment, his movements faster and faster until he closed his eyes, bared his teeth, and whispered her name. "*Allison.*"

She held on while he continued to press into her, as if emptying every bit of himself inside her was the most important thing he'd ever done in his life. When he stopped, she found herself still up against the shower wall, legs around his waist, his lips against hers.

She had the vague realization that it must've taken a huge amount of physical strength for him to have held her up so long, to have made love to her so passionately, and to keep her in place while he found his breath—and she found hers. With their lips—no, their bodies—so intertwined it was hard to figure out whose breath was whose.

"Sweet heaven's biscuits," he murmured against her lips. "I'll never be able to walk again."

She shut off the shower, not sure when the hot water had turned cold. "I know the feeling."

He raised his head to look at her. "I've never seen anything as beautiful as you."

"Probably because you never look in the mirror."

He opened the shower door, swung her around, and dropped her feet to the floor. Thank goodness for the fluffy bath mat because goose bumps were forming on her arms and legs. He found a towel and wrapped her up. Then he found another for her hair. The entire time, not only was he wet and naked, but he didn't appear cold.

"How do you never get cold?" she asked as he dried her arms with a hand towel.

He tossed the towel into the hamper and then began to dry himself off with a bath towel. "I'm always hot."

Yes, he is. She pretended to dry her face with the edge of her hair towel while he wiped off his arms and legs. It was like God had chiseled Zack's muscles and tendons into perfect proportion in order to build the ideal masculine form. Tanned skin over hard muscular curves, wide shoulders centered on top of a narrow waist, thighs and calves Michelangelo's *David* would've given up his slingshot for. And covering that perfection? A beautiful dusting of dark hair that added the perfect amount of masculinity to an already incredibly virile man.

Then there was his dragon tattoo, long dark hair, and intense brown eyes: the three attributes of her own personal wild man.

When he was dry, and before a sudden attack of shyness could kick in, he picked her up and carried her to the bedroom. He'd already started another fire, pulled down the covers, and now placed her on the bed. His gun lay on the bedside table. The shotgun was propped against the wall.

He sat next to her, on the edge that sagged beneath his weight. "We have a few hours before the service. From there, we're leaving for the airport."

With one hand, she traced the hairs on his arm. "We should probably take a nap."

"Probably." He leaned his elbows onto his bare thighs and stared at the floor. "I feel so guilty, like all of this is wasted time while my sister is a prisoner."

Allison touched his shoulder. She didn't take his frustration the wrong way. The fact was there wasn't much for them to do until they got on that plane. "We'll go to New Orleans, find the treasure, and save your sister."

He stood and leaned an arm on the mantel above the fireplace. He'd also drawn the blinds to close off the room from the midday sun. The only light came from the flickering flames. Shadows danced around, making him appear larger. She'd never known a man so at ease with himself—his body and his physical strength. Just the fact that he stood in front of a fire stark naked amazed her.

"I can't fail, Allison," Zack said in a low voice. "Not again."

She got out of bed and dropped her towels. She found her short silk robe on her dressing chair and slipped it on. Without tying it closed, she went over to him and pressed her front against his back, her breasts against his muscles. She wrapped her arms around his waist and laid her head against his shoulder. "We won't."

He covered her hands with his and shuddered. "I need to tell you something."

She stood on her tiptoes to kiss the back of his neck. "What?"

"I love you."

❧

I am an idiot.

Zack sat in a wing chair by the fireplace and pulled Allison onto his lap. He stared at the fire because he couldn't look at her. He'd admitted his feelings and she hadn't said a word.

What the hell were you thinking?

I wasn't thinking. I was feeling. That's the problem.

"Zack?" Allison shifted and he felt her cold, wet hair against his warm skin.

"Yes?" The word burst from his chest on a giant exhale because he had, up until that moment, been holding his breath.

"I'm sorry."

He swallowed hard. "You have no reason to apologize." He reached for the comb on the table nearby. "Let me comb your hair before it dries."

She pulled away to meet his gaze, her green eyes shining in the firelight. Although it was still light outside, he'd drawn the blinds more for the intimacy than the privacy. Here in the shadowed room, they were truly alone. If he could push away all of the outside worries, he could allow himself to imagine what it would be like to live in this room forever—just him, her, the enormous bed, and a crackling fire.

"Did you grow your hair for that rescue mission?" She touched his chin, then his hair that hung around his shoulders. He was so used to wearing it back all the time, it always surprised him to see how long it'd gotten.

"Yes. I started growing it the night our A-teams were ambushed in the Pamir River Valley and sent to the POW camp. I was part of a team that went ahead to gather intel. Because my skin is darker and my hair is black, I blend in better."

"Do you speak the local languages?"

"Some of them." He kissed her nose and slid her down to the floor. He tried to ignore her silk lavender robe that barely covered her breasts and framed her beautiful naked body. But his physical reaction was impossible to hide. "Linguistics and history major. Remember?"

She smiled and turned so he could start combing her hair. "My hair is thick. Don't worry about yanking it."

"Yes, ma'am."

"Zack?" Her head jerked back as he dragged the wide-toothed comb through the blond tangles. "How many of your men are in prison?"

"Ten, including one of our commanders who wasn't supposed to be on the ground the night of the ambush but..."

"But what?"

"One of my buddies, Nate Walker, was leading the operation. His plan included two teams, his and mine."

She turned sideways while he continued to undo the tangles. Her profile was outlined by the firelight. "What Vivienne said was true? You should've been leading that second team? You should've been ambushed and sent to a POW camp? You should be in prison right now?"

And because regret and guilt tasted bitter, he almost gagged on his own spit. "Yes."

What must she think of him?

It couldn't be as terrible as what he thought of himself.

He kept combing while she stared into the fireplace. She'd pulled up her knees and circled them with her arms. Her robe floated around her body, pooling on the floor next to her naked thighs, and she barely moved as he tugged her hair.

And again, she stayed silent. Was it because she couldn't form the words? Had no idea what to say? Was she embarrassed by his confession?

"It wasn't your fault, Zack."

"You sound like Nate."

She rested her chin on her knees. "Nate is right."

"Nate is wrong. Nate is also lucky. He should be in prison, but... things happened and he was released." The comb's teeth caught a knot and she winced. But she didn't ask him to stop.

"Why didn't you go with Nate and your team that night?"

"I asked to stay behind at the command post because I was waiting for a personal phone call. Another man offered to take my place, said he needed field time." Zack's laugh reeked of self-condemnation. "He said he was tired of sitting behind a desk. Since the men on my team trusted this officer with their lives—especially since he'd trained most of us—everyone was happy. He got to leave the tent; I got to wait for a call. The operation was only supposed to last twelve hours. Kells, our commander, signed off on the entire thing."

"Did you ever get the phone call?"

"I did." When he didn't continue, she turned to look at him, one arm draping across his knees while her breasts pressed against his bare legs. "It was my fiancée."

Allison's eyes widened and he heard her sharp intake of breath.

"Yes, I had a fiancée. She'd been trying to reach me for weeks and I'd gotten a message she was going to call again that night."

"The night of the operation."

He nodded. "Like I said, the men were fine with my staying behind. In fact, I think they saw what I couldn't."

"What's that?"

"She'd been trying to break up with me."

Allison wrinkled her nose. "Who'd ever break up with you?"

He reached down to cup her face gently. "I can't blame her. We hardly ever saw each other, and when we did, I was always distracted."

Thinking about you.

Allison rested her cheek on his knee, and he ran his fingers through her damp strands. "I had no idea you had a fiancée."

Because I didn't want you to know.

"How did you meet her?"

"She was a war correspondent. I met her when she was embedded with a unit we were supporting. Things between us got intense quickly, and we understood the life the other led. I was lonely. Getting engaged to someone who understood my job and its requirements seemed like the right thing. Yet all my buddies knew from the start that it was the wrong thing. They told me, and I ignored them."

"Do you think your buddy who led your team made up that story about wanting to be in the field so you could take that call?"

"It's possible." And didn't that just make the guilt so much worse.

"Why did your friends think your engagement was the wrong thing?"

"They knew..."

She squeezed his knee. "Knew what?"

"They knew she wasn't you."

Allison turned until she was kneeling in front of him. Her blond hair hung over her shoulders in long damp curls. Her green eyes shimmered with unshed tears. "Zack, I'm not the woman you believe me to be. That girl drowned when she was eleven."

He held her face again, this time less gently. "That's not true. I've spent days with you, and do you know what I've seen? A woman who remembers her students' names even though it's been years since they've sat in her classroom. A woman whose dog is so beloved he has autograph days and his own calendar.

"When I watch you walk through this city, I see a woman who is part of something larger, a woman who cares about the people—including mimes—she lives and works with, a woman who worries so much about the reputation of her ancestor who lived three hundred years earlier that she's made it her life's work to tell Mercy Chastain's story. You've even turned down an amazing career opportunity to find Mercy. Hell, you even protect her ghost by telling us to ignore her."

A tear fell and traced the curve of Allison's cheek. "How do you do that?"

"Do what?"

"Make me feel loved and cherished when I can't even…" Her voice broke and she looked away. "When I can't give you what you want."

"Have I told you what I want?"

"You've told me how you feel."

Yes, he had. "Did I ask you if you feel the same?"

She shook her head.

"I didn't ask you how you feel because I know. I know how deeply you love. And I know from that kiss seven years ago that you love me—even if you can't say it."

"I may never be able to say it."

He lowered his hands until he held her breasts. "Then we're going to have to figure out another way for you to show me."

She licked her lips. "Do you still keep in touch with her? Your ex-fiancée?"

"No." Zack opened his legs and pulled her body in closer. "I never wanted her, or any other woman, more than I wanted you."

She ran her fingers over his thighs, running her nails over the tops and using her fingertips on the more tender, inside skin. "I have no right to be jealous."

"Trust me, sweetheart"—Zack smiled wide as he dropped the robe off her shoulders—"your jealousy is a good thing."

As her fingers trailed along his thighs, up the outside, over the top, and down the insides, he relaxed into the chair and closed his eyes. For once it felt good not to have to control everything, not to have to make the decisions that left someone dead or in prison.

When her fingers paused, he opened his eyes to see her watching him. Gently, she reached for his cock and held it between her palms. Slowly, oh so slowly, her fingers closed around his shaft and she began an up-and-down movement that sent heat from his balls to his heart. His toes clenched and his calf muscles tightened. He spread his legs, planted his feet on the floor, and gripped the armrests.

Her eyelids lowered as if she were contemplating something. It wasn't until her tongue traced the head of his cock that he realized what she was doing.

Fuuuuuck. Her mouth closed over him, and he threw his head back. Between her hands pumping and her mouth sucking, he felt like his entire body was going to short-circuit and explode into an electrical firestorm. His arm muscles began to spasm, probably because he was about to rip the arms off the chair, and his hips moved involuntarily. Up and down, meeting the rhythm she set, he drove himself into her mouth, deeper and harder than he wanted to—but he was so beyond any kind of control, he couldn't help himself.

To save the chair, he grabbed her hair. He didn't want to take control, but the contractions in his lower stomach took over and his balls tightened and rose. He pushed and pulled, driving in and out of her mouth, until he was almost at the point of no return—when he stopped himself. "*Allison.*"

Was that his voice? The one that sounded like Darth Vader?

He pulled her head up, releasing his cock, to look into her green eyes. He didn't want her proving anything to him, didn't want her to do this because of insecurities over a woman whose name he could barely remember. In fact, he didn't want her to do this at all. If he was going to come inside her, he wanted her to come with him. Wanted to watch the joy on her face when they climaxed together.

She touched her lips. "Is anything wrong?"

Now it was time for a hoarse laugh. "Wrong? Oh, hell no. It's just that I want...this."

A moment later, she was on her back next to the fireplace, and he was between her legs, his cock deep in her core. He was driving and bucking like a man out of control. Sucking her nipples, kissing her lips, holding her thighs open so he could fill her so completely he touched her womb.

Her hair spread out on the white rug, her eyes closed, her lips red and bruised from his kisses. She wrapped her legs around his waist and raised her hips, meeting him thrust for thrust. When she arched her back and cried out his name, he let go of what little self-control he had left and released everything he had into her over and over again, until his toes curled and his arm muscles protested from holding his own weight.

When he felt her last gasps, he collapsed and used his elbows so he wouldn't crush her. He still lay between her spread legs, his half-erect cock buried inside her, his breath on her forehead. He'd never get enough of her. Not even if he spent every hour of every day, for the rest of his life, making love to her.

"Zack." She nibbled his ear and wrapped her arms around his shoulders. "I'll never get enough of this. Never get enough of you."

"I feel the same way." He withdrew and picked her up to carry her to the bed. After adding another log to the fire, lowering the AC temp to compensate, and setting the alarm clock, he crawled in next to her. Even though she was already asleep, he pulled her into his arms and dragged the blankets over them. Just as he was about to drift off, his phone buzzed.

He almost threw it against the wall. Instead, he checked the text, then wished he hadn't. It was a text from Nate to both Alex and Zack.

> *Kells received a phone call. He knows you're in Charleston and he's furious. He wants you both home. Now.*

CHAPTER 31

Zack parked in front of Saint Philip's church, and Allison waited until he opened her door before getting out. She adjusted the skirt of her black linen dress and slipped on her black sweater. It was seven p.m. and the church bells rang on cue.

Zack watched the area around him, always searching and surveying. She knew he wore his weapon in a leg holster and had a knife hidden on his body.

She took his arm and let him lead her into the churchyard. Another surprise this afternoon? Zack was wearing a dark gray suit, white shirt, and a blue silk tie, and even had on new leather dress shoes, courtesy of Vivienne. Allison would never tell Vivienne, but Zack had fussed like a three-year-old. Everything was too tight, too constricting, too itchy.

She squeezed his arm. "You look wonderful."

"I'm hot."

She was going to respond with a flirtatious *yes you are*, but then she saw the somberly dressed people entering the church. What kind of woman had sex with an incredibly hot man—*her wild man*—and then went to her dead husband's memorial? She felt like a character within a play. And not a Broadway musical. More like an epic tragedy where everyone suffered until they died at the end.

Clouds covered the afternoon sky, casting shadows around the churchyard stuffed with old trees, new wildflowers, and hundreds of tombs.

"Your mother's here." Zack pointed at Rue, in a long black skirt topped with a black lace camisole and matching sweater. "With your uncle Fenwick. Still in combat pants."

Allison squinted at the couple. From the way Rue's hands and mouth were moving and how Fenwick's eyebrows pulled together, they appeared to be arguing. "Let's go inside before they—"

Rue waved and headed over, dragging Fenwick. When she stopped a foot away, she nodded. "Lovely dress, Petal."

Allison gripped Zack's arm. "Thank you."

After a moment of awkward silence, Rue took Fenwick's arm and they turned toward the church. "Petal, I'll save you a seat."

Heat flooded Allison's body and Zack covered her hand.

"Miss Allison!" Susan, in a sailor dress and white sandals, ran through the iron gates separating the churchyard from the street. Nicholas Trott followed with Maddie holding his leash. "Nicholas Trott slept with Mrs. Pickles on my bed for two hours!"

Maddie handed the leash to Susan. "Why don't you take him inside? Pastor Tom has a special place set up for Nicholas Trott to sit."

"Thank you for watching him, Maddie." Allison walked between Maddie and Zack. "Would you mind taking Nicholas Trott tonight?"

Maddie held Allison's hand. "Of course not."

"Allison?" Zack touched her arm. "I'll meet you and Maddie inside."

Allison looked behind her and saw Alex striding up the sidewalk. "Alright."

Zack kissed her cheek and left to meet Alex.

"What do you know of Alex?" Maddie took Allison's arm.

"Not much. Alex went to Ranger School with Zack and now they work together in Savannah. Why?"

"Just curious." They stopped in the back of the church. Everyone was seated. Susan sat on the left side, near a blue pillow that'd been set up for Nicholas Trott.

Lawrence stood in the front, pointing Allison toward the first row on the right, next to Rue and Fenwick. Maddie sat with Susan, leaving Allison to walk down the aisle alone. As she reached the front, she noticed one other person sitting in her row. *Isabel.*

ᖫ

Zack waited for Alex, and once he pulled the apotropaic tracings from his back pocket and handed them to Zack, they returned to the church. They'd both received Nate's text ordering them back to Savannah and agreed to ignore it.

"Nice suit," Alex said.

"Fuck you." Zack adjusted his too-tight tie. "Any idea how Kells found out what we're doing?"

"Nope."

Zack stepped into the church and saw Allison in the front, sitting next to Rue, Fenwick, and...Isabel?

Fuck.

Alex moved a stack of red hymnals and planted himself in the last row. Zack followed. He and Allison hadn't talked about where he'd sit. While he wanted to support her, he wasn't sure it was appropriate for her lover to sit next to her at her dead husband's memorial.

As if reading his thoughts, Vivienne glanced back from her third-row seat and nodded, probably approving his clothing. Years ago, when Vivienne pushed the benefits of the corporate life over the soldier's life, one of his reasons for choosing a rifle instead of a law book was the wardrobe. He hated suits.

The clouds outside filtered the sun, filling the church with an eerie light. Distant thunder rumbled, heralding another summer storm. Since the church doors were still open, the scents of damp earth and ozone filled the room. Dusk was moving into night.

A photo of Stuart had been placed on an easel at the front of the church, and Lawrence paced near it.

Something was wrong.

Finally, Lawrence went to the podium. "We're waiting for Pastor Tom. In the meantime, I'd like to say some words about my brother."

After a few anecdotes extolling Stuart's propensity for numbers, the choir in the loft sang a song. Zack pretended to sing, and Alex leaned forward, hands clasped.

When the song ended, Lawrence spoke again. "I apologize for this unusual situation. We still can't locate Pastor Tom. While we wait, I'd like to introduce Isabel Rutledge."

Alex looked at Zack and mouthed, *What the fuck?*

Zack shrugged. He had no idea what was going on.

Isabel stood behind the pulpit in a dark purple skirt and suit jacket that fit her curves perfectly. Even her ridiculously high-heeled shoes had been dyed to match. Her necklace sparkled in the candlelight: Allison's engagement brooch.

"Thank you, Lawrence, for letting me speak today." Isabel took a letter out of an envelope. "I wanted to share something with you all, something that means a great deal to me and something I hope will ease your grief. Despite the fact that Stuart died so young, he died a happy, fulfilled man."

"Uh-oh," Alex whispered. "This can't be good."

Zack agreed but short of pulling a fire alarm—which he considered—he wasn't sure what to do. He could see the back of Allison's head. She'd twisted her blond hair into a braided bun and added crystal daisy hairpins to keep the stray hairs in place.

"My dearest Isabel…" Isabel's voice, both polished and sophisticated, wavered with emotion as she read a love letter Stuart had written her. Unfortunately, the letter veered off into private territory that made the congregation murmur.

When she finished, she folded up the letter. The congregation and choir had, apparently, been shocked into silence. Zack sat in his seat, horrified, stunned, and heartbroken on Allison's behalf. Stuart's affair had just been made public in the most awful way.

"Isabel is a monster," Alex whispered.

So true, brother. So. Fucking. True.

Before Isabel left the podium, Detective Waring strode into the church and down the aisle. In jeans, white collared shirt, and blue blazer, he looked both hot and annoyed. Once in front of the congregation, he held up a hand and said, "I'm sorry to inform you that Pastor Tom has been taken to the hospital."

As people started talking, Detective Waring gave a sharp whistle.

When they quieted, he continued, "If any of you saw Pastor Tom earlier today, please talk to me."

Lawrence's face turned red. "What happened?"

"This is an ongoing investigation," Detective Waring said. "Again, if any of you would like to speak to me, I'll be outside."

Lawrence nodded, turned on Isabel, and said, "Get out. Now."

Isabel flinched and left the altar. Nicholas Trott stood with his tail between his legs and barked at her.

"Nicholas Trott!" Susan ran over to him but the dog's countenance changed. He bared his teeth and stalked Isabel who stepped backward and stumbled on a step.

The growling dog moved closer to Isabel, who was struggling to get up in those heels.

"Susan!" Maddie's panicked plea cut through the room's tension.

"No, boy!" Susan grabbed the dog's collar, but he was too strong and she was too little. When he jumped toward Isabel, he knocked Susan over.

Zack, Alex, and Detective Waring moved quickly. Zack ran up the left aisle, Alex jumped over rows, and Waring took off down the middle. At that same moment, everyone in the room seemed to realize the danger and scrambled out of their seats. Some screamed and others ran toward the door.

Zack tackled the dog. Alex grabbed Susan around the waist and held her out of the way. Detective Waring got Isabel to her feet. It took all of Zack's strength to hold the dog back until Waring could get Isabel out of the church. When Isabel was gone, Zack felt the tension in the dog's body ease. His growls stopped, his tail relaxed.

"Nicholas Trott!"

Zack saw Alex holding a squirmy almost-eight-year-old. "You can let her go."

Once Susan's feet hit the ground, she ran over and threw herself onto the dog and started crying. "Nicholas Trott! Are you okay?"

Maddie scooped her daughter into her arms and sat in the closest pew.

Alex moved into the shadows near a stained-glass window.

"That dog needs to be put down." A man in a dark gray suit appeared in front of Maddie. "I don't want my daughter touching that mongrel."

Allison had told Zack about Maddie's almost-ex-husband, but Zack had expected him to be bigger. And less...thin.

"No!" Susan faced her father with tears streaming down her face. "You can't touch him! I won't let you!"

Maddie stood and let Susan go back to hugging Nicholas Trott. "Stop yelling, Heyward. You're upsetting Susan."

Heyward pointed at Susan. "When my new lawyer and the family judge realize the danger you've put her in, I'm going to win custody."

"*Enough.*" Detective Waring returned and pointed to the open doors in the back of the church. "Take your arguments outside. *Now.* Or I start arresting someone for something."

Thunder rolled again, and the church felt darker, probably from the incoming clouds.

Maddie took Susan's hand and led her outside. Nicholas Trott followed the little girl, dragging his leash, as if knowing she was his only ally. Heyward went out the opposite door.

Lawrence pulled a handkerchief out of his back pocket and wiped his brow. "Detective, what happened to Pastor Tom?"

"Earlier today," Detective Waring said, "someone beat up Pastor Tom. His housekeeper came around before the service and found him unconscious on the floor of his rectory."

"Any ideas who did it?" Zack asked.

"None." Waring nodded to Lawrence. "I'll be outside, hopefully talking to people who may have a clue as to what the hell happened."

CHAPTER 32

HALF AN HOUR LATER, ALLISON SAT ON A BENCH IN THE BACK OF the cemetery, near two yellow backhoes behind her brother's grave. Despite the drama in the church, she was focused on something else: someone had carved a broken daisy in the back of Danny's headstone and planted rosemary, thistle, and lilies of the valley around the base.

Then she remembered Stuart's receipt from the garden center.

While she rubbed her forehead, hoping to ward off a headache, Nicholas Trott lay at her feet, a vision of contrition.

Maddie and Susan stood by the entrance of the graveyard. Heyward was waving his hands around, yelling at Maddie. Across the street, Detective Waring talked to a tour guide—and twenty tourists—in front of Pirate House. The other congregants had gone home. Probably to share Isabel's letter all over social media.

Thunder clapped so loudly the ravens in a nearby tree took flight. Allison raised her face to the incoming storm. From the flashes of lightning in the distance, this one would be intense.

A bolt of lightning hit nearby, followed immediately by an enormous thunder clap, when Vivienne appeared to pet the dog. "How is Nicholas Trott?"

"Very unfulfilled, I expect."

On cue, Nicholas Trott wheezed.

Vivienne sat next to Allison. "How are you?"

That was a hell of a question. She had so many words to choose from: *embarrassed, humiliated, horrified, broken-hearted, angry*. But instead of going with a descriptor, she chose an action. "Ready to end this."

"I can only imagine you want to find that treasure and shove it up Isabel's bony ass."

Allison burst out laughing. "I'd like that, actually. Once we save Emilie, of course."

Vivienne took Allison's hand. "Tonight should give you hope. This was a desperate move on Isabel's part. She humiliated you, but she also showed a side of herself to the very society from whom she craves approval."

"Isabel doesn't need anyone's approval."

"Nonsense. We all seek approval, Isabel more than most. She's trying to throw you off-kilter. She knows that if you work with Zack, stay close to Zack, you may actually succeed in finding the treasure and saving Emilie."

Zack came out of the church and strode through the cemetery in their direction. Even from here, she could almost hear his deep, forceful breaths.

Vivienne squeezed Allison's hand. "I do have one favor to ask you, dear."

Allison squeezed back. "What is it?"

"Don't break my godson's heart."

Isabel stood in the cemetery on the other side of the church and waited for Clayborne.

While reading Stuart's letter might have made her a pariah for the rest of the social season, it wouldn't last long. In fact, she expected the ruckus over her affair with Stuart to end by Halloween. Thanksgiving at the latest.

"I have to say, Isabel Rutledge"—Clayborne appeared behind her—"you don't disappoint."

She turned and felt a single raindrop on her cheek. There wasn't much time before this storm hit, and from the dark cloud cover, it promised violence. "I think the dog's reaction, and my tripping, worked in my favor."

Clayborne took out a cigarette and lit it. "It did add to the drama."

"What happened with Pastor Tom?"

"He's in a coma. I interrogated him harder than I realized. Unfortunately, he had no new information regarding the appendix."

"If he wakes, will he be able to name you?"

"No." Clayborne studied her with narrowed eyes. "Do you hate Allison so much that you're willing to risk Remiel's wrath? You may be his favorite, but that doesn't mean he won't punish you. He doesn't like this kind of spectacle."

And what did Clayborne know of Remiel that she didn't? "I can handle Remiel."

"You haven't answered my question. Why do you hate Allison? Is it because she's everything you're not?"

Isabel waved a hand as another raindrop fell on it. "Allison is weak, and I despise all weak things. She broke Stuart's heart."

"So did you. When Stuart realized you were only using him to find the treasure for Remiel, he was devastated. You betrayed him. He died knowing he'd betrayed his wife for a woman who doesn't understand the meaning of love."

Isabel took the cigarette out of his mouth, tossed it down, and ground it out with her shoe. Who was Clayborne to lecture her about anything? "Any word on the appendix?"

"No. Although I saw Horatio hovering around the other side of the church. I have a man following him now."

She closed her eyes and chewed her bottom lip.

"And," Clayborne said, "scuttlebutt on John's Island says that Vivienne Beaumont has filed a flight plan for her newly acquired private jet parked at the airfield. Manifest lists Zack Tremaine and Allison Pinckney. They leave for New Orleans in thirty minutes."

Isabel opened her eyes and texted her New Orleans crew.

Clayborne came closer. "Do you think they tracked the appendix there?"

"No idea." Isabel slipped her phone into her purse. "Can you follow them? See if they both get on that plane and text me when you know."

"Do you think your little stunt here tonight will tear the lovers apart?"

"My stunt was designed to remind Allison that risking her heart will only lead to humiliation. Even if they go to New Orleans together, Allison will pull away from Zack emotionally. It's what she does."

Clayborne started to leave only to pause at the gate. "Did you make that phone call?"

"I did. Kells Torridan should be busy proving to his overlords that he can control his men, while at the same time realizing he can't."

"Remember, Tremaine is part of a team. Teams stick together and help one another. Especially Green Berets. It's their jam."

Their jam? "What are you saying?"

"I'm saying that while you try to destroy Allison emotionally and turn Kells's unit into chaos, you may want a backup plan."

One thing about Clayborne? He was a forward thinker. She glanced at the church and saw Alex inside, alone, on his phone. "Got it."

Alex sat in a back pew of the church and answered his phone on the third ring.

"Alex? It's Luke."

"Just so you know," Alex said, "we're not coming back until this thing is done."

Now that the church was empty and someone had dimmed the lights, he craved the quiet peace offered by the cold space and lighted candles that still illuminated the perimeter.

"You and Zack have to get back here. Kells got a call from one of his contacts. He knows—kind of—what you're doing and is on the warpath. If you and Zack don't get back here soon, Kells may burn this place down. He's that angry."

"Then make sure you don't tell him that Zack and Allison are on their way to New Orleans to find that appendix or Mercy Chastain. Maybe both."

"Jeez." Luke sighed heavily. "What am I going to say to the rest of the men?"

"Tell them Zack is getting his happy on and will be home as soon as possible. They won't begrudge him that."

"You don't think that Zack and Allison are...*happy*. Do you?"

"Does it matter?"

"It does to Kells. He wants you and Zack to come home *without* Allison."

"And Emilie? I'm guessing he knows about that too?"

"Kells doesn't believe the Fianna will give her to Remiel."

"Kells is wrong." Alex saw Vivienne Beaumont enter the church and added, "Buy us twelve more hours. Make shit up. I gotta go."

Vivienne Beaumont sat next to Alex and used a prayer card to fan herself. "Alex, did you encourage Isabel to do what she did tonight?"

Will I ever find any peace? "Fuck no. That bitch stole five years of my life. Why would I have anything to do with her?"

"Because once upon a time, while your brother was fighting for his position as Prince of the Fianna, you begged me to introduce you to Isabel. Determined to get to Remiel, you became her lover. You were quite besotted."

"If you believe I had any feelings other than contempt for Isabel, you're not nearly as good at your job as you believe." Disgusted, Alex headed for the side door. She followed and he added, "Have you told Zack that you introduced me and Isabel? Helped me get close to Remiel?"

No, Alex hadn't mentioned it because Zack was a good guy who believed in those he loved.

"Of course not. Zachariah knows very little about the people with whom I do business."

Alex slipped into the cemetery and chose a spot where he could watch Susan and Nicholas Trott deal with Maddie's ass of an ex-husband. Then he got a text from Zack.

> On our way to the airport. Left the dog with Maddie.
> Will check in once we land.

Alex responded: OK.

Vivienne stood next to Alex. Detective Waring was talking to a group of people who stood near the cemetery gates twenty yards away. The thunder was getting louder.

They had ten minutes, maybe less, before the rain started.

Then there was Maddie in a black wraparound dress that tied at the waist. The kind that fell off with one tug of the bow. "What do you know about Maddie's husband?"

"He's an adulterer and a liar." Vivienne grabbed Alex's arm with a surprising amount of strength. "Stay away from them. Maddie is a friend of mine, and I adore Susan. They don't need the kind of trouble that comes with you and this struggle between the Prince and Remiel."

Unfortunately, Vivienne was right. "I have to agree with you."

She backed up a few steps. "If there's anything you need…"

"Like what?"

"According to my sources, you were in solitary off and on for five years. You must be lonely. I know women who'd be willing to help."

She has to be kidding. "I can find my own dates, Vivienne. Besides, the last thing I need is to be on the other side of a favor from you."

Because he understood, even if Zack didn't yet, how the favor game played out. When it came to people like Aidan, Remiel, Isabel, and Vivienne, leverage was everything. Alex had tried to warn Kells, all those years ago, but Kells believed in right and wrong with no space in between for compromise. Unfortunately, that space in between the trenches— that no man's land—was where one found most of the casualties.

"Alex, may I make a suggestion?"

"Why not?" She was going to anyway.

"Go back to Savannah. Leave Remiel alone."

"You know what he *is*, Vivienne. You know what he *does*."

"I do. I also know that, so far, you've paid the steepest price in this war."

He'd once believed that, but after seeing the suffering Remiel caused Kells's men, Alex had changed his mind. "I may have lost five years, I might also be the most antisocial and most violent of all of Kells's men, but I haven't lost hope. If I'm going to kill Remiel—for real—I need all the hope I can muster."

"If that's your goal, then I'm not asking you to leave Maddie alone. I'm telling you. If you go near her, encourage her in any way, I will find a way to stop you."

He frowned at Vivienne. "Encourage her? What kind of man do you think I am?"

She smiled up at him. "Antisocial. Violent. According to Isabel, the best lover she's ever had. Oh, and determined to commit murder."

He scoffed. "Murder as a public service. There's a difference."

"Remiel won't think so."

Alex heard loud voices. Heyward had taken Maddie's arm and she shook him off.

"Are we done, Vivienne?"

"For now." Vivienne left him and he watched as her driver pulled up across the street, near Detective Waring with that mob of tourists.

Vivienne's car drove away. Maddie and her husband were still arguing.

"I've been waiting to talk to you, but you're quite popular tonight."

You've gotta be kidding me. Alex turned to see Isabel behind him and said, "Go. Away."

Isabel ignored him, of course. "Are you *interested* in the Ashton women?"

"No. I'm watching the crazy across the street."

"Apparently, those tourists and their tour guide saw a ghost. Detective Waring is trying to calm everyone down."

"What do you want, Isabel?"

"Maybe I just need a friend."

He snorted. "Call Remiel."

"Heyward may be wealthy and connected, but he's a selfish, arrogant ass." Isabel came closer and whispered, "Heyward has a violent streak. He reminds me of Remiel."

Alex moved away from Isabel's sickening sandalwood scent just as Maddie's husband grabbed Susan's wrist.

Alex stomped over. He wasn't sure what he was going to do or say.

He wasn't even sure why he was getting involved when he knew it would only cause problems. He just couldn't watch another man act like his father.

Maddie reached for her husband's arm. "Let go of Susan."

"Mom." Susan pulled her mother's skirt. "I want to go home with you. Nicholas Trott *has* to sleep in my bed with me and Mrs. Pickles or else he cries."

"That's absurd," her father said. "Stop being a baby. You're coming home with me."

"No!"

Maddie held Susan against her body. "We need to reschedule, Heyward. Susan is upset and I won't force her to go with you."

Heyward pointed at Maddie. "This is why I'm going for full custody."

"You'll never get full custody," Maddie said in a barely there voice. "I won't allow it."

He took Susan's wrist again and yanked. "Get in the car."

Alex stepped out of the shadows. "When a woman says no, she means no. Even if she's only almost-eight."

"Who the hell are you?" Heyward released Susan. His face twisted into a mask of contempt, exposing his insecurity and arrogance—two dangerous traits that turned a man into a bully.

Alex never could abide bullies.

"That's Mr. Mitchell," Susan said with her face against Maddie's dress. "He's my friend."

Heyward's laugh sounded menacing. "Why would a grown man want to be friends with a little girl?"

Alex's fist slammed into Heyward's jaw with the force of a rocket launcher. Heyward fell to his knees. The pain in Alex's knuckles and arm made him blink a few times. Other than that and a few shakes of his hand, he was the pin-up boy for *calm and collected*.

"Alex!" Maddie took his wrist. "Why did you do that?"

"Because your ex is an ass."

"That ass"—Maddie waved at Heyward on the ground—"is going to file for full custody."

Heyward struggled to stand, with a red mark forming on his jaw. "I'm going to win, too."

"What's going on?" Detective Waring crossed the street and did the gaze-dance between Alex and Heyward.

Heyward pointed at Alex. "He hit me."

The last time Alex had been ratted on had been in the prison yard, after a knife fight with a rapist. But because no one in prison liked tattletales, the ratter never made it back to his cell. Unfortunately, in the real world where everything was upside-down, tattlers were the good guys.

Detective Waring looked at Alex. "Did you assault Heyward?"

"No." Alex rocked back on his heels. He didn't need SAT words to redefine his actions. "I hit him."

Waring looked at Heyward. "Do you want to press charges?"

"Hell yes."

"That's ridiculous," Maddie said. "Heyward was hurting Susan and accused Alex of awful things."

"I would never hurt my daughter," Heyward said.

"I didn't see what happened." Waring took out his handcuffs, and Alex turned around. "But we can talk about it down at the station. Mr. Ashton, meet me there."

Alex held his hands behind his back and winked at Susan.

Susan cried and looked up at her mother. "I don't want Mr. Mitchell to go to jail."

"It'll be okay, Susan." Maddie lifted her gaze and met his. "Do you need a lawyer, Mr. Mitchell?"

"No, thank you. I'll be fine."

Waring dragged Alex to the patrol car. Once they drove away, he noticed two things. On the right side of the road, near the iron gate that led to Pirates Courtyard, he saw Horatio hit his chest with his fist and bow his head.

High praise from a Fianna warrior? *Perfect.*

On Alex's left, he noticed Isabel holding up her phone. She was filming him and had probably recorded his fight with Heyward. As they drove by, she dropped the phone into her purse. He didn't need to ask what she'd done. He knew. She'd sent his defense of Susan and Maddie to Remiel.

Now Remiel would know Alex was *interested*.

CHAPTER 33

ZACK STARED OUT THE WINDOW OF THE TINY PRIVATE AIRPORT hangar on John's Island, listened to the hailstorm wreaking havoc around them, and knew they were screwed.

"I just spoke with the pilot." Allison handed him a vending machine coffee, black with no sugar. "It'll be hours before we take off. Since this storm is affecting the entire southern U.S., we may not arrive until tomorrow."

Fuck. He fisted his free hand and watched the hail hammer the tarmac.

What were they supposed to do now?

Allison took his wrist and led him to a hard plastic seat against the wall, not far from Vivienne's private plane. Along the way, he tossed his bitter coffee into the trash. "I can't just wait here. I can't just do *nothing.*"

Once they sat, she asked, "Do you have any friends in New Orleans that can help us out? Maybe visit this restaurant for us?"

He shook his head. "I'm not very good with keeping in touch with people. It's not easy being gone all the time. And I suck at social media."

She kissed the back of his hand. "Luckily, the pilot said we can wait—and sleep—on the plane. I'm not sure how, maybe with a generator, but the plane has enough power on the ground to run the AC until we take off."

With no other choice, he nodded and let Allison lead the way to the plane.

✍

A few hours later, Allison left Zack in the bed in the back of the most luxurious airplane she'd ever seen and took a bottle of water out of the small refrigerator next to a leather couch.

She'd slept a bit, but Zack's restlessness kept waking her up. She understood his frustration and his worry, but she was antsy from something else.

She found her tote bag, sat on the couch, and covered her lap with a soft blanket. Since she'd gone to Fenwick Hall, she felt like she'd missed something. The twitchy feeling in her mind had nothing to do with what'd happened at the service. It had everything to do with those apotropaic marks they'd been collecting throughout the city.

She took out all the rubbings: the combined daisy wheel from the Pink House and planner that Alex had retraced this morning, the daisy wheel from the Fenwick Hall barn, and the one Alex had rubbed at the church.

She stared at the three complete daisy wheels. She even turned them upside down.

What am I missing?

She ran a finger over the church rubbing. Alex's heavy hand with the charcoal pencil had also picked up a broken daisy and random markings around the perimeter of the wheel. They were similar to the markings around the other two apotropaic marks.

Starting from scratch, she took three pieces of fresh tracing paper and sat at the desk. One by one, she retraced the rubbings—everything except for the daisy wheels. There was a surprising amount of engraved graffiti around the perimeters of apotropaic marks but it wasn't until she laid the three pages of new tracings on the table that she realized what those random markings were: rectangles.

Still not sure what it all meant, she found a pair of scissors in a desk and cut out the shapes. When she was done, she laid out the three pages on the table. She had three pages of rectangular cutout windows and two swirly calligraphy lines.

Then she remembered the seventeenth-century calligraphy lines that'd divided the Pirate's Grille into three parts.

It didn't take long to trim the three pages and tape them together. She just wasn't sure they were in the right order.

"What are you doing?" Zack appeared next to her in his gym shorts and nothing else. Despite the plane having some power, it was still hotter than she knew he preferred.

"I think I figured out the mystery of the apotropaic marks." She pointed to the pages she'd taped together. "When Mercy Chastain carved these daisy wheels in prison, she added these rectangles. I know it's been a few days since I've seen it, but I'm sure these cutouts form the Pirate's Grille. I think she embedded the Cardan grille into the apotropaic marks."

He held up the taped page with the cutout windows. "That means—"

"If we can find the witch's examination's appendix in New Orleans, we can find the treasure."

On Saturday morning, when the storm *finally* stopped and their plane *finally* landed, a car had been waiting for them courtesy of Vivienne. Zack had parked in a garage near the river, not far from the French Quarter. Unfortunately, since the restaurant didn't open until six p.m., they'd had hours to play tourist.

Normally, Zack wouldn't have minded spending the day in the city he adored with the woman he loved. They'd even done touristy things like eat beignets at Café du Monde and tour the cathedral, just to kill time.

But that was the problem. Time was dying.

While he was grateful for the full night's sleep, Allison's brilliance at figuring out the mystery of the apotropaic marks/Pirate's Grille, and the luxury of the plane, the clock had been ticking away.

Now that it was almost six p.m., they had sixteen hours left. Marcellus had said the Prince wanted the treasure by Sunday morning. As far as Zack was concerned that meant ten a.m., not six a.m.

The other nagging problem? He'd not been able to get in touch with Alex.

Maybe Alex had returned to Savannah to appease both Nate and Kells and keep them off Zack's ass. Throughout the day, Zack had thought about calling Nate but decided not to. Zack simply didn't have the headspace for more stress. He just hoped Alex had dealt with the Nate/Kells/Savannah situation.

Zack stopped at the corner of Saint Ann Street and Bourbon Street in the French Quarter. He took Allison's tote bag with their research and held her hand.

Zack maneuvered them across a street packed with drunk revelers. She usually wore dresses or skirts, but today she had on jeans and a white blouse, her hair in a ponytail. If it was at all possible, she looked even sexier.

They'd not only been able to sleep on the plane. They'd also showered and changed clothes. When they'd landed, he'd driven to Emilie's apartment, found her hidden key, and searched her house. Her place was tiny and neat. And they'd found nothing that would tie her to Remiel, the Fianna, or anything else from Zack's life as a soldier.

Now they passed colorful restaurants and noisy clubs with outdoor music before turning down a dark alley that smelled like awful things he didn't want to name.

"Where are we?" she asked. "The address Vivienne gave us is on the other side of the quarter."

He paused behind a dumpster and pulled his phone out of the back pocket of his jeans. "You grew up in this city too."

"No." She crossed her arms as if she were cold despite the summer humidity that blanketed the city. "I moved to the Irish Channel when I was fourteen. Then I went to an all-girls Catholic High School until going to Tulane where, as a scholarship student, I stayed in most nights. Unless I was with you."

He smiled to put her at ease and dialed his phone. When he'd met her in college he'd been surprised—no, shocked—that they'd grown up in the same city. Whereas she'd been sheltered by her grandmother, Vivienne had allowed him to run wild. He'd explored every nook of this city and knew which crannies to stay away from.

She wrinkled her nose, probably against the overwhelming stench of urine and vomit. "Who are you calling?"

"Rafe."

Rafe picked up on the first ring. "What's wrong?"

It was sad that whenever he and his buddies called each other, that was the first question they asked. "We're being followed."

"We are?" Allison spun around until Zack drew her in close.

"You sure?" Rafe asked.

"I know when I'm being tailed, brother." Zack had been in enough hot zones around the world as both the tail-er and the tail-ee. "About half an hour ago, we picked up a black van."

"Where is it now?"

"We lost the van once we entered the pedestrian area of Bourbon Street. I don't know what he—or they—look like, so I'm not sure where they went."

"Fuck."

"Agreed." Zack watched the street they'd come off of. Two men paused at the alley's entrance, then moved on. At the other end of the alley, he heard a homeless man singing in French. "Any chance we're being followed by the Fianna?"

"I don't think so." Rafe paused for a long moment. "Alex mentioned this man you're searching for—"

"Mack McIntyre."

"He worked for Remiel. I asked a few questions but haven't learned anything. But Detective Garza checked his sources. Mack lived in Terrebonne Parish with his grandmother until joining the Marines. Years ago he returned to New Orleans and ran an illegal fight club until he couldn't pay his prizefighters. Someone bailed him out, and Mack had to start working for the guy. My guess is that guy was Remiel."

"Thanks, Rafe. I appreciate it."

"No problem." Rafe paused. "Zack, when a Fianna warrior is assigned to a city, he spends months learning every in and out before starting a mission. You're ahead of the game there. You know that city better than most. Use that knowledge. And remember, always listen for the birds."

Meaning get to know the native sounds around you because when things changed, the sounds were often the first sign. "Hey. What's that noise where you are?"

"I'm in the Charleston police station with Pete and Detective Garza. We're meeting with Detective Waring."

Zack's heart began a loud *thud-thud-thud.* "Why?" *Please don't let it be about Alex.*

"We have another problem. And, no, I haven't told Kells. I don't think his temper could handle it right now. He's so pissed you haven't returned to Savannah I think he may actually start bleeding from his eyeballs."

Fuck. Zack closed his eyes and rested his chin on Allison's head. How he wished he were home in her bedroom, making love to her in front of the fireplace. "What problem?"

Allison shifted in his arms. "There's a problem?"

"Last night"—Rafe sighed—"Alex was arrested."

◌

Allison held Zack's hand outside the address Vivienne had given them. It'd taken them longer than expected to work their way through the quarter without being followed. On the corner of Cabildo Alley and Pirate Alley, near the back of the Saint Louis Cathedral, they stared at a closed-up shop on the corner. All the doors and windows were shuttered. The sun hadn't set yet, but had lowered in the sky.

"Where is this place?" she asked.

"Vivienne said it's on the second floor of this address, but I don't see a way to get up there."

A couple appeared from a door on their right, ten yards down the alley. Zack held Allison close and used his body to press hers against the brick wall. "Play along."

His lips found hers and he began a slow, tender kiss that gave and took. They were hidden in the shadows, just another couple finding happiness in the city known for debauchery.

"The food was *amazing,*" the female half of the couple said as she came closer. "How can I thank you?"

"We could go back to my place for a nightcap," the male said.

The female giggled, and they turned the corner and disappeared.

"Now what?" Allison whispered.

He kissed her forehead, her nose, and one final peck on her lips. "Follow me."

They entered the alley and stopped in front of the green shuttered door the couple had emerged from. No doorbell, no doorknob, no way to enter without—

Allison stepped up and knocked. "Play along."

The shuttered doors opened out, and they had to back up. A tall black man in a dark suit stood in the entrance. "May I help you?"

Allison smiled. "Please tell Mack McIntyre that Allison Pinckney would like to speak to him."

"He won't—"

"He will if you tell him I'm Stuart Pinckney's wife." Allison handed him Stuart's planner that she'd taken out of her tote bag. "Show him this. Please."

The man took the planner and said, "Wait here," and shut the door.

"I hope this works," Zack said.

"Me too."

They waited ten minutes before the door opened again. The man said, "Follow me."

Allison went first, with Zack's hand on her lower back, down a narrow hallway. At the end, they climbed two flights of stairs before going through another door and passing another guard in a black suit. Compared to the dark hallway, the restaurant with its low lights and candles seemed bright.

Small tables were staggered throughout the room, allowing each table an optimal view of the only wall with windows, built high into the brick wall, that looked out on the cathedral's bell tower. Light jazz music came from a trio in a corner, near the bar. All the tables were filled, and the smell of Cajun spices and warm cornbread made her stomach growl despite the fact that they'd been eating all day.

Luckily Zack had gotten over his aversion to having her pay for everything, since he'd left Charleston with nothing but a few singles in his pocket.

"This place is amazing," Allison said to their guide.

"The building has been redesigned with brick walls, high windows, and skylights, so from the street you'd never know the restaurant was here."

Suddenly, the bell tower's lights turned on and filtered in through the glass skylights. The hazy colors of sunset and the bell tower's light amplified the restaurant's intimate, private vibe. She figured the restaurant had to have one of the best views in the city and—from the tantalizing scents—it had fabulous food as well.

How she wished they'd been there for a date instead of a mission. They'd eat, dance, and go back to some beautiful room where they could be alone again.

Their guide nodded toward the bar. "Wait there."

Allison sat on a leather stool and Zack ordered them both club sodas with lime.

"Why was Alex arrested?" It was the first chance she'd had to ask.

"Not sure. Rafe, Pete, and Detective Garza—buddies of mine—are in Charleston dealing with the situation before my boss, Kells, finds out."

"Will Kells be mad?"

"Oh yeah."

They drank their club sodas and she was grateful for it. Her throat felt dry and she wasn't sure what else to say. They were running out of time and ideas and hope.

The bartender placed two bowls of stew in front of them, along with spoons and napkins. "The owner says he'll see you in a few minutes. In the meantime, he sent bowls of the house's famous gumbo, gratis."

"Thank you," she said, trying not to drool. She was going to have to try not to eat like a barbarian. She never ate like this, but somehow this city brought out her appetite.

Zack said his thanks and dug in.

At first bite, she closed her eyes—sausage, chicken, and shrimp in a tomato-based gravy. It was heaven.

"This," Zack said with his mouth full, "is better than Bayou Saint George's gumbo."

She opened her eyes just as the bartender dropped off a basket of cornbread muffins and pats of butter. She wanted to cry. They didn't speak as they ate, but she studied Zack as he watched the room. He was one of the tallest men, and with his tattoos and long hair, he stood out. She even noticed other women sending him sideways smiles. One slid onto a nearby barstool, so her skirt rose up, exposing her thighs.

To his credit, he seemed focused on everything *except* the women. While he buttered his muffin, he studied every exit, every camera, and every other man. It was as if he was evaluating all the variables involved, in case they had to run.

She finished her second muffin and wiped her lips with a napkin. "Do you always check out every room you're in?"

"Habit." He mopped up his last bite of gumbo with the buttered muffin. "I'm always looking for escape routes and other men who are armed."

When they were done, the bartender cleared their plates.

"How long?" Zack asked him.

"Soon."

Zack hopped off the stool and led her to the dance area near the trio. He took her in his arms and held her close. The tune, a Creole lullaby, was a slow-moving waltz. She rested her head against his shoulder and closed her eyes again. She let him lead while she drifted to the sound of his heartbeat.

"May I help you?"

Allison opened her eyes to find a man standing near them in black slacks and a black silk shirt, holding Stuart's planner. The same man in the photo with Stuart and Isabel.

Zack held out his hand, keeping his other palm on her lower back. "I'm Zack Tremaine. This is Allison Pinckney from Charleston. We're looking for Mack McIntyre."

The man frowned. "What do you want?"

Allison took a step forward. "I need to talk to him about my husband, Stuart."

The man looked away. Then sighed. "We can talk in private."

"I'm Mack McIntyre." He led them up a flight of stairs to the empty roof. He motioned to a table with four chairs near an unattended bar. High brick walls surrounded the area that held six tables and a dance floor. LED lanterns along the floor lined the walls. White lights hung from the pergola above the tables. She sat while Zack stood nearby.

With the sun almost set now, the view of the lit-up church's bell tower was even more spectacular.

Mack laid the planner on the table. "I'm sorry about Stuart."

"Thank you." Allison nodded at Zack. "I'll get to the point. Before he died, Stuart sold the witch's examination. But the appendix is missing. We were hoping you could tell us where to find it."

Mack shrugged. "I didn't know there was an appendix or that it was missing."

Allison gripped the edge of the table. "Do you have any idea who sold the witch's examination to Stuart? Maybe they kept the appendix."

"A few months ago, a woman named Tarragon found the witch's examination in an old barn and gave it to Stuart after he promised *not* to give it to Remiel." Mack looked away. "The last time I saw Tarragon, Remiel had taken her hostage. If she's alive, she can't be…right."

Zack paced between the bar and the table. "The Prince has my sister, Emilie. If I don't find that appendix and Henry Avery's treasure, he'll send her to Remiel."

"I'm sorry." Mack turned to leave. "I can't help you."

"That's it?" Zack grabbed Mack's arm. "You worked for Remiel, and you're fine letting him torture my sister?"

Mack threw off Zack's grasp. "It's not my fight anymore. And a word of advice? If you don't want to end up dead, leave your men behind and start a life on your own. Kells Torridan will not protect you."

"What are you talking about?"

Mack scoffed. "Why do you think two years passed before your unit could put together a rescue mission? The commanders of the two A teams were being tortured daily, yet it took twenty-four months for your team to plan an extrication, get approval, and save your men. Then when you got to the POW camp, most of the guards were gone."

"We had resistance."

Mack shook his head. "Two days before you showed up in that Afghan POW camp, there were three hundred guards. When you arrived, there were less than forty. You didn't save your men until Remiel was ready to let them go. And your boss knew that. Kells *waited* for that."

Zack took a step back. "That can't be true."

"Yet it is." Mack's phone buzzed and he checked his text. "If you can't find that appendix, your only chance to save your sister is to find a fifolet."

"You're joking about ghosts guarding treasure?" Zack asked. "My sister's life is at stake."

Mack sent a text before saying, "My granny believed that Mercy Chastain was Henry Avery's fifolet because he killed her and buried her with his treasure in Charleston. That's why everyone in that town claims to see Mercy's ghost."

"That's absurd," Allison said. "Why would Henry kill Mercy? They were lovers."

"Henry Avery and Mercy Chastain disappeared on the same day." Mack took an envelope out of his jacket and dropped it on Stuart's planner. "I can't help you find the treasure, but there are things you should know about your husband."

"You mean like his affair with Isabel Rutledge?" Allison snorted. "I know about that."

"I'm talking about the spreadsheet in that envelope."

Allison opened the envelope and took out a sheet folded into thirds.

"That spreadsheet contains numbers for private offshore accounts," Mack said. "That's proof Stuart was helping your mother embezzle money from her absinthe business. He'd set up her Pink House gallery as a shell corporation and moved the money into offshore accounts."

"Why?" Allison asked.

"I believe to get away from her husband."

Was this what Rue had been looking for in Pirate House?

Zack took the spreadsheet and his eyes darkened. "Stuart's accounts are held by RM Financial. They're owned by the Fianna."

Allison sat and stared at the planner. "Stuart was supposed to find the treasure for the Prince in exchange for something. Were these accounts that *something*?"

"Yes." Mack took the spreadsheet out of Zack's hand, shoved it into the envelope, and slipped it into the planner. "Stuart was indebted to the Prince because the Prince helped him move this money quietly."

Zack snorted. "Something that's hard to do nowadays with the antiterrorism financial laws in place."

"Exactly." Mack crossed his arms and leaned against the pergola. "In exchange for the Fianna's help, Stuart not only told the Prince what Isabel and Remiel were looking for, but Stuart also agreed to find the treasure before anyone else. Stuart was working for the Prince to help your mother, and now so are you."

CHAPTER 34

ALLISON CLUTCHED THE PLANNER. "I DON'T UNDERSTAND."

Mack sighed as if he were dealing with teenagers. "Stuart started his affair with Isabel but ended up involved with Remiel. When Stuart realized the danger, he went to Vivienne Beaumont, who contacted the Prince, who made Stuart an offer. In exchange for finding the treasure, the Prince would help Stuart embezzle money for Rue and protect him from Remiel."

"Why would Stuart help Rue?" Allison asked Mack.

"From what Stuart told me, he felt sorry for her. Apparently her husband is an ass."

"Except," Zack said, "Remiel found out and killed Stuart."

Mack nodded. "My guess is Stuart realized what the Fianna were doing to him and protected Allison by hiding the appendix. He didn't want the Fianna using her like they'd used him, and he needed to give her leverage over everyone. The only other thing he told me was that he had another man helping him. A man named Danny." Mack's cell phone rang and he answered. A moment later, he said to Zack, "Were you followed here?"

"No." Zack went to the edge of the brick wall and peered over it. "Why?"

"Because my guards said there are two suspicious-looking men in the alley."

Allison bit her lip and threw the planner into her tote bag.

Stuart had had Danny's help? Her dead brother? What the hell did that mean?

The lights overhead, as well as the lights in the church's spire, flickered and went out. The sun had set and clouds obscured the half moon. Except for the battery-powered lanterns lining the perimeter, the city had gone dark. They were in a citywide blackout.

Minutes later, Mack led Zack and Allison down a different staircase and stopped on the landing. "The power in the city is out," Mack said, "including cell service and Wi-Fi. According to my guards, the men following you work for Isabel and are still in Cabildo Alley. This door will lead you to Saint Peter street. From there, you're on your own."

"Can you make a call for me?" Zack asked.

"If my landline works."

Zack rattled off a number and a message, shook Mack's hand, and pulled his gun from his leg holster. "Our car is near the river. If we can get there, we should be fine."

Allison's eyes widened at the *if* and *should,* and he squeezed her hand.

"Good luck." Mack opened the door to expose a street that was surprisingly busy. Panicked people wandered around with their cell phones. "The outage may work in your favor."

"I hope so." Zack held his gun close to his body and with his free hand took Allison's wrist.

The door behind them closed, and he whispered, "If I release your hand, stay close. If we get separated, head toward the cathedral. I'll meet you there."

From the noise, it was hard to determine if people were panicked, partying, or rioting.

"Let's go." He kept her behind him and held his weapon low. The only light came from cell phone flashlights.

He turned right onto Royal Street, which was even busier. He forced his way through a group of young men who were whooping and hollering and blocking the entrance to Saint Ann Street. In the crush, he lost Allison's hand and his heart rate ratcheted up.

Once he broke through, she stumbled out. He noticed one of the men, wearing a long-sleeved Boutique du Vampyre shirt, eyeing her. Only tourists and people trying to blend in wore things like that. When the man spoke into a radio on his wrist, Zack took her hand again. "Run."

By the time they made it to Jackson Square, which was filled with panicked people, his heart was racing and Allison was breathing heavily. Helicopters flew overhead and a dozen cop cars appeared on Decatur Street. Red and blue lights flashed around them, sirens blasted.

"They're going to start blocking off the city." Zack spoke against her ear. "We need to get to the car. Whatever you do, don't let go of me."

She nodded and glanced back. "Zack?"

He turned to see the vampyre-shirt man, along with a buddy in a Reverend Zombie T-shirt, working their way through the crowd.

"Let's go." Zack's goal was to get through the square and across Decatur Street.

More helicopters flew by, and the cops were trying to get everyone to move back toward the cathedral. When they were halfway across the square, he accidentally bumped into a woman. She turned, saw his weapon, and yelled, "Gun!"

People screamed and scattered, leaving Zack and Allison in the open, where Isabel's men noticed them.

Zack ran, pulling Allison along with him. Cops shouted, people cried, and the bad guys gained. Once they reached the edge of the square, Zack dropped his weapon into Allison's tote and hurried toward the only cop protecting the square's gated entrance.

"Over there," Zack said to the cop. "Those men have guns!"

The cop spoke into his shoulder radio and ran toward the bad guys. Once the exit was clear, Zack and Allison raced across the street and paused behind a palmetto tree. Café du Monde was on their left, the parking area a block away, down the incline, toward the river on their right.

Zack reclaimed his gun and noticed Isabel's men talking to the cops and pointing in their direction. "Stay here." He moved into the shadows of Café du Monde, found a storm drain hidden behind a delivery van, and fired a shot into the water below.

The harsh sound of the gunshot set off another round of screams and sirens.

Zack took Allison's hand and hurried in the opposite direction, toward the parking area. Once they found the car, he ordered, "Get in!"

ဢ

Alex tried to stretch out his shoulders. An act made difficult by the fact he was handcuffed to a ring bolted into a table in the Charleston Police Department's interrogation room. At least he was out of his cell.

Bright lights overhead gave the room a bluish tinge. Or maybe it was the gray cinderblock walls and chipped blue linoleum on the floor.

He hadn't been there twenty-four hours yet so couldn't cry about his constitutional rights. Apparently the city was having trouble keeping cops and judges on their payroll, which might have been why Detective Waring, originally from Boston, had taken his job.

Detective Waring came into the room, sat, and tilted his chair back. "Heyward Ashton has filed charges. He said you two were arguing and you accused him of hurting his daughter, which he denied. Then you hit him. He said he was defending his honor by having you arrested. I then reminded him that dueling became illegal in South Carolina in 1880."

Alex smirked. He wasn't saying a word until his public defender appeared.

The door opened and a man entered. *Rafe Montfort? In a suit?*

Detective Waring stood.

Alex saw Pete White Horse and Detective Garza outside the door just before it shut. Since there was no way in hell Kells had sent them, they must've come on their own. For him.

"Good evening, Detective Waring." Rafe held out his hand and introduced himself as Alex's public defender.

Detective Waring shook and dropped. "I don't believe we've met, Mr. Montfort."

Rafe smiled. "I'm new."

Good grief. They were in trouble now.

"I heard," Rafe said, "about Mr. Mitchell's incident. I've also met with Mr. Ashton and he's agreed to withdraw the assault complaint. The two men just had a misunderstanding."

Detective Waring rose to his full height. "I need to check this out."

Rafe smiled. "Please do."

Detective Waring left the room and Rafe motioned to the two-way mirror. That meant there was no talking or any other kind of communication until they were out of the station.

A few minutes later, Detective Waring appeared with a frown. "It appears Mr. Ashton has dropped the charges. Your client is free to go."

Alex raised his hands, still in handcuffs.

Detective Waring produced a key. "Mr. Mitchell, I suggest you leave town and don't return."

"Sounds good to me." As Alex left the room, he bumped against the detective. "Excuse me."

Detective Waring's frown turned into a scowl.

Rafe waved toward the door. "After you, Mr. Mitchell."

Alex and Rafe left the station and headed for a white truck parked behind a gray sedan. Garza sat in the sedan's driver's seat and Pete was next to him. Both wore facial expressions similar to Waring's.

Rafe unlocked the truck. "Get in."

Alex hopped into the front seat and leaned back. The sun had just gone down and shadows lined the sidewalks.

Rafe turned the ignition, switched on the headlights, and pulled into the street. "What happened?"

"I allowed Isabel to manipulate me. Then I hit an asshole and got arrested." Alex studied Rafe's granite profile. "How'd you find out?"

"Horatio told us. I think he was worried."

"I doubt it. Did my brother send you?"

"No. I came on my own. That's why it took me so long."

Alex stared at the passing houses. It must've rained while he'd been inside because everything glistened like it was shiny and new. "Aidan didn't send anyone the first time either."

"I know." Rafe turned left, then right, and headed toward the battery. "Most of the warriors argued on your behalf, but the Prince refused."

Of course he did. "How'd Pete and Garza find out? Did you call them?"

"Yes." Rafe turned right and drove through a puddle. "Thank God Nate picked up the phone, realized what was going on, and convinced Pete and Garza to come along without telling Kells."

"Kells doesn't know?"

"He knows you and Zack are in Charleston." Rafe sent him a sideways glare. "But not about your arrest."

Alex went back to staring out the window streaked with raindrops. "Where are we going?"

"Vivienne Beaumont's house. She told us we could use it. And her housekeeper is providing food."

Great. Alex was starving.

Rafe made a sharp right and turned into a hidden driveway. He parked and pulled the emergency brake. "I had to terrorize Heyward Ashton into dropping the charges."

They both got out and Alex shut his door. "How?"

Rafe locked the truck. "You don't want to know."

Alex followed Rafe into the house. "Now what?"

"Pete and Garza are behind us. Then we need to decide what to do next."

Twenty minutes later, Alex and the rest of the men were in Vivienne's study drinking coffee and eating sandwiches with potato chips. Pete and Garza sat in club chairs near the fireplace while Rafe and Alex stood near a desk with Rafe's cell phone on speaker.

"Alex?" Nate's voice came in clear over the phone. "You good?"

"Sure," Alex said around a bite of his turkey sandwich.

Rafe wiped his face with a napkin. He'd already changed into jeans and a black T-shirt. "Heyward dropped the charges once I threatened him."

"Really?" Pete said from the chair, obviously too lazy to lift his ass.

"Yes," Rafe said. "From what I heard at the station, Waring is looking into Alex's past."

Garza took a brownie off a silver tray on the desk. "Did you know Waring was once in military intelligence?"

Now Pete came over and took two brownies. "Are you fucking with us?"

"Nope." Garza took a huge bite and added, "My sources told me Waring was an MP officer in military intelligence. He was in for five years and got out to become a civilian cop. He has friends."

"Dammit," Nate said.

Rafe planted his fists on the desk. "You said yesterday that Kells got a phone call telling him that Zack and Alex were in Charleston?"

"Yeah," Nate said. "It set off a storm of fury and rage."

Rafe took his own brownie and ate it in one bite. "I heard, through the Fianna, that that call came from Kells's contact—the one who kept you out of jail. This contact, apparently, isn't happy that Zack disobeyed Kells's order, Alex went AWOL, and came to Charleston to work with the Fianna."

"Jeez," Garza said, "you're not in the army anymore. Why would Kells's contact care?"

"No idea," Rafe said. "But Kells's contact can still make your lives miserable."

"Nate?" Pete ran his hands over his head and clasped his fingers over the braid that was so long it hit his ass. "Didn't Kells's contact negotiate our dishonorable discharges?"

"Yes," Nate said. "Kells took the deal on our behalf."

"What was the deal, Nate?" Rafe asked.

"We were supposed to face a secret congressional committee for our actions in the Wakhan Corridor Massacre. If we were found guilty, we'd be sent to Leedsville with the rest of our men—the ones we rescued. Or we could take the dishonorable discharges, leave Fort Bragg with nothing including money and possessions, and never talk about any of this ever again."

"Is it possible," Garza said in a hushed voice, "Kells's contact could rescind those discharges and send you to prison?"

Nate answered in a low voice, "Anything is possible."

Pete threw himself into a chair and covered his eyes with one arm. "I can't believe this."

"No one is going back to prison." Rafe's strong voice cut through the room. "We'll figure it out and come up with a plan."

"Alright. I—" Suddenly, Nate's phone went dead.

The lights dimmed, flickered, but stayed on.

Rafe's cell rang again and he answered, "What happened?"

A moment later Rafe hung up and said, "*Fuck.*"

"Again with the fuck," Pete said. "What's wrong with Nate now?"

"It wasn't Nate. It was a man named Mack." The lights dimmed again then went out completely this time. In the dark, they could hear: "Zack and Allison are under attack."

CHAPTER 35

Zack looked out the rearview window again. All he could see was that his world was *fucked*. He had nine bullets in his gun, a black van was on their ass, and the city was in total power outage.

Aaaaand their cell phones didn't work.

He wound his way out of the French Quarter with speed and a fifty-dollar bribe to a rent-a-cop at a makeshift security checkpoint leading into the Garden District. The guard had wanted more, but it was all Allison had left in her wallet.

Unfortunately, the guys following them had figured out the bribe thing as well and were now a few streets behind.

So far, it was just a following. It hadn't yet turned into a chase.

Allison sat next to him, clutching his weapon. She'd turned on the radio only to learn that the airport was closed as well.

As he drove, he watched the houses of the Garden District fly by. Even though he'd grown up here, once he joined the army, he'd rarely returned. It didn't feel like home. Except he'd never tell Vivienne or Emilie that.

They passed a broken statue in a front yard, and he had an idea. "I'm going to ditch the car near Lafayette Cemetery. Once we do that, we're going to run. Hard."

She nodded. "You're slowing down?"

"I need the guys behind us to see us get out. Can you trust me? Do what I say without question?"

"Of course." She looked in her side-view mirror. "What about the car?"

"Hopefully we can get the car later." He thought of something else. "Do you have a flashlight on your phone?"

"Yes. I also have the red lens app."

"Perfect. Get ready." Zack parked in front of the cemetery's iron gates and took the weapon. "Follow me with the flashlight."

He got out first and ran toward the gate that'd been built between two brick walls. While she held the light, he knelt. On the left side, he pulled a loose brick out of the wall. *Please still be there.* He shoved his hand in and felt around for... *Got it!*

Another key in another wall. *Hooah.*

He clutched the key and withdrew his hand. The van slowed down a block away. He needed Isabel's men to see what he was doing for his plan to work. He used the key to unlock the iron gate and slipped through.

Allison followed, the red-light flashlight bouncing around. "How do you have a key to this cemetery?"

"When I was a kid, my friends and I found the caretaker's spare." He pocketed the key and held his weapon against his thigh. "We used to steal it and play hide-and-seek in this cemetery after dark. I hope it still works."

She followed his fast-paced stride. "That's strange."

"But fun." They moved quickly, using the red flashlight to dodge headstones, then hiding behind a weeping angel thirty yards from the entrance.

Once the men parked their car and entered the cemetery, Zack threw rocks in the opposite direction. The men followed the noise, and Zack ran back to the gate and locked it.

Zack returned to Allison and tugged her up.

"Why did you lock the gate?" she whispered. "With these enormous perimeter walls backed up by even larger tombs, it'll be impossible to get out."

"I know." He kept his gun ready and let Allison guide them with her light. Slowly, they wound their way through the cemetery that looked like a city made of tiny marble houses.

Allison tripped and Zack stopped. Once she was hidden behind a crumbling mausoleum, he climbed on top of a crypt to see if he could locate the men. They were forty yards away.

When he jumped down, he noticed the worry in her eyes. "We're not far from the center. We'll be out of here soon."

They heard a man curse loudly, and Zack led her toward the path that cut through the middle. It took another fifteen minutes of hiding and waiting and running around tombs before reaching the gate on Washington Avenue, on the other side of the cemetery.

Allison held the light while Zack unlocked the gate. The old key got stuck and he had to jiggle it. Unfortunately, the metal-on-metal sound reverberated throughout the cemetery and he heard footsteps coming closer.

Comeoncomeoncomeoncomeon.

Allison's red light bounced off white marble tombs and one of Isabel's men saw it.

The lock gave, and Zack swung the gate open. Once they were through, he shut the gate, reached through the iron rails, and started to lock the padlock again—until he dropped the key.

The man fired, and Zack pushed Allison out of the way, making sure she was hidden behind the exterior brick wall.

The second man appeared, running toward Zack.

Zack found the key on the ground and locked the gate.

The first man fired off two more rounds just as Zack threw himself against the wall. He reached behind to take Allison's hand.

"Hey!" one of the men yelled. "Let us out."

Zack had a decision to make. He could get into a shootout with the few bullets he had left, or take off with Allison and get to the safe house. The cemetery walls wouldn't hold Isabel's men for long, but it might be enough time for them to get away.

The men were now rattling the gate and Zack took her hand and headed toward Coliseum Street. Then he prayed his safe house was actually safe.

ॐ

Allison waited while Zack knocked on the door of an enormous house in the Garden District. The style reminded her of Pinckney House, except much larger.

A minute later, they heard a female voice on the other side of the door say, "Who's there?" followed by the distinct sound of a shotgun being loaded.

"It's Zack. And a friend. Please put down the shotgun Nate gave you."

The door unlocked and swung open to expose a tall woman with long red hair still holding a pink shotgun. "Hurry up."

Allison followed Zack inside. Once he relocked the door, he hugged the woman. LED lanterns lined the foyer and sat on every other stair leading up to the second floor.

"It's so good to see you, Kate." Zack stepped back to wave Allison forward. "This is Allison Pinckney."

Kate leaned her gun against the wall and took Allison's hands. "Welcome." Then she looked at Zack again. "What are you doing here?"

"It's a long story." Zack exhaled and ran his hands over his head until clasping them behind his neck. "I know it's a lot to ask, but can we stay here until we can get out of town safely?"

"Of course." Kate led them through the foyer and up the stairs. She picked up one lantern along the way. "I'm not sure what's going on, but you both look exhausted. Why don't you rest and clean up while I make you something to eat?"

Allison followed Kate upstairs, appreciating the pressure of Zack's hand on her lower back. Her legs dragged like lead weights and her head felt fuzzy.

On the second floor, Kate stopped near the first door and handed Zack the lantern. "Your rooms are adjoining. Despite the heat, you may want to start a fire for more light. There are also two lanterns in the bathroom. I've left them around the house because of the crazy power fluctuations."

Zack kissed her cheek. "Thank you."

Allison entered a bedroom made up in various shades of blue. Even in the lantern light, she could see the blue silk wallpaper decorated with images of herbs and flowers. The coverlet on the four-poster bed, also made of blue silk, carried the same embroidered design as the wallpaper.

Two chairs flanked the fireplace, and drapes covered the windows. "This is beautiful."

"Thank you." Kate pointed toward the door in the far corner. "Zack, your room is through there. If you need anything else, I'll be downstairs in the kitchen. When you're ready, you can tell me what's going on."

Kate left, closing the door behind her, and Zack quickly built a fire.

Allison sat in a chair near the fireplace, watching the flames. So much had happened. So many setbacks. And now they had so little time.

He leaned one arm against the mantel and studied her. "How are you?"

"I'm...shaky. Like I want to eat and throw up and run a marathon and sleep for three days, all at the same time."

"It's the adrenaline." His gaze found her lips. "It affects everyone differently."

"I suppose." She pointed to his stained T-shirt. "You're filthy."

He pulled it over his head and she stood before him. Her fingers traced the muscled indentations on his chest, disturbing the fine, dark hair. When she brushed over his pectoral muscles, near his nipples, he inhaled. Touching his body, so hard and strong and beautifully made, made it difficult for her to breathe. "Zack, what are we going to do? We don't have the appendix and we're running out of time."

"I don't know." The raw truth in his voice brought tears to her eyes.

She wanted to solve their problems, bring him the peace she knew he craved. But she had no idea what to say. As her hands skimmed his ribs, his breaths shortened and his nostrils flared. Before she could think her way out of it, she kissed him.

Her lips met his in a fiery storm of need and desire. There was nothing soft or gentle about her kisses. Nothing but the heat that coursed through her, sending her lower abdomen into a series of contractions. She might not be able to offer him the love she knew he wanted, but she could offer everything else.

"Allison—"

"No arguments." She yanked off her blouse and cami. Her bra landed on the bed. "I need you. Now."

He growled and, before she knew it, she was on the floor with her jeans and panties stripped off. He didn't even bother undressing. He just unzipped, released his erection, and drove into her. Her head hit the leg of the chair near the fireplace, and the hard floor offered no give beneath her back. His hands held her hips and he sucked her nipples until she cried out.

His lips found hers again, and she untied the leather band holding back his hair. It fell over them, keeping her in his private space. His lips, his powerful hips between hers, his body driving into hers, all of it seemed raw and intimate at the same time. Her heart swelled until the pain forced a tear to fall.

She raised her hips, and he lifted his head. He kept her gaze as he pressed her legs apart so he could pound even more deeply into her. She closed her eyes, giving herself over to the rising heat, the powerful spasms that started in her toes and ended in her core.

As her world shattered around her, he dropped his hands to the floor on either side of her head. She gripped his tattooed biceps that bulged from holding his own weight. He threw back his head and let out a primal moan. His hair fell behind his shoulders and his tattoos seemed even more prominent in the firelight, as he held himself deep inside her, his hips forcing hers even wider. He stilled and his body stayed connected to hers. It was as if he was unable, or unwilling, to let her go.

She studied his closed eyes, intricate arm tattoos, his chest looked carved it out of marble, and the pulse that pounded in his neck. *Her wild man.*

But for how long?

Now that they were on the verge of failure, would he leave her when this was over? She couldn't love him the way he wanted. And she'd never want to hurt him the way she'd hurt Stuart. Zack deserved all of her and she wasn't sure if she even knew how to do that.

He kissed her softly. "No worrying."

She closed her eyes, mostly to hide her tears. "I'm not."

He nuzzled her neck. "And I didn't just make love to the woman of my dreams."

She laughed even though she wanted to cry. What they'd done had solved none of their problems, but for some reason she felt better. She felt safer. She felt...loved.

"Come on." He managed to stand up, adjust his clothes, and carry her to the bed. "You rest and I'll bring you up something to eat."

Her eyes closed even though she fought to keep them open. She was still naked, but the bed was too soft, the coverlet too cool, the firelight too hypnotic.

He kissed her forehead. "I'll be back soon."

When she heard the click of his adjoining door, she knew she was alone.

CHAPTER 36

THANK GOD KATE'S HOUSE HAD A LANDLINE. AND A SPARE, extra-large black T-shirt.

Zack took another bite of his third sandwich, drank a huge swig of water, and dialed.

Nate answered, "Iron Rack's Gym. We now offer self-defense classes for the women in your life."

"It's me."

Nate sighed. "Are you okay? Rafe told us you were being followed by Isabel's men."

Zack told Nate everything that'd happened and ended with, "We didn't find the appendix."

"I'm sorry, Zack. You've got to come back to Savannah. ASAP."

"I can't, Nate. I'm running out of time to save my sister."

"We can help you. We'll work on it as a team. Because that's what we are—a team."

"You can't help. I'm not sure anyone can." Zack leaned back in his chair behind Kate's desk. "Besides, we can't take off until the power is restored."

Zack took more bites of his sandwich before Nate said, "Let me tell you what's been going on here tonight."

When Nate was done, Zack seriously considered going outside, finding Isabel's men, and letting them shoot him. "Are you telling me that Kells's contact—the dude who negotiated our dishonorable discharges with the secret congressional committee—knows I'm involved in this mess with Remiel and the Prince? And because of my actions, we may end up going to jail anyway?"

It was like history on repeat—because of him and his actions, his men were screwed.

"Yes," Nate said. "That's why you need to come in. Now."

"Fuck."

"Again, yes." Nate lowered his voice. "This isn't your fault."

"No? Whose fault is it?"

"It's Kells's fault," the female voice said from the doorway.

"Who's that?" Nate said. "Her voice sounds… Oh, hell no."

"I had no choice." Zack stared at the woman in jeans and a white T-shirt, with a mass of reddish-blond hair.

"There's no coming back from this," Nate said. "When he finds out—"

"I'll call you when we're on our way home." Zack hung up and said to Kate, "Nate knows where I am. He guessed."

She shrugged. "Honestly, Zack, I don't care. I'm done with the lies, secrets, and violence."

"You're wrong." He moved toward the woman he'd known for years, the woman who'd saved them tonight. "Leaving him isn't going to make you safer; it's not going to change who you are or where you fit into this story. If you loved us"—Zack pressed his hands over his heart, hoping to appeal to her lighthearted side—"you'd come back."

She broke into a smile. "Of course I love you all. It breaks my heart that half of you are in prison, that I'm losing all of you as well as him."

"Then don't let him go." Zack took her hand and squeezed. "Please, Kate. We're desperate. If you care at all for us, reconsider your decision to divorce Kells."

"Allie! I painted my treasure box." Danny tossed his metal lunch box into her tree house and scrambled in. His blond hair stuck up everywhere. "Want to know why?"

She glanced at the white and green broken daisies he'd painted along the sides of the lunch box, in between the superheroes. Then she turned the page of Wuthering Heights *and ate another handful of popcorn. "No."*

"Mercy Chastain used her broken daisy to protect herself from her accusers. It was her tally man."

"Talisman."

"Right!" His green eyes shone with excitement. "I read it in the witch's examination before it went missing. I'm doing the same thing to protect us from Fenwick."

Allison threw popcorn at him. "Don't let Mama hear you say that."

He sat crisscross-applesauce and held the treasure box on his lap. "I also overheard Mama talking to Fenwick about the dread pirate Henry Avery. He killed Mercy, and in return she cursed anyone who looked for Henry's treasure."

Allison rolled her eyes. "That means the daisy didn't work for her."

"Or she didn't use it properly."

"If you spent more time on schoolwork and less time reading about pirates, Mom and Fenwick wouldn't yell at you so much."

Danny's lips trembled. "I hate them."

She closed her book. "No, you don't."

Mama and Fenwick weren't kind, but they didn't beat their kids. At least, not Danny.

"I do!" Danny fisted his hands. "I think Fenwick killed Dad. If Dad had used the broken daisy, he might still be alive."

She sighed. They'd been having this conversation a lot lately. "It was an accident while Dad was looking for me in the woods." Which was all her fault because she'd had a fight with her mother and had run away. "Dad tripped and his gun went off. Even the police said so."

"Then why did Mama marry Fenwick so quickly?"

She scooted back until she rested against the tree house wall, dragging Danny and his box with her. She blinked away tears. She missed her father horribly and wished she could go back and change things. "I don't know."

"I can prove it, Allie," Danny whispered against her shoulder. "I mean, I can almost prove it. You should keep the treasure box. You need protection more than I do. They're meaner to you."

She breathed in his scent of puppies and pine. "If you keep fighting them, things will get worse."

"*Some things are worth fighting for, Allie.*" Danny sniffled. "*We're worth fighting for.*"

She rested her chin on his head and closed her eyes. "*You're worth fighting for, Danny. Me, not so much.*"

"*You can't believe what Mama says about you.*" His voice deepened, startling her with its sudden maturity. "*She's changed since she married Fenwick. He's changed her.*"

"*It doesn't matter. Remember, we have a plan.*"

His voice hitched. "*Are we still running away to live with Nana in New Orleans?*"

"*Shh.*" She opened her eyes and touched his lips with her finger. "*You can't tell anyone. You have to pretend like everything is still the same. Go to school and have your friends over. But, yes, once we have enough money, we're leaving here. Forever.*"

He wrapped his arms around her waist and hugged hard. "*I love you, Allie!*"

"*I love you too, Danny. I'll never let anything happen to you.*"

Allison was drowning. She opened her eyes and couldn't move. Her arms and legs were frozen. She couldn't even blink. Worse, every gasp for breath left her choking.

The memories of the day before Danny died kept her paralyzed. Those moments replayed in her mind over and over again. She'd promised to protect him and yet he'd drowned.

Find a path back.

Zack's words called to her. She was strong enough to fight this half-waking nightmare, to reclaim her life. She focused on one finger at a time.

I can do this.

She closed her eyes, the only function she could actually control, and went back to her fingers. This time she imagined her fingers tracing Zack's tattoos. Along one arm, around his back, and down the other arm. Every one of the dragon's scales, his green eyes, the golden hilt of the lance striking its heart.

One finger moved.

She changed her mental image to one of his hard chest. The cuts and indentations of muscles so unlike her soft stomach. The feel of hair covering warm skin. The dark line that led from his belly button down to... Her toe moved.

As her visual exercise became more erotic, she swallowed. Remembering his powerful body deep inside hers, filling and stretching and claiming, made her lower abdomen clench. Remembering the moment he climaxed, the way his eyes darkened, allowed her to fist her hands. Remembering the way he said *I love you* loosened her chest and brought a rush of air into her lungs.

With every memory of their lovemaking, she reclaimed more of her own body. A few minutes later, she was able to sit up in bed and wonder why her entire body ached.

Of course. Everything rushed back in vivid color. She glanced around the room, realizing she was alone.

Once she'd put herself back together, Allison went downstairs, following the lanterns. She'd showered and put her clothes on. Thank goodness the bathroom was stocked with toiletries. It was amazing what a difference a toothbrush and a comb made in a girl's life.

She followed the voices to the back of the house. Despite her sleep paralysis, she'd only slept for twenty minutes.

"Kells is pissed at me because I won't follow his orders, and your pending divorce is making him even angrier." Zack's voice came out of the kitchen.

Allison paused in the shadowed hallway, one palm against the wall. She didn't want to interrupt the heated conversation.

"My divorce isn't about you," Kate responded. "I have to do this."

"No, you don't. There are things going on that you don't know. Those of us still free may end up going to prison after all."

Allison heard a loud clanging, like a porcelain mug hitting a steel sink.

"That's not possible," Kate said. "Your discharges were approved—"

"Kate, when will you understand that the rule of law doesn't apply here? It has never applied. Our teams were set up, our men imprisoned without due process, there was no real defense, and our futures were negotiated by Kells's contact without our input. That means Kells's contact can do whatever he wants to us."

"You're worrying about nothing, Zack."

"Really? Kells is freaked."

"Once Kells signs the divorce paperwork and realizes we both need to get on with our lives, he'll feel better."

"You couldn't be more wrong." Zack's laugh was short and harsh. "Kells loves you. He will never get over losing you. That's the truth of it."

"Loves me like you love Allison?"

"My feelings for Allison have nothing to do with this."

"Zack, they have everything to do with this."

"Am I interrupting?" Allison entered the room lit with lanterns and flashlights. If she was going to reclaim her life, she needed to do it with honesty and dignity.

Zack smiled when he saw her. "Are you hungry?"

She pressed a hand against her rumbly stomach. Despite eating her way through the French Quarter, she was hungry. "Yes."

Kate brought a tray of sandwiches to the table and then went to the two-burner camping stove on the counter. A saucepan sat over one of the propane-fueled flames; a coffeepot sat on the other. From the saucepan, she ladled out a bowl of soup. "I hope you like tomato."

"I do." Allison sat in the chair Zack pulled out for her. "Thank you."

Kate came over with the bowl and a smile.

Allison took a sip. "It's wonderful."

Zack brought her a glass of water. "You didn't sleep for very long."

"I slept a bit."

Zack met Allison's gaze, but his was unreadable. "I explained the situation to Kate. She's married to Kells, my boss."

Allison nodded. "Thank you for taking us in, Kate."

"Not at all." Kate graced her with another one of those killer smiles. "Would you like some coffee?"

"Yes, please. With cream and sugar."

Zack glanced at his watch. "Kate, I'm going to try your emergency radio again."

"Here." Kate handed him a cup of coffee.

When Zack left, Allison wasn't sure what to say so she started with, "This is a beautiful house."

"Thank you." Kate came over with two more mugs of coffee, both with cream and sugar. "It belonged to my mother. When she married my father, she moved to Boston. After her death, she left it to me."

"You didn't grow up here?"

"No. My father hates New Orleans. Too hot and buggy."

Allison started on the sandwich. Eating was good because it helped quell the awkward pauses.

"I know this sounds weird"—Kate stared into her mug—"but I know a lot about you."

"Me?" Allison wiped her lips with a napkin. "How?"

"I've known Zack since he joined the Seventh Special Forces Group at Fort Bragg. The unit was close."

"Your husband, Kells, was in charge?" Allison took another bite of her sandwich.

"Yes. And I made it my mission to get to know all the men." Kate stared out the dark window, as if remembering something. "I'm not sure if I should tell you this, but Zack has been in love with you since I've known him."

"He also had a fiancée."

"Not for long." Kate sat across from Allison. "You were the only one he ever talked about. You have always been everything to him."

The bread suddenly tasted dry, like sandpaper. She had no business being anyone's *everything*. She wasn't even sure if she wanted that job. Although she and Zack were intimate and he loved her, she knew in her heart that she couldn't love him the same way. She'd never loved anyone that way. And when she'd tried, her husband ended up having an affair with a murderess.

And having wild sex every night with Zack? That wasn't love. It was solace.

"Allison?" Kate touched her hand. "I'm sorry about your husband."

She met Kate's gaze, and it took everything inside her to act normal despite the fact that she'd just realized: if she didn't want to break Zack's heart, she had to tell him they didn't have a future. Not a long-term one, anyway. "Zack told you?"

"Yes. It's awful what happened. Zack also told me what you two are trying to do." Kate got up, turned off the burners, and shut the valve on the small propane tank. "With any luck, you'll never meet Remiel Marigny."

"We can't find the appendix. And we may not be able to save Emilie."

Kate gripped the counter, her back toward Allison. "I know. I hate what's been happening to my...Kells and his men."

Allison finished her soup and sandwich and brought her dishes to the sink. She hated what this was doing to Zack and would give anything to be able to fix it. Especially since his career might be the only thing he had left. "We have one remaining clue."

Kate looked at Allison. "What's that?"

"The man we met tonight mentioned Stuart may have hidden the appendix to protect me and that he'd had help from someone named Danny."

"Do you know who this Danny is?"

"He's my brother who drowned when I was eleven."

Kate took Allison's hand and squeezed. "I'm sorry."

Allison nodded and noticed her tote bag on a chair. "Danny believed my uncle killed our father to marry our mother. Danny was so obsessed by the possibility that our uncle would hurt me, he reread *Hamlet* daily. The irony is that he's the one who drowned." She took out Stuart's planner and flipped through the pages again until she came to the quote. "'When sorrows come, they come not single spies, but in battalions.'"

"That's from *Hamlet*?"

"Yes. It's engraved on Danny's tombstone." She wiped her eyes. "I guilted my mother into having that quote put on his tombstone. She wanted something else, but I insisted. The interesting thing is that earlier today I noticed something new—a crude engraving of a broken daisy on the back of Danny's tomb. Someone had also planted flowers and herbs."

"Why a broken daisy?"

"It was Mercy Chastain's talisman."

"Zack told me about your ancestor, the unnamed accused witch from 1703."

"Danny believed the broken daisy was supposed to keep Mercy safe." Allison flipped through the calendar pages. "Three months ago, I planted violets on Danny's tomb. Whoever carved that broken daisy and planted rosemary, thistle, and lilies of the valley had to have done it since then."

"Any idea who?"

Allison spun the planner around and pointed to a particular calendar block. It was marked *St. Philip's Churchyard*. "In a box of Stuart's things, I found a receipt for a garden center dated the same day—the same day he'd borrowed a hammer and a chisel. I think Stuart bought those flowers and planted them behind Danny's grave after he carved that broken daisy."

Kate read the planner. "Do you think that broken daisy is a message?"

"Maybe. Although I don't know what the plants mean."

"They're plants found in Marian gardens." Kate glanced at Allison and shrugged. "I'm a historical horticulturalist. My company restores historical gardens. Here in New Orleans, there are a number of abandoned churches with attached gardens that were once dedicated to the Virgin Mary. They were called Marian gardens, designed with specific plants symbolizing different moments in her life.

"Rosemary, thistle, and white lilies of the valley represent three of Mary's dolors, also known as sorrows. Rosemary represents the flight from Egypt, thistle represents her son's passion, and the lilies of the valley represent her tears at the crucifixion. All three flowers are also powerful symbols of protection: physical, emotional, and spiritual."

"That's interesting, but why would Stuart plant them? Why carve a broken daisy on Danny's tomb?" Allison stared out the dark window. She didn't even react when the lights turned back on. "Danny believed

Mercy's broken daisy was a symbol to ward off her accusers. Kind of like apotropaic marks are symbols to protect from curses."

Kate touched Allison's shoulder. "Did Danny ever use an image of a broken daisy to protect himself?"

Allison pressed the heels of her palms to her eyes. "I think I know where Stuart hid the appendix."

∽

Zack found the women in the kitchen, hovering over Stuart's planner. Instead of checking the emergency radio, he'd rescued the car. Isabel's men had disappeared, and since it was dark out, he'd been able to run with his weapon ready without anyone noticing. "What's wrong?"

Allison smiled but didn't meet his gaze. "I think I found the appendix. It's in Charleston."

Zack picked her up and spun her around. "Now that the power is on, our plane can leave. You can tell me in the car how you figured it out."

Allison left his embrace and picked up her tote bag. "Thank you for helping us, Kate."

"Of course." Kate gave Allison a hug. "Safe travels. I hope you find Emilie soon."

So did he. "Turn on the house alarm after we leave, Kate. And make sure that shotgun Nate gave you is loaded."

"I will." She followed them toward the foyer, turning the lanterns off along the way. "I keep the knife Pete gave me, along with Luke's whistle and Ty's pepper spray, in my purse. And tell Cain while I appreciate his gift of brass knuckles, I'm not sure how to use them."

Zack chuckled. "Please reconsider the divorce, Kate. It's killing Kells."

Kate opened the door. "I've already filed the paperwork and am waiting for a court date."

Zack paused near the open entrance. A breeze blew through, and he could smell ozone in the air. It was about to rain again. "Is there anything I can say to change your mind?"

"No."

Zack kissed her cheek and walked Allison to the car. For the first few minutes after they drove away, Allison told him why she believed the appendix was in Charleston. While he wasn't sure about her logic, it was possible.

The other thing he wasn't sure about? She seemed…distant. Or maybe she was just tired.

Once they hit I-10, his phone buzzed with a text and he dug it out of his pocket. "Fuck."

"What's wrong?"

He held the phone so she could read Kells's text.

Don't come back to Savannah. Ever.

"What does this mean?" she asked.

"I've just been fired."

CHAPTER 37

NATE PACED THE BACK ROOM OF IRON RACK'S GYM.

Over the past two months, he'd been turning this storeroom into their unit's command post. So far he'd scored folding tables, six chairs, and a metal filing cabinet they used as their armory. The room reeked of chemical fumes from their desperate attempt to get rid of mold.

The gym was still undergoing renovations, so their real issue was power. Until they redid the wiring and got better internet service, it was impossible to use the equipment and put up the kinds of firewalls a computer geek like Luke required.

Luke, Ty, and Cain came in with sullen faces and coffee mugs and sat at the table. They'd had a long day dealing with gym members and Kells's mood. Being down two men had been harder than Nate had expected.

"What now?" Ty said with so little enthusiasm one would think he'd just had a root canal.

"We have a problem." Nate was too worked up to sit, so he paced. "Where's Kells?"

"Gone," Luke said around a yawn. "Don't know where. He took Vane with him."

Of course Kells took Vane. Because Vane, despite being a highly trained and experienced soldier, was a suck-up. If Kells needed something from coffee to a listening ear, Vane provided it.

"Any idea when Kells will return?" Nate asked the men.

They shook their heads.

"Good." Nate rubbed the back of his neck. "That's good because

I have something to tell you and something to ask you and Kells can't know any of it. At least not right now. Oh, and there's also some distressing news. I should've told you earlier, but I didn't."

Cain leaned back in the chair that was too small for his frame. "Let's get the telling over with first."

"Last night, Detective Waring arrested Alex in Charleston."

Ty's exhale sounded long and tired. "Why?"

"Alex was protecting a child and hit a man. Except the man was the child's father and filed charges. Luckily, Rafe handled it and got the charges dropped."

"How?" Luke asked. "Rafe isn't a lawyer."

"He plays one for the Fianna." Nate pressed his palms on the table. "Kells wasn't here, so I made a command decision to send Rafe, Pete, and Garza to fix the situation."

"Wait." Ty squinted. "Half of our unit is in Charleston?"

"Yes." Nate went through why Alex and Zack were in Charleston and everything about Emilie and the treasure. "While Alex was waiting to be released, Zack went to New Orleans to search for the witch's examination's appendix. While there, he ran into trouble with Remiel's men. He may have fired a weapon in public."

Cain raised an eyebrow.

Ty rested his head on his arms on top of the table.

Luke stared into his coffee mug.

Nate continued, "Things got spicy when the city's power went out. Zack lost cell service, and he had to find a safe place to stay. Remiel's men followed Zack until he ditched them. Zack couldn't go to Vivienne's because he knew they'd look there first."

Luke drank his coffee and grimaced. Probably from the bitter aftertaste caused by the cheap beans. "Where'd Zack go?"

"To Kate's." Nate stopped talking because he needed that little detail to sink in. It took a moment, but one by one the men sat up and stared at him with wide-open eyes.

"*Whaaaaat?*" Luke drew out the word until it hit three syllables.

Nate nodded. "Zack had Allison with him—"

"Whoa." Cain threw up his hands. "Zack took Allison with him on a mission? What the hell is wrong with him?"

"Dude." Ty laid his head on his arms again. "Zack's been off the rails since Stuart died. He's spent more time in Charleston than Savannah. Which sucks because we need the help here."

Nate agreed but that wasn't their main concern. "Zack is on his way back to Charleston and called before takeoff to fill me in on what he's learned and what he needs help with."

"Is this the asking part?" Luke looked around the room at all the men who weren't there. "There are only four of us."

Nate took another breath and told them about why Kells had been such an ass lately: Kate filing for divorce and Kells's contact finding out about Zack's unauthorized mission. The only two things Nate left out were the bit about Kells's potential actions that may have held off rescuing their men, including Nate, for two years and the fact that Kells's contact was so pissed he could send them all to prison.

That intel was simply too fucking much for them to deal with at that moment.

Nate ended with, "Zack needs our help rescuing Emilie."

"How are we supposed to do that?" Luke asked. "We don't know where she is."

"I'm waiting for Zack to arrive in Charleston and call us back. Then we'll make a plan."

"We did the tell and the ask." Ty finally lifted his head. "What's the distressing part?"

Nate crossed his arms and stared at his men. "Kells knows that Zack went to New Orleans and fired him."

Two hours later, Allison ran into her house and headed for Stuart's study. It only took a moment to open the safe and pull out Danny's treasure box. She ran her fingers over the broken daisies her brother had painted along the sides of the lunch box.

Zack appeared with their bags. "Have you opened it yet?"

She clutched the box to her chest. "I was waiting for you."

He dropped their bags on a chair in front of the desk and said, "I'm ready."

She placed the box on the desk and opened it. The scents of pine and puppies filled her lungs and tears stung her eyes. She took out a manila folder with two words printed in Stuart's perfect handwriting: *For Allison.*

Zack undid the metal clasp. She held her breath as he pulled out a set of yellowed pages, each one wrapped in archival plastic. Gently, he laid seven pages on the desk next to each other.

Allison took the magnifier out of the desk drawer. "It says appendix on top, but the entire page is filled with words. They're not even in sentences. Just line after line of random words. This doesn't make sense."

Knocks sounded on the front door and Zack went to answer it.

When he left the room, she exhaled loudly. She was a coward. She had to tell him what she'd realized, what she had to do, but she couldn't. She couldn't be in the same room with him without wanting him. But while she desired his touch, his kisses, his body moving over hers, she would not be so selfish as to break his heart.

Once her phone had worked again, she'd even texted her UVA colleague about that job.

Using the magnifier, she studied the writing on the other pages. Every page was filled with words in no order with no sentence structure. And on various corners of every page, someone had drawn a tiny broken daisy.

Zack returned with Alex and three men she'd never met.

"Allison?" Zack motioned to the first man, who was wearing a blazer, dress shirt, jeans, and a holstered weapon. "This is Detective Garza."

She nodded and a second man stepped forward, hand out. He looked like a convict. Tall, brown hair, the most intense gaze she'd ever seen, and one arm tattooed with words in an elegant script that were barely covered by his black T-shirt. "I'm Rafe."

She turned to the last man with long plaited black hair that reached his waist. While not as tall as Zack, the third man was wide as a door and made of solid muscle. He wore black combat pants and T-shirt, and had tribal tattoos on his arms.

He didn't just shake her hand. He kissed her cheek. "I'm Pete. I can't believe I'm finally meeting you."

She had the distinct impression all the men were armed.

"Hi." Because that was totally lame, she cleared her throat and added, "Thanks for helping Alex."

"No prob." Pete placed his fists on the desk and said, "What've we got?"

"We have the appendix and…" Zack held up the tracing paper with cutout windows that Allison had taped together on the plane. "A homemade copy of the Pirate's Grille."

"Except," she said, "I'm not sure I put it together properly."

For all she knew, she'd taped the three sections backwards.

"Let's give it a try." Garza took off his jacket and tossed it on a chair. "What do we do with it?"

"We lay the Pirate's Grille over the appendix. The words that you see through the cutout rectangles will hopefully expose a message." Allison pointed to an appendix page. "The Pirate's Grille is smaller than the appendix pages, and I don't know how to align them."

Pete held the magnifier over an appendix page. "None of these words make sense. They're not even in sentences."

"I know," Allison said. "It's possible it's gibberish to throw off treasure hunters."

Pete handed Zack the magnifier. "Have I mentioned today how much I hate pirates? I hate their maps, their treasures, and their bullshit psy-ops games."

"Gotta give this old pirate credit though." Rafe leaned over the desk to study the pages. "Henry Avery pulled off the largest pirate heist in the history of the world and hid his treasure in a way that no one has ever found it."

Allison placed the Pirate's Grille over an appendix page and… nothing. Words appeared through the holes, but none of it made sense. "Huh. This is supposed to work."

"Maybe it's upside down," Pete said.

Garza turned the Pirate's Grille upside down, and still none of the exposed words made sense together. "That didn't work."

"Fuck you."

Rafe took the tracing paper and laid it over another appendix page. "Why are there bent flowers on the corners of each appendix page?"

"How the hell should I know?" Pete shot back.

Minutes later, the men were still arguing about which side of the Pirate's Grille was up or down. Allison went toward the window, where Alex sat with Danny's treasure box on his lap. She was exhausted and could no longer look at the appendix pages without the words blurring.

"Are you okay, Alex?"

"It wasn't the first time I've been arrested and won't be the last." He winked. "I even got a present out of it."

"Oh. That's interesting." She wasn't sure she wanted to know about any *present*.

"What is this stuff?" He held up a Jolly Roger black bandana and a metal skull-and-crossbones key chain he'd taken out of the lunch box.

"My brother's treasures." She took the keychain and ran a finger over the indentations. "When we were kids, we found carvings of pirate skulls on the upper floor of the barn. My dad said they were late eighteenth century. Danny and I used to make up pirate stories and act them out in our tree house."

She glanced at the men who were arguing over whether or not the sentence *She laid waste to a headless son in the pasture* was a clue.

"Allison?" Alex poked her arm. "What barn?"

She looked at him. "The barn at Fenwick Hall. Now it's used for storing bottles of Raven's Retreat Absinthe and drying herbs."

Alex's eyes narrowed. "How far away is it?"

"Depending on traffic, thirty to forty minutes." She put the bandana and key chain back into the treasure box. "Why?"

Alex handed her the box, returned to the desk, gathered the appendix pages and the Pirate's Grille and shoved them in the envelope.

Pete reached for the envelope that Alex held above his head. "What are you doing?"

"We don't need to find the treasure," Alex said. "I know where Emilie is being kept."

"Where?" Zack demanded.

"Fenwick Hall." Alex looked at Allison. "In the barn."

Zack tried to take the manila envelope out of Alex's hand, but he wouldn't let it go. "Why do you think my sister is in the barn at Fenwick Hall?"

"When I saw Emilie, she was in a rustic building. I wasn't able to determine where I was, but I smelled lavender and rosemary and other herbs—including something that smelled like licorice. And I saw carvings of skulls on a beam. Allison said she and Danny found skulls carved in the barn near Fenwick Hall."

Zack looked at Allison. "Do you think Rue would hide my sister for the Prince?"

"If the Prince is holding Rue's money hostage." Allison went to the tote bag, took out the spreadsheet, and handed it to Detective Garza. "The Fianna were helping Stuart and Rue embezzle money."

Garza stared at the page. "Why?"

"Supposedly Rue was trying to leave her husband. Although we don't know Mack enough to trust him." Zack had already filled the men in on their trip to New Orleans—including the part where Kells fired him.

"Dude." Pete spoke to Zack but stood next to Alex as if in a show of solidarity. "This is a good thing. Why are you discounting it?"

"Because we don't know for sure." Zack dug through the desk drawer and found a map of Charleston he'd seen the other night when he'd searched the room. He laid it on the desk and pointed to Hoopstick Island, the small spurt of land off of John's Island. "We've no resources. If we do this—plan a raid and she's not there—we've tipped off the Fianna. They'll know we don't have the treasure, and they'll hand my sister over to Remiel."

Garza looked at Rafe. "Will the Prince really do that?"

Rafe crossed his arms. "Yes."

Zack looked at the men in the room. "Whatever we do, we have to be smart about this."

"I say we vote," Alex said. "We raid Fenwick Hall and save Emilie or stand here and scratch our balls. In private, of course."

Zack chewed the inside of his cheek and stared at the map. If they were wrong, it could mean Emilie's life.

"It's also the only thing we have to go on," Pete said. "Since we're voting, I'm in."

"As am I," Rafe said.

Garza nodded. "Me too."

Everyone looked at Alex, who said, "It was my idea."

"Do you have weapons?" Rafe asked.

"Yes," Allison said. "There's a bunch to choose from."

Zack knew exactly what was in the gun safe. "Four pistols, three rifles, a twenty-gauge shotgun, and a twelve-gauge shotgun. There's also a crossbow and a ton of ammo."

Allison raised an eyebrow and Zack shrugged. It was his job to monitor the weapons.

"It'll have to be enough," Rafe said.

"Alex?" Zack said as he started marking up the map with a pen. "You're not coming."

Alex slammed his hand on the desk. "Why?"

"You have to stay with Allison, and I can't let you get into any more trouble."

"This is bullshit," Alex said.

"Zack is right," Rafe said. "Someone has to stay with Allison."

Alex pointed at Rafe. "Then you do it."

"*Enough.*" The men turned to Zack with shocked stares, but he didn't care. "My mission, my rules. We load up and leave in ten minutes."

"We can take my truck," Rafe said.

Allison was looking at her phone. She hadn't said a word about not going and Zack had expected a fight—or at least a fuss.

He studied her in her jeans and white blouse, her blond hair piled high in a messy bun. She glanced at him and a chill went up his back.

There was something else about her...that distance cloaked in sadness that he still couldn't identify. While he'd much prefer to stay here and figure out what the hell was wrong, he had to save his sister. "I'll be back soon."

She placed her phone on the desk and nodded.

Zack clasped his hands behind his neck and exhaled. "Let's roll."

CHAPTER 38

A FEW MINUTES LATER, ALLISON FOUND ZACK GRINDING HIS TEETH in front of the open gun cabinet in the pantry. The men had packed up Stuart's hunting weapons, and she'd drawn Zack a map of the hidden gate near the river that would get them onto the Fenwick Hall property.

"Zack," she said softly. "What's wrong?"

He placed ammo boxes on the counter. "Nothing."

She knew that wasn't true because in the last few minutes, he'd been terse and distant. "I know something's—"

He slammed the door and faced her. His clouded eyes were filled with hurt and anger. "Why didn't you tell me you were considering that UVA job? Why didn't you tell me you were leaving Charleston?"

She swallowed and licked her lips. "How do—oh. My phone." She'd left it on the desk right after they'd voted to save Emilie, and he probably saw the text that'd come in from her UVA colleague. It'd been filled with excited emojis. "It's not decided yet."

"You haven't asked me if I'd go with you." He gripped the cabinet handle and his knuckles whitened. "Does that mean you haven't decided whether or not to break my heart?"

"No. I mean..." She clasped her hands behind her neck and stumbled over her words. "I don't know what I want."

He grabbed her shoulders and pulled her against his chest. "Then let me remind you."

His lips met hers with force, like a silent plea to be seen, to be understood, to be loved—a plea she wasn't sure, right now, she could answer.

When his lips softened, she wrapped her arms around his neck and clung to him. She might not know what she wanted, but she knew who she wanted—*her wild man.*

Zack ended the kiss, picked up the ammo, and left the room.

She followed him, but by the time she got to the foyer, the men had left, slamming the door behind them.

She blinked to clear her blurred vision and locked the door.

"Where's Nicholas Trott?" Alex asked when she entered the study. He sat near the window, reading a book, with her handgun on a nearby table.

"Spending the night with Susan and Mrs. Pickles." Allison touched her lips and moved to the window. The garden lights were on, but it was dark outside.

Zack's kiss hadn't just been forceful yet gentle. It'd been…fearful.

It'd been a silent plea to wait.

While she wanted to go after him now, she knew it was best if she stayed behind.

At first, she'd been annoyed that he hadn't wanted her to help save Emilie, but while watching the men—professional soldiers—organize their mission with such efficiency and calculation, she'd realized she'd only be in the way.

Besides, she had the feeling Zack *needed* to save his sister without her.

"Zack was a sourpuss before he left," Alex said as he turned a page.

She crossed her arms tightly around herself. "He found out I'm considering a teaching position at the University of Virginia."

Alex moved toward her and stared into the garden as well. "Are you leaving Zack behind?"

"I don't know." She pressed her fist against her forehead. "It's a great job and a chance to start over again. I also know Zack has commitments to his men in Savannah. I don't want to hurt him, but I honestly don't know if I want him to come with me. All I do know is that I want to find Emilie and end this nightmare."

Alex's breaths sounded harsh. "Can you guess what the problem is with running away?"

She shook her head and brushed away a stray tear.

"You take yourself with you." Alex bumped her shoulder with his. "I speak as a man who's run away and been put away."

She exhaled heavily. "I don't know what to do."

"In a situation like this, you're not supposed to. And while I hate to break up your personal pity party, we have real things to worry about. Like Zack leading an operation with no idea what he's walking into. Hell, for all we know, there could be a company of Fianna warriors there protecting Emilie."

She hit Alex's massive bicep with her small fist. "Why didn't you say something?"

He didn't even have the decency to rub his arm like it hurt. "Zack is a Green Beret. He'll figure it out. Unfortunately, he's almost out of time."

She swallowed back the tears that made her vision blur. She hated that she was such an emotional mess. "Do you think Kells meant it when he told Zack not to come back?"

Alex shrugged. "Kells gets frustrated when men don't do what he says or question his orders. The irony is he's known in SF circles to be calm, cool, and completely in control. Since the discharges? He's been under tremendous stress and acting like a dick. Probably because he's beholden to this super-secret contact who's keeping his men out of prison. Being an ass is his way of coping."

She could see why a man like Kells might act like that. And she could also see why Zack would chafe. "I think Zack is trying to redeem himself. To prove he's not a coward."

Which was crazy because he was the bravest man she knew.

"Probably. Male pride and all that."

She gave her most dejected sigh, went to the desk, and found Stuart's planner. "Alex, what did you find at the Charleston Architectural Board?"

Alex came to the desk and shoved the envelope containing the appendix and homemade Pirate's Grille into the tote bag. "Stuart borrowed a book, *Notorious Pirates and their Secrets, 1650–1781*. It hasn't been returned, so he must've put it somewhere."

Allison flipped through the planner. "I've not seen anything like that in the house."

"Maybe at his office?"

"No. The bank delivered..." A flash of heat rushed through her body. With shaky hands, she dropped the planner and grabbed Alex's wrist. "Get your gun."

"Why?"

"We're going to Pirate House."

Zack led the way through the woods around Fenwick Hall, trying not to worry about Allison's text. Not only was he shocked by her consideration of that job, but his heart was shattered. Even though they'd never once talked about their future past the Fianna-driven deadline, he'd just assumed...because he was a selfish bastard.

When was he going to remember that about himself?

Why wouldn't she take the job? Why wouldn't she leave all of this heartache behind?

Why wouldn't she want to start a new life with new people in a new state?

While a part of him wanted this opportunity for her, another part knew the futility of running away. Hell, he was living that futility every moment of every day.

Including that exact moment, as he dodged a spiderweb only to step near a nest of copperheads.

He moved carefully, silently ordering himself to let go of his worry about Allison. He had to keep his focus sharp and his physical responses sharper.

He held up a hand and stopped behind an oak tree fifty yards from the barn. Pete and Rafe squatted nearby. Garza waited on the causeway, where they'd hidden the truck. Being a cop, they decided it was best for him to stay as far outside of this operation as possible.

Their other concern was Rafe. He'd gotten no information from the Fianna about this situation. They had no idea what they were walking into, how many—if any—Fianna guards were there. Yet if the warriors discovered Rafe was helping Zack, the Prince could rain down hell.

"Getting here," Pete whispered, "was too easy."

Zack glanced at Pete and Rafe. Since they both wore black combat pants, black T-shirts, field jackets, and boots as their regular-day dress, they were more prepared. This wasn't the first time he'd ended up running an op with little preparation, wearing jeans and carrying borrowed weapons. But he was determined to make it his last.

"I agree," Rafe said.

Allison had been right about the opening in the ten-foot-high wall surrounding Raven's Retreat. What she hadn't mentioned were the brambles, snakes, or spiders.

"The only cameras are on the front gate and the trees down the driveway," Rafe said. "Which is strange."

"Allison said her mother and Fenwick rely on the walls, the river, and the impassable land for protection."

Pete peered into the dark. "Is this place really a cult?"

"Yes." Zack wished they had night vision, but they'd have to manage with two flashlights they were hesitant to use. Luckily, the half-moon's reflection off the river provided ambient light. "Fourteen men and twenty women live here with Rue and Fenwick."

"That's fourteen men too many," Rafe said. "Still, I don't see any of them. There were no guards at the front gate. No perimeter patrols. Something doesn't feel right."

Zack pointed to the barn near the river. "Pete, you and I will get into the barn. Rafe, you stay behind as watch. Signal if anyone shows up."

"What if there are warriors inside?" Pete asked Rafe.

"Pray. Kneel. Submit."

Zack nodded. "Let's go."

A few minutes later, Zack opened the combination lock and led Pete inside the barn. There was no movement, no sounds other than the river lapping at a faraway dock.

"What's that smell?" Pete whispered.

"Herbs." Like the last time he'd been there, he smelled lavender and licorice. Unlike last time, the fan sound was off and the upper door was no longer barricaded.

Once they cleared the bottom floor, they met at the steps. Zack went upstairs first and used his rifle to push open the unlocked door. He went in, surveyed the scene, and exhaled.

"Well, shit," Pete muttered.

A lit flashlight lay on the floor, beneath a blanket, giving off a muffled beam. A mattress in the corner had a plate of food next to it. Pete picked up a newspaper. It was the same one Emilie had held in her proof-of-life photo.

They heard an owl hoot twice. Then a third time.

Pete gripped Zack's shoulder. "That's Rafe. We need to leave."

Emilie was gone. Zack had failed. Again.

"Come on!" Pete dragged Zack down the stairs and stopped.

Two flashlights came on, blinding them. Zack raised his hand to shade his eyes, and one of the lights lowered enough for him to see the situation.

Horatio and another warrior he didn't recognize blocked the exit.

Horatio turned off his light and came forward, his gun's red laser sight pointed at Zack's chest. "Offer your swords to Fortinbras."

When the red laser sight from Fortinbras's gun hit Pete's forehead, Pete threw down his rifle. Zack tossed his on top.

Horatio raised an eyebrow.

"Fuck." Pete pulled out his pistol and knives and tossed them.

Zack did the same. "Now what?"

Horatio pointed to the door. "Now, you attend us."

Fortinbras came over with plastic zip ties and bound Zack's and Pete's wrists behind their backs. Fortinbras gagged Pete with a blue bandana.

Before Fortinbras could gag Zack, he demanded, "Where's my sister?"

"Safe for now." Fortinbras shoved a gag into Zack's mouth and dragged him toward the door. "Although you may have forsaken Lady Emilie's life because you've chosen to fight instead of search."

"Fuff foo." He tried to kick Fortinbras only to trip and fall to his knees.

Fortinbras yanked Zack up and pain ripped through his shoulder. He ground his teeth on the gag. He wouldn't give them the satisfaction of a grunt.

Horatio walked ahead with the flashlight until they reached a white van near the river. He opened the back and forced Pete in. Then Zack. Not an easy thing to do when one was bound and had to hop in ass-first.

Horatio pushed Zack, and he landed on his side. It wasn't until he managed to get into a seated position that he saw Detective Garza, also bound and gagged, a few feet away.

Horatio sat on a bench bolted to the wall and pointed his gun at Zack. "Pray that your love will find the pirate king's treasure in time."

The door slammed, and Zack kicked the metal door, leaving a dent the size of a cannonball.

CHAPTER 39

Allison led the way through the gate leading to Pirates Courtyard with a penlight, and Alex followed with his weapon ready. He'd not been happy about her plan, had bitched as she wrote a note to Zack telling him where she was going. Had complained so much that she'd even let him drive, although she doubted he had a license. While it was close enough to walk, she didn't want to waste time.

In the car, she told him about the boxes from Stuart's office that she'd had delivered to Pirate House because she didn't know what to do with them.

They entered the patio, guided by lights strung though the trees and around the fountain. She was surprised when the motion-sensor floodlight didn't turn on. She was even more surprised to find the back door unlocked.

Alex opened the door for her. "Why is the house unlocked?"

"I don't know. That's been happening lately." She entered the kitchen but didn't turn on the main lights. It just seemed safer keeping them off. "Over here."

"Why are we whispering?"

"It feels like we should." She used the flashlight to illuminate the boxes on the floor. Alex moved them to the kitchen table so she could start going through them. It didn't take long to find the book. While she checked the other boxes, Alex flipped through the book's pages.

A loud noise sounded on the second floor, and Alex raised his light to the ceiling.

When they heard the noise again, Alex ran down the hallway. He only slowed as he climbed the tight, narrow staircase. Allison came up behind him, tote bag on her shoulder. Her breaths shortened and her heart beat so loudly it was all she could hear.

The noise sounded for a third time, and Alex pushed on the door. It was locked.

Allison handed him the house key. "It works on all the locks."

He slipped it in and turned the bolt. Keeping his weapon ready, he put the penlight in his mouth and used his other hand to push the door open. They heard another bang.

Alex went into the room and stopped so quickly that Allison ran into his back. That's when she saw, in the beam of their light, Emilie on the floor near the fireplace. She was gagged, and her hands were handcuffed to an old iron ring attached to the mantel. Nearby was a wood box she'd been kicking. The velvet curtains hanging over the windows had been pinned together to keep the room dark.

Allison ran over and took out the gag. Emilie fixed her gaze over Allison's shoulder and yelled, "Watch out!"

Allison and Alex spun around at the same time as a woman with white hair and in a pale blue nightgown appeared. Allison stumbled back. *Mercy Chastain?*

The woman's wild, unkempt curls floated around her shoulders, and her face was covered with tiny scars.

The woman rushed Alex, except he subdued her easily and ended up holding her back to his front with his arms around her. And he still held his weapon. "What. The. Fuck."

"I don't know her name." Emilie coughed on the words, and Allison found a half-full water bottle nearby. She held it up for Emilie to drink. "But she lives here. These strange men take care of her. Since I've been here, she hasn't spoken at all. I think she's mute."

In response, the woman struggled against Alex again—in complete silence.

"What men?" Allison checked the handcuffs and iron ring. She had no way of getting Emilie free.

"These men with a strange walk who talk like they're from another century. There's usually one with us at all times. They only tie me up when they leave us alone."

"Allison." Alex grunted as he kept the woman under control. "In my back pocket, there's a handcuff key."

She hurried over and found it. "Why—"

"My present from the police station." He pulled the woman to the floor and got her to sit between his legs. His arms were around her middle, keeping her from flailing, and his legs were over hers. And he still held his weapon.

Allison unlocked Emilie and helped her up. "I'm so sorry we couldn't find you sooner."

Emilie gave Allison a hug. "I'm grateful you found me at all."

"Uh," Alex said with more groans and grunts as he kept the struggling woman from kicking him. "What now?"

"I will tell you, my lord and ladies." The male voice came from the doorway, and they turned to see Marcellus blocking the way, a handgun pressed against his thigh. "'Tis time for the madness to end."

Isabel sat on a bench in the back of Saint Philip's east churchyard and checked her phone. The electricity and cell service had returned earlier, and her crew was using the construction equipment again. Fluky power wasn't conducive to treasure hunting.

Neither was the cloud cover, another threatening storm, or her pounding stress headache.

Clayborne strode in her direction, dodging a sleeping angel statue embedded in weeds and wildflowers. While she didn't care how the church honored its dead, she was grateful for the cover. For the past few weeks, she'd had a crew disguised as a pipe restoration company digging around the graves, and no one had said a word. Now, with Pastor Tom in the hospital, they could work at night.

The annoying thing was that she had to pay her men overtime—not because they were working in the dark, but because they were afraid of seeing Mercy Chastain's ghost across the street.

Clayborne stopped in front of her. "There's nothing here. Stuart gave you wrong information."

She looked up at him. "Stuart loved me. He wouldn't do that."

Clayborne wiped his forehead with his arm. "Toward the end of your affair, Stuart knew you'd betrayed him. It's possible he betrayed you first by giving you false information."

No. It wasn't possible. Stuart had loved her. She stood, walked to a construction hole, and stopped near a headstone carved with a broken daisy. "Stuart gave me the information in bed. Before he knew I worked for Remiel."

Clayborne kicked a rock—or maybe a bone—into the hole. "Earlier today I asked a historian to look at Mercy's headstone. While old, it might be a forgery."

She frowned. "What are you talking about?"

"I believe Stuart found an old, unnamed headstone in the back of this cemetery and added that carving of a broken daisy. Stuart wanted you to believe that Mercy was buried here as a fifolet to protect Henry's treasure."

Isabel wrapped her arms around herself. Had Stuart betrayed her? If so, then all of this time had been wasted. "If the treasure isn't here, where is it?"

"I don't know." He took out his buzzing cell phone. "It's a text from my man following Horatio."

She read over Clayborne's shoulder. "Your man lost Horatio but found Marcellus."

"Yes." Clayborne whistled to the crew and they turned off their equipment. "Marcellus just entered Pirate House."

Isabel smiled and stared through the darkness toward the house beyond the iron gates. Then, she embraced the relief that eased her headache.

Pirate House was across the street. And it was time to end this.

CHAPTER 40

WELL, FUCK.

Alex released the woman and stood, making sure the three women were behind him and his weapon was pointed at Marcellus. "I'm leaving, and I'm taking *all* of the women with me. Whatever game you're playing"—he nodded toward the woman in the blue nightgown silently sobbing in a corner—"it's over."

"This play within a play ends when the Prince wills it." Marcellus floated in with that eerie walk and stopped in front of Alex. "I require your phones."

Alex was so sick of this shit. "Do you not see my gun? It's pointed at your fucking face."

Marcellus laughed as another armed warrior entered the room. This one, a tall black man with green eyes and wearing combat pants, held a gun with a red laser sight pointed at Emilie's forehead.

Alex placed his gun on the floor and kicked it to Marcellus. He could take one man in the space of a gunshot, but that second would kill Emilie. Of that he was sure.

Allison and Alex threw their phones on the floor. Marcellus tilted his head until Alex tossed his second phone as well.

"Well met." The new man with an Australian accent hit his chest with his free fist and bowed his head. "They call me Laertes."

"Laertes?" Allison's voice sounded hushed, and she stared at him with wide eyes.

Laertes nodded. "My lady."

Allison frowned.

"Laertes watches over the mute woman," Emilie said in a muffled voice. "He's her keeper."

"Who is she?" Allison asked.

"Lady Tarragon," Marcellus said.

Allison glanced at the woman who now sat on the bed. "Mack McIntyre told us Remiel killed Tarragon because she gave Stuart the witch's examination."

"The Fiend failed." Laertes, still holding his gun, went to Tarragon and placed a hand on her shoulder. "The Fiend tortured her with his box."

Alex inhaled deeply. When this was over, he was going to finish what he'd started five years ago. He was going to kill Remiel, even if it meant going back to prison for the rest of his life. "Instead of getting her medical help, you keep her prisoner?"

"Lady Tarragon is no prisoner." Laertes folded a blanket that had fallen to the floor. "She's a selective mute and has chosen to be here."

Emilie pointed to the corner from where Tarragon had emerged. "She comes and goes through a back staircase."

"The hidden doorway," Allison said. "It leads to Pirates Courtyard—except it was boarded up years ago."

Laertes dropped the blanket onto the cot, took a white cloak off a hook on the wall, and draped it around Tarragon's shoulders. "When Master Stuart requested help from the Prince, one of his tasks was to restore this room and the hidden entranceway for Lady Tarragon."

Allison sighed. "The termite remediation he was taking care of for me."

Between Tarragon's white-blond hair and the white cloak over the pale blue nightgown, she appeared otherworldly.

"Oh my gosh." Allison finally realized the truth. "Tarragon is the ghost of Mercy Chastain people have seen roaming the courtyard and the cemetery next door."

"Yes." Laertes walked Tarragon toward Marcellus. "Nighttime is the only time she feels safe outside, the only time no one can see the damage the Fiend inflicted."

Allison moved in front of Tarragon and reached for the key that hung on a chain around her neck. "This is a key to Pirate House and the gate between Pirates Courtyard and the cemetery."

Laertes bowed his head. "A gift from Master Stuart."

Marcellus checked his watch. "'Tis late. Ladies Emilie and Tarragon will accompany us. Lady Allison must search for the treasure."

"And what do I do, Marcellus?" Alex's sharp tone could slice granite. "Sit on my ass while you take the women away?"

"You do nothing." Marcellus tilted his head. "'Tis what you do best."

Alex ground his molars. He knew bait when he heard it. "I have another offer. In exchange for the women's freedom, I'll return to the Prince."

Laertes laughed, his arm around Tarragon's shoulders. "'Tis a foolish—"

"Ask him." Alex kept his gaze on Tarragon's terrified face. "Ask my brother which he'd rather have—two women who are nothing more than leverage, or me."

"Wait." Allison grabbed Alex's arm. "The Prince is your *brother*?"

Alex met her surprised gaze with a shrug. "Yep."

Laertes nodded at Marcellus. "We accept."

"I don't understand." Allison squeezed Alex's arm. "What just happened?"

Alex handed her the car keys and whispered, "Take the women and drive to Savannah. Don't stop until you get to Iron Rack's gym. Nate will help you."

"I can't—"

"You have to." Alex removed her hand from his arm. "Marcellus, how do I know you'll let the women go?"

Marcellus bowed his head. "You have our word."

Tarragon shook her head, and Allison said, "I don't think she wants to go with us."

"She doesn't have a choice." Alex turned to Tarragon and held her scarred face within his palms. Using his softest voice, he said, "It'll be okay. If you go with Allison, you'll be safe. But you have to leave now."

Tarragon shook her head again until Emilie gripped her hand. "We can go together."

"I don't like this," Allison said to all the men. "You have no right to take Alex."

"Allison!" Alex hated yelling, but she had to get with the plan. "Leave. *Now.*"

A short pause later, she and Emilie helped Tarragon toward the exit.

"Lady Allison." Marcellus stepped in front of the doorway, blocking them. "Do you have any words for your lover?"

"What are you talking about?"

"He and his brothers-in-arms have been taken. If you want to save him, find the pirate king's treasure."

Allison's wide-eyed gaze found Alex's. "What—"

"Allison!" Alex ordered in his sharpest voice. "Go. *Now.*"

Nate tossed his coffee into the trash. Luke hovered over a laptop looking up any information he could find on Henry Avery and his treasure. Ty slept on a couch in the corner. Cain was working off his angst on the punching bag in the gym.

This waiting for info sucked. The only bright spot was that Kells hadn't returned yet. The longer he stayed away, the more time Nate had to fix things.

He was winding his way through the gym to get a bottle of water from the office when his cell phone rang. "Rafe? What the fuck is going on?"

"We have a problem."

Nate stopped near the front desk, put the phone on speaker, and closed his eyes. "Tell me."

"While looking for Emilie at Raven's Retreat, two warriors took Garza, Pete, and Zack. I tried to follow, but I lost them."

"And?" Because there was always an *and*.

"When I returned to Allison's house, I saw a letter."

"A letter." Nate opened his eyes to find Cain a few feet away, listening. He had stripped off his T-shirt and was panting from exertion. The sweat had soaked the waistband of his gray gym shorts and made the tattoos on his arms shine.

"Alex and Allison went to Pirate House to find some book. By the time I got there, two warriors were taking Alex away."

Nate rubbed his forehead with his fist. "You're telling me that Alex, Garza, Pete, and Zack—half of our unit—were taken by the Fianna *and* the women are missing?"

"Yes."

"Fuck."

"The treasure?" Cain spoke loudly, as if not aware of how speaker-phones worked.

"No idea." The sound of a truck engine came through the phone. "There's something else. Since the night of Hezekiah Usher's murder, I've been asking other warriors for intel, but I've come up with nothing. I think I'm being shunned because I've been helping you."

Nate closed his eyes again. "Where are you now?"

"On my way back to Savannah. I have the distinct feeling—"

"Uh-oh." Cain tapped Nate's shoulder and he opened his eyes to find Kells and Vane a few feet away, arms crossed, listening.

Fuuuuuck.

Kells focused his gray gaze on Nate. Kells didn't need to say anything. His flared nostrils and narrowed eyes told Nate everything he needed to know about his boss's rage level. And Vane's smirk? That just made Nate want to use his fists.

"Rafe?" Kells spoke into Nate's phone. "Distinct feeling about what?"

"Isabel, by manipulating Alex, has cut your force in half."

When the dashboard clock told Allison it was almost one-thirty a.m., she stepped on the gas and passed the sign for 17 South. Emilie sat next to her, and Tarragon was curled up in the back seat. She'd refused to wear a seat belt, and Allison hadn't fought her. At some point, they'd have to stop for gas and get directions to Iron Rack's Gym.

Unfortunately, none of them had cell phones. If she could find a gas station that sold burner phones, maybe she could call the gym and let Nate know what had happened. Thank God she'd kept her purse in the car. If she'd not had a wallet, they'd be in even more trouble.

And the fact that Laertes was the warrior she'd met seven years ago in New Orleans? Almost too insane to accept.

"Allison?" Emilie sorted through the appendix pages on her lap. "If we want to save my brother, do we really have to find a pirate king's treasure?"

"Yes." She passed a truck and returned to her lane. Now she remembered why she hated this road: no streetlights. She turned her beams on high.

"How?"

Allison stopped at a stoplight and took out her homemade Pirate's Grille. "When you place this over the appendix pages, the cutouts expose a hidden message in the text."

Emilie shoved the documents back into the envelope and opened the book. "This is insane."

"That doesn't mean it won't work." The light turned green, and Allison stepped on the gas again. "I know you've been through a lot. I haven't even asked you—"

"I'm fine." Emilie flipped a few of the book's pages. "I was terrified, of course. And I'm sure, once we save my brother, I'll cry for days. But until we save Zack, I'm solid."

"Thank you."

"You're welcome."

Tarragon made a croaking sound from the back seat. She'd moved forward to stare at the book in Emilie's lap. Emilie handed her a water bottle Allison had in the car.

Allison noticed a sign for a gas station. "Are either of you hungry?"

Tarragon nodded and drank her water.

Emilie wrinkled her nose. "I'd love to get a toothbrush and maybe some deodorant."

"We'll get whatever you need." Allison pulled into the station, parked the car in front of a pump, and glanced in the rearview mirror.

Tarragon had laid down again. "I have some extra T-shirts in the trunk, if you don't mind wearing a photo of my dog."

"I'll wear anything as long as it's clean." Emilie opened her door, got out, and stretched.

Allison came around and gave Emilie a hug. "We were so worried."

Emilie hugged back. "I'm so grateful you found me."

There'd been no time for any kind of emotion, and Allison was beginning to feel tired and headachy, probably the letdown from the adrenaline and stress.

She popped the trunk and grabbed a bag filled with T-shirts. "I'll get some things from the convenience store. Pick whatever T-shirt you want. While I'm inside, can you watch over Tarragon?"

"Of course."

Allison found her purse and went into the store. A few minutes later, she emerged with four bags filled with supplies. She handed one to Emilie. "Toothbrush, toothpaste, liquid soap, deodorant, and a brush. I also bought some food and scored a burner phone."

Emilie clutched the bag and a pink Nicholas Trott T-shirt to her chest. "Tarragon went to the bathroom while you were inside and is asleep again. I'll be right back."

Allison started filling up the car's tank and checked on Tarragon again. She'd slipped a blue Nicholas Trott T-shirt over her nightgown. Sighing, Allison leaned against the car door and dialed 411 on the burner phone. Luckily, they were able to connect her to Iron Rack's gym.

"Hello?" The male voice sounded hesitant and stressed.

"Hi, uh, this is Allison. Is Nate there?"

"Thank God." The man's exhale carried through the line. "I'm Nate. Where are you?"

"We're forty minutes away, I think."

"We?"

"I have Zack's sister, Emilie, with me, and another woman named Tarragon. She was tortured by Remiel and captured by the Fianna. I also think the Fianna have Zack and the other men."

"Allison? Listen to me," Nate said in a firm-yet-gentle voice. "I need you to drive safely for forty minutes. Can you do that?"

She swallowed. "Yes."

"Are the Fianna following you?"

"No. They let us go because Alex offered himself to the Prince in exchange for our release. But they took our cell phones."

"Wow. Okay. Was not expecting that. Here's the address." Nate rattled directions, and she wrote them down on the back of a Nicholas Trott greeting card she found in her purse.

"Got it," she said. "I'm leaving now."

"You can do this. We'll find Zack and all will be well. I promise."

His voice, so calm and confident, eased her racing heart. Her "thank you" came out in a rush of gratitude.

Once she hung up, she finished pumping the gas and Emilie appeared wearing the T-shirt and a big smile.

Allison twisted on the gas cap. "It always feels good to brush your teeth, doesn't it?"

"It does." Emilie got into the car and dropped her bag into the back seat.

Allison slid behind the wheel. "I called Nate. It's going to be okay."

Emilie nodded and Tarragon moaned in her sleep. Allison drove out of the station and turned the radio to something classical to keep everyone—including herself—calm.

All will be well.

Just as she settled into a good speed and her eyes readjusted to the shadowy road, she noticed a large SUV with its flashers on stopped in the middle of the road.

Had there been an accident?

Emilie reached for the dashboard. "What's going on?"

"I don't know." Allison shifted into reverse just as a truck tapped her bumper from behind. The SUV drove closer until her car was trapped.

Tarragon sat up, and Emilie pulled the tire iron from beneath her seat.

Allison, blinded by the headlights, drove forward and back in short increments, trying to maneuver a way out. "Where—"

"I took it out while you were in the station." Emilie's voice sounded strained.

Emilie's window smashed and she fell over onto Allison's lap. Someone had broken the passenger side window with a sledge hammer. Allison stepped on the gas until the driver's side window exploded. The force threw her to the side, and she landed on top of Emilie.

Although Allison was dazed and covered with shattered safety glass, she was aware enough to realize someone was carrying her out of the car.

"Put Allison in the SUV," a familiar voice said. "You take the other two."

"Did you find anything?" The female voice cut through the sounds of boots crunching broken glass on the road.

Isabel?

"There's a tote bag on the front seat." The familiar male voice again.

Allison kicked at the man shoving her into the car. He threw her face-first onto the seat and bound her hands behind her back. When she fought, someone gagged her.

She choked and struggled to sit up. Through the window, she saw another guard locking Emilie and Tarragon into the pickup truck. Just before the guard blindfolded Allison, she noticed something else. Isabel stood in a circle of headlights. She wore black combat pants, a tan T-shirt, and her hair had been pulled into a tight bun. Besides her gun holstered on her waist, she held the tote bag with Allison's research and was talking to a man in jeans and a black motorcycle jacket.

Clayborne Fenwick. Her uncle. Her father's murderer.

CHAPTER 41

Isabel held the tube with the Pirate's Grille in one hand and, with her other, laid out everything from the tote bag on the hood of the car.

"So." Clayborne held the flashlight for her. "You didn't destroy the Pirate's Grille."

She ignored him. She had everything she needed now. Allison was trussed up in the back, and the other two women were in the truck. Isabel hoped that receiving Tarragon and Emilie would appease Remiel until she found the treasure.

She and Clayborne had followed Marcellus into Pirate House and heard the exchange between Alex and the warriors. She could've made herself known, but she decided her best chance of finding the treasure did not include open confrontation with two Fianna warriors. Her best chance lay with following the women.

Clayborne moved his flashlight beam over the papers. "Attaching a tracking device to Allison's car was a brilliant idea."

Isabel glanced at him. Did he not realize that this was why she was the boss? "I did that when Allison parked on her street during the fire. I figured if she took off suddenly—like she did tonight—it meant she found something."

Isabel was grateful the device had worked. The other thing she was grateful for? Everything in the tote bag including duct tape, scissors, a history book, and the witch's examination's appendix pages. She even found a crude homemade Pirate's Grille. From the way it was taped, it was off about an inch. But it was close.

"Well, aren't you clever?" Isabel whispered to herself.

Allison made struggling sounds in the back seat, and Isabel nodded to one of the guards. He slapped her and she stopped moving.

"Be a good girl, Allison," Isabel said loudly enough for the other woman to hear. "Or I'll hand you over to Remiel when we're done."

Clayborne pointed to the Pirate's Grille. "Do you know how this all works?"

"Yes." She took out the original Pirate's Grille and laid it over an appendix page, making sure to line up the broken daisies. "The holes in this grille aren't symmetrical, so it can be turned over and upside down. Stuart told me to line up the broken daisy on the grille with the broken daisy on the appendix page to get the right alignment."

A minute later, she put on her glasses and read the words showing through the grille's mask. "'I grieve for you, O Mary most sorrowful, in the affliction of your tender heart at the prophecy of the holy and aged Simeon.'"

Clayborne leaned over to see. "What the hell?"

Isabel covered the second appendix page with the grille and read, "'I grieve for you, O Mary most sorrowful, in the anguish of your most affectionate heart during the flight into Egypt and your sojourn there.'"

Clayborne took the third. "'I grieve for you, O Mary most sorrowful, in those anxieties which tried your troubled heart at the loss of your dear Jesus.'"

Isabel took off her glasses. "These sound like the Seven Dolors of Mary."

Apparently, her expensive parochial high school in Savannah had had value after all.

She read the last four appendix pages. "They *are* the seven dolors. But why go to all that trouble to hide them in a cipher?"

"No idea. This is fucked up. I thought we'd be getting directions, like some kind of eighteenth-century GPS system."

She'd thought that too. She walked to the car's open back door and looked at Allison. With her gag and blindfold, her hair hung in chunky strands around her sweaty face. "Do you know what the seven dolors mean?"

Allison shook her head.

"Of course she's going to say no," Clayborne said.

Isabel motioned to the guard. "Get out." When he did, she sat next to Allison, took off the gag, and whispered, "How about a trade? You tell me what the seven dolors mean, and I'll give you the information Zack needs to save his men."

Allison sniffled and wiped her mouth on her upper arm. "I don't know."

Isabel grabbed Allison's hair and yanked her head back. "I could torture you instead."

Allison grimaced. "Like you tortured Stuart?"

"*Yes.*"

"I don't know what it means."

Isabel re-gagged Allison and got out. Isabel had done enough interrogations in her time that she could tell Allison wasn't lying.

Isabel found Clayborne flipping through the book they'd found. "Somehow, these dolors are supposed to lead us to the treasure. We just have to figure out how."

Clayborne scratched his head. "Henry Avery wasn't a church-going man."

"Henry Avery was a brilliant, paranoid opportunist who trusted few people." Isabel put the papers into the bag. "He was also a unique, out-of-the box thinker."

"You think this is an out-of-the-box message?"

"I do." She just didn't know what kind yet.

"Look at this book about pirates and their secrets." Clayborne had stopped at a page with a yellow Post-it note with the words *Mercy's grave?* written on it.

"That's Stuart's handwriting." She read the chapter title: *Thomas Toban and the Ironworker.* "It says here that in 1702 the pirate Thomas Toban hired the Charleston iron and glassworker Joshua Linguard for a project that took two years to complete and cost ten thousand pounds."

Clayborne pointed to a sentence. "The project was completed in May 1704, and Joshua disappeared a few weeks later."

"The same time that Henry and Mercy disappeared." Isabel looked off into the distant darkness. "Hezekiah said that Thomas bought Henry Avery's ship when he retired. So Thomas and Henry knew each other."

"Maybe this project was the hiding of Henry's treasure?"

"Possibly." She turned to another page and her heart raced. "Here's a scanned image of the eighteenth-century receipt. It's signed by Joshua Linguard, Thomas Toban, and Mercy Chastain."

"Mercy was definitely in on this gig, then."

Isabel grabbed the flashlight to look at the Joshua Linguard Workshop logo on the receipt—a *JL* in the middle of a lily. "This logo is on the doorknob of the Usher Society building."

"Turn the page. There's another photo of that logo."

She turned to see a close-up photo of church doors with the doorknobs carved with the *JL* logo. The year 1704 was marked below. "I know this church."

She threw the book into the tote bag and got into the car.

"Where are we going?" Clayborne asked as he started the car.

"To find the treasure."

The van stopped, and Zack opened his eyes. They'd been driving for... Hell, he had no idea how long they'd been driving. It was dark and hot in the back of the van with no windows or ventilation.

Or maybe it was the heat of Horatio's contempt.

Fuck you, buddy.

The van door opened and Horatio got out, rifle over his shoulder, flashlight on. Zack was grateful for the breeze, even if it meant an incoming storm.

Zack pulled off his gag. Pete's and Garza's eyes went wide until Zack held up a metal bolt he'd found beneath his ass. While they'd been driving, he'd cut through the zip tie. Luckily, it'd been dark and bouncy, so Horatio hadn't noticed.

Pete turned, and Zack cut his ties. Then Pete freed Garza.

Horatio was talking to Fortinbras. They spoke so softly Zack couldn't hear.

"Now what?" Pete asked.

"We run."

"No. We don't even know where we've stopped." Garza lowered his voice even more. "*You* run. They won't all go after you because they'll need to take care of us as well."

"We separate them?" Zack liked the idea. "What about you two?"

"We'll pretend we're still bound. When we start moving again, we'll figure out a way to take control."

"It's dangerous," Zack said. "They're Fianna warriors."

"Fuck that," Pete whispered. "We'll meet you back at the gym."

This was one of those plans that seemed destined to fail—pretty much like every plan he'd made lately. "We've no idea where we are. It could take hours to get back to Savannah."

Pete gripped Zack's shoulder. "Then you better start running."

Zack nodded and moved toward the door. The warriors were talking near the driver's side door. The woods were on his right, and he saw a sign for the town of Levy.

Thank God. "We're close to the Georgia border."

He shimmied out—the only time in his entire life he'd ever shimmied anywhere.

Once clear of the van, he scrambled down a ravine. Although the woods looked close, there were still ten yards to clear before he hit the tree line. He ran faster than he'd ever run in his entire life. He only paused once, a few minutes later, when he heard two particular sounds. Loud male voices and...*gunshots.*

Nate sat in the gym's office while Kells paced the room. So far, Nate had been called irresponsible, rash, reckless, as well as other words he'd never repeat in polite company.

Yes, maybe the decision to send Pete and Garza to Charleston hadn't been well thought out. Adding Rafe to the mix when Kells still didn't trust the ex–Green Beret/Fianna warrior might not have been Nate's best idea. But the truth was Kells had gone off without telling anyone where and had left Nate to deal with the crisis.

Rafe, who stood in the corner, cleared his throat. "The women should've arrived by now."

Nate sent Rafe a *Really?* glare. Because stating the obvious wasn't helping.

Rafe's response? A shrug.

Kells stopped near the window overlooking the street and crossed his arms. "Nate, are you sure you gave Allison the correct directions?"

Oh. Come. On. "Yes, sir."

The office door opened, and Luke's head appeared. "Pete and Garza are—"

Pete pushed by Luke. Garza followed. While Pete strode to the window near Kells, Garza stayed back, near the filing cabinet that held the printer.

Kells's eyes widened in surprise. "I thought you were taken by warriors?"

"We were," Pete said. "Me, Garza, and Zack. But we got away."

Kells glanced at Garza. "*How?*"

That single word carried a number of questions, including *Did anyone die?*

"While looking for Emilie, we were taken by two heavily-armed warriors and tossed into a van. When we stopped near the Georgia border, we broke free and Zack got out to run—"

"Wait," Kells said, "Zack left you behind?"

"It's not what you think, sir," Pete said. "We decided he should run and divide the warriors. One ran after Zack while we took down the other and grabbed the van."

"Pete," Nate asked, "You didn't pass a car with three women in it, did you?"

Pete frowned, then Garza frowned, and both said, "Why?"

"Allison called an hour ago. She, along with Emilie and a woman named Tarragon, were driving here after escaping two Fianna warriors. Except they're late."

"Do you know what kind of car Allison drives?" Pete asked.

"Yes," Rafe said. "A silver Honda Accord."

"I told you." Garza pointed at Pete. "It had a bumper sticker that said *Nicholas Trott for Charleston County School Board Supervisor*."

"This isn't my fault." Pete pointed back at Garza. "Nicholas Trott is a common name. I mean, who elects a dog to a school board?"

"That's enough," Kells said. "Did you see Allison's car?"

"Yes." Pete ran his hands through his hair that had been plaited hours ago but now hung straight down his back. "Off to the side. It looked abandoned."

Fuck. "Where?"

"A few miles north of the Georgia border."

"And you didn't check it out?" Nate asked Pete.

"I didn't know it was Allison's car. We wanted to get back here as soon as possible. We also had no way of knowing Allison was anyplace other than at her house with Alex."

"Wait," Garza said. "How did the women get away from the Fianna? And what happened to Alex?"

Rafe stepped up for this one. "Alex traded himself to the Fianna in order to let the women go."

"So," Kells said slowly as if he were speaking to children, "Zack is on foot, running from a Fianna warrior. Allison, Emilie, and another woman are missing. Alex is with the Prince."

"There's one more thing," Pete said. "That Fianna warrior we overtook in order to get the van? We didn't kill him."

Kells frowned. "I'm very glad about that."

Pete grabbed two water bottles from the small fridge and handed one to Garza. "We had to do something with him though."

Luke's head appeared in the doorway again. "Sir? Did you know there's a man tied up in the back room?"

Kells glared at Pete. "The Fianna warrior is *here*?"

Pete took a drink, almost finishing the bottle. "We had to bring Fortinbras with us."

Garza took a gulp of water and added, "He's your hostage."

CHAPTER 42

ALEX SHOVED THE BOX INTO HIS BROTHER'S CLOSET IN THE MILLS House Hotel suite and dialed Nate. When Nate didn't answer, Alex left a detailed message and hung up. Then he returned to the living room to finish the dinner he'd ordered from room service.

Even though he was stuck here, with Marcellus in the hallway guarding the door, the information he'd just learned was worth being traded for the women.

Finally, just as Alex stacked his dishes on the tray, Marcellus opened the door and Aidan walked in. Although he wore a suit and still appeared tall and strong and formidable, there was a tiredness about him that Alex hadn't seen the other day.

"My lord," Marcellus said to Aidan. "Your brother has returned."

Aidan dropped a leather briefcase on a polished credenza. "Thank you, Marcellus."

Marcellus left and Alex said, "You heard what happened?"

"Yes." Aidan went for the bar and opened a bottle of water. "You gave yourself up to save those women. Commendable, yet as usual you acted without understanding the consequences."

Alex sat on the couch and propped his boots on the coffee table. Now that his stomach was full, he yawned. "I'm not interested in another lecture on my lack of impulse control."

"You can't lack what you never had."

Alex clasped his hands behind his head. If Aidan was going to lecture, then Alex was going to respond with insolence. "I saved them."

"You put them in even more danger."

"Horseshit."

"Do you know where the women are now?"

"On their way to Savannah where the great Kells Torridan can protect them."

"They were until they were intercepted by Isabel Rutledge. Now they, along with your buddy Zack, are missing."

"Wait." Alex stood. "*What?*"

"Isabel has Allison and has sent Emilie and Tarragon to Remiel. My guess is that by dawn, they'll be dead." Aidan pointed toward a door across the room. "Get some sleep. You're going to need it."

"Aren't we going after the women?"

"No." Aidan headed in the opposite direction, toward his own room.

"You and Kells are so much alike it's weird that he's not your brother."

Aidan came back, anger flashing in his eyes until his phone rang. He answered on the first ring. "Yes?"

Aidan's face turned red. "I'll be in touch."

After he hung up, Alex pressed even though he shouldn't. "Who was that?"

"Kells." Aidan headed for his room until Alex grabbed his arm.

"What's wrong?"

"Kells has one of my warriors. If I want him back, I have to give Kells what he wants."

"What's that?"

"*You.*"

Zack paused near an oak tree. Horatio had been hunting Zack for miles.

Zack's lungs ached and his legs felt like they were going to fall off. He pressed his forehead against the bark and took in as many deep breaths as he could in the shortest amount of time.

I have to keep going.

Except the problem was he had no idea where. His only hope was to find a river or a road he could follow. He took in more breaths and listened to the sounds around him. When he didn't hear anything, he moved again. A hundred yards later, he noticed a road.

A light flickered ahead and he ran. A car sat on the side of the road. Its headlights were off but a man with a flashlight was searching it.

Horatio?

Zack crouched while Horatio went through the car. It wasn't until Horatio moved to the trunk that the flashlight lit up the back bumper. A silver Honda Accord with a Nicholas Trott bumper sticker.

Allison's car?

Horatio shut the trunk, leaned his ass against the metal, and held his cell phone to his ear. He held the car keys in his other hand. "I've lost Tremaine yet have reclaimed Lady Allison's carriage."

Where was Allison?

"Isabel has Lady Allison?" Horatio closed his eyes and responded, "Yes, sir."

Horatio hung up and went around to the driver's side door.

Zack picked up a dead branch and came up behind Horatio. Horatio turned just as Zack swung. The branch hit Horatio on the temple and he fell to his knees.

Horatio recovered enough to grab Zack's legs and throw him to the ground. The force knocked the air out of his lungs. Horatio straddled Zack and swung a right hook into Zack's jaw. Pain shot through his head and his vision starred. He reached for the nearby branch and swung again, knocking Horatio off. Zack straddled Horatio and threw so many punches he lost count. He only stopped because his fist had gone numb and his arm hurt like every bone had been broken.

Zack rolled off, his chest aching as he dragged in oxygen. He placed his palm on his own heart and discovered he was hyperventilating. Between the running, the fighting, and the worrying, he was a mess. Here he was, a former Green Beret, lying on his back in the middle of a rural road, barely able to breathe.

Hooah.

When Horatio groaned, Zack got to his knees and found the flashlight beneath the car. In the process, he found the car keys and discovered the front side windows had been smashed. He had to get himself together. Allison was missing and he had no idea where she'd gone. And what was he going to do with Horatio? Zack could leave him in the road, but that seemed cruel. Even for a Fianna warrior who'd been nothing but a pain in Zack's ass.

He used the car to pull himself up and found a dog leash in the trunk. After tying Horatio's hands behind his back, and spending another ten minutes dragging the enormous man into the back seat, Zack brushed away the safety glass and got into the driver's seat. Luckily, he'd found a bag with water bottles and snacks. He also had Horatio's cell phone, but it was locked. "Horatio? What's your phone's password?"

Horatio tried to spit at him.

Zack thought about everything he knew about Horatio. The man ran around hitting people, kidnapping women, and spouting Shakespearean verses.

Of course.

Zack used the keypad to spell out a word and…it unlocked! Since Nate wasn't answering his cell, Zack called the gym's phone.

"Hello?" Nate's hesitant voice came through in pieces, probably because there was little cell service.

Zack put the phone in the cup holder and drove. "It's Zack. I found Allison's car. I'm thirty minutes away."

"Allison called me earlier. She was with Emilie and another woman. I gave her directions to the gym, but we have no idea what happened to them."

"Isabel has Allison. I don't know about Emilie." Zack blew out a breath. Knowing Emilie was free of the Prince was a huge relief. But the fact that she was missing again made him feel even worse. "Pete and Garza?"

"They arrived with a Fianna warrior as hostage. Kells is concerned."

"Tell Kells I'm making it a twosome. I have Horatio."

"Great."

"What about the fact that Kells fired me?"

"Don't worry about that. Drive safely and get back ASAP. We'll figure out what to do next. Rafe just left to meet a contact. He's hoping to find something out as well."

"Thanks, brother. I'll see you soon." Zack tossed the phone out the window and sped up. The phone probably had a tracking device.

When Horatio moaned, Zack glanced in his rearview mirror. "Hey, Horatio. May flights of angels sing thee to thy rest."

Horatio raised his head and dropped it again.

Zack readjusted the mirror and thanked God for the gift of stupid cell phone passwords like *Hamlet*.

Allison couldn't breathe, couldn't see, couldn't move. But she could smell the distinct odor of gasoline.

Her frozen body refused to move and not just due to her bound hands, gag, and blindfold. She was also squished between two armed guards. It felt like she was trapped beneath ice, flowing with the cold current yet unable to let anyone on the surface know she was alive. The rag in her mouth made it impossible to swallow. She was completely immobile. She was shocked that she'd even dozed off.

Find a path back.

She moved a finger, but her hands, tied behind her back, had gone numb.

Slowly, she flexed each toe. At first, only her big toe twitched. Then feeling returned to her feet. As her body released the paralysis, she realized they were still driving and she'd no idea where they were going.

"The truck has arrived at Remiel's safe house," Isabel said softly from the front seat. "How many gas cans did you bring?"

"Four," Fenwick said. "Are you still reading that book?"

"Yes. I found documents folded in the back. They're the photocopied eighteenth-century records Stuart showed me proving that Thomas Toban bought two headstones in St. Philip's a few days after Mercy and Henry disappeared. One with a broken daisy carved on the front, the other with a skull and crossbones." Her sigh carried a bitter edge. "Forgeries, probably made by Hezekiah, to keep me away from the Isle of Grace."

"You betrayed Stuart, Isabel. You lied about working for Remiel and why you wanted Stuart to find those documents. Then you threatened Allison's life. What did you expect?"

"He loved me."

"Not enough to give you the treasure," Fenwick said.

"Be. Quiet," Isabel said.

"*Sooooo.*" Fenwick elongated the word as if trying to change the subject. "When we get there, what do we do?"

Allison leaned forward slightly.

"My guess is that Henry Avery had Thomas Toban and Joshua Linguard manage a project that hid the treasure."

"Except," Fenwick added, "if I were an evil pirate like Henry Avery, once this project was done, I'd kill everyone involved, including the manager and the builder. Since I'm also a paranoid fuck, I'd kill my lover and use her as a fifolet."

Allison heard the sound of flipping pages.

"Fifolets are mentioned a lot in this book," Isabel said. "If Henry Avery killed Mercy to protect the treasure, he may have also killed Joshua Linguard. Two murdered souls doubled the protection."

"And the treasure?"

"I assume buried beneath Mercy Chastain." A book slammed shut and Isabel said, "Once we get there, we look for her grave. Ten thousand pounds would buy a hell of a mausoleum."

"We have to dig up a woman who's been dead over three hundred years? Whose spirit might be a vengeful ghost?"

"You're afraid of vengeful ghosts?" Isabel's laugh sounded almost cruel. "The man who killed his own brother, married his brother's wife, and allowed his stepson to drown because he had proof of his father's murder? The man who stole the Witch's Examination of Mercy Chastain on the day of his brother's funeral, hid it for sixteen years, only to allow his lover Tarragon to steal it from him? The lover who was not only his wife's acolyte but is about the same age as his stepdaughter?"

"Yes."

"Henry Avery isn't the only evil fuck in this story." Isabel paused. "Tarragon was right. You do have deep undercurrents."

They continued talking, but Allison was shaking so hard it was hard to concentrate.

Fenwick had killed her father and Danny?

She struggled not to vomit into her gag.

"Turn onto that dirt road," Isabel said many minutes later.

The car stopped, and the guard dragged Allison out of the back seat with the warning, "Fight me and I kill you. Got it?"

Allison nodded and walked with him. The ground beneath her sneakers felt sandy yet gravely. The acrid smell of marsh mud, with a hint of pine and gardenias, burned her nose.

Finally, the guard said, "Sit."

Her legs stiffened and she sat on something hard and cold.

"Stay," the guard added.

"We need to search the cemetery for Mercy's grave." Isabel gave the guards more details and finished with, "Clayborne, the guards and I will search while you watch Allison. And turn off those damn tree lights."

Allison heard the sound of boots breaking twigs and walking away.

"Allison," Fenwick said in a voice that reeked of snarl, "if you promise not to move, I'll take off your blindfold."

She nodded. A moment later, she blinked to adjust her eyes. It'd been black behind the blindfold. Fenwick had left the flashlight on top of a tomb, and she could see she was in a cemetery she didn't recognize with a small white church behind her. The one visible side was dominated by three arched windows flanked by enormous shutters, and someone had strung white lights through the trees.

Construction equipment was lined up nearby, along with a generator and red gas cans. In the distance, she saw flashlights leading deeper into the churchyard.

Something rustled and she looked down. A water moccasin glided by. She whimpered and lifted her feet onto the tomb. She hated snakes.

"Where am I?" She tried to speak through the gag but her words came out garbled.

Instead of responding, Fenwick zip-tied her ankles together, retrieved his flashlight, and disappeared through the back door of the church. A minute later, the tree lights turned off, leaving her in darkness.

CHAPTER 43

ZACK HALF CARRIED, HALF DRAGGED HORATIO THROUGH THE back door of Iron Rack's gym. He'd parked in an alley nearby, and no one had noticed one man carrying another. If anything, a casual observer would think that Zack was helping a drunk friend home.

Pete hurried over. Once they got Horatio tied to a metal chair next to Fortinbras, they blindfolded him.

Pete grabbed Zack's arm and whispered, "What happened to Horatio's face?"

"It ran into my fist."

Pete picked up empty water bottles and a pizza box, tossed them into a nearby recycling bin, and led the way out of the back room. As they strode through the dark gym, Pete told Zack about Rafe being shadow-banned from the Fianna and how they were waiting for a call about where to trade Fortinbras—and now Horatio—for Alex.

"Where is everyone?"

"Squeezed into Kells's office, waiting for you. Except for Garza and Ty, who are sleeping upstairs, and Rafe, who went to meet a contact."

Zack paused in front of the door to Kells's office. Inside he heard Vane talking to the other men in his know-it-all voice that drove Zack insane.

"Sir," Vane said, "Zack took Allison on an operation to New Orleans. He's out of control."

Zack stormed in and the door banged the metal filing cabinet. The temp made his face bead with sweat, and his nose burned with the smell of ramped-up testosterone. "You wanted to see me?"

Kells turned away from the window overlooking the street. He stood taller than the other men in the room, his arms crossed over his wide chest. "Can I assume you have another Fianna warrior tied up in the back room?"

Zack nodded. "Horatio."

Kells pointed at Cain who was seated near the desk. "Please watch our hostages."

Cain took off, closing the door behind him. That left Nate standing in a far corner, shoulder against a filing cabinet. Luke sat at the desk behind a laptop. Vane had the chair near the desk and stared at Zack like he was the neighborhood kid about to get grounded. Pete sidled up to the coffeepot and started pouring.

Kells's fingers tap-danced on his bicep. "Tell me everything that's been going on in the past few days. Every moment. Every detail."

"Sir, with all due respect, Isabel has Allison and possibly my sister. The interrogation can wait."

"No, it can't."

Zack started to leave and Kells said, "Where are you going?"

"You fired me. Remember?"

Kells closed his eyes and squeezed the bridge of his nose. "We're all stressed—"

"I believe your exact words were *don't come back*. I interpret that as being fired."

"You disobeyed a direct order," Vane said from his seat. "What did you think was going to happen?"

"How about trusting me for a change?" Zack spoke directly to Kells because none of this was Vane's business. "You could've trusted me to make the right decisions and get the job done."

"You were—are—being led around by a woman," Kells said. "Again. The last time—"

"I know what fucking happened." Zack added a last-ditch "sir" to soften his tone.

Before Kells could respond, Nate moved into the center of the room. "None of this is helping us find Allison or Emilie. Now, I suggest we let Zack tell us what he knows and maybe we can figure this out together."

Zack sighed and stared at the ceiling covered with brown water spots. It was a miracle this dump didn't fall in on itself. It took Zack exactly six minutes to lay out everything he'd done and learned—except for the romantic parts. And the part about seeing Kate. Because *that* would've started a war.

When the heavy breathing of his men became too intense, Zack added, "I have no idea where Isabel took Allison or Emilie. I have no research. No clues. Nothing."

Nate rubbed his forehead. "Maybe if we found the treasure, it wouldn't matter. We could trade it for the women."

"Without the witch's examination's appendix and Pirate's Grille," Zack said, "our only option is finding Mercy Chastain."

Nate took out his phone. "Alex left me a rambling message about Mercy Chastain. It didn't make sense until you told us your story." Nate put the phone on speaker and replayed the message.

Alex's scratchy voice came through. "Nate. I'm in my brother's hotel room reading the Witch's Examination of Mercy Chastain. Part of the proof she offered for her innocence were the apotropaic marks she'd carved in her cell along with the Marian garden she'd planted around her home. Witches couldn't live anywhere with apotropaic marks and couldn't grow herbs in a garden devoted to Mary. Mercy mentioned growing rosemary, lilies of the valley, and thistle.

"It's also clear the charges were made up. In the notes at the end, she mentioned that in return for her release, Nicholas Trott—the chief justice, not the dog—wanted to know the location of Henry Avery's treasure. Since she didn't know where it was because it was being *built*—yes, that's the word she used—she told him she'd leave him a way to find it. That's why she came up with the cipher of the apotropaic marks—aka the Pirate's Grille—and the appendix.

"There's one more thing. In a book Allison and I found, I saw a receipt from 1704. Thomas Toban and Mercy Chastain spent ten thousand pounds to *build* something. FYI, I told my brother I'd go with him to Italy in exchange for setting the women free. Don't know if I'll ever see you again. If not, it's been...real."

Nate hung up the phone. "Obviously Alex, when he left that message, didn't know we were going to make a trade for him."

Zack ran his hands over his head. This whole thing had become a nightmare of epic proportions.

"Zack?" Kells took his turn in the center of the small room. "You mentioned Stuart planted thistle, rosemary, and lilies of the valley behind a grave for Allison to find?"

"Yes." Zack paused, not wanting to talk about Kate's role.

"Those plants," Kells said, "represent the Seven Dolors of Mary."

Luke grimaced. "The what, sir?"

"The sorrows of Mary's life." Kells clasped his hands behind neck. "The flight to Egypt, the passion of her son, crucifixion. My wife once wrote an article about them."

Aaaaand no one wanted to touch that.

"Sir?" Vane raised his hand. "What do these plants have to do with finding the women?"

"I don't know. It's possible Stuart knew more about Mercy and the treasure than he told Isabel or the Prince. It's even possible he knew the location of the treasure."

Zack closed his eyes. He'd never considered that.

"Alex mentioned the treasure being *built*," Nate said. "And a receipt for something that cost ten thousand pounds."

"That's two million in today's currency," Luke said.

Kells went back to staring out the window. "What cost the pirate Thomas Toban ten thousand pounds in 1704? And how does that tie in to Mercy's Marian garden?"

"Thomas Toban was from the Isle of Grace," Luke said. "Maybe it was something Thomas built out there."

A hot flush rose up Zack's neck at the same time Kells spun around to face them. "Luke?"

"I'm checking now." A moment later, Luke said, "There's no information on who paid for it, but the church known as Saint Mary of Sorrows on the Isle of Grace was completed in 1704. It cost ten thousand pounds. That's a lot of money for that tiny church."

Zack followed Kells and his men into the gym. He needed to leave now. "Sir—"

"Zack." Kells stopped by the door to the back room and held up one hand. "Before we do anything, I want to talk to Horatio."

That was a pointless task. "Horatio won't say anything."

Kells ignored Zack, entered the back room, and stopped.

They all followed, and Vane shook his head.

Yeah, Zack had been worried about this.

Kells looked at Zack, frown locked and loaded. "What happened to Horatio's face?"

Cain, who sat nearby reading the newspaper, said, "An accident."

Kells's sigh filled the room. "I'd like you to leave me, Luke, and Cain alone with Horatio."

There wasn't time. "Sir—"

Pete took Zack's arm and dragged him into the gym. Vane and Nate joined them by the fighting ring.

Zack turned to Pete first. "I'm leaving now. Are you in or out?"

"I'm in, but—"

"Wait!" Vane moved between them, hands on his hips. "Someone has to stay here with Kells and protect Horatio and make the trade for Alex."

"Kells has Luke and Cain to help him."

"But"—Vane pointed to the darkness outside the glass front doors—"Rafe has disappeared. Ty and Garza are asleep—"

"No, we're not," Garza said as he and Ty came down the stairs. Garza beelined for Zack and gripped his shoulder. "Whatever you need, I'm in."

Ty came over and crossed his arms. "Me too."

"I'll stay here," Nate said. "To mitigate the freak-out."

Vane scoffed. "There's no way Kells will authorize this operation."

"That's why we're not asking him." Zack pointed to Garza, then Pete. "Get what you need. Because the bikes are still in Charleston, and I don't want to piss off Kells even more by taking the unit's cars, we'll use Allison's and Garza's. We leave in five minutes."

Pete glanced at the closed door leading to the back room. "Our weapons are in there."

Zack pulled out his gun and checked his magazine. "I have mine."

"I'll swing by Rafe's apartment," Garza said. "I have a key and know the combo to the gun safe."

"A cop having access to an ex–Fianna warrior's weapons?" Pete shook his head. "Because that's not fucked up."

"We live in a fucked-up world," Garza reminded them.

Zack stared at the building's exposed steel beams that were probably covered with asbestos. Garza's words were so true.

"Zack?" Vane asked in that annoying way of his. "Kells will fire you again when he discovers you're choosing the personal over his orders."

"Honestly, brother, I don't care."

"I don't like it," Vane said.

"I didn't ask you to come."

Vane's mouth opened and closed like a hooked fish taking his last breath. Then he glanced at the door hiding Kells and Horatio.

Yes, brother. A choice between Kells and the rest of the unit. *Which one will you choose?*

Vane swallowed and said, "I'll meet you out front. With the weapons."

CHAPTER 44

ALEX STRETCHED IN THE BACK SEAT OF THE BLACK SUV AND watched the outside world go by. He wasn't that familiar with the roads between Charleston and Savannah, but he had the feeling they weren't going in the direction they should've been.

He flexed and unflexed his hands. It wasn't that he didn't want to go back to Kells and the gym; it was just that the women were still missing. And maybe, if given the chance, he could help.

The tires ground gravel and bounced so hard Alex's head hit the ceiling. "Marcellus? Where the fuck are we?"

"Attending to another purpose." Marcellus turned onto a dirt road. "We have one of the Fiend's men."

"The guy Zack found at the Usher Society?"

"Aye. He offered information in exchange for his life." Marcellus shifted the car into a lower gear to drive through a ditch. "Now my brothers and I have anointed our swords and prayed for time."

"Time to do what?"

"To save Lady Emilie from the Fiend. To save her from death." Marcellus stopped the car next to four other black SUVs, got out, and slammed the door. Then he went around to open the back and shut it. When Alex heard the distinctive sound of a magazine clicking into a rifle, he tried the door handle. Locked.

They'd parked along a river facing an old farmhouse. Swampy woods hid them from the rest of the world. It was dark, but in the choppy moonlight, he could see the house with broken shutters, holes in the roof, and a sagging porch covered in kudzu. Even with his windows closed, Alex smelled the stench of rot and decay.

It reeked of Remiel.

Sixteen warriors surrounded the house, and one group of four entered the front. The warriors moved without light, without sound, and in perfect coordination, as if each were simply part of a whole. Muffled shots cut through the air and flashes lit up the windows from the inside. A few minutes later, warriors reconvened near the SUVs.

One warrior carried a woman in his arms. Another warrior escorted a woman out. Marcellus came back, opened Alex's door, and a woman in a pink Nicholas Trott T-shirt slid in.

Emilie?

Emilie gave Alex a tired smile and then held out her arms for the other woman, who appeared unresponsive.

Tarragon.

Once the women were settled, with Tarragon lying on Emilie's lap, Marcellus got in and drove away.

Alex had a million questions, but instead he wrapped an arm around Emilie's shoulders and let her rest against him. She closed her eyes and her breathing evened out.

Yeah. Dealing with Remiel's bullshit would exhaust even the strongest soldier.

Isabel was running out of time and patience.

"What do you mean," she said to the guard in front of her, "you can't find the grave?"

"There's nothing—"

"Ma'am!" The second guard ran over. "You gotta see this."

With her flashlight and tote bag, Isabel followed the guard through the winding path. Her other man carried a digging stick, shovel, and sledgehammer. A few minutes later, she stood in front of a ten-by-ten mausoleum carved with broken daisies and skulls along the top. Two weeping angels, each with a broken daisy on its lap, guarded the iron door. The doorknob was etched with the *JL* logo.

She pointed to the guards. "Break it open. And remember, fifolets are buried *on top* of the treasure."

A guard wiped his brow with his arm. "You mean we have to desecrate the grave?"

"It's a treasure worth millions. Did you think it would be buried a few feet underground? For all we know it's *in* a coffin *beneath* a body." His eyes widened and she pointed to the door. "Hurry."

It took another few minutes before they pried the door open. With the flashlight guiding her way, she entered the crypt first. A horrific smell assaulted her, and she gagged on the stench of decay. From all four corners, weeping stone angels faced the center. There were two stone coffins, both with carvings on top. She traced each one with a finger, sending clouds of dust into the air. One had a broken daisy; the other had the initials JL. "This must be it."

A guard came in with a sledgehammer; the other carried the digging stick.

"Open these tombs." She blew more dirt away on one coffin and saw the initials MC below the broken daisy. "This one first."

One of the guards used his flashlight to expose carvings above their heads. Dozens of daisy wheels had been cut into the ceiling. "These are witch's marks. If we do this, we'll be cursed."

Isabel took out her gun and aimed it at the guard's chest. "If you don't, you'll be dead."

Both guards got to work, and Isabel smiled. She'd done it. She'd found Henry Avery's treasure, and Remiel would be pleased.

The other benefit? She didn't need Allison anymore. Now Isabel could kill her.

Fenwick cut the ties on Allison's ankles and forced her up the back steps of the church. He'd taken off the planks that had covered the doors and hustled her through the sacristy, into the main church.

The building was stifling due to the scents of orange oil and freshly cut plywood in the stale, hot air. Bricks and construction debris lay everywhere.

He placed the flashlight on the stone altar and forced her to sit next to a pile of bricks. He took out his weapon and yanked back the slide. Then he removed her gag.

She tried to lick her dry lips. She'd do anything for some water.

"Regardless if Isabel finds that treasure or not, she will kill you." Fenwick paced the shadows in front of the altar, moving in and out of the dim light. "If she succeeds, she returns as Remiel's second-in-command. If she fails, she'll have to disappear. Either way, leaving you alive would mean you'd won. She could never live with that."

"Won?" Allison tried to move her numb arms enough to get the blood flowing again. "This isn't a game."

Fenwick smirked. "You haven't been paying attention."

"If Isabel fails, won't Remiel kill you too?"

"No. Remiel and I have a separate arrangement." Fenwick crossed his arms. "I'll become Remiel's second, return to Raven's Retreat, and manage the absinthe business."

Allison snorted. "Rue embezzled the money out of the business and hid it."

"What are you talking about?" His words sounded low and deadly.

Allison swallowed, but her mouth was still too dry. "Stuart helped Rue move money from Raven's Retreat to an offshore account. They did it behind your back with the Prince's help. Rue was planning on leaving you alone and bankrupt."

"Rue would never do such a thing."

"Maybe she realized you killed her husband and her son, stole the witch's examination, and had an affair with her acolyte." Allison wiggled, desperate to regain feeling in her arms. "I heard what Isabel said in the car. Is it all true?"

"Fenwick Hall was my birthright, and Danny was a pain in my ass." Fenwick hit his chest with his fist. "Rue was always supposed to be mine. I met her first, but once she learned my brother inherited Fenwick Hall, she married him instead. And my affair with Tarragon wasn't my fault. She started it. I fucked her. Nothing more. Then, before I could dump her, she stole the witch's examination and gave it to Stuart."

"The witch's examination disappeared during my father's funeral. Rue blamed *me*."

"I stole it during the funeral. I took it with me as I traveled the country, learning how to distill absinthe, and showed it to various experts. I'd hoped someone could decipher the appendix that would lead to the treasure. Unfortunately, that attracted unwanted attention from the Prince. And then Remiel."

"How did Tarragon know about the witch's examination?"

Fenwick laughed. "Tarragon is no innocent girl. She's Remiel's niece. He planted her in my home to seduce me. Once she did, Isabel appeared. If I didn't want Rue to know about the affair, I had to do whatever Isabel asked."

Allison stared at the man she'd never called stepfather. "Isabel's requests dragged you deeper into Remiel's world?"

"*No.* Once I met Remiel, I *begged* to join his organization." Fenwick knelt in front of her and pulled out a knife. "Remiel has such plans. If you only knew, you'd slit your own throat."

She tried to spit at him but couldn't.

"No one expected Tarragon and Stuart to betray Remiel. I have to give them credit. That took serious balls." Fenwick rested his knife along the neckline of her white blouse, just above the swell of her breasts. "Now, you're going to tell me where the treasure is, or I will kill you."

"It's buried with Mercy Chastain. Haven't you heard? She was Henry Avery's fifolet."

He pressed the knife against her skin, and she winced. "Thomas Toban spent ten thousand pounds hiding that treasure. There's no way it's buried in some old tomb."

Allison had no idea where the treasure was, but that answer would only anger him more. "I'm sure you can come up with more positive reinforcement. Isabel offered me information."

"What are you talking about?"

"Isabel told me if I helped her find the treasure, she'd give me information that would save Zack's men."

Even in the dim beam of the flashlight, she saw Fenwick's face turn red. "She would never do that. Remiel would kill her first."

Allison shrugged, except the movement made her arms cramp. She breathed deeply until the muscles relaxed. "Why don't you ask Isabel? The offer sounded sincere."

Isabel appeared from the small room behind the altar. "What's going on?"

"Fenwick is trying to find the treasure on his own," Allison said, "so he can become Remiel's second."

Fenwick slapped Allison and she fell sideways onto the bricks. Her head spun and she tasted blood from her split lip.

Isabel came closer, holding her gun against her thigh. Her combat boots echoed on the stone floor. "Is this true?"

Fenwick scoffed. "Of course not."

Isabel stared at Fenwick for a long moment before saying, "Secure her and the church. I need you at the tomb. We're close to finding that treasure. I want to take it and get out of here before dawn."

Fenwick took a plastic zip tie from his back pocket and bound Allison's ankles together. Then he blindfolded and gagged her again.

Once they left, she chose a sketchy plan with little chance of success.

It took a lot of time and scooting around in the construction debris to find something metallic and sharp. Slowly, she cut through the plastic ties that held her hands behind her back.

Once free, she struggled to take off her gag and blindfold with numb hands. Then she curled into a ball because pins and needles tingled in her arms as the blood flow returned. While she lay there, she waited until her eyes adjusted to the darkness.

Fenwick had taken the flashlight with him.

Once she could sit, it took more minutes to cut through the ties around her ankles. She stood carefully, waiting for the feeling to come back to all of her extremities. Then she stumbled down the aisle toward the front door that was bolted shut from the outside.

She turned toward the altar and saw three enormous arched stained-glass windows set into the side walls. It was still too dark to see outside, but there were a few rays of moonlight. Inside, she could just make out the shadows of pews covered in canvas, paint cans stacked in the corners...and a hammer at her feet.

She picked it up and went to the first arched window. She pounded, but there was no way to open or shatter the heavy-duty glass that protected the stained glass. All of the other windows were also covered.

Disappointment made her hands shake, but she forced herself to keep going.

Feeling her way through the shadows, she made it to the wall behind the altar. That led her to the sacristy, but the back door was barricaded from the outside as well.

She returned to the sanctuary and fell to her knees behind the altar.

What was she going to do?

She was alone in a church on some isolated sea island where no one could find her.

The worst part? Zack believed she was going to leave him. Believed she was going to take some stupid job at a stupid school without him. Believed she didn't care for him.

She hadn't trusted him. She'd withheld herself from him. And he'd not said *don't go*. He'd kissed her and walked away. Still, she wasn't going to wait around for Isabel to come back and kill her.

She moved and, beneath her knee, felt an engraving in the stone floor. She used her hands to trace it and found a curvy line that led from the altar to the wall behind her. The moonlight shone a bit brighter, and she could make out the carvings attached to the line. They almost seemed like...leaves?

She brushed away the dust and stood. The line looked like a flower stem that started beneath the altar and led to the wall. She rubbed the dust off on her jeans and studied the church again. From the back to the front, there was the narthex, the nave, then the sanctuary. Three large arched windows made up the two side walls. Above the narthex door, there was a rose window.

The altar was in front of her, and she turned to see the paneled wall behind her. Now why wouldn't there be a window behind the altar? Or at least an altarpiece?

She stood between the altar and the wall and stared at the floor. The carved stem ended *beneath* the wall. Considering the church's architecture, it was almost as if the wall were an add-on. Maybe covering a window, definitely covering the engraving.

While interesting, this wasn't going to save her. She needed to find a way out or at least be prepared to fight. She tightened her hold on the hammer. Fenwick might have a gun, but she had surprise on her side.

And now she was armed.

CHAPTER 45

On the Isle of Grace, Zack stared at the church across the street knowing he needed a plan. ASAP.

Unfortunately, at that moment he had nothing close. He couldn't even confirm that Allison or his sister were in Saint Mary of Sorrows or even on the isle.

He left his hiding place behind a shed and returned to where he'd parked on the back side of Mamie's Café, across from the church. The roof of the café, a former Texaco gas station, gave them a perfect vantage point from which to gather intel. The cloudy night had that blessing/curse thing going on: it hid him well but randomly obscured the moonlight and everything else.

He had to admit that he was surprised by Vane's decision to tag along and that he'd taken charge of the aerial recon on the café's roof. Then again, just because he sucked up to Kells and could be extremely entitled and annoying, that didn't make him useless. The truth? Vane was, and always had been, a powerful, professional soldier who could do the hard things and be counted on when things got hot.

Zack found Detective Garza resting his elbows on the top of his car and staring at his phone. "Do you have a connection?"

"Nah." Garza slid his phone into his jacket pocket and opened his car's trunk. "The cellular is spotty and I can't believe this place doesn't have Wi-Fi."

"There's not enough people in this town to make it worth the cost." *Town* being a generous description, since it consisted of Mamie's Café, a modular shed for hurricane evacuation supplies, the rectory/sheriff's office, and the church.

Pete climbed off the café's roof. "I don't see any perimeter guards."

Zack hadn't either. And that just added to his stress. Were they not in the right place?

Garza dug into a duffel bag in his trunk and dragged out a rifle with a scope. "These clouds are going to keep it darker than normal when dawn hits."

Zack took the shotgun. "There's a parked SUV near the rectory, and I thought I saw brief flashes of light inside the church."

But they'd disappeared in the space of a blink.

"Dudes!" Vane's head popped over the edge of the roof. "You need to see this."

One by one, they climbed the exterior metal fire escape ladder to the second story. Zack slung the shotgun onto his back and went last. Once on top, he crawled to the edge overlooking the church on the other side of the street. He lay between Vane and Pete while Garza crawled to the corner.

Pete took Vane's binoculars. "What are we looking at?"

Vane pointed to dark woods behind the church. "Lights in the far side of the churchyard."

Garza used his rifle's scope to survey the area. "I don't see anything."

Pete held the binoculars up to his eyes. "Nope."

Zack took the binoculars and looked for himself. Nothing.

Garza crawled closer to the men. "Now what?"

"Dudes!" Vane took back his binoculars. "There *are* lights deep in that cemetery."

"We have to get a visual," Zack said. "I'll go first. You three stay up here and I'll use my flashlight to signal. One light means danger and I'm coming back. Two lights mean all is clear."

"I'm coming too," Pete said. "You always need backup."

Vane swung his rifle off his shoulder. "I'll cover you. Garza can cover Zack."

At least they had a plan. He had no headspace right now to consider the fact that this was a waste of time.

༄

Isabel stood inside Mercy's crypt and held her breath while Clayborne and the guards struggled to move the two stone coffins. The guards had opened them, but they'd been empty. Not filled with bones or dust or remnants of clothing. Just...empty.

Now the men were moving the coffins so they could see what was beneath. The tomb's floor was made of stone, but there had to be a way to dig.

The treasure had to be here.

While they worked, she used her flashlight to check out the angels. They were the only other things in the room, but they didn't appear to be made out of anything other than marble.

"Isabel."

"Keep looking." She'd never trusted Clayborne. He was as evil a monster as Remiel. She'd just not expected him to challenge her outright. That meant she had to kill him. She coughed and covered her nose and mouth from the dust and mildew.

"Ugh." One of the guards pushed hard and a coffin finally moved. And beneath it? The same stone floor she stood on.

"Use the sledgehammer and break up the floor." She took a breath to steady her increasing heart rate.

"It's not here, Isabel." Fenwick wiped his brow with his arm and tossed the digging stick down. It hit the floor with a loud *clang*. "It's time to leave."

She glanced around the tomb again. They only had a few flashlights. Maybe that's why she wasn't seeing what was probably in front of her.

"Did you hear that?" One of the guards pointed outside.

She turned to Clayborne. "Allison—"

"Bound and locked in that church. We need to take care of *that* problem and leave. Cut our losses."

"No."

Clayborne waved his hand in disgust and left the tomb.

Unfazed by his attitude, she picked up the sledgehammer and

started hammering the floor until one of the guards offered to do it for her. "It has to be here."

Her life depended on it.

∽

Zack ended up behind a tall limestone column, shotgun ready, breathing heavily. A few yards away, he saw faint lights moving in a large tomb with Isabel and two guards inside.

Pete whistled from his position three feet away behind a tree. They were going in.

Zack led the way until they took up positions on either side of the door. From his vantage point, Zack could see one guard trying to move a coffin while another took a sledgehammer from Isabel and struck the floor.

Pete threw a rock into the tomb, hitting the wall, and all three looked up.

Isabel pointed to the guard. "Check that out."

When the guard came out, Zack hit him with the butt of his shotgun and dragged the unconscious body behind the tree. Luckily, the guard had plastic zip ties in the pocket of his combat pants, and Zack borrowed them. After securing the guard, he motioned to Pete by raising one finger at a time.

One. Two. Three.

Zack and Pete raised their weapons and entered quickly, with Zack ordering, "On your knees. *Now.*"

The guard dropped the sledgehammer and fell to his knees, hands behind his head.

Isabel, on the other hand, stood there with her hands on her hips. Disgust lined her beautiful face. "What the hell is this?"

Since Pete covered the guard, Zack focused his aim on Isabel. "This is me telling you to get on your damn knees."

Isabel's eyes widened. Then, slowly, she moved toward him. "No man says that me."

Before Zack could respond, Isabel drew her gun and fired at Pete and the guard, then pointed her gun at Zack.

The sound reverberated through the stone room, leaving Zack with ringing ears and flooding his veins with adrenaline. Nate had said she was a quick draw, but Zack hadn't believed it. Now they stood opposite, weapons aimed at each other. Her pistol against his twelve-gauge loaded with buck shot. At this proximity, they'd both be dead in a second.

Pete dropped and rolled to his side; blood soaked his T-shirt. "*Fuck.*"

"Brother?" Zack adjusted his grip on the shotgun. He'd already hesitated once because he didn't want to kill a woman, but he would if he had to.

"It's not fatal," Isabel said. "But he'll bleed out if you don't help him."

"I'll be okay." Pete gasped. "The guard is dead."

Zack sneered. "You shot your own man?"

"I killed your leverage."

Because that's what these games between the Prince and Remiel and Kells were always about—leverage.

"Drop your weapon, Isabel. End this now. Tell me where Allison and Emilie are, and we'll help you get away from Remiel."

She laughed and moved toward the open door. His aim followed her. "You're insane. No one gets away from Remiel. Just ask Kells."

"Isabel—"

"No, Zack. You have a choice. Come after me or take care of your man." She took one step out of the tomb. "I wonder what it will be this time? You have a history of seeing to your own needs before those of your men."

"Don't listen to her." Pete struggled to sit but he ended up on his side. "I'll be okay."

Isabel smiled and took another step back into the darkness. Then another and…she disappeared.

"*Fuck.*" Zack took off his T-shirt and pressed it against Pete's wound. The bullet had skimmed the side of his chest. It wasn't serious, but it was bleeding. "Hold this." Zack muttered curses. He was such a pussy. He couldn't even shoot a woman.

"Go after her." Pete coughed and tried to roll into a ball.

Zack swung the shotgun onto his back, then the rifle, and dragged Pete until he stood with his arm over Zack's shoulder. "We're either walking out of here, or I'm carrying you."

"Walking." Pete pressed the T-shirt to his side and grunted. "You don't lift like you used to. I don't want you dropping me."

Zack adjusted Pete's weight and the weapons and headed out into the dark. "Maybe if you didn't have me taking stupid-ass refresher self-defense classes—"

"Says the man who"—Pete paused to spit—"can't shoot a woman."

"So true, brother." *So very fucking true.*

CHAPTER 46

ALLISON HEARD SOMETHING IN THE SACRISTY AND PRESSED herself against the wall behind the altar. She tightened her hold on the hammer's handle and held her breath.

A flashlight beam appeared, and she swallowed hard.

Fenwick stepped near the altar, and Allison swung, clipping Fenwick on the shoulder. He dropped to his knees and the flashlight skidded away. She jumped over him but he grabbed her ankle. She fell, and the breath rushed out of her lungs. Fenwick grunted as he struggled to stand. She rolled over, swinging wildly.

He disarmed her and pointed his gun at her head. In the dim light, his face was twisted into a fierce mask of hatred and disgust. She lay on her back, panting.

Fenwick, who wasn't even breathing deeply, kept his weapon aimed on her. "Where is the fucking treasure?"

She used her elbows and heels to scramble away. "I don't know."

Isabel rushed in, her flashlight and gun out as well. "Shoot her. It's time to leave."

Fenwick moved quickly. He disarmed Isabel and pulled her against his chest, her back against his front. He kicked Isabel's gun behind him. It landed near the sacristy, so Allison's only chance to get it would mean passing by Fenwick.

"Let go!" Isabel elbowed him until he pressed the gun's barrel to her temple and she stopped struggling.

"Allison?" Fenwick snarled. "Get the fuck up."

Allison used the pew to stand and saw the hammer nearby. "What do you want?"

"The treasure. You've been searching for Mercy your entire life. You know where she, and the treasure, are hiding. If you don't tell me, I'll kill Isabel."

"I don't." Allison held out her hands. "I swear."

"Don't play games, *Petal*. You may hate Isabel, but she's the only person on this earth who can exonerate Zack and his men. If I kill her, your lover will never reclaim his life. He'll have to live in a run-down gym forever. No redemption. No honor. Just a life of nothingness surrounded by moldy pirate flags, sweaty wipe-down towels, and memories burning with regret."

"Please," Isabel pleaded. "Listen to me—"

"No." Fenwick focused his gaze on Allison. "Where is it?"

"I don't know. I swear."

Isabel stomped on Fenwick's foot and he dropped his arm. It wasn't much, but it gave her a chance to grab his arm, spin him around, and kick him in the groin. He dropped to his knees, and she reached for his gun, but not before he shot her in the shoulder.

Isabel cried out and fell to the floor. Allison hurried toward the other gun until Fenwick pointed his weapon at her.

"This is your last chance."

She held out her hands. "I swear I don't know."

"Pity." Fenwick found Isabel's gun and trained both of them on Allison. "You could've saved your lives and Zack's honor. Now all three are forfeit."

"I swear—"

"No point in swearing, Petal." He backed away. "If I were you, I'd start praying."

Fenwick left the church and she ran for the back door. It slammed shut and she heard him boarding it up with an electric drill from the outside. She pounded and screamed, but he laughed until the noise stopped. It was then that she realized he'd walked away.

She leaned her back against the door and saw an electrical panel on the wall. She hit all of the switches, praying for an alarm, but nothing. The church lights didn't even go on.

She ran back in to find Isabel on the floor, her eyes closed. Allison took off her white blouse, grateful she had on a white cami, and moved Isabel until she could press the bunched-up cotton against the wound. From what she could tell, the bullet had ripped through Isabel's shoulder and come out the other side.

Except for a few moans, Isabel didn't say a word.

What am I going to do?

Allison wiped her forehead with her arm and sat against a pew, her arms around her pulled-up knees. She closed her eyes and thought about their options. She had a hammer and Isabel's flashlight. From the lighter sky, dawn would be here soon. Maybe, once the day started, someone would find them.

She glanced at Isabel and the blood that had already soaked through the blouse. Isabel might not have that long.

"Do you smell smoke?" Isabel leaned against a pew.

Allison stood. "I do."

She saw spirals of smoke coming from outside the church. With Isabel's flashlight, she hurried to a window and saw yellow and orange flames. Gas cans lay on the lawn.

Fenwick had set the church on fire.

Zack, carrying Pete, reached the far edge of the cemetery near the road, when Rafe's security lights lit up the trees. Not white lights. *Blue* lights.

"Sorry about this, brother." Zack adjusted Pete's weight and switched to a fireman's carry. Then he ran toward the café until Garza and Vane raced out and passed him.

Zack turned to see where they were going and, when he saw smoke coming from the direction of the church, laid Pete on the ground, propping him against a headstone. "Stay here."

Two shotgun shots rang out. Then a third.

"Sure." Pete reached for the rifle. "I'll watch the perimeter."

Zack handed Pete the weapon and took off. Once Zack entered the churchyard and jumped over a shovel, he saw the flames. Garza and Vane were already filling construction buckets via a hose that came from the rectory. "Is anyone in there?"

Garza handed him a bucket. "Yes. We saw a flashlight inside."

"We were on the way to check it out when we realized it was on fire. We tried to open the doors." Vane tossed water onto the flames licking the side of the church. "They're blocked with planks screwed to the frames."

"I fired on the doors with a shotgun," Garza said, "but they're at least six inches thick."

"There's a hydrant in front of Mamie's Café," Vane added, "but no hose."

Zack took Garza's bucket and used his bare arm to wipe the sweat out of his eyes. The air was heating up quickly. "Garza, drive over the bridge until you get a signal. We need a fire truck and an ambulance. Pete has been shot."

"It'll take too long," Vane said. "We need to open those doors."

"There's a shovel in the graveyard." Zack threw water on rising flames. "Maybe we can use it to pry open the doors."

Vane tossed another bucket onto the church. "What about the windows?"

"They're covered in bullet-proof, hurricane-proof glass."

A loud whoomph sounded, and the church's outside paneling started to burn.

Zack heard a vehicle screeching on gravel. Rafe jumped out of his truck and raced toward the prefab modular building next to the café. Garza and Vane followed.

Zack ran back to get the shovel, returned, and took the church's front steps in one leap. The goal was to use the handle as a crowbar behind the planks shuttering the doors. Despite the intense heat, he pushed and pulled until the shovel's handle broke, throwing him onto his ass three steps down.

Rafe, Vane, and Garza had found a fire hose in the hurricane shed and were hooking it up to the fire hydrant.

Please let the hose be long enough.

Zack booked it to the other side of the church. It'd just started to burn, but he got close enough to look in the window. Standing on a pew near another window, he saw Allison hitting the glass with a hammer. He pounded his fist against the window to get her attention but she didn't notice.

He hurried back to the other men. "Allison is in there."

"Watch out!" Rafe yelled a moment before a huge surge of water hit the church over Zack's head. Rafe sprayed the church but the flames grew. At this rate, even if they put the flames out, the smoke would suffocate anyone inside.

Zack found bricks on a pile of construction debris and threw them at the windows. They didn't even dent the high-tech glass. He barely noticed when a minivan appeared and Nate got out.

He barely noticed when Cain and Luke appeared and started filling buckets and throwing water at the church.

He barely noticed when Ty forced water down Zack's parched throat.

"Zack." Ty's voice sounded years away. "Emilie is okay. She's safe."

Zack bent over and pressed his hands into his thighs until a loud *whooshing* sound had both Zack and Ty running around the church. Flames engulfed the back door. While his sister was safe, Allison was inside that inferno.

Allison jumped off the pew and hurried to Isabel, still holding the hammer as if that would magically save them.

"It's not supposed to happen this way." Isabel's black hair hung around her shoulders in a tangled mess of dirt and blood. "This is how we were to end it, to hide your body. Remiel wouldn't do this to me. He *needs* me."

Fenwick and Isabel had planned to shoot her and set her body on fire?

While Allison wanted to kick Isabel's wounded shoulder, she didn't have time. She coughed on the smoke as rays of early morning sunlight filtered into the room. First it streamed through the rose window, detailing the intricate design that reminded Allison of a…multicolored daisy wheel. Then the light came through the side windows.

Allison studied each of the six windows and their brightly colored stained-glass designs: *Saint Simeon's prophecy. Escape to Egypt. Lost in the temple. Carrying the cross. The lance. The burial.*

Six of the Seven Dolors of Mary?

Allison moved behind the altar. Now, with the light pouring in, she could see the engraving below her feet. It was, indeed, a stem with leaves that ended beneath the wall behind her.

She coughed on the smoke and ran toward the wall with her hammer. It got stuck in the paneling. She quickly searched the church and found a hatchet and a piece of drop cloth she could use to cover her mouth and nose. The hatchet wasn't big enough to touch the thick church doors, so she started chopping the wall behind the altar. If there was a window behind this wall, then it might not be covered with unbreakable plastic.

It was her only chance.

After a few good hits, the wood began to splinter.

"What are you doing?" Isabel coughed.

Allison didn't answer because her lungs hurt and the axe handle was heating up. She wasn't about to waste any oxygen on Isabel. But Allison didn't want Isabel to die either—not if she had information on Zack.

After twenty hits, Allison dropped to the ground. The smoke darkened the room and her arm muscles contracted painfully.

She tried to pull away the lower half of the paneling. After a few tugs, she fell backward, wall in hand. The lower half of the wall had split off, and she saw the rest of the engraving on the floor—a broken daisy with an inscription.

Requiescat in Pace

Mercy Chastain

She inhaled and coughed on the smoke that was now burning her lungs and eyes.

Had she just found Mercy's grave?

She moved closer and, through the hole she made in the wall, she saw an altarpiece against the original structure.

A wooden ladder in the sacristy caught fire and dropped to the ground. The flames seemed to realize their purpose and burned through the sides.

She found her hatchet and banged the paneling again.

They were running out of time.

CHAPTER 47

ZACK'S THROAT FELT HOARSE. HE'D BEEN SCREAMING ALLISON'S name while also breathing in smoke and tossing buckets of water. This business of filling five-gallon construction buckets with a garden hose to put out a fire was not just useless, it was exhausting. His arm muscles were permanently contracted and he couldn't feel his legs anymore.

Cain now held the fire hose and was making progress on one side. Ty, Garza, and Luke were tossing buckets on the other side when Rafe and Nate ran toward the front door with heavy pry bars. Zack dropped his bucket and followed them, meeting Vane along the way. The front door wasn't engulfed in flames yet, but it was hot as Hades.

"We found these in the hurricane shed." Rafe took his bar and shoved it behind one of the three heavy planks that had been secured across the double doors.

Nate did the same. Zack stood behind Nate and grabbed the upper part of the bar, while Vane took Rafe's side.

Rafe held the lower half of his bar. "*Pull.*"

All the men groaned and, despite the force of four ex–Green Berets, the board refused to budge.

"Again," Rafe ordered.

Zack lost track of how many times they pulled, but just as his arms were about to fall off, the board moved.

"Again!" Nate yelled.

They strained again and again and again until the board gave way. Nate tossed it aside and they went to work on the second.

Precious moments passed until, finally, this board splintered off.

Then it was onto the third. When it broke in half, they all tumbled down the steps. Zack jumped up and yanked the doors open. The flood of fresh air fed the flames and blocked his view—but not before he saw Allison up on the altar, chopping—like a girl—at a wall.

The fire roared down the aisle, and she turned. When she met his gaze, she ran toward...someone on the floor.

Nate handed him a wet cloth to cover his mouth and nose, and he raced through the flames. He'd forgotten, until that moment, that he was shirtless. The fire was burning the hair off his chest.

Allison reappeared, holding the arm of a limping woman. Isabel?

Heat and smoke blinded him, making everything around him hot and dark. But he didn't care. Not about Isabel or fire or treasure. All that mattered was Allison. And she was alive.

Allison struggled to hold on to Isabel and breathe at the same time. The heat burned her face and hair, and her eyes watered. When the door had burst open, all she'd seen were flames and smoke—until Zack appeared with his bare chest, soot-covered muscles, tattooed arms, and his hair undone and smoking, as if it'd been singed. *Her wild man.*

He wrapped something around his face and forced his way in as if not caring about the flames and smoke and imminent danger. She stumbled off the altar and into the aisle. The pews were burning now, and one of the windows cracked. Smoke swirled, sending her and Isabel to their knees.

"Allison!"

She heard his voice but couldn't see and couldn't move. Isabel crawled ahead but Allison's breath got caught in her dry throat. Panic began and her hands and legs shook.

Suddenly, she was airborne. Someone had picked her up and was carrying her outside. Fire reached for her, heat melted the rubber soles of her sneakers, and the hair on her arms burned off.

"I've got you."

Zack? She wrapped an arm around his neck and pressed her face against his neck. "Isabel?"

She coughed out the word and wasn't sure he even heard until he said, "We have her too. You saved her."

Zack carried Allison toward the rectory, where Rafe had parked his truck. Rafe had Isabel already on the ground, his emergency medical kit out, and was seeing to her wounds. Pete lay nearby, shirt off and a bandage around his chest, eyes closed.

One good thing about ex–Fianna warriors and ex–Green Berets? They had decent combat medic skills.

Zack laid Allison on the ground near Rafe and fell onto his back next to her, his arms wide. The morning light had appeared and he'd hardly realized it.

Nate came over to check Allison, and Zack forced himself upright. "How is she?"

Nate helped her sit so she could cough, and he wrapped a blanket around her shoulders. Then she drank two bottles of water, four gulps each. "We should get her, Pete, and Isabel medical attention. The women may have suffered smoke inhalation. And Isabel has been shot."

"I'm okay." Allison coughed for another thirty seconds.

Zack pulled her into his arms and he could hear her labored breathing.

While Zack held her, Nate took off her sneakers. The soles had melted and he needed to check her feet. They weren't burned, but they were red, like her arms and the rest of her exposed skin. Even her hair had been singed. "Do you feel faint? Or nauseated?"

"No." She coughed again. "Emilie?"

"Safe." Nate brushed her hair out of her face "We need to get you checked out by a doctor. Just to be sure. We have one we trust, but we have to take you to him."

She burrowed against Zack and shook her head.

Zack glanced at his buddy still lying on the ground. "How's Pete?"

"He'll be okay—oh shit." Nate pointed across the street.

Zack turned to see three men step out of an SUV. "Why is Kells here with Horatio and Fortinbras?"

"Don't worry." Nate gripped Zack's shoulder. "Take care of your woman. I'll deal with Kells."

Nate crossed the street, and Kells walked with the warriors who, despite having their hands tied behind their backs, moved freely, with no gags or blindfolds.

Nate and Kells engaged in a convo that required lots of hand motions.

Many minutes later, Allison asked, "Where's Isabel?"

She moved against his chest and he bit his bottom lip. His skin wasn't severely burned, but it was sensitive. Like a bad sunburn. Still, no amount of pain would make him release her.

"Rafe tended to her shoulder and Luke took her to the rectory. It's also used as the part-time sheriff's office and there's a one-person cell in there."

"She's locked up?"

"Until we get her medical treatment, we need to keep her safe from Remiel and figure out what to do with her."

Allison flung her arms around his neck. Her tears soothed his skin. He knew, in a then-and-there kind of way, that even if he had to move to Virginia, he was never ever letting her go.

CHAPTER 48

ALLISON TIGHTENED HER ARMS AROUND ZACK AND HELD ON for at least twenty minutes. She didn't care that her skin felt like it was melting off or that her breathing sounded raspy and labored and hurt like knives in her throat. Together, they watched his men put out the fire. As the group moved around with buckets and hoses, Zack told her each of their names. The way he said them, with so much pride and love in his voice, proved how much they meant to him.

She withdrew from his arms, stood, and grabbed his wrist. Despite her bare feet catching on the rocky ground and the blanket irritating her sensitive skin, she dragged him closer to the church. The fire was out, but Rafe and three other men were still soaking everything, trying to put out embers in the grass. The steps hadn't burned completely and she went up and stood in the doorway. The cold water soothed the soles of her feet.

Zack had told her that he and his men had put out the fire because there was no fire department on the Isle. The Isle's local law enforcement—a sheriff and part-time deputy who were also brothers—had gone out of town, and Detective Garza wasn't officially helping them. Apparently, the Isle was too remote and too poor for anyone to care about and the people of the Isle were good with that. They preferred to be left alone.

She was just so glad Zack and his men had found her.

"What are we doing?" He kept one hand on her waist as they entered the building. Everything was soaked and smoke still rose from the ashes. They made it down the aisle together, dodging charred debris and puddles.

"You'll see."

"Hey," Rafe said from the doorway. "This isn't safe."

She turned and saw Rafe standing with Detective Garza, Vane, Cain, and Ty, all wearing variations of combat pants, T-shirts, and concerned frowns. "I want to show you something."

Despite her bare feet, she didn't stop until she stood near the altar. "Does anyone have a flashlight? And I need some buckets of water."

Vane and Ty went to get the water while Detective Garza handed her a penlight. The wall behind the altar had disintegrated. She shone the light on the window high above an altarpiece covered in soot. Because the back siding outside the church had partially burned off, some light peeked through.

"Hey." Rafe moved ahead of her. "I didn't know there was a window here."

"It was sandwiched between a false wall inside and the back siding outside." She moved the light around so they could make out the design. "This church is called Saint Mary of Sorrows. Mary had seven sorrows, but there are only six windows. Three on each side."

Zack took the light from her so he could aim it higher. "This window—it's the crucifixion."

"The seventh sorrow," Rafe whispered. "I got married in this church and never realized."

She coughed again but didn't want to tell Zack that her lungs hurt. "Look at the floor."

They all did, and she heard their collective gasp.

"Mercy Chastain is buried here?" Zack said, the exhaustion competing with the awe in his voice.

"Yes," she said.

The men returned with two buckets of water each, and she asked them in between coughs, "Can you rinse off the altarpiece beneath the window?"

Vane shrugged. "Sure."

Vane and Ty dumped two buckets of water on the altarpiece, and black, sooty water ran onto the floor. She stepped aside to protect her feet. While they drained the other two buckets, she raised her face to the sky visible through the burned-out ceiling. Clouds had moved in.

"What are we doing?" Zack whispered in her ear.

She rewrapped the blanket around herself. The shadows around them floated away and rays of bright light warmed her head. "When the sun hits, look at the altarpiece over Mercy's tomb."

Zack tightened his arm around her waist.

The floor in front of her lightened, and she said, "Just watch."

The sun's rays traveled across the dirty floor, highlighting Mercy's name in the stone, and up the altarpiece. Set in three pieces, with the middle protruding out farther than the side pieces, it spanned the width of the window above it. In the middle, the tabernacle had gold doors, while the panels above and beside it had been decorated with images of Mary and the three archangels—Gabriel on the right, Raphael on the left, and Michael in the middle, above the tabernacle.

The piece could've come out of a Middle Ages church—until the sun hit it.

Through the rays, there was no mistaking the brilliant sparkling colors. Gold, reds, blues, pinks, greens, and every other color one could imagine, shimmered.

Like treasure.

"Wait." Rafe moved closer. Then stopped. "What the hell?"

Vane touched the tabernacle doors. "Is that gold? Set with…diamonds?"

"The entire thing is made with Henry Avery's treasure," Allison whispered. "Melted down, reworked, ground down, and reset into an altarpiece—technically called a retable—by Joshua Linguard in 1704."

"It's incredible." Detective Garza ran a hand over a panel representing the Annunciation set with rubies and sapphires and amethysts. "I can't believe this has been hidden here for centuries."

"Wow," Cain said with his hands on his hips. "Just wow."

The sounds of car engines came from outside, and Rafe said, "Alright, gentlemen. Recess is over."

"What are you talking about?" Zack asked.

Rafe pointed to five large black SUVs that had parked in the road between Mamie's Café and the scorched church. "There's still work to be done."

Allison, Zack, Rafe, and the rest of Zack's men left and stood on the unburnt grass near the rectory and part-time sheriff's office.

Horatio and another man, who introduced himself as Fortinbras, bowed their heads, their hands zip-tied together. The last man stood off to the side with his arms crossed. The *very* tall ginger set his gray gaze on her. He didn't even try to hide his dislike. He had to be Kells.

The SUV doors opened and men got out.

"A few of the Prince's men," Zack whispered in her ear.

A few? She swallowed and her throat ached.

A moment later, Rafe was moving her and all of Zack's men into one line, shoulder to shoulder, with Horatio and Fortinbras behind them.

Kells stood off to the side, still glaring at her.

Sixteen warriors moved gracefully to make a similar wall opposite Zack and his men. Two sides lined up across—and against—each other. With at least twenty yards separating them, Kells's men stood on one side, the Prince's warriors on the other.

"We're not going to fight." Allison pulled on Zack's arm. "Are we?"

Seriously? She had no shoes, no weapon, and was still nauseated.

He moved her so she was slightly behind him. "I hope not."

Nate, who stood next to her, chuckled. "We're making a trade. Rafe is doing the honors."

When the men were settled on both sides, Rafe walked to the center. As hard as she tried, she couldn't stop watching the way he moved. It was both beautiful and terrifying.

Rafe held up one hand. "We're here to make a trade. First, Alex Mitchell, brother of the Prince, in exchange for the warrior Fortinbras."

Laertes opened one of the SUV doors and Alex stepped out. He wasn't bound and he walked with purpose and determination. He wore the most annoyed scowl she'd ever seen, and she tried not to smile. Alex stopped in front of Rafe.

Behind her, Kells cut Fortinbras free and the warrior walked to the middle as well. He bowed his head to Alex as they passed, but Alex ignored him and beelined for Zack.

Once Alex positioned himself on Zack's other side, Alex said under his breath, "You fucking owe me."

Zack nodded.

"The second trade will be the warrior Horatio in exchange for Lady Tarragon."

"What about Emilie?" Allison whispered.

"I don't know." Zack moved toward Rafe. Except Rafe held his hand out in a *stop* motion. Zack ran his fingers through his hair until Allison took one of his arms, lowered it, and held his hand.

All gazes focused on the same SUV Alex had just gotten out of. Laertes opened the door and Tarragon emerged. He took her arm and escorted her to Rafe.

Rafe's gaze widened and he started flexing and unflexing his hands.

That's when the murmuring started among Zack's men.

"Dear God," Nate whispered. "What happened—"

"Remiel," Allison said in a loud enough voice for all of Zack's men to hear. "Remiel is what happened to Tarragon's face. And she's Remiel's niece."

A few of the men coughed, and Zack started swallowing and blinking like he'd just choked on Red Hots. "I've seen her before. In the window at your house in Charleston. I thought she was a ghost."

Allison rested her head against his warm arm. "A lot of people thought that."

Luke whispered something in Nate's ear. Then Nate sent Zack a strange look.

Meanwhile, Kells undid Horatio's ties and the warrior with the swollen face moved forward. When he reached Tarragon, he kissed her hand. Then he walked until he was reunited with his men.

While Rafe spoke softly to Tarragon, Nate gently disengaged Allison from Zack and drew him back behind the men. "We have a problem."

"*Noooooo!*" Tarragon picked up the skirt of her dirty sheer blue nightgown and ran in the other direction—right into the arms of the warrior Laertes.

Rafe hurried over to talk to Laertes and Tarragon.

Zack and Nate reappeared on either side of Allison. Both of their faces had gone hard and angular. Something was definitely wrong.

Rafe came back to the center and cleared his throat until everyone focused on him. "The Lady Tarragon has asked the Fianna for asylum and they've agreed to care for her. The trades have been made. May we all go in—"

"Wait!" Zack strode toward Rafe. With his long black hair undone, full arm tattoos, and bare chest covered in dirt, blood, bruises, and cuts, he was an imposing figure.

At least Allison thought so.

She glanced at the other men and wondered if they were used to stuff like this.

"Where is my sister?"

Kells left his line of men and hurried to the center. Once there, he grabbed Zack's arm. She couldn't hear what the men were saying, but it didn't matter. The world around her wobbled and she felt nauseated. "Nate? Is there a bathroom in the rectory?"

"Yes." He took her elbow. "Are you okay?"

She nodded and said, "I'll be right back."

Since everyone was focused on Zack, Kells, and Rafe, no one noticed her running to the rectory. She made it just in time. Once she finished throwing up and the dry heaves eased, she washed out her mouth and returned to the office. It was a basic room with some cabinets, a gun case, a desk, two chairs, a few windows, and...a cage in the corner.

"Isabel?"

Isabel sat in the corner of the cell, her legs drawn up and her head resting against the wall. Her shoulder had been bandaged and the white pressure gauze contrasted with her black hair that hung around her shoulders. "What do you want?"

Honestly, Allison wasn't sure. "Do you need anything?"

Isabel slowly turned her head until their gazes met. "Let me out."

Allison touched the cold metal bars. "I can't do that."

"Even if I give you the information about Zack's men?"

Allison knelt. "If you have information to help Zack and his men, you have to tell them. The Fianna are here. They can offer you asylum like they offered Tarragon."

"Tarragon is a fool. The Fianna can't be trusted."

"They're more trustworthy than Remiel."

Isabel used her good hand to grip a bar and stand. "One isn't better than the other. Men who are beautiful, brilliant, and unloved are the greatest purveyors of the truth. That makes them the most dangerous."

Allison stood. "I don't understand."

Isabel shook her head. "When you have nothing else in your life, objective truth—the reality that can be ignored but never be denied—becomes your only solace. Your only reason for living. Even if it breaks a man's heart and turns him into a monster."

"That's not—"

"True?" Isabel laughed until she coughed. "It's the *only* truth. Hell, Mercy Chastain knew that."

"What do you mean?"

"Mercy Chastain was a poor woman during a time when that was a dangerous proposition. A barmaid in a brothel. A woman who had an affair with the most wanted, most notorious pirate in history. A woman who had a baby out of wedlock, who took a house from a man she wasn't married to. A woman who was accused of witchcraft not because she was guilty but because she could lead those in power to the greatest treasure ever stolen. A woman who negotiated her own release by promising a cipher leading to the treasure."

"How did you—"

She laughed roughly. "Stuart told me." She gripped the rail and pushed herself closer to Allison. "Mercy knew the truth about men. She played their game—no, she *outplayed* their game. She understood there was a chance Henry would kill her once her accusation was dropped, so she came up with a cipher that would keep men running around in circles for centuries. A cipher—and a hidden key—meant to protect her child but ended up protecting *you*."

Shouts started outside and Allison wondered if there *was* going be a fight. "Mercy did what she had to do to survive. That's her truth."

Isabel raised an eyebrow. "Then how are we any different? I've been abused by men, betrayed by those I believed in, lost everyone I've ever loved. Yet when I *act out*, I'm the one imprisoned."

"*Act out?*" Now it was Allison's turn to grab the bars. "Mercy embedded a cipher in her own witch's examination, and then engraved the cipher's key in her apotropaic marks, in a desperate attempt to save her life and protect her child. You're a murderer."

"Says the woman who can't love and hurts everyone around her." Isabel sneered. "At least I've known great passion and fierce love. One of those men is outside ignoring me, while the other is dead. What about you? What are you willing to fight for? What's your truth?"

Her truth? She loved Zack with her whole heart. She'd just never recognized that feeling deep inside—the one that makes you hold your breath until your lover walks in the door, that makes you willing to sacrifice everything for his happiness—as love. "My truth is I will do anything to save Zack and his men. To save their future."

Isabel nodded to the key ring on the desk, then she reached into her back pocket. "Let me go and I will give you this."

She held a flash drive in her palm.

"Don't do it." Alex strode into the room, took Allison's shoulder, and drew her away from the cell. "She's an evil bitch."

Isabel batted her eyes at Alex. "Here to save me, lover?"

"I'm here to check on Allison. There's been a complication. We only had two warriors to trade."

"Wait." Allison went to the door to see Zack and his men talking in a circle. "The Fianna won't give back Emilie?"

"Not without another offering."

Isabel laughed, then coughed. "The Fianna can't be trusted."

Allison ignored Isabel and faced Alex. "How do we fix this?"

Alex sat on the corner of the desk. "Give the Fianna something they want."

"Isabel?"

"*No.*" Isabel shook the bars. "I'd rather you kill me first."

Alex shrugged. "Just as well, since they said no."

"Isabel has information on Zack's men that could save them." Allison pointed to the flash drive Isabel slipped into her pocket. "Or…I have an idea."

Allison took Alex's hand and dragged him outside.

A loud car engine made everyone turn toward the road. Another black car stopped and a man emerged from the back seat. He had dark hair, wore a tailored suit, and moved with a confidence that propelled him forward.

All of the men returned to their lines, Kells's men on one side and the warriors on the other. Even Rafe bowed his head when this man entered the center area.

Kells walked out to meet him.

Allison dragged Alex back to where his men stood. "Who's that?"

"The Prince," Alex said.

Alex's brother.

Rafe and Kells and the Prince spoke in murmurs.

"They're negotiating," Alex muttered. "Always negotiating."

Nate frowned. "Alex, how well do the Prince and Kells know each other?"

Alex scoffed and walked toward the minivan. "Wake me when it's over."

Zack and Nate shared a long look until Rafe waved Zack to meet him in the center.

Allison had no idea what was happening. "Why are those men yelling at Zack?"

Nate muttered a curse. "Once upon a time, Zack was engaged. It didn't last long. She caused trouble and was a huge source of friction in the unit."

"What's does that have to do with everyone being mad at Zack?"

"Tarragon?" Nate pointed at the woman in the blue nightgown still clinging to Laertes on the other side of the field. "She was Zack's fiancée. Her real name is Theresa."

Allison drew in a deep breath and ran toward Zack. No way would she let him face this alone. Besides, she had an idea that could end this nightmare.

CHAPTER 49

ZACK TRIED NOT TO SIGH TOO LOUDLY.

In fact, he had to force himself to pay attention. Both Kells and the Prince were upset because his ex-fiancée was Remiel's niece Tarragon. Although he'd known her as Theresa.

Apparently, almost six years ago, Zack had walked into Remiel's trap. Theresa buying him a drink at that sleazy bar. Their on-and-off relationship. Her call the night of the doomed mission, the same night he allowed his men to go into combat with another commander. All of it had been planned by Remiel.

Now Kells and the Prince were talking to—no, yelling at—each other and ignoring him. All he wanted was to figure out a way to get his sister back. Then, when the women he loved were safe, he wanted to wrap Allison in his arms and go to sleep.

And when he woke up, he'd take Allison and leave Savannah.

Maybe Virginia was the better option.

Yeah. Kells was now dropping the blame for the entire doomed mission onto Zack's lap. While he was willing to take his share—enough that it felt like he was carrying an M1 tank on his back—he wasn't the only one who'd screwed up.

Kells leveled his fiercest gaze at the Prince. "Leave my men out of your fight with Remiel."

The Prince crossed his arms. "They're in this fight whether they want to be or not. This situation with Tarragon proves what happened to you and your men was more thought-out, more planned than you could've imagined."

Kells took a step back when Allison ran up to them.

She was out of breath. Her feet were bare and dirty. Her burned hair hung in singed strands over her shoulders, and she clutched a gray blanket around her. One would think she'd feel embarrassed, but she stood tall, her head high, and faced the Prince. "Is it true that we need to trade something for Emilie?"

The Prince focused his brown gaze on Allison. "It is."

"Then I have something you want. Something that, as the descendent of Mercy Chastain and Henry Avery, belongs to me. Something I'm offering in exchange for Emilie's freedom."

The Prince tilted his head. "You found Henry Avery's treasure?"

Allison pointed to the church.

"It's true, sir," Rafe said. "It's behind the altar."

The Prince walked toward the scorched church and stood in the entrance, shading his eyes because of the sun. It took a minute, but when he returned to them, his wide-open gaze told them he'd seen it as well.

She straightened her shoulders and spoke to the Prince again. "No one except for the men here know about the treasure. I trust Zack's men. Do you trust yours?"

The Prince raised his hand and dropped it.

An SUV door opened and Marcellus helped Emilie out of the car.

"Are you sure," the Prince asked, "that you're aware of what you're giving up?"

She smiled at Zack. "I've found my treasure and my truth."

The Prince motioned to Kells. "I'll have the altarpiece removed to a safe location today. I'll also rebuild this church."

Kells nodded.

The Prince moved aside so Emilie could rush into Zack's arms.

He picked her up in a giant bear hug until she hit his shoulder and said, "Put me down, brute. You don't even have a shirt on."

Allison met the Prince's gaze one last time. "Have I paid Stuart's debt?"

"Aye." The Prince raised his hand again, and Marcellus escorted another person into the center. A man shuffled with hands bound and his head bowed. He had a bruise on his temple.

"What's this?" Kells asked.

"One of Isabel's guards," Zack said. "Isabel killed the other one."

"Yes," said the Prince. "We took care of him as well."

When the shuffling guard saw the Prince, he fell to his knees.

Zack cleared his throat. "I hit this one and tied him up because I was looking for the women. I'm not apologizing."

"I'm not asking you to apologize." The Prince nodded at Marcellus. Marcellus handed Zack his pistol, a bullet already in the chamber.

"Years ago," the Prince said, "my predecessor, who knew your grandfather, sent a messenger asking you to reconsider your decision to become a Special Forces officer."

"I remember."

Allison tugged his arm. "It was Laertes, the warrior with Tarragon." Why was Zack not surprised?

The Prince pointed to the weapon in Zack's hand. "Today I'm offering you a chance to redeem your honor. To prove you're not a coward."

"By killing an unarmed man?" Zack snarled at the Prince. "That doesn't prove anything."

"This unarmed man had every intention of killing, and burning, the woman you love. He would've done the same to your sister and your ex-fiancée if ordered to. He was also in the POW camp. He tortured your men." The Prince touched the guard's head. "He admitted it."

Allison held her breath and watched Zack's eyes darken and his nostrils flare. Slowly, he pointed the gun at the guard's head, his finger on the trigger.

She touched his arm and his muscles bunched. He gripped the weapon until his knuckles turned white. His body shook and sweat beaded his forehead as he stared down the gun's barrel into the guard's terrified eyes.

She glanced back at Zack's men, all of them focused on Zack. Emilie's face lost color and she closed her eyes.

The Prince moved closer. "What kind of man are you, Zack Tremaine? What will you do for those you love?"

A fierce protectiveness swept through her body. No way would she let the Prince have the last word. Standing on her toes, she whispered in Zack's ear, "Remember your truth."

Zack blinked, shook his head, and tossed the gun onto the ground. The guard fell forward and his shoulders shook with his sobs.

"I'm done." Zack's voice sounded husky and strained. "Done with the secrets, the lies, and the violence. Done with having to prove to everyone around me how much I regret my past decisions and how much I love my men. Most of all, I'm done proving myself to *you*."

Allison wasn't sure if Zack was speaking to Kells, the Prince, or to himself.

Emilie took Zack's hand and Allison pressed her head against his shoulder. She was so proud of her *wild man*.

Marcellus retrieved the gun and dragged the guard away. Then the Prince nodded.

Rafe cleared his throat and announced, "This night has been wondrous strange, yet 'tis time to remove ourselves in peace."

"Wait!" Luke raced into the center and said to Kells, "Isabel. She's... gone."

Isabel grabbed the tote bag, left Mercy's fake tomb, and clawed her way through the woods behind the cemetery. She had no idea what had happened to the guard she'd killed and didn't care. Her shoulder ached, but Rafe had given her painkillers while he'd stitched her arm. It'd been a field surgery and would hold for now.

She stumbled over a grave and ended up on her knees. She had to hide before anyone found her. Before Remiel found her. She could still remember the fire's heat and her throat felt like it'd been charred. Her cough sounded raspy and harsh.

Her goal was to hide in a safe place and, eventually, sell the Pirate's Grille and the witch's examination's appendix. No one would know the treasure had been found. And by the time they did, she'd be long gone with the money.

"My beautiful Isabel." Remiel's voice came from behind. "What have you done?"

Her stomach tightened and she used a palmetto branch to help her stand. He wore jeans and a white collared shirt, covered by a black leather jacket. His dark hair was styled and his blue eyes reminded her of the sapphires in the altarpiece. "I found the treasure."

He shoved his hands in the pockets of his leather jacket. "And set it on fire."

"No." She coughed until they became dry heaves. "Clayborne. He set the fire to kill me and Allison."

"Clayborne told me you offered information to Allison."

"I only said that to learn more about the treasure." Isabel's voice came out husky and pleading, not her usual forceful, confident self.

Remiel's smile made her step back. His smile wasn't like normal people's. His lips tightened over his teeth and his eyes narrowed. It was the smile of a man who believed inflicting pain was the only way to control others. "Clayborne told me you were also planning on selling the Pirate's Grille and the witch's examination's appendix."

"No." She held out the tote bag. "I can make this right. We lost the treasure but the documents are still worth millions."

He circled her slowly, and she turned to keep his gaze. "You've been with me from the beginning. You know my past, my present, my secrets. You know everything about me."

"I would never—have never—betrayed you."

"I know you believe that." Suddenly, he walked away.

Was he giving her another chance?

Should she let him?

She tightened her grip on the tote bag and exhaled deeply. Did she have a choice but to follow him? If she didn't, he'd just hunt her down like he'd done to so many others. And that hadn't ended well for any of them. If she did, well, it seemed like he was offering her a way out. A way to redeem herself. After all, she'd been by his side since the beginning. Since the accident.

She walked quickly to catch up to him. As she fell into step behind him, he held up branches so they wouldn't strike her in the face. They hiked through the woods until they reached a clearing with his car. Remiel had always preferred to drive himself instead of having a driver.

He opened the back door. "There's a blanket and water bottles."

"Thank you." She crawled in and collapsed on a blanket. He shut the door and the locks clicked. After drinking the water, despite a slight bitter aftertaste she attributed to smoke, she closed her eyes. There wasn't a single part of her body that didn't hurt. "Now what?"

He slipped into the front seat. "I have something for you. It's in the seat pocket."

She pulled out a cell phone. "What's this?"

"Turn it on."

She pressed the on button and a photo appeared. She sat up and her shaky hands almost dropped the phone. It was a photo of her getaway accounts she'd hidden from Remiel. "Where did you get this?"

"Stuart. He never really loved you."

Remiel had known for months? It was hard to talk, hard to think. The water bottle rolled off the seat onto the floor and she remembered the bitter aftertaste. *Oh. God. No.*

"Please. Remiel." Her tongue felt thick and her head spun until everything appeared to be painted in shades of gray. "I can explain."

"I'm sure you can." Remiel glanced at her in the rearview mirror while the window between the front and back seats went up. The last words she heard were: "Except I don't care."

Her eyes felt heavy, her body tightened, and she knew the truth. *Poison.*

CHAPTER 50

HOURS LATER, ALEX PUSHED AWAY FROM THE TABLE THE MEN had set up in the back room of Iron Rack's gym. They'd returned and ordered breakfast from the diner around the corner. None of them had cleaned up yet, other than washing their hands, and they were covered in varying amounts of soot, dirt, and blood. Yes, they were *that* hungry.

Alex had no idea how they were paying for this meal, but that wasn't his problem.

Although it was still midmorning, it felt later. Possibly because he was so exhausted. Or maybe because clouds had chased the sun away. Either way, he wanted to sleep for a million years. But now that he was back with the group, he didn't want to leave.

He didn't want to be alone.

"I knew Zack wouldn't pull that trigger." Nate poured an insane amount of syrup on his seven-stack of pancakes. "Zack is too smart to fall for the Prince's bullshit."

Alex agreed. Although he also knew that sometimes the drive for revenge obliterated everything else in a man's mind, hence the monster known as Remiel.

"I can't believe the treasure was in the altar," Pete said with his mouth full of bacon. "Who thinks of these things?"

"It's craziness," Cain stuffed his mouth with sausage biscuits. "And the woman with the scarred face was not only Remiel's niece but Zack's fiancée. That is messed up."

Alex finished his orange juice. "Everything having to do with Remiel is messed up."

The room went silent, probably because that truth meant Remiel wasn't finished with the men of the Seventh Special Forces Group. While Nate picked at his eggs, Ty wiped his sooty face with a white napkin. Vane excused himself to use the bathroom. Luke moved asparagus around his plate like a three-year-old. Cain cleared his throat before drinking more water.

Finally, Nate said, "I wonder what's on that thumb drive Alex found."

Not found. Traded. For Isabel's freedom.

Yeah, Kells was going to hold this one over Alex's head for a long time.

"Probably shit," Pete said as he ate more bacon. "No matter how close we get to finding intel, it always ends up as shit."

"Maybe not." Vane returned to the table and took more pancakes. "Alex let Isabel go for that information. It has to be worth something."

Nate raised a glass with the fakest smile plastered on his grim face. "Let's hope so."

The other men chimed in with weak optimism. Alex didn't have that kind of hope, but he'd still do it again. Letting her go for that flash drive was a chance he'd had to take. He, in all sincerity, hoped she'd gotten away. From the Prince. Kells. And Remiel. She was a coldhearted bitch, but she'd earned that truth the old-fashioned way—through abuse, neglect, and betrayal.

And Alex's truth? He'd felt sorry for her.

After the hubbub over Isabel's disappearance, they'd packed up their gear and left the isle just in case any cops or firetrucks arrived. Although, given the Savannah PD's indifference to the isle in the past, Alex would be shocked if any cops showed.

While the details were being handled, Alex also knew that their actions today were superficial. Until they dealt with the emotional issues, nothing was going to change.

Remiel wasn't going away.

"The Prince may have won this round, but Remiel didn't lose," Alex said. "According to Zack, Isabel took the witch's examination's appendix and the Pirate's Grille when she kidnapped Allison. Now they, and Fenwick, are missing."

"The treasure's been found." Luke used his fork to point at Alex. "The Prince has it."

"As far as the world's concerned, Henry Avery's treasure is still out there. That means those documents will bring in a lot of cash. There's no reason for the Prince to buy them since he has the treasure. But another buyer would be eager to pay...thousands?"

"I read online that together they're worth millions." Luke stabbed a sausage and ate it in one bite. "The question is, what will Remiel do with that money?"

Cain laid his head on his arms on the table. "Can we sleep now?"

Zack entered the room and beelined for the coffee. Once he had a full cup, he sat. His scorched hair hung around his shoulders, his dark eyes had a grayish veil over them, the lines around his mouth looked like someone had cut them out with a putty knife.

He'd showered and changed into jeans and a black T-shirt. White gauze covering cuts on his arms were a startling contrast to his dragon tattoo. He had butterfly bandages on one eyebrow, and his knuckles were bruised and swollen. "Allison and Emilie are both asleep." He nodded toward Alex. "In our room."

The men started asking questions and it wasn't until they realized Zack hadn't said a word that they went quiet. They had a friend—Doc Bennett—who doctored on the side. Kells and his men were just some of Doc Bennett's off-the-books clients. Doc Bennett had already checked Pete out and praised Rafe's combat medic skills.

Zack drank his coffee and started answering. "Doc Bennett says Emilie is in better physical shape. She's dehydrated and has some cuts and bruises, and she's exhausted. Although I have no idea what she suffered with the Fianna, so that's a wait-and-see situation. Allison is dealing with smoke inhalation and dehydration. With rest and IV fluids, she'll recover as well."

The men offered a collective sigh of relief.

"How did this happen?" Nate asked. "How did Emilie end up on her way to Remiel and how did Allison end up in that church with her stepfather and Isabel?"

"Tracking device," Luke said. "I did a sweep of Allison's car once we got it back to the gym and found it under the back wheel well."

"What about Garza?" Pete asked. "Has anyone heard from him?"

Nate shoved eggs into his mouth. "Garza is at the station and as we suspected no one was around to call in the fire. The Savannah PD, as well as the rest of the State of Georgia, has a hands-off attitude toward that Isle. The Prince took care of the guard Isabel killed, and there's no word on Fenwick."

"Isabel?" Cain asked. "If she's still out there, we have to find her."

"Agreed." Nate used his executive officer voice. "Once the women recover and we sleep, we'll come up with a plan."

"No." Zack stood and looked at each man directly. "Since Kells fired me, and I'm no longer part of the unit, finding Isabel is all on me."

Allison rolled over in a soft bed and opened her eyes. The room was dark and not just because the lights were off. The half moon shining through the window told her it was nighttime.

Blinking lights came from the machine next to the bed. She was still hooked up to an IV as well as the pulse/blood oxygen monitor. Before the doctor had checked her out, she'd insisted on taking a shower and washing her hair. It wasn't until she was rinsing the shampoo that she'd felt dizzy and nauseated. Luckily Zack had been close by to catch her and carry her to bed. Unfortunately, that also meant she'd fallen asleep with wet hair. Now it was a snarled mess.

She sat up in the twin bed in the tiny room and took off her oxygen cannula. She could make out duffel bags on the floor and an empty twin opposite hers. What she didn't see? *Zack.*

She pulled the meter off her finger and got out of bed, holding on to the IV pole. She wasn't brave enough to take the IV out by herself. Her feet hit a wood floor and the AC'd air left chills on her arms. She wore two hospital gowns. One tied in the front and one tied in the back. Beneath that she wore nothing.

After using the bathroom in the hallway, she was determined

to go downstairs and find Zack. Except with every breath, she felt queasy.

"Whoa." Zack came upstairs and hurried over. Carefully, so he wouldn't dislodge her IV, he picked her up and carried her to the bed. Once he placed her beneath the blankets and adjusted the IV pole, he laid down next to her. Because they were in a twin, she ended up curled around him.

"How's Emilie?"

"She's downstairs eating. She was scared, but now she's angry."

A sentiment Allison understood well.

"I explained as much as I could about Remiel and the Fianna and why we couldn't go to the police. Surprisingly, she was okay with that. Fortinbras took decent care of her. He also told her a lot of what was going on—what happened to my men in Afghanistan—and how if she went to the cops, they wouldn't believe her. And if the cops did believe her, it would put me, my men, and herself in even more danger."

"She's okay with all of that?"

"She agreed to keep quiet but gave me hell for not telling her about what had happened to us in Afghanistan and that I was dishonorably discharged. I reminded her it was classified. Still, she called me an obfuscating lout. I left the room before she threw a plate at me."

Allison laughed for the first time in...she couldn't remember. She had so much to say to him but her eyes refused to stay open.

He tucked her next to him, making sure her head was on his chest so she could listen to his heartbeat. "You need to rest."

She yawned. "I'm sorry."

"For what?"

"For not telling you about the UVA position. For allowing you to find Emilie while believing I might leave you. I shouldn't have left the house with Alex. I wanted to save you."

"Shh." He kissed her head. "You found my sister and the treasure. As for the rest, we'll work it out. I've always liked Virginia."

She chuckled, coughed, and closed her eyes, loving his warmth and his heartbeat.

"Allison?" His breath tickled her head. "Will you marry me?"

She raised her head. Even in the dark, she could see his glittering eyes. "Are you sure?"

He rolled until she was on her back and he was over her, propped up on one arm. His free hand smoothed stray hairs off her face. "Yes. I'm sure I'm asking you to marry me."

She couldn't hide her smile. "I'm afraid I may hurt you."

"I'm afraid I won't be enough for you. That makes us even."

"You will always be more than enough for me."

"No matter what happens, I will never leave you. Never betray you. Never let you go."

She touched his face, covered in a day's worth of stubble. "Yes, Zack. I'll marry you."

CHAPTER 51

THE NEXT MORNING ZACK STOOD IN FRONT OF THE WINDOW OF Kells's office and stared across the street at the boarded-up T-shirt shop. Although he was relieved Emilie and Allison were okay, he was still reliving the moment he hadn't pulled that trigger on the guard.

Because he almost had. Just the thought of that man hurting the women he loved, torturing the men he'd failed, sent him into a rage. It would've been so easy to take out his anger on the unarmed guard. It would've been so easy to pull that trigger and prove to everyone he was no coward.

Then Allison whispered *remember your truth*.

Suddenly, visions of everything he and Allison had endured over the last few days, the memories of their lovemaking and their argument before he left to find Emilie, even that night seven years ago at Le Petit Theatre flooded his mind, leaving him two options.

Pull that trigger or forgive himself.

He'd suddenly understood that while revenge satisfied a man's anger, it fed his self-hatred—a self-hatred that led to death and destruction. Remiel exemplified that equation.

Since a dark side always has a light side, Zack also realized that the act of forgiving oneself was the real test of a man's courage. A brave man would never fear offering mercy to an unarmed one.

So his truth? He was a brave man seeking the gift of self-forgiveness. A gift that only came from love. Love for his woman. Love for his men. Love for himself.

The question now was, where would that seeking lead him?

Alex and Nate arrived with take-away cups from the coffee shop down the street.

Zack took one and drank deeply. It was hot and surprisingly not bitter. "Thank you."

Nate nodded toward the coffeemaker on the filing cabinet. "Luke has surrendered. No matter what beans he buys, the coffee tastes like sludge."

"I'm telling you"—Alex sat on a metal folding chair and propped his boots on Kells's desk—"it's the water. The taps in this place put out pure chlorine."

Zack took another drink. He wasn't sure why they were talking about coffee, but he was grateful. Kells came in and Alex lowered his feet to sit upright.

Nate closed the door and took another metal chair. That left Zack by the window. Alone. And he was fine with that.

Kells placed the thumb drive on the desk. "Luke and I went through a combination of audio files and images. The audio is between Isabel and Stuart. She's admitting Remiel set up the ambush that took down our unit in Afghanistan. That he ran the POW camp. She told Stuart about the torture and how, when we"—Kells nodded at Zack—"were given the go-ahead to rescue them, Remiel let the guards go ahead of time."

"That's why there was no fight?" Zack leaned his shoulder against the glass and focused on the cracked sidewalks outside. "Remiel knew we were coming."

"Yes." Kells, still standing, shuffled pages on his desk as if he needed time to think before speaking.

"Sir?" Zack exhaled before asking, "Did you deliberately drag out the time it took between the men being captured and their rescue?"

"That's *insane*." Nate almost spat the words.

"*No.*" Kells fisted his hands. "Why would you think that?"

"It's…nothing." Zack sighed. Although Mack seemed so sure Kells had been playing games, Mack wasn't the most trustworthy source. And Horatio's insinuations? Fianna bullshit. They were always trying to rattle the ranks. Hell, they'd tried to rattle him seven years ago. He just hadn't realized it.

"Sir." Nate stood to pace the small room. "Who told Remiel you were coming to rescue us? Even we didn't know Remiel was alive and doing all these things until a few months ago."

"That's the million-dollar question," Kells said. "Few knew about the mission. Zack, Vane, and I planned it. We didn't tell the other men until we were on our way."

Alex tossed his empty cup into the trash. "Did anyone above you know?"

Kells nodded. "Although we did the planning, we couldn't execute it without funding or permission."

"Your contact." Zack moved until he stood behind Alex. "The one who negotiated our discharges and kept us out of prison. Did he know about the mission?"

"Yes. But I don't think—"

"With all due respect," Nate said, "someone tipped off Remiel. It must be someone else who had access to your plans."

"I'm not disagreeing with you, Nate." Kells clasped his hands behind his head. "I've been through the list of those who knew about the rescue mission. They all came forward in our favor during those secret congressional investigations. They all approved the discharges instead of prison time."

Alex sighed heavily. "That means someone is playing the long game."

"Yes."

Zack gripped the back of Alex's metal chair. "*When* did these people who approved our rescue mission learn about Remiel's heartbeat?"

Kells looked directly at Alex. "No one knew Remiel was still alive until after the rescue. I learned Remiel might be alive from evidence found at the POW camp and informed them."

"Yet it still took years to get me out?" Alex snorted. "Thanks."

Zack gripped Alex's shoulder until he threw it off.

"Sir." Nate sat again and leaned his forearms on his thighs. "Anything else on that drive?"

Kells handed Nate a stack of papers. "Financial statements. Stuart

Pinckney gave Isabel money in a secret account. Probably for an emergency getaway."

Nate sifted through them. Since Nate was a math guru, most of the unit's financial matters went through him.

Alex stood. "If that's all we get for letting Isabel go, it's a bum deal."

"Why?" Nate looked up from the pages. "We have Isabel admitting—"

"Admitting what?" Alex waved an arm at the map of Afghanistan covering the wall. "That Remiel ambushed your men and held them in a POW camp? That's awful, but it's not something that can be prosecuted. Your men aren't in prison because they lost a battle. They're in prison because they're taking the blame for the Wakhan Corridor Massacre."

"Which Remiel did not admit to." Zack picked up the thumb drive. "Isn't that so, sir?"

Kells nodded. "Isabel's admission doesn't absolve our men still in prison. She doesn't mention the Wakhan Corridor Massacre at all."

"Everything that's happened in the past few days is meaningless," Alex said. "We found the treasure, gave it to the Prince, and got shit in return."

Zack returned to the window and used his fist to rub the center of his chest. His burned skin itched, and every muscle felt like it'd been stretched and snapped back into shape hundreds of times.

Yes, as far as his men were concerned maybe all the trouble in the past few days had been for nothing. But he couldn't say that about himself. There was so much in his heart that wasn't about his unit or Remiel's war or the never-ending cycle of lies he and his men had been told.

Allison was healing and she'd agreed to marry him. Yet since she'd woken the second time, she'd been distant. She'd agreed to wear his ring—which he hadn't gotten yet—then said she wanted to wait to get married. That it was too soon after Stuart's death. While she might be right, Zack knew there was something else. She seemed happy yet…she was putting him off.

And she wouldn't tell him why.

Zack shook out his arms and flexed his fingers. His body hummed with a restlessness he couldn't name or ignore. "Now what?"

Kells came over to the window. "I didn't mean to fire you. I was... frustrated and angry and worried about the men. I took it out on you."

"No, sir." Zack spoke directly. "You were projecting. And if we're going to talk about this, we're going to be honest."

Kells's gaze darkened. "Excuse me?"

"You might've been worried about everything going on. But that's been happening for years. You took out your anger and worry on me because I spent the last two months in Charleston watching over Allison. You assumed because I once chose a woman over my men that I was doing so again. You blame me because I didn't take my A team to join Nate's. You blame me for the ambush, as if my being there would've changed the outcome."

Kells stared at Zack with such palpable anger that Zack could feel the heat.

Zack pointed to the thumb drive on the desk. "While I will regret, for the rest of my life, not taking my own team into the hot zone, it wouldn't have changed anything. I had no way of knowing that Theresa/ Tarragon was Remiel's niece and that he was getting me out of the way. I had no way of knowing that our teams were about to be ambushed and sent to a POW camp."

The room was silent.

Zack wasn't backing down. He'd made mistakes, but he was done feeling guilty about them. He was ready to move on with his life, even if it meant leaving the unit.

Could he do that? Could he walk away from his friends? His brothers? While they were still upside-down in this war between Remiel and the Prince? "I'm moving to Charleston. Maybe Virginia."

Kells's chest deflated. "Excuse me?"

"You fired me."

"I didn't—"

"You did. I'm not in the army anymore. None of us are. We're playing at being a unit. We're desperate to cling to what we had, to be what we were, but we're not. We're never going to be reinstated in the army. Our discharges will never say *honorable*. Our lives, as they are now, will never be our own."

"We still have a chance to reclaim what we once were. You have to remember—"

"I do remember, sir. That's the problem. This past week has been nothing but remembering. And I remembered that I want to be a man who can be proud of his work, love his woman, and raise a family."

"I never said you couldn't do that. You can marry Allison. Hell, Rafe, Nate, and Cain are married."

"That's not what I mean, sir. I'm sorry you miss Kate. And since you're going to find out anyway, you should know I saw her in New Orleans. She's as lost without you as you are without her. But taking your anger out on me—on us—is wrong. Kate didn't leave you because she stopped loving you. She left you because she loves you but couldn't bear the weight of these secrets anymore."

"That's absurd." Kells went back to his desk. "What we do is classified. What goes on between Remiel and the Prince has to remain secret."

"Secrets are keeping us, and the people we love, in danger. Secrets are coming between the men in the unit, which makes things even more volatile. And I'm just as guilty. I kept secrets from you. I knew you didn't want me in Charleston watching Allison. When I needed your help, I didn't ask for it because I knew you'd say no."

Kells crossed his arms over his chest. "If you want to leave, I won't stop you."

"I don't want to leave." Zack moved to the front of the desk. "I have to leave."

"Time-out." Nate waved a hand between Kells and Zack and spread the financial documents on the desk. He pointed to a line at the bottom of a page. "Isabel had over three million dollars in this account. She had no family, yet look at the name of her beneficiary."

When they all squinted, Kells pulled out a magnifying glass and held it over the name.

Vivienne Beaumont. "Why would Isabel Rutledge leave her money to my godmother?"

"Interesting question." Kells's phone rang and he answered with a curt, "Hello."

A minute later, he hung up. "That was Detective Garza. Isabel Rutledge is dead."

Isabel was dead?

Alex exhaled the breath he'd been holding since discovering that Kells knew Remiel was alive *years* before getting Alex out of prison. Sure, Alex figured Kells hadn't run to the prison. Hell, even Aidan hadn't given a shit.

Still, knowing he'd been in prison years longer than necessary hurt. A lot.

But his ability to feel self-pity meant he was still alive. Unlike Isabel.

"What happened?" Nate asked.

"Garza went back to the isle to make sure things were…clean. That's when he found Isabel's body in a desecrated tomb. She'd been left near a weeping angel statue. She's at the morgue. His guess is poison."

Alex closed his eyes and said a silent prayer. No one deserved a death by Remiel.

"Good God," Nate whispered. "That's monstrous."

Hence why I tried to kill him, brother.

Kells pointed to the financial sheet again. "This has left Vivienne Beaumont an even richer woman. Garza is leading Isabel's death investigation, so you may want to talk to Vivienne."

"I will," Zack said.

Alex rubbed his forehead. He hadn't liked Isabel, but he had slept with her. Despite her evil tendencies, she hadn't deserved this. The truth was this chaos wasn't about Kells and the Prince. This chaos was all about Remiel. What Remiel wanted. Who Remiel hated. When Remiel would strike next. That was a lesson Isabel had learned the hard way. That was a lesson Alex was worried Kells and his men had yet to understand.

"Zack?" Alex stood. "I know you want out. I know you're pissed at Kells. Hell, I've been pissed at Kells since I was sixteen. But you can't leave the unit."

"Alex—"

"No." Alex pressed his fist against Zack's chest. "I understand you want to go to Charleston, maybe even Virginia, with Allison. I also know that leaving the unit down one man could make Kells's operation crash and burn. But I have a plan. I promise, when I'm finished, it's an idea that'll work for all of us."

CHAPTER 52

ALLISON SAT AT HER DESK IN THE PINCKNEY HOUSE STUDY AND wiped her palms on her jeans. It'd been ten days since her ordeal, and she and Zack were in Charleston—temporarily.

Although she was happy, she still felt detached from everything and everyone. Including Zack. He'd been kind and gentle with her distance, but she could tell from his frowns that she'd used up his patience allotment. The problem was she didn't know what was wrong with her. Since the fire, she felt like a daisy petal floating on a breeze—unable to land yet unable to return to what she'd once been.

It didn't help that not only had she not decided whether or not to take her UVA offer, but she wasn't sure about Alex's alternative plan either. That left Zack in a difficult position with his men. It wasn't fair of her, but until this detachment disappeared, she couldn't fix it and they couldn't move forward.

Her brother-in-law, Lawrence, sat in a chair, and Zack stood in the corner, near the window overlooking the garden. Nicholas Trott lay in his bed. Since their return, the dog hadn't left their side. Loud noises outside proved that the new gardening staff Lawrence had hired were helping the grounds recover from months of neglect.

"So we're agreed." She opened the social calendar she kept for the house. "Zack and I will live here until we decide what to do next. In return, I'll help manage Pinckney House's social calendar. Participation in the Autumn Garden Festival, the Haunted Mansion Tour—"

"Is this place haunted?" Zack winked at Allison and she tried not to laugh.

"Of course it is," Lawrence said. "It's why I started my Got Ghosts? tour company."

She continued, "The Historic Home Tour and the annual reception for the Charleston Architectural Board. They're both held in the garden in September. Once I move out and you move in"—she turned to December and January—"there's the Christmas Historic Home Tour, the neighborhood's New Year's Progressive Dinner, and the Robert Burns Society Supper."

Lawrence grimaced. "Okay."

"After that, I haven't committed the house to anything. Although if you don't open the gardens on the Fourth of July, the mayor will be upset. He loves Nicholas Trott's punch."

Lawrence scoffed. "The dog makes punch?"

"No." She ignored Zack's laughter. "It's a punch named after Nicholas Trott. Once Nicholas Trott walks in the parade, people come to the garden, where we serve punch and the dog poses for selfies. Last year I sold tote bags, the year before that coffee mugs, and the year before that note cards. All profits were given to the Charleston Public Library." She closed her planner and stood. "We're done. Are you staying for the party tonight?"

"No." Lawrence stood and straightened his suit jacket. "Have you set a date?"

"Not yet," Zack said harshly.

The lack of a wedding date was another source of friction between them. She exhaled and handed Lawrence his briefcase.

Lawrence took it and paused. "I'm not supposed to tell you this because Rue wanted to speak to you first. It's something the auditor found."

Rue had taken Fenwick's disappearance hard, especially after learning that he'd been accused of murder and arson and no one knew if he'd return. When Allison had seen Rue a few days ago, she'd seemed less... angry. "What did he find?"

Lawrence opened his briefcase, took out a form, and handed it to her.

It was a copy of the spreadsheet Mack had given them. "I've seen this before. Rue asked Stuart to help her move money."

"Stuart also moved his own money into the account."

"Money he took out of the trust?"

"Only the money that belonged to him. He was protecting it." Lawrence pointed to the bottom number with many zeroes. "Half of that is yours. Your mother is stopping by my office today, and together we'll move your money into whatever account you'd like. Apparently, Rue had been looking for this document."

Allison had been right. That was why Rue had been searching Pirate House.

"I don't understand." It wasn't a huge amount, but it would help her renovate Pirate House or move to Virginia. "Why would Stuart do this?"

"Stuart wanted to shield his money to protect you." Lawrence took the document and shoved it into his bag. "And for some reason, he trusted Rue."

After Lawrence left, Zack took her hands. "Despite his mistakes, Stuart was a good man."

And he'd loved her.

"Come on." Zack, still holding her hand, dragged her out of the study. "There's something we need to do before the party."

She tried to stop him but he was too strong. "What?"

"Say goodbye."

৩

Zack was worried.

For all of Allison's kisses and the time he'd spent in her bed, she refused to set a wedding date or talk about that job at UVA. While it was true Stuart had died only a few months ago, they hadn't been truly married for years. Zack wasn't asking her to marry him tomorrow, although that'd be fine with him; he just wanted any date. In the future. On the calendar. In permanent marker.

And screw what the rest of the world thought.

He took Allison's hand and led her through Saint Philip's east churchyard. In his other hand, he carried her tote bag filled with Danny's treasure box, a trowel, and small pots of daisies he'd gotten from Pastor Tom. Pastor Tom had been released from the hospital and gone back to giving sermons and watering the cemetery.

When Zack had spoken to Vivienne about the money Isabel had left her, she'd deflected by telling him that on the day after Stuart's service, after the storm ended, she'd overseen the placement of Stuart's gravestone.

Zack stopped in front of Danny's grave and started digging, being careful not to disturb the violets.

"What are you doing?" she asked.

When the hole was large enough, he placed the treasure box in it and covered it with dirt. "Letting Danny go." Zack glanced up at her and saw her wiping away tears. "It's time."

She nodded and helped him replant the purple flowers.

When they were done, Zack moved to the tomb next to Danny's. Plastic still covered the headstone, held down along the edges with stones. Rainwater filled the dips and valleys in the sheeting. The humidity beneath obscured the words. "You never spoke at Stuart's service."

Allison took the daisies out of the bag. "I had nothing to say. Especially after Isabel's speech."

Zack squeezed her hand. "If we're going to have a life together, we owe it to ourselves to lay the past to rest."

Another tear traced down Allison's cheek and she wiped it away. "I loved Stuart, but I never should've married him. A Fianna warrior even tried to warn me."

"Rafe told me that the previous Prince was not only a master manipulator, but he also knew this war was coming. He knew Mercy Chastain would play an important role, which was why he sent Laertes to warn you and discourage me. It wasn't a message of truth—it was a message of war."

"Laertes was correct. I made the wrong choice."

"You can never defeat the impossibility of uncertainty."

She rolled her eyes. "I still feel guilty about getting engaged to you so quickly."

Yeah, he'd figured that was why she'd been so distant. "Stuart knew your heart wasn't all yours to give. He knew you loved me too and still asked you to marry him. This is not all your fault."

"I did love him too. Just not in the same way."

Zack handed her a Nicholas Trott bandana so she could wipe her nose.

"Does that make me a terrible person?"

He smiled. "It makes you a woman with an enormous capacity to love. A woman who wanted all of the men in her life, including her brother, to be safe and happy. That's a gift, Allison. It's your truth. You need to accept that part of yourself."

The tightness in her stomach eased and the invisible weight she'd been carrying lightened.

"Although, I think you should take Pete's self-defense class for women."

She smiled and wiped her face on his bandana again.

He knelt in front of the gravestone and smoothed the dirt. Although it'd been less than two weeks ago, the rain and humidity had encouraged the growth of morning glory vines and ivy. Palmettos grew beneath ancient oaks. Tiny birds hopped from headstone to flat tomb. "Why are the cemeteries in this city overgrown?"

"It's part of the culture and history." She knelt next to him. "Death is so disconcerting. A tear in the world that can't be healed but can be covered up by flowers and trees. Nature provides the bandage for the wounds death leaves behind."

He dug holes in the sandy soil. "I prefer to think they can't pay their gardening staff."

She laughed and wiped her forehead with her arm, leaving a streak of dirt across her face. Her smile lifted his heart and the fact that she was willing to do this meant she might be able to let go and accept the inevitable: He loved her. She loved him. They were getting married and would have an incredible life together. Whether they stayed in Charleston, moved to Virginia, or returned to Savannah.

They worked in silence until the daisies were planted. While he collected the pots, she gathered pine straw and used it to mulch the flowers.

He dumped the pots and trowel into the bag and removed the stones from the plastic sheeting. "Did you choose the headstone?"

"No." She stood and wiped her hands on her jeans. "Lawrence ordered it."

Zack stood next to her. "Ready?"

At her nod, he swept off the covering. A skull with wings had been carved into the top of the gray marble.

"A winged death's head." She traced the detailed edges. "It represents the soul's flight to Heaven."

Zack held her hand and read the inscription. Below Stuart's name, birth and death dates, the stonemason had carved BELOVED BROTHER AND HUSBAND. Zack, still holding her hand, drew her around to the back of the tomb, where another inscription had been cut.

He read aloud: "'Live in this fair world behind, honor'd, beloved, and, haply, one as kind.'"

Allison picked up a stone and placed it on top of the marble. "Now I can breathe. I feel alive. I feel whole."

"So do I, love." Zack grabbed the bag and led her out of the shadowed graveyard, toward Pirate House, shimmering in the daylight. "So do I."

CHAPTER 53

A FEW HOURS LATER, ALLISON STOOD NEAR THE WINDOW IN THE drawing room of Vivienne's mansion while Vivienne directed waitstaff, the string ensemble, florist, and caterer.

"You look beautiful." Zack came up behind her and kissed her head. Nicholas Trott lay at her feet. After leaving the cemetery, they'd gone back to the house to shower and change. They'd had three hours before the party, and they'd barely made it.

"Thank you." She blushed when she remembered their time in the shower together after she told him she'd declined the UVA offer. "Did you tell Alex that we agree with his plan?"

"Yes. We'll tell the men later tonight."

Through the window, she saw the strands of lights strung through the garden blink on.

Allison rested against Zack's chest. "It's sweet of Vivienne to hold this engagement party for us."

"She's been waiting for this for years. No doubt there'll be showers and cocktail parties and oyster roasts."

She kissed his chin. "Will you be okay with that?"

He kissed her cheek. "I don't care as long as I don't have to pay for it or dress for it."

"Yet you do look nice when you dress up." Tonight he wore lightweight black wool pants, a dark blue button-down shirt, and a red-and-blue silk tie. His long hair was tied at the nape of his neck, and only part of his tattoo could be seen over the collar. The clothes had, of course, come from Vivienne. She'd insisted that all of Zack's men dress for the occasion.

"There you two are." Vivienne swept into the room on gold Jimmy Choo heels and wearing a gold lace sheath hemmed below the knee. A sheer gold lamé jacket covered her shoulders, and a dazzling diamond-and-gold necklace matched the diamond drops in her ears.

Emilie came into the room in a stunning red silk halter dress and high heels decorated with sparkly straps. Her long black hair had been twisted into a complicated braided knot at the base of her neck. "Is there anything we can do?"

"No, dear. That's why I hire help." Vivienne drew Allison out of Zack's arms. "Don't wrinkle your dress. The guests will be arriving shortly."

Allison smoothed down the skirt of her peach silk chiffon dress. With a full skirt, tight bodice, scooped neckline, and fluttery sleeves, she felt like a perfect picture of femininity on a hot summer's night.

Vivienne went back to shut the doors so the four of them would be alone. "I want to talk about the money Isabel Rutledge left me."

Zack frowned until Emilie gently touched his arm.

"Go ahead, Nénaine," Emilie said. "We're listening."

Vivienne straightened her diamond necklace. Twice. "I was as surprised by the money as you were, Zachariah. Then Isabel's solicitor—who does not work for Remiel—sent me a letter explaining things that happened when she was a young woman."

"What—"

Vivienne held up a hand, interrupting Emilie. "Her letter was sent in confidence so I won't share the details. Suffice it to say that when Remiel tortured his poor niece Tarragon, it brought up bad memories for Isabel. She started a getaway account. Isabel, knowing that her chances of leaving Remiel alive were small, willed the money to me with instructions to transfer the money to Tarragon. That money is now in a trust for Tarragon set up by the Fianna."

"They're no better than Remiel." Zack said harshly.

"Not better, but different. I spoke to a warrior named Laertes assigned to watch over Tarragon. Tarragon is in Italy at a Fianna safe house, receiving medical care. Now she'll have money of her own if she chooses to reenter the world."

Emilie touched Vivienne's hand. "Maybe Isabel wasn't all evil."

"No one is all evil," Vivienne said.

Zack stared at the ceiling. "Oh good Lord."

Emilie hit him in the stomach just as the doorbell rang.

Zack rubbed his stomach and asked Vivienne one more question. "Did you tell Detective Garza this?"

"I did. Now." Vivienne took Emilie's arm, then Allison's, and led them into the foyer. "Let's enjoy the party and think only of happy things."

Allison glanced back at Zack and smiled. Vivienne was right. Now was not the time to stress. Tonight was about being grateful. Tonight was about new beginnings. Tonight was going to be the first night of their new life together. Tonight was the night of happy things.

An hour later, Zack put his empty champagne glass on the passing waiter's tray and found Allison talking to Emilie and Maddie in the sitting room, near the string ensemble. His buddies milled around eating appetizers and drinking from real glasses instead of plastic cups. Even Alex stood in a corner with Garza, pretending not to watch Maddie.

So far everyone, except for Kells, had shown up. The few married men brought their wives, and Zack was glad for that. The more of his friends Allison met, the closer he could draw her to him.

He wasn't worried about her feelings anymore, just restless. Now that they'd agreed to Alex's plan, Zack wanted to be married now, not later.

Nate clapped Zack on the shoulder. "It's time. Where do you want to do this?"

"Dining room."

"I have to admit, I had no idea your godmother was so…"

"Wealthy?" Zack caught Emilie's gaze. She was smiling, and he gave her a brotherly wink. "It's not my money."

Nate touched Luke's arm. "Gather everyone in the dining room."

Luke nodded because his mouth was full and both hands held plates of salmon canapés and onion toasts.

A few minutes later, all the men, including Garza, stood in the dining room. Nate whistled until they stopped talking and focused on him. Alex was near the fireplace, a part of the group yet separate.

"Zack has a few things to say." Nate nodded at Zack.

Zack cleared his throat. "I'm leaving Savannah."

The room went silent until Cain said too loudly, "What?"

Zack swallowed and started again. "Kells fired me." *Jeez, I'm one with the words today.*

"Kells didn't mean it," Luke said. "He was in a mood. He fired Cain last week."

"I ignored it," Cain said from the back of the group.

The men laughed, and Zack said, "I just... Hell."

Nate stepped up like the good XO they all counted on. "This is the deal. Zack is going to stay in Charleston until Allison finishes teaching at the College of Charleston. Because Fenwick is still on the loose, Kells and I agreed it would be a good idea to have someone in Charleston."

"We need Zack at the gym," Ty said. "There's too much work to do."

Nate held up a hand. "Zack has agreed to commute to Savannah. To spend at least three, hopefully four, days a week with us until he and Allison can move to Savannah permanently."

"I don't like it," Vane said. "Zack is supposed to start teaching Krav Maga classes. How the hell am I supposed to train him and schedule his classes if he's not there?"

Male voices started up again until Nate whistled. "Zack isn't leaving us. This situation is not permanent. Once things are settled here, he and Alex will return."

Luke raised his hand. "Will Alex live in Charleston too?"

The dining room door opened and Kells entered.

Kells had come?

The men faced Zack again. "Alex is staying in Charleston temporarily to help me watch things here. Vivienne has offered Alex a room. In a few months, depending on how things go, we'll reevaluate the situation."

The men shuffled, a few whispered, but there was no outright rebellion. Zack knew this wouldn't be a popular decision, and not just because of the work that needed to be done. Zack *was* leaving. Even if it was temporary, their unit would never be the same.

Maybe that would be a good thing. Because right now, with their near-wins over Remiel, they were a mess on every level: personal, financial, operational.

"I know things have been hard lately." Kells came forward and addressed the men. "I've been…difficult. Secretive. I thought withholding information would allow you to settle into this new life none of us wanted. But I was wrong. I've been making decisions for you instead of including you. And that has left some of you feeling isolated and put others in danger. While I can't promise to change completely—"

The men laughed.

"—I promise to start working with you instead of above you."

The men smiled. A few clapped.

"There's one more thing. We've won three battles over Remiel, but barely. We still don't know what his end game is, nor do we have evidence to free our men from prison. The only thing we do know is that Remiel has been planning this for far longer than any of us expected."

A few men looked at Zack, and he just took it.

"In the last few months," Kells continued, "Nate has improved our operational security and has been working on our finances. While money is an issue, we have to up our intel game."

"How?" Rafe asked from behind the group.

"I don't know yet, but I'm open to ideas. If you have them, come see me or Nate. Now." Kells went to the tray of champagne flutes on the sideboard and, with Nate's help, handed out glasses. "I'd like to propose a toast to Zack and his future bride." Kells raised his glass and said, "'Doubt thou the stars are fire, doubt that the sun doth move, doubt truth to be a liar, but never doubt I love.'"

EPILOGUE

Hours later, Zack and Nicholas Trott found Allison in her bedroom near the window overlooking the garden. The garden lights were on, and she'd lit the room with candles.

He came up behind her and took her in his arms. She'd changed into a white silk nightgown. "You sure you're okay giving up that position at UVA?"

"It was an easy escape, but I realized that the things worth having are the things worth fighting for. I'm not sure what I'll do when we eventually move to Savannah, but we'll figure it out." She rested against his chest. "Although we don't know what happened to Fenwick, I've no doubt you'll defeat anyone who comes against you. In fact, I feel sorry for them."

He chuckled. Her faith in him made him feel like he could load a Howitzer with one hand while fighting zombies with the other. "Why the mulling?"

Nicholas Trott yawned and stretched in his bed near the fireplace.

"I've been thinking. About us."

"Okay..."

She turned so he could see her shimmering green eyes. Had she been crying? "I want to ask you a question." Her finger traced his lips. "I'd like you to say yes first."

He gently bit the tip of her finger. "Anything."

"Tonight, Rafe told me the church on the Isle of Grace was being rebuilt and should be done in a month. So I was thinking, once that church is complete, I want to get married there."

Zack's heart lodged in his throat. "You don't want to get married at Saint Philip's?"

She shook her head. "I want to marry you in the church where I realized how much I love you. The church where you saved me. The church where I found my treasure."

He took a ring Vivienne had helped him choose out of his pocket and knelt.

She touched his head. "What are you doing?"

He slipped the diamond solitaire on her left-hand ring finger. "I will marry you anytime, anywhere you want. As long as you'll promise to be mine forever."

She drew him up, threw her arms around his neck, and pressed her soft body against his hard length. Somehow her nightgown ended up on the floor. "Forever and ever and ever."

Hours later, Allison laid her head on Zack's bare chest. They were curled up, naked, in her bed. Her hair covered the tattoo on his arm, one of her hands rested on his lower stomach. He'd made love to her in such a way that if she died in that moment, with only the moon as a witness, she'd have no regrets.

Non ruta non dolor.

So much had happened since that night it was difficult to relive it all in her mind. Yet all that mattered was this moment with Zack. There was no point in dwelling on the woman she'd once been. No point in fussing about the choices she'd made and the years they'd lost. The only thing that mattered was that she and Zack had found each other. They'd fought for each other. Now, they'd live for each other.

That made her the luckiest woman in the world.

"Are you worrying?"

She kissed his chest. "Just being grateful. So very grateful."

He rolled until his body was on top of hers, his leg between her thighs. "I still can't believe I'm here, with you, and this is real."

She untied his hair so it fell forward, trapping them in this private, intimate space. She kissed his eyelids, his cheeks, and his lips. She felt his strength and his length and smiled. *Again? Really?*

"We only have a few hours, and I want to spend all of it like this with you."

She kissed his nose. "A few hours until what?"

He nuzzled her neck. "Didn't I tell you? Some of my men stayed in Charleston overnight at Vivienne's. I invited them to breakfast. They're coming in a few hours."

"The men are coming?" She laughed, not sure if he was serious. "In a few hours?" No, he hadn't told her.

"Uh-huh." His lips moved lower. "You're not mad?"

No. But that just added an urgency to her caresses.

"Your men are your family, which makes them my family." She smoothed back his hair and met the brown gaze of her wild man. "I want a family. With you. Because I've finally realized that while certainty is an impossible truth, it can be fought for, won, protected, and treasured."

Zack's breath hitched and his eyes darkened in the candlelight. "Meaning?"

She smiled and pulled him down for a kiss. "Zack Tremaine, I'm certain that I love you."

ACKNOWLEDGMENTS

I can't believe I'm writing the acknowledgment for my third book, and I want to thank my extraordinary editor Deb Werksman for this amazing opportunity. I so appreciate your guidance and patience while I wrote this book. This story took everything out of me and you made sure I didn't lose sight of my characters or this story. I am so blessed to have you as my editor!

I'm also sending hugs to my agents Deidre Knight and Kristy Hunter for their support and love. No matter what I need, or when I need it, you're both there to help me. Thank you!

I also want to thank the rest of the Sourcebooks staff, including Susie Benton, Stefani Sloma, Gretchen Stelter, Jessica Smith, and everyone else for the hours of hard work you've all put into this book and series. I couldn't have done this without you.

A huge thank you to the Sourcebooks art department. I love this cover and all of the covers in this series. They are amazing!

To Kieran Kramer, Kim MacCarron, and Nadine Monaco, thank you all for reading an early version of this story and helping me smooth out the rough parts. It was a long draft and I am eternally grateful!

To my critique partner and dearest friend, Mary Lenaburg, thank you for not letting me give up.

To my girlfriends Jean Anspaugh and Jackie Iodice, thank you for always answering the phone when I call.

To my brother-in-law and Charleston lawyer, Bill Hanahan, thank you for sharing your family surnames and stories, especially those that took place in 17th and 18th centuries.

I've done a huge amount of research for this book and series and want to thank the Charleston Public Library, Historic Charleston Foundation, Charleston Library Society, and the Historic Savannah Foundation for your extensive research collections.

To Dr. Michael S. Overholt, PhD in Classics at the College of Charleston, thank you for checking my Latin grammar!

To Sandals South Coast Resort in Jamaica, I was under deadline and spent most of my vacation typing while sitting on the beach. Your staff couldn't have been more wonderful as they brought me meals and non-alcoholic drinks. Thank you so much!

To my one-eyed rescue dog who sleeps all day by my side, thank you for not sharing with the world those times when I'm either crying or bingeing on Oreos. It will always be our secret!

To my twins who remind me of everything that's truly important in this world. I'm so grateful to be your mother.

To my husband, who's always believed in me, thank you for being my best friend, my biggest fan, my maker of maps, and my teacher of military weapons and explosive compounds. I will always love you.

Finally, to my readers. Thank you for loving the world of Kells Torridan and his men as much as I do. These books wouldn't be the success they are today without you. I hope I will never let you, or my characters, down.

ABOUT THE AUTHOR

Sharon Wray is a librarian who once studied dress design in the couture houses of Paris and now writes about ex–Green Berets and their smart, sexy heroines who teach these alpha males that *grace* always defeats *reckoning*. She lives in Virginia with her husband, twins, and one-eyed dog.

She also loves to interact with readers. While you can find her on all social media sites, she especially loves spending time on Instagram as @sbwray and on her website at sharonwray.com.